you're so bad

FINDING YOU

ANGELA CASELLA

also by angela casella

Finding You

You're so Extra

You're so Bad

You're so Basic (November)

Fairy Godmother Agency

A Borrowed Boyfriend

A Stolen Suit

A Brooding Bodyguard

A Reluctant Roommate

Bringing Down the House (Nicole and Damien's story)

Highland Hills

(co-written with Denise Grover Swank)

Matchmaking a Billionaire

Matchmaking a Single Dad

Matchmaking a Grump

Matchmaking a Roommate

Bad Luck Club

(co-written with Denise Grover Swank)

Love at First Hate

Jingle Bell Hell

Fraudulently Ever After

Matchmaking Mischief

Asheville Brewing

(co-written with Denise Grover Swank)

Any Luck at All

Better Luck Next Time

Getting Lucky

Bad Luck Club

Luck of the Draw (novella)

All the Luck You Need (prequel novella) by Angela Casella

one

SHAUNA

I SWEAR under my breath as my phone buzzes. It's face-up on the coffee table, next to the sweating beer that's waiting for me to finish dessert, so I can already see his name.

Colter ASshole, changed when I was drunk and never updated to the proper capitalization.

Damn it.

I'm in my pajamas at six-forty on a Saturday night, eating a pint of ice cream while watching a bad dating show with my grandmother's Corgi. The last person in the world I want to hear from right now is my ex-boyfriend. Shouldn't that be understood?

It doesn't help that my grandmother, whom I live with, is gussying herself up for the wrap party for a made-for-TV movie she appeared in. I mean, no girl wants to be out-foxed by her grandmother. Nana was a background actress, an extra, but Constance Murphy has never been the type to blend in. She's even sharper and snappier than she was at twenty, I'm sure, and she has the kind of presence and authority that makes people take notice. If I told her that, she'd insist no granddaughter of hers could possibly be a wilting violet either, but I feel like one lately, down to my fading, overgrown purple pixie cut and the zit on my cheek.

1

I'm a little depressed, I guess. That's what happens when your boyfriend leaves you and promptly gets engaged to your best friend.

Former best friend.

Sighing, I stuff a final spoonful of ice cream into my face and then present Bertie, who's snuggled up next to me, with the remainder of the pint, holding the bottom for him. Vanilla, purchased so I could share, because I am this dog's bitch. Fine by me. I'd rather be his bitch than some man's girlfriend.

"I shouldn't look, should I?" I ask him. "It's just going to piss me off, isn't it?"

He's nose-deep in the pint and clearly could care less. Fantastic. Not only am I talking to a dog—I'm talking to him and he's not listening.

Still holding the pint mostly stationary for Bertie, I lean forward and ditch the spoon in favor of the phone. I unlock it with a finger while paying half-attention to the douchebag on the screen—a guy with teeth so white they could probably be seen from space. He's saying something about the dangers of opening his heart to new love, as if it's a real boo-hoo hardship to be presented with multiple hot single women who want to bang him. The show's called *Time to Settle Down*, and the premise is that Tooth Guy has gotten too old to continue being a playboy. So they're giving him one last hurrah before he has to propose to one of the ten women living in his temporary harem with him.

"I dislike you," I say, pointing the phone at him. Bertie grumbles at me because I jostled the pint I'm still holding. I could put it down for him to feast on, but it's cozy having him this close, so I'd prefer for him to stay.

Finally, sighing, I look at the phone and read Colter's message.

> When do we get to meet him, Bean?

I'm tempted to reply that he doesn't get to call me that anymore, and I didn't particularly like it in the first place, but I'm silenced by his next message. A photo that was taken in my basement several weeks ago. It's of my grandmother and one of the much-younger friends she made while filming the movie.

Leonard has wavy brown hair, slightly too long, and hazel eyes with long lashes. He's tall, muscular, and tattooed, although he really missed the mark in choosing which ones to get, because I knew within five minutes of meeting him that "trouble" should be scrawled right in the middle of his forehead. It's this air he has–like he's always five minutes away from making his next mistake or banging someone in the bathroom of a Wendy's. Of course, *that* would be a mistake for whoever he'd tricked into banging him. The man may be gainfully employed, but he has the air of a vagrant. A *hot* vagrant. The kind who might trick a single mother into taking him home, only to run off with her...

I don't know, people don't really have silver silverware anymore, do they?

Besides, from what little I know about his past, he's the kind of guy who throws grenades and then runs—not exactly the sort of person you want to hang your hat on.

Still, credit where it's due. My grandfather ran off a while back to shack up with his much-younger water aerobics instructor girlfriend. When he found out, Leonard offered to take this photo—and a few more—with Nana so she could pretend she'd attracted a partner even younger and hotter than Grandpa Frank's pretty young thang. Up the photos went on social media, and my grandmother has spent the past several weeks deflecting thirsty questions from everyone she knows. She's loved every minute, but as far as I know she's declined to explain herself to anyone.

Is Colter trying to get the goods on my grandmother?

He's not the type of guy who likes gossip, as a rule. So is this coming from Bianca?

Yes, I decide, *that tracks.*

She always *did* enjoy gossip. It was all fun and games until she turned on me and swooped in on my boyfriend. You'd think six years of friendship would have given her pause, but Bianca believes in going for what she wants. That was something I'd admired about her once.

Teeth on edge, I mute Mr. Whiney Pants on the TV and type:

> What do you mean?

> I'm happy for you. I've always known you'd meet the perfect person when the timing was right.

Wait, *what?*

The ice cream container escapes my grip, and Bertie grumbles at me again before inelegantly jumping off the couch, his little Corgi legs really no help to him.

I fumble with my phone as I try to figure out an appropriate response.

> Are you under the impression that there's something going on between me and this man?

> Very funny, Bean. Your grandmother has been spreading the word. She says he's a great guy. A doctor, huh?

A doctor? That should have been his first clue it was a lie. The only "doctors" who look like Leonard are strippers in white coats.

> You're bringing him to the wedding, I hope. AND the Sten party.

Dread washes over me.

"*Nana,*" I shout, my voice unhinged. I get up off the couch. "*Nana!*"

"For God's sake, child," she chides, emerging from the back hall-

4

way. Bertie pauses in his ice cream massacre to wag his nub tail at the sight of her. She *does* look good in her blue sequined gown, her hair swept up in an elegant do. I'd be more appreciative if she hadn't just screwed me over.

I shake the phone at her. "Did you tell people that your friend Leonard is my boyfriend?" I hiss. "My *doctor* boyfriend?"

She pales in the way of someone who knows they fucked up.

"Maybe a few," she admits. "I didn't appreciate the way they were talking about you. My friend Marsha said something about it being a pity you didn't drag Milquetoast to the altar while you had a chance, and I might have lost it a little. They've all been asking me about the photos, and I–"

"You made him a *doctor*," I say, because I really can't bring enough attention to that point. "Who the hell would even believe that?"

"Have you met Dr. Rose?" she asks, pretending to fan her face. "He's a smoke show."

I have no idea who she's talking about—indeed, there's a fifty-fifty chance she's making it up—so I just scowl at her. "You're evading the point. Colter knows, Nana. Someone told his mother, and now he wants to meet my boyfriend. The *doctor*."

"Pediatric surgeon," she corrects, but from the way her eyes have widened I can tell she wasn't expecting her game of telephone to go so far.

I continue to scowl at her. "Well, he expects my pediatric surgeon boyfriend to come to his wedding," I say through my teeth. "And the Sten party."

"What the hell is a Sten party?" she asks, her lips tipping up as if she's prepared to be amused.

This is why I haven't told her yet. Normally, I'd laugh with her, because it's truly ridiculous, but my tone is tight as I say, "Colter and Bianca are having their bachelor and bachelorette parties together. They're just *that* in love. I told you I had something going

5

on next weekend." I wave a hand. "It's an all-weekend thing. It's supposed to be fun. I guess a lot of people are going."

Including a lot of people I know. People who have given me the cold shoulder for months, as if my bad luck might be catching. If it seems perverse of me to want to go to such a thing, let it be known that I *don't* want to go. The thought of attending the wedding, and especially the Sten party, makes my stomach turn over. I know Colter only wants me there to soothe his guilty conscience, so he can keep being seen as a good guy. Bianca's playing a darker game, though, and I'm not going to be the one to tap out. I won't let her rewrite history and make me a victim...or a villain.

Her lips thin. "What on God's green earth prompted you to say you'd do any of this?"

I stare back at Nana. "Maybe the same thing that prompted you to make up such a stupid lie."

"I didn't want to let them embarrass you." She props a hand on her hip. "As if you lost out by not marrying a man who works for his mother."

"So you decided it would be better for *you* to embarrass me," I say, suddenly beyond done with all of it. "Don't you think it's going to be worse when I have to tell Colter that you made it all up?"

"So don't," she insists. "I can't think why it would be any of his business in the first place."

"And if he sees Leonard making out with some other woman in a Wendy's restroom?"

I'm not sure why the Wendy's thing keeps coming up. I'm not even hungry, although they *do* have good fries.

"That seems highly unlikely." Nana sniffs. "Milquetoast would never deign to set foot in a fast-food restaurant." Shifting tactics, she asks, "Why don't you come with me tonight? It'll be fun. Your friends are going to be there. You need to get out more."

"You mean *your* friends," I say tightly, although it's not entirely true. Leonard and I may not have formed a beautiful friendship, but

I *have* gotten acquainted with another of my grandmother's movie extra friends, Delia. My friend Rafe is also engaged to Sinclair Jones, the star of the movie, who was Nana's in with the casting director. Sinclair is the one who organized the party tonight. She's also the person who is making my dreams come true.

My work dreams, to be clear—it's not a threesome situation. I've been trying to be a full-time clay artist for years now, but I've never made enough money. Up until now, it's always been the second and less well-paying of my jobs. For a long time, Rafe and I worked together as personal trainers, both of us wannabe artists who couldn't make the cut. A good fifty percent of my clients were men who wanted to watch my ass in my lycra shorts. But Sinclair's new art collective, The Waiting Place, is paying me a modest salary for teaching. Started paying me last month, in fact, even though it's September and we don't open until October 1st. That, in addition to what I'll get from selling my art there, will mostly pay my bills. Same for Rafe, although realistically he won't have to worry about the bills much now that he's marrying a movie star.

Quitting the gym was a banner moment, but it happened a few weeks ago, so I've already burned off the high.

"I'm wearing novelty pajama shorts," I object.

"You can change." She shrugs. "Or not. Pretend it's a fashion statement. For God's sake, it probably is. I wouldn't be the least bit surprised if—"

"Just go, Nana," I say, suddenly exhausted. "Have fun." I lift a finger. "But don't you dare tell Leonard about any of this. He'd find some way to twist it to his advantage."

She clucks her tongue. "You've got that boy all wrong."

"The only reason he posed for those photos with you was because he liked the thought of causing trouble. He admitted as much."

To be fair, I thought it was fun too. Right up until I got a text about my pediatric surgeon lover.

7

"Did you give him a different name?" I ask.

"I felt it was best to stick as close to the truth as possible." She says it with a straight face, as if she hadn't promoted him from being a construction worker to a pediatric surgeon.

"So I'm madly in love with Leonard the pediatric surgeon?" I ask, groaning as I consider what to tell Colter. Is Nana right? Is it possible I don't have to correct the story? I can tell him Leonard's out of town or working for a Doctors Without Borders office in Mozambique or something. It sounds like a fake excuse, but better that than admit *he's* fake.

"I don't want to leave you like this," Nana says worriedly, sharing prolonged eye contact with Bertie as if they're both worried about me and are working out a strategy for my betterment.

"I'd prefer it if you did. I'm going to be pissed about this for at least twenty-four hours. Possibly twenty-four years, depending on the fallout."

She nods slowly. "That's fair. I'm still going to hug you, though."

Sighing, I walk into her open arms, and breathe in her perfume —a different scent than the one she wore for fifty-some-odd years, because after my grandfather left she declared she was embracing new beginnings. At the time, I figured that was just the kind of shit people say after something bad happens, but she's held to it. When Rafe's fiancée said they were looking for extras for her film, Nana was first in line, and then she learned crocheting from a YouTube video and started making sweaters for Bertie. Finally, the cherry on top—the three thirty-something friends she made on the movie set. Delia, her boyfriend Lucas Burke, and Burke's friend Leonard.

My grandmother's switching things up from her perfume to her social life, and I'm stuck in a rut. If anything, I'm digging my way in deeper.

Nana swats me on the ass. "You need to be a little bad for a change."

"Not the party line you gave me when I was a kid," I tell her as I retreat to the sofa. Bertie, the little traitor, trails her to the door. "Have fun, Nana."

I'm still pissed, but I don't like the worried look in her eyes as she glances back at me. It's been there for months because of my grandfather, and now it's back because of me. Maybe it never really went away.

"I feel the need to point out that my career is going great for the first time ever," I call out as she leaves and shuts the door behind her.

She doesn't dignify that with a response, so I slump back into the cushions and turn on the volume. Whiney Pants is now making out with someone on the beach. Maybe it was the teeth that did it for him.

"Come to Mama," I say and grab the beer waiting for me on the table. It's starting to feel like a two-beer kind of night. Maybe three.

I'm near the bottom of it when a knock lands on the door.

Bertie stirs to attention in the dog bed he settled onto after Nana left, then darts toward the door, suddenly barking up a racket. I follow him, feeling cautious suddenly, because Bertie doesn't typically bark at people.

"There is a life alert in this house," I call out as I make my approach, "and I'm not afraid to use it."

Then I look through the peephole, and the air whistles out of me.

It's *him*.

Leonard's wearing a button-down shirt that covers all of his tattoos. But nothing conceals the mischief in his hazel eyes or the chaos of his always messy hair. Still. This is the closest to looking like a doctor he's ever going to get.

"No need to use the life alert," he says through the door. "I'm a pediatric surgeon."

I don't know whether to laugh or cry. I *definitely* shouldn't open the door.

two

LEONARD

I PROBABLY SHOULDN'T BE HERE.

Maybe that's exactly why I came.

I've been good lately, doing and saying what I should. Sometimes it feels like a pair of too-tight boxer briefs strangling my balls.

Ten minutes ago, I was in a very sweet vintage Rolls Royce on the way to a wrap party for the movie in which I was human scenery. I was with my buddy Burke and his girl, Delia, both of them dressed to the nines—Burke in a tux and Delia in one of her colorful dresses you can't look at too long if you want to keep your eyes working right. I was feeling pretty fly, because I was dressed in pants that didn't have a single hole in them, and I'd convinced the driver of the car to let me have a turn behind the wheel. There's nothing that makes my blood sing quite as much as doing something I'm not supposed to. The driver, a geezer with a huge mustache, had moved over to the passenger seat. He had all the marks of someone who was feeling regret, but hey, he'd agreed.

When we picked up Constance, I could tell there was something off with her. Normally, she would have nearly shit herself over being in a car like that—same as me—but she barely said two words.

Then, a couple of streetlights later, she confessed to the whole shebang about Shauna and the photo...

And I nearly wrecked the car.

Here's the truth: I've got a thing for Constance's granddaughter. Shauna's small but athletic and curvy, with short purple hair and an attitude that makes her ten times as sexy. Then there's her art. She's a clay artist, and most of the bowls, mugs, and vases she makes are monsters. They have sharp teeth. Tentacles for hair. You name it. They're cool as hell, and the fact that monsters live inside that pretty little pint-sized woman interests me.

And I'd just been hand-delivered an excuse to spend time with her.

Nothing can happen between us, of course. I might have started talking to Constance on the movie set out of boredom, but she's become important to me—important enough that I don't want to fuck up our friendship to see if her granddaughter tastes as good as she looks.

Not that I'd be offered the chance.

This thing I've got for Shauna isn't mutual. If anything, she's taken a dislike to me. Seems like she has a smart reply to everything I have to say and a judging gaze that's always on me. Still, I wouldn't mind getting to know her better, even if it's as bad of an idea as it was for that driver to let me take a turn behind the wheel.

Speaking of him—he shrieked, "Pull over now, sir!"—and then threw us out as soon as I'd parked at the curb.

Once we'd all filed out in our finery, he shouted, "You'll never rent from us again," which we all agreed was fair. I don't like it when people mess with my toys either, and it *was* a very nice car.

Burke said he'd grab us an Uber, but from the way he was eyeing me, he already knew what my next move would be. He let me stew on it though. My buddy was raised by a couple of rich assholes, so he can be pushy as hell, but he knows what makes

11

people tick. Getting bossed around doesn't it do it for me. So he doesn't try it all that often.

Still, he obviously wasn't surprised when I announced I was bouncing on the wrap party, on account of I had to go see my girlfriend.

"Say hello to Shauna for us before she knees you in the balls," he said with a smirk, wrapping his arms around his girl.

"Oh, she wouldn't do that," Delia said, because she is both sweet and naïve. I have every expectation that Shauna might punch me if she opens that door. She certainly won't be rolling out the red carpet.

"I can't say I'm sorry for any of it," Constance said as a group of tourists pushed past us, arguing about directions. They were wrong, but I felt no need to say so.

"Nobody thought you would be," I said.

She shrugged, looking delighted with herself, and Delia and Burke shared this knowing glance you only see between two people who've been foolish enough to fall in love.

"Stop it with the lovesick glances," I said. "I got a weak gag reflex."

"Yes, me too," Constance added. "All of this pecking and mooning is all very good when you're young and everyone's pretty, but wait until you're in your eighties and everything sags—"

"Good God, Constance," I said, giving her arm a gentle shove. "I just got done saying that thing about the weak gag reflex."

She laughed wickedly. "Tormenting you makes me feel young again."

A woman walking by with a stroller gave us a worried look, like she thought our crazy might be catching. When I saluted her, she nearly broke into a run.

Burke rolled his eyes at us, although he should have been used to us carrying on. It's what we did the whole time we were on that movie set. There's not much fun to be had when you're told to sit or stand places like you're a potted plant, so Constance and I made our own fun.

"We weren't mooning over each other," Burke objected. "We had a feeling something like this would happen."

"What, that Constance would send a photo of me around to her friends and say I'm Shauna's pediatric surgeon boyfriend?" I asked. "That's a very specific thing to have foreseen. Maybe you should bail out on L&L Restoration and start a phone psychic business."

L&L Restoration is the house flipping business that Burke and I are running.

To be clear, he's the one with the bones and business smarts to get this ball rolling. I'm as broke as the day I was born—and if I had any business sense, I'd have a bank account with a few zeroes in the balance.

I didn't ask Burke to put that kind of trust in me, and part of me didn't want him to. It's a burden, someone else's trust. Especially when you have to bust your ass to be worthy of it. At the same time, he's giving me a chance to make something of myself. I can't throw that away, even if sometimes, in the middle of the night, I wake up wanting to pack a bag and drive off to somewhere where no one is dumb enough to give me responsibilities.

"The psychic thing sounds like fun," Delia said. "Maybe it could be a side hustle."

"Look at you making jokes." I grinned at her, pleased as punch. "I'm rubbing off on you."

"Yeah, probably for the best if you take an uber away from here, so we can make sure that stops," Burke said.

So that's exactly what happened. They went on their merry way to the party, and I headed over here to talk to Shauna.

I found myself whistling in my uber, because Constance had just given me the best gift possible—an excuse to get into trouble and pretend I was only doing it as a favor. Maybe she'd known I'd react this way. She's a wily one, my friend.

That's what brought me to this moment: standing at Shauna's door, reporting for fake boyfriend duty.

When the door swings open, I can feel a grin stretching my face. Shauna looks like she just crawled out of bed. She's wearing boxers decorated with characters from a cartoon that got cancelled when we were kids and a T-shirt that very obviously doesn't have a bra under it.

Hallelujah, the sight of her beaded nipples through her shirt is better than a shot of fine whiskey.

"Did you convince Nana to do this, Leonard?" she asks through her teeth.

Forcing my gaze away from those pretty points is hard enough that someone should give me a medal for it, but I meet her glare and grin. Lifting my hands up, palms out, I say, "Hell, no. If I'd come up with it, I would have given myself a cooler job."

"This is a disaster," she mutters.

"Probably," I agree. Her pint-sized dog ambles up and settles at her feet, giving me the evil-eye. I've always had a thing for dogs. Never got another one after I lost my girl Gidget, but that doesn't mean I don't like them. Dogs don't truck in bullshit. A dog likes you, you know it. A dog hates you, you know it. There's something to be said for that.

Unfortunately, this particular dog hates me. Maybe he's right to. If Shauna weren't Constance's granddaughter, and I didn't like Constance more than I do the majority of people, then I already would have tried to fuck her.

"You gonna invite me in?"

She snorts and puts a hand on her hip. "No. We can talk out here on the porch."

"You aren't concerned about your neighbors overhearing?"

She glances pointedly at the empty porches around us. There's something wrong about an empty porch in the thick of summer, like a hand that's gone unshaken.

"You never know when people are listening," I say. "Why, this one time—"

"I'm having a beer," she blurts. "Do you want a beer?"

"I'll never answer that question with a no," I say, parking myself in one of the two rocking chairs on her porch. It's pretty nice out here, and I can't say I regret missing the wrap party for the movie. Not when the alternative is porch sitting with a beer and a sexy woman.

Sure, she has no more regard for me than her dog does, but it's not off-putting. I've always had a thing for smart women who can see right through me.

Shauna disappears through the door, muttering to herself, and I swear to Christ that little dog growls at me when he catches me watching her ass disappear into the house.

"I come in peace," I mutter, then get to rocking. He must decide it would be too much trouble to try to nab me in the balls, because he disappears into the house through the open door. A minute or so later, Shauna comes out solo with two cold ones and shuts the door behind her. She hands me one of the beers before sighing and settling into the other rocking chair.

"That sigh of defeat isn't like you," I comment after I take a swig of the beer.

She lets out a pfft of air that flutters her bangs. They're dark at the root. "How the hell would you know? You know nothing about me. You've been to my house all of two times."

"Three. I came by a couple of days ago to help Constance move her dresser when she got a bug up her ass about trying feng shui. You weren't home, but Bertie came running out with your bra in his mouth, so it felt like you were spiritually present."

Another pfft of air. "She's taking this whole post breakup life reinvention thing too far."

"You think?" I ask after taking a swig of beer. "Maybe you haven't been taking it far enough."

She glowers at me, and I can't help but laugh. Based on her expression, it was definitely the wrong thing to say. "What? Constance likes to talk, so yeah, I've heard a thing or two about your ex. Seen some pictures too." I cock my head. "You really wanted to marry that guy? He looks like someone who sells used cars. The really bad ones that wouldn't get you two blocks."

A snort escapes her, like she wanted to laugh but didn't let it happen. "He and his mother run a craft store, actually."

I shrug. "Crafts, cars. Same difference. He looks like a salesman."

"You're one of those people who uses 'literal' for things that aren't literal, aren't you?"

"Nah, that's a five-dollar word. I prefer not to blow my load that quickly."

She shakes her head and then takes a swig of beer, her expression too sad for my liking. "You don't know me, Leonard. And you don't know Colter. You barely even know my grandmother."

I ignore the sting of that last sentence and say, "I forgot that was his real name. Why didn't his parents save everyone some trouble and just call him Douchebag? Because they all but ensured he'd be one with that name."

"You don't have to get involved," she says with a sigh. "This is my life, and my grandmother had no right to tell you anything about it. But, for the record, it's incredibly weird to me that you'd want to be friends with a woman in her eighties. You know she doesn't have any money to speak of, right?"

That accusation doesn't sit well either, but I don't let it show.

Raising my eyebrows, I say, "My best friend is a millionaire. If I wanted to steal from someone, why go any further? Hell, Burke and I are in business together. It would be easy."

She rubs between her eyes and curses under her breath. "That was a shit thing to say. But you have to admit it's weird that you and my grandmother—"

16

"Oh sure, it's weird as hell," I say, rocking. "But she's my friend, no question. And being a good friend to her, I obviously care about her personal life. So, your business is my business. I'm going to help you."

Her nose crinkles with amusement, and fuck me, it's cute. "What are you going to do to help me? Put a hit on Colter?"

I lift my hands. "Whoa, that's not the kind of trouble I like to get into. But if you decide you want to stir up a little shit and get even, I'm your guy." I grin at her. "Let's give these jokers a wedding to remember."

"You really want to go with me?" she asks, seeming surprised. "I figured I'd pretend you were off saving lives overseas or something."

"I'm going to save you from the trouble of making up a shitty lie and give you a better one."

She makes a sound like a growl and runs both hands through her purple hair, instantly making it messier—and hotter. That sound does things for me too. "What's the point? I don't even like Colter anymore. It might have taken me a while to realize it, but Nana's on to something with the whole milquetoast thing. To be honest, I have no idea how I let things go on so long. I definitely wouldn't want to be with him if they broke up. So shouldn't I just keep pretending I don't care?"

"Why don't you start off by telling me what happened?" I say.

She angles her head and gives me an almost sly expression that I like more than I should. "I thought you already knew everything."

"Probably about 75%, but Constance always thinks she knows more than she does. Except about cheese. She knows a lot about cheese."

She gives me a blank look, decides she doesn't care about the cheese, and then shakes her head. "My story is more pathetic than epic."

"All the better. I live for other people's pathetic stories. It makes me feel better about my own life."

17

three

LEONARD

SHAUNA SWIGS HER BEER, then says, "I don't know why I'm telling you this."

"I'm guessing it's because you need to talk to someone, and I stumbled along at the right time."

She nods slowly. "I met Bianca at a craft fair about six years ago."

"You sell your stuff at craft fairs?" I ask. I like the thought. It's... wholesome, and Shauna's not a wholesome kind of broad. I can see it in those monsters she makes, in the gleam in her eyes when she's putting me in my place. There's something wicked about her, like she's just waiting for someone to push her over the edge, or maybe up against a wall...

I get a flash of her like that, her head tipped back, her throat begging for my lips and teeth, her tits—

Constance's granddaughter, I remind myself.

"What the hell else am I supposed to do with a hundred mugs?" she asks.

I shrug. "Your grandmother said you were part of some sort of art collective with that actress Sinclair."

"I am, but we haven't really gotten up and running yet. The

grand opening for The Waiting Place is on October 1st. Sinclair's been busy with..." She waves her hand.

"That shitty movie your grandmother and I were in?"

"Exactly. So certain details needed to...well, wait."

"What's the deal with the name, anyway? Reminds me of the clink."

"You've been to jail?" she asks, wide-eyed.

"Only lockup."

She nods slowly, chewing on that, then says, "It's from a Dr. Seuss book. We're a bunch of artists who are going to teach people at all different levels of ability to craft. The focus will be on helping people find their form of artistic expression."

"You gonna show me how to make an ashtray?"

"Why am I not surprised you smoke?" she says, rolling her eyes.

"Only 420." The look she's giving me says she doesn't think that's any better, and maybe it's worse. It helps me settle down, but I'm not about to say so. I don't tell people about the dreams. Not even Burke knows, and he's the person I've told the most. "So what happened at the craft fair?"

"Bianca was there selling her handmade pompoms." I laugh. She continues speaking as if I hadn't. "She calls them Queen Bee Pompoms, maybe you've heard of them."

I laugh again. "I sure as shit haven't."

She shrugs, but there's a slight smile on her face. "They've become pretty big over the last couple of years. Anyway. I'd seen her around a few times before, but this time we got to talking. We sort of hit it off. Fast forward four years. A little while after I started dating Colter, she met this guy Carter. We weren't as close by then, because her business had started blowing up, and mine... Let's just say I was working at a sweaty-ass gym to pay for my shitty studio space before Sinclair came along. Bianca had found other friends, but we did a lot of couple stuff together for the next year and a half or so. And then she and Carter—"

"Has a type, huh?" I ask.

This gets me a small smile. "They broke up, and she asked me to get drinks with her. Lift her up, you know? Obviously I wasn't going to say no to that."

"What she'd do, roofie you?"

She gives a shake of her head, her lips turned up. "No, she got me drunk and told me about Carter being an ass, then asked me to tell her all the things that bothered me about Colter. Turned out there were a lot."

"Like what?" I ask, unable to help myself.

She looks at her beer, then takes a sip. "He wanted me to be more like him."

"Boring?"

She gives a half-hearted laugh. "Maybe. And he didn't get my art. He encouraged me to make something more commercial. Bianca had been on that party line for a while. Maybe they were already fucking."

Probably, but I don't say so. "They're wrong. I don't even like art, and I like yours."

Her lips lift up slightly. "Thanks. Anyway, she convinced me to call him out on a few things over text, and it led to this huge fight. We decided to take a break, and the next thing I know, Bianca's calling me up. She'd never planned on it happening, she said, but she and Colter had hit it off. They were in love, and she'd do anything to get me to forgive her. Anything but give him up, obviously."

"Huh, ballsy," I say.

Shauna shoves my arm and frowns at me.

"Shitty too." I lift my hands. "But there's no denying she's got some balls. That means you've gotta show her yours are bigger."

"Those pompoms she makes are fucking enormous. I don't know if mine are bigger."

She surprises me into laughter, and it's even more of a surprise when she laughs with me. I feel a twinge of...something, but maybe it's just that old impulse to ruin things. I've got a good thing going, being friends with Constance. I don't want to fuck that up.

I shake off the thought. "When did she make that call to you?"

"Eight months ago," she says, rocking aggressively in the chair. "They got engaged after three months of dating. Colter and I were together for two years."

"Amateurs. So what are we going to do to destroy their joy?" I grin at her. "Tie-dye the wedding linens, crash-bomb the cake, fill them with crushing doubt? Ooh, you want me to seduce the bride?"

She shoves my arm. "Why would I want you to do that? Then she'll think she can steal anything she wants from me."

"Huh. Guess you have a point. Too bad. I'm envisioning Bianca as this Type-A blond chick. You'd be surprised how wild they can be."

"You're gross," she says, giving me a look of disgust.

"Never claimed otherwise. You didn't say I was wrong about the Type-A blond thing."

"This is a bad idea," she blusters.

"Probably. If you don't want to go through with it, you can always say you've changed your mind about being in their wedding. Might want to add that it was pretty fucked up of them to ask in the first place."

"I won't give them the satisfaction," she says tightly, and the look of determination on her face reminds me of her grandmother. Constance is one tough broad, and I respect the hell out of her. Shauna too. "Especially not Bianca." She purses her lips for a moment, thinking, then says. "I haven't really told anyone this part, but it's like we're playing a game of chicken, and she's daring me to be the one who taps out."

"She wants a reaction from you."

"Yes," she says, leaning forward. "She wants me to cry and put up a fuss. I don't understand why, because we were close before shit

21

went down, but it seems like she wants to destroy me. I mean... there's the wedding date for one thing—"

"What do you mean?" I ask. "That it's so soon?"

"Sure," she says, blowing out a breath that makes her bangs sway. "And then she asked me to be a bridesmaid."

I whistle.

"And not just any bridesmaid—her only bridesmaid, which makes me the de facto maid of honor. She said it was because I'd introduced them. But it goes deeper than that. She's having all these wedding-related events at places I love, and she's inviting me to them. That's fucked up, right?"

"Deeply."

"I can't give her what she wants."

"No, you definitely can't let her see you break," I agree.

She sighs and takes a sip of her beer. "It still hurts, though. I mean, I thought she was one of my best friends."

"You get manicures together?"

She rolls her eyes, then lifts a small, undecorated hand. "I work with clay, so nothing ever stays on my nails."

There's something sexy about her bare hands, no rings or polish, just her soft, smooth skin and a small scar near the base of her thumb.

"But sure, we did some girly shit if that's what you're getting at. We also drank bourbon and closed down bars, had crafting competitions, and made-up scavenger hunts for things we could find around town. We were *friends*. We let each other in. I mean...she had this competitive streak that could be a bit much, and sometimes she could be mean to people, but I never thought she'd turn it on me."

"Maybe she feels bad about the whole thing, and it'll boost her ego if you flip out and act crazy. She could be trying to drive you to it."

"Maybe," she grumbles.

"You seem like you care more about what she did than what Dumbass did."

"Because I do," she says, picking at the skin near her thumbnail. I'm tempted to stop her, but I don't. "He wasn't right for me anyway, so it was just a matter of time."

"But you thought she was forever."

She nods, her jaw tight. "It hurts worse because I have to keep pretending I'm bored of the whole thing."

"I'll bet you give a good bored face," I comment.

"You should know, you've seen it plenty."

I laugh, because she really is something else, then rub my hands together. "On to Plan Chaos. You know, I'm not so good at planning. I'm more of an on-my-feet kind of guy. What do you say we take it as it comes? Seed little bits of fucked-up fun wherever we go without looking like we're the bad guys. And, of course, I'll be the most devoted doctor boyfriend you could hope for."

"What do you want for helping me?" The look on her face says she won't accept that I want to help for no other reason than that I *like* her. And Constance, of course.

"Pay me in clay. You can teach me how to make something."

She gives me a you're-full-of-shit look. "You want to learn how to use a wheel?"

I lift my hands. "Chicks dig a man who can use his hands."

"Fine," she says with a sigh. "Why do I think you're going to want to make a huge clay dick?"

"Because you're an excellent judge of character," I say with a bark of a laugh. "So when's the wedding, sugar?" Sugar tits almost comes tumbling out, but I have some self-control.

She bites her lip, and it looks so damn luscious, I feel a sucker punch to my chest. There's no denying I want her. I've wanted her since the first time she threatened me with physical harm, within minutes of meeting me, but that's not what this is about. It's been too long, is all. I've been in Asheville for a couple of months now, and I haven't brought a single woman home. I'd promised myself it was going to be different here—*I* was going to be different—and the first step is to stop repeating old patterns. Still, there's a pretty big damn difference between a man's hand and a soft, wet—

"It's not just the wedding."

"Oh?" I ask, cocking my head.

"There are events all next weekend. They're calling it a Sten party—stag and hen."

"Excuse me?"

"There's an event on Friday night, then an adult sleepover at Camp Smileshine on Saturday. And we wouldn't want to forget the photos at the flower farm the following weekend. The wedding is two weeks later at the NC Arboretum."

"Smileshine?" I ask in disbelief. "Sounds like a place where people go to get murdered by killer clowns. What if their relationship falls apart on Friday night? Then we won't have to do that other shit. Maybe I can infiltrate enemy lines, find out if Douchebag is dicking around on her."

She laughs. "I guarantee you he's not. She'd kill him."

"That would solve our problem, wouldn't it?"

I get another laugh from her, which makes me feel pretty damn good.

"I don't necessarily want to ruin the wedding," she insists. "I'm cool with them getting married and making each other miserable. I just..." She blows out a frustrated breath. "I can't back down, like I said, but if I have to be subjected to all of this bullshit, I wouldn't mind making them a little uncomfortable."

"I can do that," I say, wanting the gig more than I should.

"You're really going to do all of this shit with me?" she asks in disbelief. "For a couple of clay lessons?" She shakes her head. "I'll pay you, Leonard."

"Sure, whatever," I lie. I'm not going to take a cent from her. It's not that I have an objection to money, but her money? Hell, no. If I take it from anyone, it'll be Ole Douchebag. If I told her that, though, she'd deny me.

She turns in her rocking chair and studies me for a long moment, our eyes locking. "Thank you for being good to my grandmother," she finally says. "Even if I don't understand why. Doing the movie helped her a lot...even with the trouble."

The trouble being that someone in the crew tried to kill Delia. It has made what would have been your average D+ romantic comedy into something people are excited about. I'm just glad she's alive. I was the one who saved her from that fucker, and sometimes when I wake up at night, my heart racing, it's because of that, not all of the stuff that came before.

"You don't need to thank me," I say slowly, trying not to be drawn in by those lips, slightly parted, or that messy lilac hair. Her big brown eyes are still watching me, seeing God knows what. "It's like I told you. I like Constance. She'd be hard not to like."

"I agree with you there," she says with a slight nod.

"She raised you, huh?" I ask softly. I know that much from Constance. Shauna's parents died in a car wreck, and she moved in with Constance and the asshole formerly known as Mr. Constance. "You were lucky."

She nods again. "She's the best. My grandfather's a bit of a disappointment. But what can you do?"

"You're one of those women who think all men are fuckers, aren't you?" Admittedly, from what Constance has told me, Shauna's ex isn't a prince among men—he's just one of those posers who likes to seem like one.

A side of her mouth lifts. "Maybe I'd like someone to prove me wrong. But no, I don't think all men are like that. Rafe, Sinclair's fiancé, is one of my oldest friends. He's not a fucker." Her gaze doesn't leave me. "What about you? What are Leonard Smith's parents like? It's hard to imagine you as a kid."

Smith isn't the last name I was born with, but I'm used to going by names that aren't mine. "My father's someone everyone would be better off not knowing, and my mother thinks he's the second coming. I guess they're kind of like Burke's parents, except shittier and much poorer."

My friend Burke's parents aren't a gold standard, so she'll understand what I mean.

I've only been back in Asheville for a few months, but I lived here for a long stretch eight years ago. Burke's folks ran me off. At the time, I was working for them at Burke Enterprises. I found out they were responsible for a building collapse that killed people, and instead of copping to it, they tried to cover it up. When I confronted them with what I knew, they hired someone to dig into my past. He connected the dots that I've done my damnedest to hide, and they told me a truth I couldn't deny—I had no iron proof, and no one was going to believe a piece of shit like me once they knew all the details of my past. They offered me a payoff, and I took it.

But they didn't trust me not to run my mouth, so they hired someone to follow me around. My paranoia didn't much like that, and I got to thinking they wanted to rub me out. I didn't tell any of my friends because I figured Burke would side with his folks, and our buddies would side with him. So I ran. And I kept on running until Burke found me and brought me back.

Now, the secret about Mama and Papa Burke is out. Burke found the evidence I couldn't, and his parents are going down. Even if they don't get jail time, they've lost their shine and their company. Fucking good.

Still.

My father makes them look like they should be sainted.

Shauna seems alarmed by the mere mention of my waste-of-space dad, so I can only imagine how she'd react to the rest of my past. Thank fuck she can't read minds. "My father's in jail. He's not going to bother anyone anymore."

I'm not sure why I offered up so much information, but the

words are already out, so I slap the arm of the rocking chair, and say, "Well, this has been a pleasure, sweetness and light. We better exchange phone numbers so we can get our story straight before next weekend."

"Are you going to keep calling me stupid names?" she asks.

"Until I find one that feels right, little bit."

She rolls her eyes but takes out her phone. Our fingers touch, and there's a little zip, like the kind you get when you mess around with an electrical socket, except more pleasant. It's unexpected, but I shake it off, smiling when I see the little goblin dog on her lock screen.

"No wonder he doesn't like me messing with you," I say. "He figures he's got it locked down."

I give her my number, and she sends off a text. I pull out my phone when it vibrates and grin at the middle finger emoji in my inbox.

I snap a photo of her, catching her with one eye half closed, the other wide open, then save it to my contacts under Light of My Life.

She leans in to see, then skewers me with a glare that makes me laugh. "I'm going to take one of you too."

She gets her phone out and snaps it, then immediately glowers. "Why the hell are you so photogenic?"

"One of my many blessings. When's my first clay lesson?"

Shauna studies me for a moment before answering. "You were serious about that?"

"My buddy Danny's birthday is coming up in October. What better gift that a foot-high clay dick? He'll love it. It'll be the center-piece of his home."

Her lips twitch. "Sure. I'll teach you. How about we see if you show up to the first Sten event first?"

"You're on," I say, holding my fist out for a bump. She gives it to me. "In the meantime, I better read the idiot's guide to pediatric surgery."

"Yeah, I'm pretty sure that doesn't exist. Maybe just pretend you don't like talking about work because it brings up traumatic memories."

Traumatic memories are something I know a thing or three about. I nod. "You got it, boss. Text me about the first nightmare event. I can't wait."

She smiles at me, and I feel a tugging in my gut. Maybe because this is one of the first times she's given me a real smile, and I like it.

"It's at the event space at Buchanan Brewery." She rolls her eyes. "My favorite brewery, not hers."

"You like that campground too?"

She shakes her head. "Nope, she comes by that one honestly. I hate camping. Get this, though. We're all going to be making pompoms on Friday night."

"There you go," I say with a grin. "Our chance to prove, once and for all, that your balls are bigger."

four

SHAUNA

MY GRANDMOTHER GETS home after midnight, laughing as she shuts the door behind her—and I hide in my bedroom with a final beer, feeling like the troll under the bridge. The last thing I want is for her to catch me scrolling through old Facebook photos of Colter, Bianca, and me. Bertie must feel bad for me, because he doesn't scratch the door to leave despite wagging his little nub of a tail for all he's worth at the sound of my grandmother's voice.

Am I an asshole for wanting Colter and Bianca to suffer a bit? I meant what I said to Leonard. I don't want to ruin their wedding or stop it from happening—they deserve each other. But I wouldn't mind pricking a pin in their happiness balloon. A slow leak seems to be just what the doctor ordered.

Doctor Leonard, that is.

I guess that's why I said yes.

I certainly didn't agree because I liked the way Leonard looked at me earlier. I was a hot mess, from my hair down to my toes with the chipped green polish, but his smoldering gaze suggested he'd like nothing better than to bend me over the porch railing and...

God Almighty, I need to get laid. It's been eight months since

Colter and I broke up, and even though I've gone on a couple of dates, none of them have progressed beyond dinner or drinks. Usually drinks to get through the dinners. The only action I've gotten was a goodnight kiss that left my mouth tasting like garlic and regret.

The thing is, despite his obvious unsuitability, Leonard is an attractive man.

Okay, fine. Attractive is the word you'd use for a silver fox in a sweater vest. Leonard is hot. He's as hot as a flaming Cheeto soaked in sriracha and lit on fire, mostly because he's a little grungy and unsuitable. Which is probably why my natural reaction to him is to focus on every last thing that's wrong with him.

Lucky for me, he usually gives me plenty of material.

Sighing I throw myself back onto my bed, a queen bed with a soft dove-gray duvet, because if you're going to live in your grand-parents' house, you'd better have an adult-ass bed.

It must be true that you dream of the last thing you were thinking about before you go to sleep, because in my dreams Leonard is railing me from behind against the porch, well, railing while my next-door neighbor, the sour-faced Mrs. Applebaum, watches with pursed lips from her Adirondack chair. When we finish, she lifts a sign ranking us two point five stars. Based on her sour expression, I'm guessing it's out of ten, like with figure skating. She obviously doesn't like me very much, because the dream sex *absolutely* ranked an eleven out of ten.

The next morning, I wake up with a headache, a zit that's expanded to the size of a bee sting, and a lady boner so persistent that I have to shoo Bertie out of the room so I can take out my vibrator.

Can a person go through a mid-life crisis at thirty-one? Because it certainly feels like that's what's happening. I don't even *like* Leonard. The only possible explanation for this madness is the sexual desert I've been marooned in.

After I cover up the zit to the best of my ability and get dressed, I head to the kitchen to sit with my grandmother, hoping she made me some coffee. She did, thank all that's holy, because the kitchen looks aggressively yellow this morning, and it's not helping my head. The only person who's home is Bertie, who's rooted beside his empty food bowl, giving me accusatory and hopeful looks.

There's a note on the table saying,

Off to my wet felting class. Have a nice day. I'm sorry again about last night, Shauna, but it sounds like it worked out for the best. Leonard told me you had a nice talk!

"I'll bet he did," I grumble before finishing the note—

P.S. Don't let Bertie fool you. He has been fed and walked.

"I knew it, you little stinker," I say, pointing a finger at him. He grunts, as if he knows the gig is up, and books it to a fluffy bed by the table. It's printed with a design of green eggs and ham, and it annoys me to remember that I picked it out with Colter at Craft Me, the store he runs with his mother. I'd burn it, but Bertie's fond of it, and the practical side of me won't allow it.

After half a cup of coffee, I've managed to bury the sex dream, somewhat, so I check my phone.

There are texts from Delia and Grandpa Frank, whose name my grandmother changed on my phone while *she* was drunk, to Grandpa Fruckface. I'm guessing she didn't keep the r on purpose, but I kept it that way because it makes me laugh.

31

Apparently drunken phone meddling is a thing that the women in my family do. Or at least my grandmother and me.

I wouldn't know what my mother might have done.

I was thirteen when she died, but I barely knew her. The only thing I knew for sure was that she didn't want me. It's hard to admit that about someone who's gone, because it means nothing can be fixed. But it's no less true.

I check out Delia's text first:

> I want to hear everything about Doctor Leonard! Can you meet Mira and me tomorrow night at the bar? It's her night off, so it would be just the three of us.

I'm halfway tempted to say no, except it occurs to me that Delia must know Leonard pretty well. They worked on that movie together, and he and Burke have been friends for years. Nana has plenty of Leonard knowledge, too, but if I ask too many questions about him, she'll become suspicious. Delia doesn't have a suspicious molecule in her body, so she's the perfect person for me to interrogate. Maybe she knows more about his past. There was this bleak look in his eyes when he told me his dad was in jail. It made me curious, I guess. It made me feel an unexpected flash of...connection, though I certainly won't be admitting that to anyone.

I send off a yes, then take a long sip of coffee before reading my grandfather's latest mea culpa—which doesn't sound like a mea culpa at all. My grandmother and I aren't the only stubborn ones in this family.

> I sent my last message seven days ago. It's been twenty days since you sent any kind of response.

I itch to text him a confirmation, nothing more or less, just to piss him off. But that's probably what he's angling for.

Sighing, I start to set my phone down when another message rolls in. This one's from Leonard.

> I'm guessing you have a hangover. Am I right? I like being right.

I think about ignoring him too, then write:

> Maybe you should open up a phone psychic business.

> No way. I was just telling Burke he should do that last night, because he said he predicted this whole thing with our fake relationship.

> Sorry to Burke and his imaginary business, but I think phone psychics are bogus.

> You don't believe in the mystical beyond, donut?

> Never call me that again.

He doesn't need to know his nicknames amuse me. If he knew that, or that I had a dream about him screwing me over the front railing of my house, he'd see it as an open door. What he'd do with that open door, I don't know, but I have a feeling it wouldn't end well for me.

My phone buzzes, and I lift it with a little more interest than before. Sure enough, it's him.

> I'm going to find the right nickname. It just takes practice. But I'm more than willing to practice until I get to perfect, my peach.

> Nope, that name's worse than the rest.

> But you do have a good peach.

> Of course I do. I don't need to be reminded of it.

Still, it doesn't hurt. I ditch the phone, smiling, happy, and feeling better than I have in weeks, and take Bertie out for a walk he doesn't need.

The next day, after spending the morning hauling boxes around at The Waiting Place, I head over to Glitterati, Delia's sister's bar. It's the kind of place that takes its name seriously, because everything inside is bright and covered with glitter. The bar itself is made of purple resin filled with ribbons of glitter, and the drinks are served on trays made out of old records. The first time I came here, I knew I'd found a place that spoke to my heart. So do the Evans sisters. There's Delia, with her red-gold hair and colorful outfits, and Mira, who has pitch black hair and light brown eyes. They come off as such opposites, but they both have a thing for color. This place is proof enough of that.

I knock on the door—locked, with a bedazzled Closed sign in the window—and Mira opens it.

"Well, you look like shit," she says.

"Thank you." I try not to lift my hand up to cover Zit Mountain, but my will power is a fragile thing these days. "I always try to look like I feel. It's my form of radical honesty."

She grins at me. "And telling it like it is, is mine. Come in, you have a drink waiting for you."

"Music to my ears."

Delia's sitting at the bar already, wearing a bright yellow dress that would look hideous on ninety percent of the population—

maybe ninety-five. Her face lights up when she sees me, and I already feel better than I did five minutes ago.

I may have only met the Evans sisters a couple of weeks ago, but it always does my soul good to see them. There's something so genuine and warm about them, and even though they're very different, they both are the kind of people who listen because they want to hear—not because they're waiting for their chance to speak. It has only made me realize how hollow my friendship with Bianca had become toward the end. And, also, how isolating it had been.

Bee wasn't my only female friend, but she has a habit of driving away people she doesn't like. Or people who threaten her. Or people who take up the time of the friends whose focus she wants for herself. I didn't even realize how bad it had gotten until she'd moved in on Colter, and I was left alone.

Rafe's my oldest friend, but he's still a dude. Sometimes you need female companionship and nothing else will do.

"I was worried you weren't going to come," Delia tells me, pushing a drink toward me. It's blue with edible glitter floating in it.

"That's a My Fake Boyfriend is Loki," Mira says, joining us. "I made each of us a signature drink."

"You gonna trademark that one?"

"I think Disney would have something to say about that." There are already three drinks on the counter, but she slips back behind the bar.

"Why don't you sit with us?" I ask. "I know that's your safe space, but I promise we won't bite."

"Something tells me it'll be a multiple round kind of night," Mira responds.

"Speak for yourself," I say, picking up the blue drink. "It's Monday, and the last thing I need is to roll into Tuesday with a hangover."

"Maybe I *am* speaking for myself." And I realize she's not

looking her best either. She's much better with makeup than I am, but there are circles under her eyes.

"What's up?" I ask.

"Nope, nuh-uh." She pulls up a stool behind the bar and leans her elbows on it, looking like James Gandolfini does in *The Sopranos* before he makes someone an offer they can't refuse. Admittedly, I don't think James Gandolfini ever touched a glitter bar in his life, but if he had, I'm sure he could have made it look intimidating.

"We want to know what happened with Leonard the other night," Delia says. "He said he's going to the wedding."

I sigh, because for someone who's pretty closed-lip about everything to do with his past, he can be as big of a gossip as my grandmother. No wonder they're friends.

"Yes," I say, then take a sip of the drink to steel myself. Damn, it's good. It's sweet and tangy and packs a helluva punch. I lift the glass toward Mira in acknowledgment. "You have a gift, my friend."

"And you have gossip." Waving a hand, she adds, "Out with it."

So I tell them about my porch sit with Leonard, leaving out the sex dream for obvious reasons.

"He's a good guy," Delia says after I finish.

I almost choke on the last sip of my Loki drink. "Seriously? I can think of many words to describe Leonard, but 'good guy' aren't two that come to mind."

"But he is," she says intently, swiveling her stool a little so she's facing me. "You know, he almost crashed the car we were in when Constance admitted to lying about that photograph."

"So he almost killed you, my grandmother, and Burke. This is supposed to convince me he's salt of the earth?"

"He was surprised," she says with a half-smile. "What I'm saying is that he instantly wanted to help you. There aren't a lot of guys who'd step into a situation like that. And no one would do it for someone they don't like."

My mind flashes to my phone, to all of the texts he's been sending me over the last couple of days. Funny messages but also memes. Photos of famous dick sculptures which he insists will have nothing on the clay dick he's going to make under my tutelage. His mind's like a squirrel's—jumping from one nut to another. It's been...entertaining.

I laugh uneasily. "Nope. No way. He flirts with me, sure, but I don't think he knows how to interact with a member of the opposite sex without flirting. It's like diarrhea of the mouth. He can't help it."

"Please never say that again," Mira deadpans. "Hearing it ruined my day. Possibly even my week."

Delia's still watching me, and she shakes her head. "You're wrong. He's not like that with me. Or your grandmother."

"Because you're banging his best friend, who he's in business with," I say. "It would be a bad look, and he does so flirt with my grandmother. She loves it. All she can talk about lately is Leonard said this, Leonard said that. I've been thinking of hosting an intervention, but the only person I knew would be a definite yes was Bertie, and let's be honest, that wouldn't do much."

Delia lifts her eyebrows but doesn't say anything, as if her silence is all the answer I need.

"So you're implying he flirts with her because she loves it. Fine, I guess that's nice enough. But seriously, what do you even know about this guy? What do any of us know? Don't you think it's weird that he's so buddy-buddy with my nana?"

"No," Delia says, tracing the edge of the bar. "I don't know much about his past, but his father was a horrible man, and from what I've heard, his mother didn't protect him."

She pauses, and I feel something sour in my stomach. Something almost protective. Maybe it's the kneejerk reaction of someone else whose parents didn't give a shit. Delia nods as if she knows what's going on inside of me. "Don't you think he sees your grandmother as a kind of mother figure?"

"Haven't you met her?" I ask pointedly. "She may make dog sweaters and doilies, as of a month ago, but she's not the most maternal person in the world."

"Yes." She smiles. "And she seems like exactly the sort of mother figure someone like Leonard would want."

There's an unwinding inside of me, because this makes sense. It makes me feel more charitable toward Leonard, less guarded. Which I'm far from sure is a good thing.

"Fine," I acknowledge. "So maybe he really is doing all of this out of the goodness of his heart..."

"I wouldn't go that far," Delia says, giving me a little Mona Lisa smile.

"No, we're pretty sure he wants to bang you," Mira adds. She's been watching us with her stool pushed back, her feet kicked up on the bar top.

My mind shoots back to that two point five score card from my dream. I'm tempted to tell them, but it feels like I'd be giving too much away.

"Having sex with him would be a bad idea," I say, because that much I know is true.

"Probably," Mira says, swinging her feet down and leaning forward against the bar, "but let's be honest, it would be a good time."

The fluttering in my belly agrees with her.

"How long has it been for you?" Delia asks softly.

"Nine months."

While the breakup with Colter was eight months ago, we hadn't had sex in weeks. Possibly because he was already with Bianca.

Rubbing the bridge of my nose, I turn to Mira. "Okay, your turn," I say. "You said you'd play story hour if I did."

"Ugh, fine." She waves a hand through the air. "I need to find a place to live. My boyfriend and I broke up weeks ago, and we're still living in the same tiny-ass apartment. It's becoming toxic. I poured lemon juice in his milk after he labeled it *Byron's milk*. I mean, seriously, did he intend to drink a whole carton of milk by himself? He was just being a dick."

My mouth drops open. "I didn't even know you had a boyfriend."

She shrugs. "Because it was over before we met. Like I said, I'm stuck with him. You know how hard it is to find an affordable place to live in this city. I think I'm going to start sleeping at the bar."

I glance around at all the color and glitter. "If you managed to fall asleep in this place, you'd certainly have interesting dreams."

"You see my conundrum. Our mother offered to let me stay with her, but—"

"She's not the most supportive person," Delia finishes.

She's overly charitable in her character assessments, so this probably means their mother is Satan reborn.

"You could live with Lucas and me," Delia offers. I get the sense it's not the first time she's said it.

"Yes, there's nothing newly single people love better than to live with people who are wildly in love. I'm going through my *love sucks* phase, thank you very much." She nudges her mostly empty drink. "This is a Love Sucks, and let me tell you, it is dee-licious."

"You're encouraging me to have sex with Leonard," I point out.

"Yes," she says. "Fuck the living daylights out of that hot piece of ass. Just don't fall in love with him. *That* would be a mistake."

I look at Delia, who surprises me by shrugging. "Undecided. Like I said, I really do think he's a good guy."

"But what solid facts do you know about him? He seems pretty closed-off."

"You know the part about Lucas's parents, right?"

"I do."

Mostly because she's told me a little about it, and my grandmother has told me a lot. The Burkes made an irresponsible decision that killed some people, and instead of manning up and admitting it, they arranged for an innocent man to take the fall and then threw a bunch of money at the problem to make it go away. Solid folks. They drove Leonard out of town because he knew their secret, and he stayed away because they'd paid him off.

Again, solid guy.

Apparently, he'd even changed his name to stay hidden. To me, that doesn't speak of a good guy or someone who has a clear conscience. Is it any wonder I don't trust him?

I wrap the thought around me like it's armor.

"Leonard's a mystery," she says softly.

Later that night, after I go to bed, a dangerous thought runs through my head.

I've always liked solving mysteries.

five

LEONARD

People are going to ask how we met, Shauna. I got an idea. Why don't we say we both joined Farmer's Only? You know, that dating site for farmers. You did it because you really wanted to fuck a man who knows how to rake up straw shirtless, like on those dirty books chicks love to read, and me because I had fantasies of meeting a milk maid with a couple of blond braids. So we arranged to meet, and hell, within five minutes it was obvious neither of us were farmers.

You think there are any actual farmers on that site?

WTF, Leonard. It's 3 a.m. on a Thursday.

A farmer would be awake at 3 a.m.

Like you said, we're not farmers.

But shouldn't we have some sort of cover story, Sugar Baby? We're supposed to go to that brewery tomorrow night, and we're very far from being able to pull this off.

As if. You're not old enough or rich enough to have a Sugar Baby.

So you're admitting I'm a hot young stud?

I guess you're right about the cover story.

I'm getting lunch with your grandmother at 12 Bones tomorrow. Or today, I guess. Want to come?

That'd be a no from me. I don't want to discuss this in front of my grandmother. But you can swing by The Waiting Place afterward to talk to me. It's not far. Now, leave me alone until a more reasonable hour. Shauna Lesson #1: I am not a morning person.

Leonard Lesson #1: I'm more of a middle of the night person, but if you're in the mood for a good time, I'll ride you right no matter what time it is. ;)

Goodbye, Leonard.

IT HAPPENED AGAIN.

It happens damn near every night.

He was chasing me in this one. The salty old bastard had just wrapped his hand around my collar, a grunt of victory escaping him, when my eyes popped open and I woke up.

Nervous energy is pounding through my veins, and it needs somewhere to *go*.

I wasn't going to think too closely about why my first instinct was to text Shauna. Reaching out to her at this hour was obviously a mistake, but I've been sending her messages all week.

I can't seem to stop myself. I keep thinking about her sitting in that rocking chair on her porch, her hair all mussed. Smiling at me with a twinkle in her eye that made me want to make some mistakes. And I'll never forget the way her nipples were poking at the shirt, like they had a mind to say hello. There are plenty of things I'd like to say back. I've been thinking about them so much, wondering what other parts of her might look like, that you'd think I'd have good dreams for once. But my old man's not so easy to shake.

Sighing, I reach into the drawer for my glass pipe and ganja. My mind wanders to those pompoms we're supposed to make on Friday night. What can I do to sabotage pompom-making? Bring a fucking cat?

Ding, ding, ding.

I'm grinning, my mind already working overtime on the crappy idea, but a sound downstairs makes me drop the pipe onto the carpet. Half the weed too. Dammit. I'm guessing Mrs. Ruiz will be able to sense the presence of a molecule of weed in her house like a homing pigeon.

I met my landlord through my buddy Drew Jones. She's his fiancée's grandmother. I only know her as Mrs. Ruiz, because she's the kind of broad who won't let anyone under the age of forty call her by her first name.

The place was a bit of a dump, although he'd already fixed it up some, and they agreed to let me stay here in exchange for fixing it up more. A good deal. I've enjoyed pulling the house into this century, although I've had less time lately since Burke and I just got started on a new flip project.

There's another sound, this one more clearly from an intruder.

My mind whirls back to yesterday afternoon. I took out the padlock that was sticking in the back door, but I haven't replaced it yet. So the only working lock is one of those thumb locks that's so easy to get past all you need is a hairpin.

Fuck, that was stupid. I was pushing my way past locks like that by the time I was six or seven. This neighborhood's cleaned up some since I lived a few streets away in my early twenties, but it's not the kind of place you want to wander around at night, especially not if you look like you shop anywhere other than Walmart.

I grab the metal baseball bat I keep by the bed and edge the door open, then creep down the stairs slowly in the dark, taking them one at a time.

There's another muffled sound, and I pin it to the kitchen. So whoever it is definitely got in through the back.

Fucking fabulous, Leonard. Great decision-making. As if you hadn't broken into dozens of houses before your balls dropped.

I creep down carefully, putting my weight on the outer edges of my feet to avoid being heard. There's a different sound, a chair scraping across the floor, so I guess my would-be thief is having a sit down.

Or lying in wait for you.

That voice in my head wants me to run. To make for the front door instead of checking the kitchen, but that voice is a coward, and I'm sick of being driven by it. So I reach the bottom of the stairs, then veer toward the kitchen. There's no light filtering out of the opening, so my buddy is sitting in the dark like some kind of asshole.

Pulse pounding, I crouch my way toward the wall leading in there. I can see the round table, the chair pulled out. The shadowy figure sitting on it. My hand flexes around the bat. Time to rumble.

I need to act quickly, because the one thing I've got going for me is surprise. And if I can get him in a headlock while he's on that chair...

What if he has a gun?

Then I'm screwed, obviously, but I'm not going to run. Not this time.

Go for his arms.

I take another breath, then charge in and drop the bat, instead torquing the intruder's arms behind his back.

And he shrieks.

It takes me all of five seconds to realize a few things.

He's a kid.

He's terrified.

He's bleeding all over my hand.

He could still have a gun, but I drop his arms anyway.

"What the fuck?" I ask, because my mind is flooded with unused adrenaline, and I'm genuinely confused.

It's his arm that's bleeding, I realize, and as my eyes adjust to the darkness, I can see the cut through his shirt. It looks jagged. He can't be more than seventeen or maybe eighteen with thick dark hair and brown eyes. Gangly, like I was at that age, and everything inside of me *hurts*.

"Are you going to kill me?" he blurts, his eyes wide.

"No, but I *would* like to know what the fuck you're doing in here, bud. It's a little late for a house call."

"I'm sorry, man. I didn't...I thought maybe I could find a med kit in the bathroom. But I was tired, so I figured I'd sit down for a minute. I didn't think anyone was home. There's no car in the drive or on the curb, and I know the woman who lives here is in Puerto Rico."

"Someone stole my truck?"

Well, damn. It wasn't a very good truck, but it did get me around occasionally. I guess Constance will be picking me up for lunch.

"It wasn't me," he says, alarmed.

"No shit, kid. Otherwise, it would be out front."

"Are you going to hurt me?" he asks, and the fear in his voice is a gut punch.

"No, I'm not going to hurt you," I say, taking a step back. "You want me to take you to the hospital?"

"How?"

It's a reasonable question. Apparently, I have no truck to speak of.

"I could call a friend to take us."

He shakes his head, pushing back in his chair as if he's about to get up and take a runner.

That's when the truth hits me.

"You a runaway?" I ask.

"I'm almost eighteen," he says defensively. "I only got a few weeks left. But if they find me now..."

I run a hand over my scruff. "They'd have to take you back to your folks?"

"I got no one, man. My mother died when I was a kid, and my dad's in jail. My foster father is an asshole."

"He beat you?" I ask, looking for bruises. There aren't any, but if the guy's a seasoned asshole, he'd know where to leave them.

The kid swallows and nods, like he feels like less of a man for admitting it. It makes me want to destroy the foster father. But I won't ask for his name yet. If I do, then the kid will spook. "His brother's a cop, so no one believes me."

"He the one who did that to your shoulder?" I ask.

"No," he says as he fidgets in the chair. "I got that climbing over a fence. Something sharp on it I didn't see in the dark."

I could ask whose fence, but I don't see the point. He's running from trouble and he's scared enough to *be* trouble.

"What's your name, kid?" I walk over and flick on the light—and wince. That cut on his arm is going to need a few stitches. Three to five, looks like.

He pauses for a moment, wary, then says, "Reese."

"You named after a peanut butter cup?" He's probably lying, but I don't resent the lie. For all he knows, I'm a piece of shit who broke into his friend's house and holed up here.

"Reese with one S, man. None of that plural peanut butter shit. What are you doing in Mrs. Ruiz's house?"

"She's letting me stay here in exchange for not making it a dump."

He swivels his head, taking a look-see. "You've got some work to do."

"Thanks for the vote of confidence," I tell him. "What do you say I help you with that cut, man? You need some stitches."

"You know how to stitch someone up?"

Yeah, just call me a pediatric surgeon. I almost grin at the thought, but I don't want to scare the kid off.

I hike up the sleeve of my T-shirt, showing him my scar. "Yeah, let's just say I've been in this particular rodeo before."

"You stitched yourself up?" he asks, sounding impressed. Then his face twists. "You didn't do a very good job, you know. It's a nasty scar."

"Chicks dig it. You'll have a chick magnet of your own." He looks a little deflated by the thought, more about the scar than the chick magnet, so I add, "You heal better when you're a kid. I came by this one a few years back. I'm old. Make sure you stop doing dumb shit before you get old too."

He gives a ghost of a smile.

"You know Mrs. Ruiz?" I press.

"Yeah," he says, rubbing his nose. "She's helped me out a couple of times."

Good enough for me.

"You hungry, kid?"

For a second, he has the look of a startled bird, maybe about to fly off, maybe about to take a shit on the truck that got stolen, but then he nods.

"I'm no chef, but there are cereal boxes over there." I gesture to the collection sitting against the counter wall. "Milk in the fridge.

You can take a bowl and spoon from the dish drainer. I'm gonna go grab my first aid kit."

"Thanks," he says slowly, his eyes on me as I head for the opening. "How do I know you're not going to call the cops?"

"You don't, I guess." I grab the side of the doorway. "Just like I don't know if you're telling me the truth about being almost eighteen. I *do* need to call them about the truck, as much good as it will do me, but I'll wait. I've been where you are before. I get it. And Mrs. Ruiz is good people."

Or at least my buddy tells me so. She took one look at me and started muttering under her breath in Spanish.

He nods once, but I wonder if he's going to jet as soon as I turn my back. I grab the med kit in the bathroom, trying to be quick about it without seeming like I'm in a hurry. When I return to the kitchen, the kid's still there, munching on some Fruit Loops.

I'm pretty sure Shauna would take it as further evidence that I'm a child, but I've always had a thing for Fruit Loops. Generic fruit loops, because that damn toucan comes with a markup.

"You're still here," I mutter.

"Thought about bouncing," he says.

"I know." I get out the alcohol wipes and the needle and thread, then get the needle toasty over the gas range on the stove.

"You sure you've done this before?" he asks, eyeing it with suspicion as he sucks down his cereal. He's eating like it's been a while since his last meal.

"Yeah, I have. You're going to have to pull them out yourself or come back here. One week. Maybe two. And if it looks infected, you'll have to find a doctor. Or a nurse. Don't wait. Infections can be a bitch."

"Sounds like you know that from experience too."

"I've spent time on the street," I confirm, carrying the needle back to the table. "Learned the hard way. Push up your sleeve a bit more."

I should probably ask him to take off his shirt, but he's already got that edge of wanting to run. I don't want him to think I'm some kind of pervert.

He pushes it up, wincing. I don't warn him that it's going to hurt —I'm pretty sure he knows a thing or two about pain—but start in with the alcohol wipes.

"You in school?" I ask.

I can feel his sidelong glance. "You sound like someone who's going to narc on me."

"I'm not," I say, still cleaning the wound.

"I'm not in school. None of that shit's going to help me."

"Maybe, maybe not. But you can always get your GED. That's what I did. You get that, you can find yourself some kind of job. Better that than trying to make it by taking other people's shit. That won't get you far."

"I don't take anything from people's houses," he says, which would be more convincing if he hadn't just broken into mine. "I took some stuff I needed from a couple of box stores, but that's it."

"You hold to that," I say, "because if you break into the wrong person's house, you'll get yourself a bullet between the eyes. Worst that'll happen to you if you steal Tampax from Target is getting pulled in by the cops."

His answer is to take a final bite of the cereal before pushing it away. The milk is a gross chalky purple color. His face isn't far off. "Like I said, his brother's a cop."

"Great motivation not to get caught. Or, better yet, to find yourself a job."

He grunts.

"I'm going to get started now, kid. You need something to bite down on?"

This gets me a half laugh—the half laugh of a kid who's more innocent than he thinks, because I wasn't joking. "You got a chew toy?"

"I can get you a rubber spatula if you need something. It's going to hurt like a bitch."

"No," he says flatly. "I can take it."

So I get started. He flinches but holds steady, which makes me think redder thoughts about that foster father of his.

"Where'd you learn this?" he asks through gritted teeth.

"YouTube."

Not true. There wasn't YouTube when I was a kid, but if I told him that, he probably wouldn't believe me. Kids these days think that shit's been around forever—all the information in the world at your fingertips. The way I learned it is that my father made me stitch him up after he got in a fight. But my answer seems to calm the kid.

I finish up quick as I can, then put some Vaseline over it and bandage it up. I give him a couple of Advil, which he washes down with the purple milk from the cereal bowl. Stitching up his arm didn't make me feel like yacking, but for some reason that does.

"You keep that bandage dry today," I say. "And start cleaning the wound twice a day tomorrow." I cock my head at him. "You got somewhere you can do that?"

The fact that he's here suggests he doesn't, but he nods.

"You have a phone?"

Another nod. "Pay as you go."

"Give it to me."

He scowls. "No man. I'm not giving you my phone."

"I'm gonna give you my number. You call me if you get into any scrapes. And if you need somewhere to stay, you can crash on the couch."

I should probably ask Mrs. Ruiz before offering, but if I lived my life by probablys and should'ves, shit would have worked out differently for me.

He rubs his nose again. "You some kind of perv?"

"Depends who you ask. But it's women I like." A corner of my mouth hitches up. "Hell, I even have a girlfriend." If Shauna gets to play pretend, so do I.

"You don't look like the kind of guy who'd have a girlfriend," he says.

"I'm not, usually. But banging random women is another thing you should stop before you get too old."

He gives a slight nod. "Okay." Then he pulls the phone out from his pocket, wincing a little.

I program in my number, text myself from his phone, then give him a look. "I mean it, kid. You stay here if you need to. Mrs. Ruiz took everything she cares about, and I don't have anything worth shit, so there's nothing you're going to make a buck off stealing."

Or at least I don't have anything worth shit *now*. I left a few good tools in that truck.

He scowls at me. "I wouldn't take anything from her."

"I notice you didn't say anything about stealing from me," I say with a snort.

He shrugs.

"I appreciate the honesty. Now, you're free to sleep on the couch, or grab some of my shitty paperbacks to sell for a few nickels, but I'm going back to bed. Try not to get yourself killed, all right? I'm not a medical doctor."

My mind supplies: *I only play one at Sten parties and weddings.*

"I thought you were going to call the police about the truck."

I snort again. "Sure, but let's be honest, they're not going to give half a shit about it, and I'd rather not deal with the chuckleheads they have working on the late shift. I'll call in the morning."

It also means he'll have somewhere to spend the rest of the night.

"All right," he says flatly. "If I need to come back, do you want me to just break in again?"

I almost laugh, but I'm too tired. "Or, you know, text. I'm going to put that deadbolt back in tomorrow."

I'm not enough of an idiot to offer him a key.

I look out the window before heading upstairs. Because if the kid were ballsy enough, he could have lied about the truck, hoping he'd get a chance to go through my things and find the key so he could grab it and adios.

He was right, though. It's gone as if it never was, another piece of my life that was taken from me. I shake my head, a slight smile escaping. "I hope she gives you half as much shit as she's given me," I say under my breath as I go upstairs.

That truck's a hunk of junk, so bad I thought it was thiefproof, but I'd become fond of it. Still, I meant what I said. I won't call until morning.

They're never going to find it anyway.

When I get up in the morning, the kid is gone, and so are my shoes.

Goddammit.

six

LEONARD

AS PREDICTED, the police officer who shows up at the house doesn't give a borrowed fuck about my stolen truck. But he *does* find it "very interesting" that I'm staying in Mrs. Ruiz's house. Officer Murray is pale and blond and looks like he doesn't get out much, so I guess he's hoping for something interesting to happen. Like catching a vagrant who's stupid enough to call the cops.

"You'll have to verify that," he says with a hearty amount of suspicion after I tell him about my living arrangements. So I call Mrs. Ruiz up on FaceTime so she can flash her license at him and confirm my story. She gives him a chewing out that I very *much* enjoy listening to.

Before Officer Murray leaves, he flashes me a photo of Reese on his phone.

"You seen this kid around the neighborhood?"

"Why?" I ask.

He lifts his pale yellow brows. "It's a yes or no question, son."

He's at least five years younger than me, but I don't want to end up in lockup for pissing him off, so I settle for a simple "no."

Maybe Reese is full of shit, but I'm not about to turn the kid in. Even if he did steal my shoes.

Seeing as he left behind a pair of falling-apart Nikes, I'm mostly glad he took them.

When I can see the cop's taillights out of the window, I text the kid:

> You forgot my wallet.

Those little tell-tale dots appear, then his message:

> I'm sorry about the shoes.

> I'm not. Come back later if you need a place to stay.

> You should be more careful with your things, man.

> Quit it with the sticky fingers, kid. You could get in serious trouble. You need somewhere to lie low for a few weeks, I can help with that.

I think about telling him the cops are asking around about him, but I don't want to scare him off. If someone had told me a thing like that when I was his age, I'd've been the next state over by lunchtime. My last text was probably pushy enough.

So I call Mrs. Ruiz back instead. She doesn't look too pleased by all the calling, but when I ask if she knows a kid named Reese who hangs out in the neighborhood, she nods sharply. "I let him mow the lawn sometimes. He does a terrible job, but his foster father's a bad man. He wears a mask for other people and turns his rage on his family."

"They live around here?"

"He's never told me, and I haven't asked," she says. "But I know he speaks the truth about that man. I can see it in his eyes."

It's a schmaltzy thought for a take-no-prisoners woman, but I know what she means. She's got a bullshit detector, same as me.

"Has the kid ever taken anything from you?" I ask, holding my breath.

"You think I'd let someone steal from me, *mijo*? Are you sick in the head?"

She hangs up without asking if I want to say howdy to Drew, and that's that.

I call up Burke and let him know that I won't be in until after lunch, on account of my distress over the lost truck. He tells me too bad, ending with, "I'll be there in five minutes."

So much for having a nap before meeting up with Constance.

Burke shows up in six minutes.

"You're a minute late," I tell him as I let him in.

He ignores me, pacing the little entryway of the house, which is much too small for both of us. He's full of the kind of nervous energy that's catching, but I just stand there and watch him, arms folded, waiting for him to come out with it. I already have an inkling of what's bothering him.

"What if it's them, man?" he asks.

I didn't need to ask him who he means. He's talking about his folks.

"It's not," I say. "Why would they steal a Chevy that barely runs?"

"They wouldn't have done it directly, but maybe…"

"It's a rough neighborhood, man. Trucks get stolen. I probably forgot to lock it."

"Would you?" he asks pointedly.

Never. I might have forgotten to replace the lock on the back door of the house, but I used the thumb lock. I'm not a total idiot. You lock doors or you lose your shit and possibly get beaten for the pleasure.

"Maybe. You know, I pity the bastard who stole it. But it wasn't your folks. It doesn't fit their MO at all."

I mean, sure, Mama and Papa Burke would probably drink

champagne while they watched me burn, but I doubt they'd trouble themselves to light the fire. I'm nothing to them. Vapor. I'm not the one who humbled them for their bad business practices—their baby boy is. Still, they know I set their downfall into motion. That can't feel good.

"Who knows what their MO is?" he says, pausing to kick the bottom step of the stairs.

"They haven't done anything to mess with you. Neither has that step."

"I know they haven't," he says, turning to look at me. "That's what I'm afraid of. They send me texts every now and then, and last week a family photo arrived in the mail. They're trying to mess with me, even if they're not being obvious about it."

"You still have that detective working for you?" He hired someone a month ago to keep an eye on them and make sure they're not plotting our doom.

"Yeah. He's found nothing, but I've got this feeling."

I feel like a damn goose is tap-dancing on my grave, but I lock it down and pat him on the back. I can't let the fear take control. Not anymore. "I get it, man, but you can't let that bring you down. That's how they win. That's the *only* way they win. Now what do you say we go over to the house and pretend to work for half an hour before having some lunch beers?"

"It's way too early for lunch," he says with a nearly there smile.

"And it's a few hours later somewhere. I think we need a win."

"And lunch beers are a win?"

"Lunch beers on the deck in the sun, the mountains spread out under us? Hell, yes, that's a win."

I have another reason for wanting to get him out of the house— I'm worried he'll notice Reese's crappy shoes and start asking questions.

I'm tempted to tell Burke about the kid, because he's a man who gets things done—a hero, something I'll never be. But at the same time, there's a chance he'll feel the need to do things "the right way." He might want to bring in the cops, and I can't let that happen. I'm going to help the kid, but I'm going to do it my way.

So we head over to the house to get some work done before Constance picks me up for lunch and our secret mission.

seven

SHAUNA

"OFFER STANDS," Rafe tells me. "I'll go to the wedding with you."

It's Thursday afternoon, and we're working in my section of The Waiting Place, called The Clay Place. This warehouse is massive, and it's arranged with five different stations, mine being one of them. Each has an open front with displays and art for sale and a workshop in the back for classes and for our own work. There's also The Paint Place, The Jewelry Place, The Glass Place, and The Paper Place, along with a large, open atrium in the middle for visitors to lounge and hang out. Yes, we went for simplistic names. Most people need things spelled out for them, so we figured we'd err on the side of obvious.

The other artists have also been unpacking and prepping for opening next month. I love walking through the hallway and soaking it in—it has the shininess of dreams on the cusp of coming true. I especially like peering in through the plate glass windows of The Glass Place, where our glass artist, Evelyn, has dozens of spinners and glass dragonflies on display, catching the light from the open glass ceiling of the atrium in different shades of purple, green, orange, and pink. It's magical. It's *ours.*

Rafe's helping me unpack a few boxes for my display shelves up front. We've already got the bigger pieces unloaded, and I'm setting out a few smaller pieces to catch the eye and inspire students. My friend has this protective look he gets sometimes, half scowl, half mother hen. He's a big guy—less big than when we both worked at the gym but plenty enough to be intimidating when he feels like it. But he's a teddy bear for the people in his inner circle, always has been, and he has the soul of a painter. Which is why he's running The Paint Place. That, and because he's screwing the woman who runs this joint. His words, not mine. I've known him for over ten years, and he's always had a talent for phrasing.

"The answer remains no," I say, throwing a piece of bubble wrap at him after I finish unwrapping one of my favorite mugs—an open maw with teeth along the edges—and place it on a shelf.

This is probably why I haven't been successful. I make monster mouths for people instead of pretty little nothings. Bianca and Colter might be dicks, but that doesn't mean they're wrong about me.

Bianca's recipe for my success was for me to make pretty pieces, inspired by nature. She was so adamant about it that she talked me around to trying.

Okay, she didn't *talk* me into anything. I lost a bet. So for one of the spring craft markets where we had side-by-side booths, I made only pretty stuff. Pieces inspired by the Blue Ridge Mountains. Puff pieces.

I sold out.

A normal person would have listened to the market, but I didn't enjoy making those pieces. While I'd prefer to make money than not, if money were the most important consideration for me, I would have abandoned clay a decade ago. Clay is my therapy. It's my way of exorcising my feelings. My demons. Of seeing them as beautiful, even.

Still, I have to admit I've been in a creative desert lately.

Monsters can be eye-catching and arresting, but the stuff I've been making lately is downright ugly. Maybe even scary. There's a vase with three mouths full of sharp teeth, a mug that would probably give someone a heart attack if they unwrapped it, and a statue of a beast with four clawed legs and a head not even a mother can love.

I'm its mother; I don't love it.

Those pieces are hidden in the back room, mostly because Rafe and I would be having a different conversation if he saw them. He knows I only put out work like that when I'm in crisis mode—just like I know he's a grumpy brute when he goes too long without painting.

I'll probably have to talk the problem through with him at some point. Classes are starting next month, and no one wants to learn how to make vessels so painfully ugly they make people cry. But I've decided it's a problem for another day.

"Is the thought of going to the wedding with me that bad?" Rafe asks, pulling me away from my monsters. "I'm not going to lie. I'd like to punch Colt, but I probably won't."

"What good are all of those muscles if you don't use them?" I ask, starting in on another wrapped piece.

"Do you *want* me to punch him?"

"Maybe. But I kind of dig pretending I don't care. It's driving Bianca nuts. You know how much she thrives on reactions."

She always has. Her mother was a cold, reserved woman who always found her wanting; her father was as much of an absence as mine. She cut ties with both of them, and now she goes through life constantly pushing people, acting out, and throwing fits—anything for a reaction. I've made excuses for her before, but I'm done with that.

"I shot her down that one time she tried to hit on me," Rafe says with a knowing smirk. "She'd probably hate it if you brought me."

It happened years ago, but he's not wrong—she always talks

about him with a hint of resentment, like a woman who's been rejected and didn't like it. Still...

"Nope, not happening." I carefully remove the bubble wrap. This mug's a couple of lovers wrapped around each other, a crooked arm on either side as a handle. I heave a sigh. "What good would it do, anyway? Colter and Bianca *know* we're not together. It would be like going to the prom with my brother."

"So, you'd prefer to go with a conman?"

It shouldn't irk me. After all, I'm the one who presented Leonard in an unflattering light. But the word feels like an unpleasant prickling along my skin.

"Leonard's not a conman," I object. "He's my grandmother's friend."

Rafe puffs out air. Hot air, I'm guessing. "Your grandmother has a screw loose lately."

I've been saying the same thing for weeks, but I'm annoyed to hear it from him. Then again, Rafe and I have known each other for over a decade, and he's always been friendly with my grandfather. They used to drink beer together in my backyard every Sunday afternoon before my grandfather discovered his passion for water aerobics. For all I know, they still do, although I'm guessing Rafe would rather spend his time with his fiancé than my flatulent, swear-happy grandfather.

"Nana's happier than she's ever been," I say in a clipped voice. "Has Grandpa Frank been whispering in your ear like some sort of consigley—" I think for a moment, then admit, "Okay, I forgot how to say that word."

"Consigliere?" he asks, his expression amused. "Have you been re-watching *The Sopranos* again?"

Short answer, yes. I figured it was good preparation for going into enemy territory. Tony Soprano dominated at every game he played, and I'd like to dominate at this one.

"Irrelevant. You *have* been talking to him, haven't you? I'm guessing he came to you with some sob story?"

He shrugs, his expression half-amused, half-wary. The wariness is smart. It's the attitude of someone who knows me. "He hasn't behaved well, but he's still Frank. You know he'd like to talk to you."

"He has my number. We don't need to play telephone through you."

He tips his head. "You don't answer your phone when he calls, and you haven't been responding to his texts."

"Yeah," I say breezily, "funny how that happens. Whenever he gets in touch, I'm busy. Go figure. He should pick better times."

"And yet you're still going to Dipshit's wedding."

"Yes, but that's out of spite."

He gives a shrug that suggests he's mystified by women, women in my family especially. "Frank's not a bad guy—just a shitty husband. I don't think you should give up on him just because he's—"

"A jerk? He's clearly been talking smack about Nana if you think she has a screw loose."

He lifts his hands and shakes his head. "No, that's all from you. You told me that she spent hours feng shuing her bedroom the other week."

"Yes, and it looks fabulous."

"What would it take for you to give him another shot?"

"Him getting amnesia. But only so I can convince him he's one of those Nascar guys."

"He hates Nascar," he says, giving me a wry look.

"He should have thought of that before he messed around."

"You've only got one grandfather left."

I smile and flick him on the chest, balancing the lovers mug in the other hand. "Sinclair's really gotten to you, hasn't she? She's turned you all gooey on the inside."

He doesn't look displeased. "Sure. What can I say? Love does crazy things to a man."

"It really does, doesn't it?" a familiar voice quips.

I drop the mug, the two lovers splitting apart with a loud, resonant crack.

A horrified gasp escapes me, and not just because it's hours of work down the drain. It feels like a sign.

I look up to see my grandmother walking in with none other than Leonard. The pile of boxes in front of the window hid them from view, but I guess they still heard us. Nana's wearing one of the bright, airy kaftans she picked up after my grandfather defected, and Leonard has on worn jeans and a band T-shirt he's probably owned since he was a teenager, judging by the way it hugs his arms. I dislike the tingling feeling inside of me, but I assure myself it's a natural reaction to a pair of muscular tattooed arms. Admittedly, Rafe is both muscular and tattooed, but looking at his arms does nothing for me.

"You made me drop my mug," I accuse, even though it's not exactly fair. I meet Leonard's eyes and feel an undeniable twinge of attraction. It's that naughty glint in his eyes and the way they're framed by those long lashes. It's the way his hair looks like he's been running his hands through it.

"You need to stop swooning every time you see me, Sugar Puffs." But he bends down and picks up the two halves. A whistle escapes him when he sees the phallus that was sculpted inside of the mug. "So you really can teach me how to make a clay dick," he says as he hands it over. I set the two pieces on the desk next to the display case I've been filling up.

"This the guy?" Rafe grunts, reverting to a caveman.

Really, where was this protectiveness when we were talking about Grandpa Frank? Admittedly, my grandfather didn't do anything to me personally, but any insults paid to my grandmother are very much insults to me.

Leonard juts out his hand. "I'm Leonard. Pleased to meet you."

Rafe shakes it, and from the way his hand curls around Leonard's, I can tell he's trying to assert which of them is stronger. "Rafe. I'm Shauna's friend. I'll be keeping an eye on her."

"No need to break my hand, bub," Leonard says with a lazy grin. "I'm not gonna touch her unless she asks nicely."

"Oh, you're awful," Nana says with a chuckle.

"Yes, he is," I agree, even though I'm not sure I mean it anymore.

"I'm the one doing a favor here," Leonard comments, his gaze finding mine and holding it. Rafe has released his hand, but he doesn't look too happy about any of this. The only person who seems completely at ease is my grandmother, but that's probably because she's been drinking a half a glass of wine at lunch lately.

Leonard's scrutiny is surprisingly intense, and I feel something inside of me growl in response, as if we're two animals sizing each other up. Maybe Bertie always barks at him because he senses something...uncivilized about him. I do too.

Maybe I like it.

"I'm paying you," I tell him through gritted teeth.

"Yes, in clay lessons. You think you could teach me how to build a truck out of clay, too? Someone stole my Chevy this morning."

"*Why?*" I've seen his truck before. It's old and rusty and only runs on a wish and a prayer.

He laughs, loud and deep, as if I said something unspeakably funny. "That's basically what the cop told me when he finally showed this morning."

Rafe grunts again, this time because he's had his own bad experiences with the police department.

"They're never gonna find it," he tells Leonard.

"Yeah, I'm not holding my breath. Too bad Colter isn't actually a used car salesman, huh, sweet cheeks?"

Laughter rips out of Rafe. "He does look like a used car sales-man, doesn't he?"

I shoot him a look of betrayal. "*Seriously?* First Grandpa Frank and now him? Do you think they deserve your loyalty just because they have a Y-chromosome?"

Lifting both hands, he says, "I'm not touching that one with a ten-foot pole." He glances at Leonard again, then nods. "Give them hell, but don't give her any. My friend here has an oven that fires up to 2000. Probably good at burning bodies."

"Sure," Leonard says. "But then all her pieces would smell like roasted meat." He glances at the monster-mouth mug on the display case and shrugs. "Though maybe you wouldn't mind so much, Tiger." He snaps his fingers, looking altogether too pleased with himself. "That's the one."

"Excuse me?" I say, putting a hand on my hip.

"Tiger. That's you."

"He's right," Rafe agrees with a muffled laugh. "And that's my cue." He turns tail and leaves. I'm surprised he doesn't high five or fist bump Leonard on the way out, the traitor.

"Are you implying I have a temper?" I ask Leonard.

"Implying?" He laughs. "I thought it was something we all took for granted."

"He's right," my grandmother says, then hands me a bag of take-out, the sight of which makes my stomach grumble. "We got you some lunch, Shauna. You never remember to eat when you're working."

She's right. Nana's always been there to remind me, ever since I was a little kid, lost in making macaroni sculptures or trying to teach my dolls to be more talkative. My grandfather was good to me too, but there's something to be said for a person who shows up when they're needed, how they're needed. My parents never did. I guess that's why I'm having trouble forgiving Grandpa Frank. Nana's one of the only people who has ever shown me that kind of love—the kind you don't have to ask for or deserve. The kind that can envelop you and make you feel almost full. So she's the one who deserves my loyalty.

"Thanks," I say as I set the bag on the desk.

"I'll leave you two to it," Nana says, patting my arm.

"But who's going to take Leonard home?" I ask in alarm.

"*You*, Tiger," she says with a half-smile. "I have my horseback-riding lesson."

She really has a way of making me feel like a slacker, what with all this feng shui, movie extra acting, and horseback riding, but I love it for her.

"Okay," I say, eyeing Leonard. "But you better not try anything."

"I was thinking of pocketing the clay dick. Is that what you meant?"

"You can have it," I scoff. "The rest of the mug too." I could fix it, but the mug feels tainted now. When I saw it lying broken on the floor, it seemed like a message from the universe that I'm cursed in the love department.

"Really?" he asks, eyes bright, like he's actually excited to have it.

"Sure. If you hold up your end of the Sten bargain, I'll even show you how to piece it together."

"I already said I was going with you," he says with mild annoyance.

"I can tell you two will have a ball," Nana says before turning her attention to Leonard. "Don't forget the cheese for the charcuterie board."

Leonard lifts a scandalized hand to his chest, his arm flexing. My eyes find the scar just above the tattoo of a dog. I wonder about both of them—and am annoyed with myself for wondering.

"I'd no sooner forget the cheese than I'd forget Tiger here's birthday." Then he adds in a theatrical whisper, "When's your birthday, Tiger? Help a guy out."

I feel a prickle down my spine. If I tell him, he'll make a big deal out of it, and I'd prefer for him not to. "A lady never tells."

"She's turning thirty-two," my grandmother offers helpfully, but she doesn't give me away.

"Thanks a lot, Nana."

Leonard's brows wing up. "Huh, I figured you were pushing forty."

"No, that's you," I shoot back, although he doesn't look forty any more than I do. Maybe thirty-five. Could be younger, but he has the look of someone who's lived hard and had fun doing it. I probably look like a doll preserved in a box.

"Why are you making a charcuterie board?" I ask my grandmother with suspicion. "Are you having a party you forgot to tell me about?"

"Burke is," Leonard says. "Tonight. But I'll take you if you ask nicely." He winks. "Might be good practice."

"We'll see."

"That's Shauna for no," my grandmother says, leaning in and kissing my cheek. The cloud of unfamiliar perfume gives my heart a squeeze.

"Don't fall off the horse," I tell her as she leaves. She's chuckling as she disappears from view, leaving me alone with Leonard.

Sighing, I shift my attention to him.

"Eat," he says, surprisingly earnest. Then, when I make no move to slide behind the desk, he adds, "I don't like my women too thin. I need something to hang on to."

"I'm never going to sleep with you." I wave a finger for emphasis. "*Never.*"

"Promises, promises." He nods to my chair again. "Sit. No one likes cold french fries."

I give a slight shudder, because he's right. French fries should be crisp and warm in the middle. Anything less is like a hot date that ends with a limp noodle.

Sighing, I take a seat behind the desk. As I pull out the food, I nod to a single chair backed up against the wall. "You sit, too. I don't want you looming over me."

He rolls his eyes but retrieves the chair and pulls it up while I open the to-go box. There's a sandwich in there, but I bypass it and take out a fry, then three, because I don't care about impressing him.

He has an amused look on his face as he watches me shove them into my mouth.

"You think it's funny to watch women eat?" I ask after I chew and swallow.

"I just got done telling you I like it." He leans back, spreading his legs in that way men do, like his dick is too big to be contained by his legs. "You this touchy with everyone?"

No.

"You'll be relieved to hear that I got to the fries soon enough," I say, evading the question. "They're still delicious."

He mimes wiping sweat off his brow.

"Did someone really steal your truck?"

"You don't think much of me," he says, his voice serious now. He holds my gaze, pausing before he continues. "But I wouldn't lie to your grandmother. I like her."

It's obvious he means it, and I feel a prick of guilt. There's no denying I haven't been very nice to him. It's just...there's something about Leonard that cuts under my skin, like he's a human sliver. He sets me off. And I'm attracted to him, which sets me off more.

I'm far from sure why I've agreed to this arrangement—except for the obvious. I already committed to going, and I'm too stubborn to back down now. So, I might as well have someone on my side.

"I'm just surprised someone took it."

"I know," he says with a grin. "The dumbass who took it is going to be real surprised too, when it breaks down after ten miles."

"So, do you need a pickup on Friday night?"

He nods. "If that's okay, Tiger."

"You're really going to call me that?"

"Does Milquetoast have a special name for you?"

My scowl returns. "Bean."

Something resembling a laugh escapes him. "He call you that because you can only come with your clit?"

I choke on a French fry and cough several times before I swallow it. "That's none of your damn business."

He waggles his eyebrows. "It is if they're supposed to think I'm the one making you come."

"There is absolutely no reason for you to tell anyone about our fictional sex life."

More brow waggling. "Don't you want to make them jealous?"

"Let's table that. And no, he doesn't call me that because of a sex thing." To be honest, Colter wasn't great at making me come, but from my experience, the only men who can make it happen every time are made of silicone and come in party colors. "He calls me that because I'm little. Like a bean."

He scoffs. "That's stupid. Beans aren't little. Those vines will climb twenty feet high if you let them."

"Thank you," I say, waving a French fry. "I hate it. And he still uses that nickname, even after everything. It's infantilizing."

He squeezes the arm of his chair, and my eyes follow the movement, soaking in how his muscles respond up his arm. The dog on his bicep seems to be winking at me. "Let's show him you're more of a tiger than a bean."

I give a slow nod. I don't want Leonard to be right, but I *do* want to show someone something. I've been holding back too much. Letting everything roll me along rather than swimming where I want to go.

"Why are you helping me, for real?" I ask. "I don't know how much I can pay you. This place hasn't even opened yet. I mean, we're salaried, thanks to Sinclair, but without the storefront open—"

"I don't expect any money. The clay lessons are enough." He shifts in his seat, glancing at my desk. "Plus the fucked-up mug."

A delighted laugh escapes me. "You want a broken mug and to learn how to make a clay dick?"

"Yes," he says leaning back further. "Otherwise, I'd have to buy Danny a present, and now that I have the idea in my head, nothing else will do." He tilts his chair, balancing one of his feet on the back of the desk. I did that when I was a kid, and my grandmother told me I was going to crack my head open. So I did it again—and fell down and whacked my head.

"You're going to fall and hit your head," I comment.

"Probably." He grins. "I figure if I hit it enough, maybe it'll be the reverse of a concussion, and I'll learn some shit instead of forgetting it."

"Fat chance."

Still leaning back like that, he says, "I'm helping you because I decided I want to be the kind of person who helps people instead of ruining everything. That's why. If you don't believe me, that's okay. I can understand why you wouldn't."

"But you're not just doing this for emotional support. You want to mess with them."

He gives me a grin that lights up his face and makes his eyes crease. It's the kind of grin only a statue could look at without grinning back, and I'm no statue. He grabs one of my french fries and eats it, and I find myself watching his throat bob and taking in the slight curl of his hair at the nape of his neck. There's a tingle of something again. "Sure. I might want to be a better man, but I'll never be a saint."

It's impossible not to smile. Still, I figure I'm doing okay on the self-control front given the dirty things I suddenly want to do to him.

eight

LEONARD

"YOU GOING to steal more of my fries?" Shauna asks.

Her tone tells me it's a dare, so even though I don't actually want more, I grab two.

She shakes her head but doesn't seem all that annoyed.

"I don't know anything about you," she reflects.

"You don't need to know anything about me," I say through the fries, rewarded by her grimace. "It's Leonard the pediatric surgeon you need to know. Seeing as he's fictional, feel free to be generous. Especially when talking about his dick."

She gives me a smartass look. "So you need me to be generous?"

"Fuck no." I rock back in the chair just because she told me not to. The expression on her face says she knows it, but hell, someone needs to get her to lighten up. "But I don't have a twelve-inch schlong, and it would be pretty funny if Dr. Leonard did. I'll bet old Colter would get a complex about that."

She shrugs her head to her shoulder, then smirks and says, "My grandmother says it's best to stay close to the truth when you're lying about things."

"It's close enough," I say, and her smirk widens into a smile.

"Besides, you're better off not knowing about most of the stuff in my life."

"Oh?"

"*Oh.* So, where'd we meet?"

"What if we say we met at the gym I worked at? You look like you workout."

"Checking out the goods, were you?" She heaves a sigh that makes me laugh, then I add, "When'd you stop working there?"

"A few months ago. We can say we've been keeping it quiet for a while."

"Sure," I say, but I don't want to commit to it. It's a boring story, and I've decided she's going to have a good time at these wedding events. We're going to show Milk Toast what an idiot he is for tossing her away. That's what Constance calls the chump, and it's got a certain ring to it.

"Sure, you're going to go along with it, or sure you're trying to change the subject?" she asks, staring at me with those amber eyes, just like a tiger's.

I wonder if she'd scratch me during sex.

"What are you thinking about right now?" she asks with plenty of accusation.

Busted.

When you're caught, you might as well be honest, so I say, "You scratching your nails down Dr. Leonard's back like a good tiger."

Her frown turns into a full-on glower, which is probably why I pick that moment to tip the chair back too far. It falls, and my head hits the floor. It fucking hurts.

I hear Shauna swear and then scurry around the desk. She leans in close, and there's no denying it's a helluva view with her T-shirt gaping enough to show me her tits, cupped in a neon purple bra.

"Did you break yourself?"

I get up and rub my head. "Nah. It would take more than that to break me." I eye her as I get up and pull the chair with me. "You're dying to say I told you so."

"I was going to wait until I'd offered you an Advil, but we can fast-forward if you'd like to get to it sooner."

God help me, there's something about this woman...

"Might as well get it over with," I ask, watching as she circles the desk again and lowers into the chair. She grabs a bottle from one of the drawers then shakes out one pill, takes a good look at me, and shakes out another. I take them from her palm.

"I told you so," she says as I swallow them down dry.

"Ah, order has been restored to the world."

She grins, then shakes her head with a mixture of amusement and annoyance as I prop up on the chair again. *Yeah, that's right.*

"Why don't you tell me what your tattoos are about?" she says, her eyes dipping to my arms. "And how you got that scar."

I lift my eyebrows. "You think someone's going to ask me about my scar? That's pretty dark. I reserve the right to tell them it's none of their damn business."

"So your tattoos. That's something a girlfriend would know."

I point at Gidget. "That was my other girl, Gidget."

"You had a dog?" she asks in disbelief.

"What, you can't believe it because that little gremlin of your grandmother's hates me so much?"

She shrugs, and I can tell what she's really getting at.

"Oh, you don't think I could take care of anyone." Old pain radiates through my chest. "I guess you're right...she's dead, and it was my fault."

"I'm sorry, Leonard," she says, and looks like she means it too. "But I didn't say that. I wouldn't."

Still, but I'll bet she was thinking it. And why wouldn't she?

It's been true for most of my life—Leonard, unable to take care of himself, let alone anyone else. Leonard, the fuck up. Leonard, the coward.

Leonard, who only knows how to run.

"How about this one?" she asks, her voice soft, as she reaches across the desk and presses her fingers to my flesh. They barely brush the skin, but she might as well have grabbed my dick and squeezed.

I glance down to where she's touching me and laugh. It's a mushroom wearing sunglasses. A five-dollar special when I was down on the beach in Florida. "That's called getting drunk. But if you want a meaningful story, you can tell people I got it in honor of penicillin."

"And this one?" she asks, pointing to a pot leaf.

I laugh again. "That's pretty self-explanatory, don't you think?"

Shauna pulls her fingers away. I swallow.

"And what prompted you to pursue pediatric surgery, *Dr.* Leonard?" she asks with a small smile.

"I don't think kids should be forced to suffer," I say, rubbing the place in my chest that still hurts. It hits me that I haven't put much thought into this story. Normally, I'd be two steps ahead, but I'm rusty. "So, what happens when they look up Dr. Leonard and pediatric surgery? Won't they be able to find out in, like, five minutes that I'm no doctor?"

Her face goes pale. It's obvious my sweet summer child has no experience in deceiving people—at least not at the level a lie this big requires. "Crap. I didn't think of that. They don't know your last name, so maybe we have time."

"I'll ask Danny to set up a website for me. He's like Columbo with a computer." He's getting ready to launch a video game with Drew. They're ambitious types, my local buddies. Danny and Drew. Burke and Shane. Back in the day, before I skipped town, the five of us used to do everything together. I was the sore thumb back then, and I still am. Burke, Danny, and Drew have all welcomed me home, but I don't think Shane's glad to see me back. He's been acting like I'm a bad penny that won't stop popping up.

The thought's like a cavity in the back of my mind, but I bury it down.

"This is a bad idea," Shauna says, looking down at her french fries like they might hold all the answers to the world. Just in case they do, I grab another and crunch into it.

"Probably," I offer. "But we've already gone this far. Might as well really lean into it. If you're worried about the pediatric surgery thing, we can tell them Constance got it wrong because she's going deaf."

"She won't like that," she says with a snort.

"She's in the shithouse with you because she made all of this up. Might as well piss her off now, when she feels too guilty to do anything about it."

Her mouth purses to the side.

"So what's the deal with the camping thing on Saturday, anyway? Am I gonna have to pitch a tent?" I waggle my eyebrows.

She ignores the gesture. "No, I guess we were already assigned a cabin. Bianca texted me about it yesterday. I'll sleep on the floor."

I lower the chair and lean forward a bit. "You don't think you can share a bed with me without throwing yourself at me?"

"Yes," she says, deadpan. "That's exactly what I thought. More like, I wouldn't be surprised if you pretended to roll over in your sleep and grabbed my ass."

"You *do* have a nice ass."

I'm surprised when she blushes slightly. I'd like to see it happen again. But there's movement in my peripheral vision, and I see the curtain to the back waving slightly. Pointing to it, I ask, "That where the magic happens?"

Her eyes widen, and she pops up off her chair. "You can't go back there."

"Why, is that where you keep the great and terrible Oz?" I ask, instantly wanting to check it out. What's she got back there? The tools for a passion party?

"A few things I'm working on. They're not ready, though. I don't show people things before they're ready."

I want to press her, but I don't, because somehow I can tell she's afraid of something back there, or at least afraid of me seeing it. I don't want to make her uncomfortable. I'd like to make her feel a lot of things, but that's not one of them.

I glance at the clock. I told Burke I'd try to get to the flip house by 1:30, and it's 1:32. "Say—"

"Let me guess," she says, catching my gaze. "You need a ride."

"Look at that—" I grin at her, "—we're already finishing each other's sentences."

nine

LEONARD

"NO, SHIT," Danny says. "Someone really stole the clunker? Burke told me earlier, but I figured he was messing with me."

We're out on the deck with a couple of beers. Delia's sister, Mira, is inside making cocktails. She can mix a mean drink, but Danny's always been all about the basics—a good breeze, a beer, the sun on his back, a T-shirt, and jeans. He's not a fancy guy, and neither am I. The best things in life are the ones you can enjoy when you have one buck or twenty. I'm not opposed to drinking what she's pouring, but I like this too. Sitting out here with my friend, shooting the shit out in the breeze. Pretending everything's okay.

The party's been running for a while now. It's a small group—Danny and me, Burke and Delia, Mira, and Constance. Shane was invited, but he's continuing his trend of avoiding me.

Danny's not a crowd guy, even when it's a small crowd, full of people he knows, so when I asked for a private chat, he was happy to bring me out to the back deck.

For now, Danny and Burke share this apartment. Burke's going to move in with Delia soon, though, so this place will just be Danny's. Lucky guy, to default his way into a penthouse. But

77

Danny's not the kind of person who accepts lucky breaks, the doofus, so Burke will have to continue pretending Danny is doing him a favor by being here. I can just hear him spouting the bullshit that'll get our friend to stay put. *Need someone to hold down the fort. Keep things clean so I can use the place when we have friends in town.*

The thought makes me smile. They're both good guys, Burke and Danny. So is Shane. He was in law school when I left Asheville all those years ago. He's a lawyer now, and Danny always deadpans that it's for an "important" firm, because that's what Shane likes to remind people of these days.

I've only seen him once or twice since I got back to town. He hangs out with the other guys, but he'd obviously prefer to keep his distance from me. I get it—if you're an important lawyer, the last thing you want is to be seen palling around with a former criminal. And sure, he doesn't know about my past, but he has a good gut and plenty of memories of all the illegal shit we use to do together—like sneaking onto the roof of the Biltmore or fast-talking our way into other people's weddings so we could try to make it with the brides-maids. Burke keeps saying he'll come around, but I've got my doubts.

I don't blame Shane one bit. He's protecting himself, just like he should. Still...I wish things were different.

"What'd the police say?" Danny asks, pulling me back into the moment. "And why are you smiling?"

"Because that old truck's someone else's problem," I hedge. "And Burke's going to buy me a new one for the business."

It still feels surreal that I'm running a business with him. Four months ago, I was in Florida, hiding from someone I'd lost money to in a stupid bet—and also from someone whose wife I'd fucked.

I hadn't known she was married, but then again, I hadn't asked.

It wasn't a life I'd cared about leaving behind, just like the other pit stops I'd made since leaving Asheville. The only one that had ever mattered was here, because of these friends I'd made. The only real friends I've ever had. The kind of friends who will start a business just to give you a damn job.

Burke and I are only on our second flip house. The first one isn't even going on the market, on account of Burke decided he was moving into it. Part of it, though, will be used as the office for L&L Restoration.

Imagine that. *Me*, having an office.

None of the many teachers who failed me in high school would believe it. My old man certainly wouldn't.

Danny laughs. "You're not worried they're going to steal a nicer truck if they lifted the Chevy?"

He has a point. "This one's gonna have an alarm system. All the bells and whistles. They try lifting it, they're going to find a spotlight on their ass."

"Still seems like a bad idea. Why don't you move in here with me after Burke leaves? I'd prefer not to have to go anywhere to socialize."

"Or even socialize when people are here," I say with a laugh, nodding toward the glass door.

He inclines his head. "You know I'm a one person at a time kind of guy."

I grin at him. "You're missing out on a world of fun, bud. Nothing like having two women in your bed at the same time."

"Sure, Leonard. We all know your bed is the party bus." He lifts his eyebrows, studying me, and I feel like I'm in the hotseat. It's his eyes—so dark brown they're almost black.

"I've had my moments." I don't know why, but the back of my neck's sweating.

"Haven't seen you with a single woman since you came back."

"Haven't seen you with one either," I quip back.

His acknowledges that truth with a nod. "None of them can come close to Daphne. What's the point?"

"That's the attitude, Sparky."

Daphne is his ex-girlfriend. They broke up over eight years ago. I love Danny, but rule number one, don't lose your mind over a woman. Rule number two, if you're going to break rule one, make sure your woman is going to stick around. Daphne is some sort of tech genius, and she left to take a job in Europe. She didn't ask Danny to come with her because she said, and I quote, 'You're too basic.'

Ouch.

"Never said I had a good attitude," he says with a small smile. "Don't you think we have enough of that going on with the lovebirds in there?" He gestures to the plate glass door, through which I can see Burke twirling Delia around in a circle, her red-gold hair flying.

"Yes, it's sickening." I don't really mean it, though. I like them together. It's like getting trashed and watching a Hallmark movie.

Something I've obviously never done before.

"Don't get me wrong," Danny says. "She is absolutely the best thing that ever happened to him."

"Huh, I thought I was," I object.

He shoves my shoulder. "You're the one who's going to give us all heart attacks at a young age. You're looking at Burke's future widow in there, because of you."

"Ha. Ha. Very funny. You know, maybe I'm more domestic than you. After all, I *do* have a girlfriend who's taking me to a wedding." He knows about the whole Dr. Leonard situation, because that's the kind of amusing shit you share with your friends. What I haven't admitted to is my interest in Shauna.

He gives an amused sniff. "And you're best buds with her grandmother. If I didn't know better, I'd say you really are going domestic."

"If I started living here, it would complete the process."

"Would that be so bad?" he asks, giving me that look again, like he can see through me.

I consider it for a moment, because, damn, this place is *nice*, then shake my head. I want to keep an eye on the kid.

Besides...if I moved here, I'd feel like I was taking advantage of Burke. I'm guessing Danny feels that way too, but Danny isn't the asshole who ran off eight years ago.

It feels like I've spent most of my whole life running from who I was, but it still doesn't feel like I've run far enough. Every night, I wake up feeling like it's all about to come crumbling down on top of me. Feeling like it's already started.

"No, man," I say, taking a swig of my beer. "Not right now, anyway. I'm not done fixing up Mrs. Ruiz's house."

He shrugs. "How are you going to figure out who took the truck?"

"I'm not, probably. I'm guessing it's some dumb kid."

"You don't think Burke's parents are behind it?" he asks, arching his brows. Danny's the armchair detective in the group, on account of he can't stop listening to true crime podcasts. It's no wonder he's going the alarmist route. "What about asking Burke's P.I. to find it?"

"I don't want to find it," I say with a laugh. "Besides, hiring him would cost more than the truck's worth. There's no way Burke's parents would think causing me a minor inconvenience is worth their time."

He shrugs again, and I figure it's time to ask him about the doctor website. I'm about halfway through the request when Constance comes out with the whole damn charcuterie board. She's in a color-block dress, her hair neatly pinned back. The smile on her face, like she knows a secret and is pretty pleased with herself, reminds me of Shauna.

"I knew I loved you," I say as she sets the board of food down on the small table between the two deck chairs. Danny immediately gets up, as if he'd planned on doing it anyway, and she takes the seat without offering the thanks he wouldn't want. He starts in on the charcuterie board, collecting some pepperoni folded to look like flowers.

"You'll love me even more when I offer you some of this," she says, pulling a flask out of her purse. I try it without asking what it is, then nearly spit it out. It tastes like a cup of coffee someone left in the cabinet under the sink for two months.

"What the fuck is that?" I sputter.

I've tried damn near every alcoholic drink under the sun, and I can't place it. I'm glad I can't because it means I haven't had the misfortune of trying it before today.

"Kahlua. I made it myself," she says, much too excited about it. "It's one of my new hobbies."

"Maybe stick with the feng shui."

"Or the charcuterie boards," Danny suggests. His eyes are shining in the dark night. "This is good."

"Thank you, *Daniel*," she says. "There's nothing like a young man with some manners. Leonard could learn a thing or two from you."

I snort. "That's Dr. Leonard to you, you old buzzard."

She laughs with me, then takes another swig from her flask before cringing and then shrugging. "I begrudgingly admit you might have a point about the Kahlua. Now, you were telling him about my granddaughter?"

"Yeah," I say, scratching my head. "It occurred to me that it's pretty damn disprovable to claim I'm a pediatric surgeon. All that chucklehead Colter has to do is a Google search. So I was asking Danny here to set me up online."

Danny starts laughing in a way that confirms he's had too much to drink. "Leonard Smith, pediatric surgeon. This will be the most fun I've had in weeks."

"Will he get in trouble for impersonating a doctor?" Constance asks. "I'm fine with a pat on the wrist, but we can't have our boy going to jail."

"Thanks," I say flatly.

"I don't think so," Danny says. "Not if he doesn't try to treat anyone or give medical advice. We'll keep everything vague to the point of absurdity, and if anyone calls us on it, we'll say it's a parody website." He looks downright happy about it. "And if anyone meets him, they'll have to agree."

Constance's eyes light up. "I think I like you, Daniel."

"Have some more of that hooch you made," I say. "You'll start liking everyone."

"Let me try it," Danny says, reaching out his hand. Clearly he's a glutton for punishment. He takes a slug and then lifts his eyebrows and hands it back. "Interesting."

I laugh and pat him on the back. "How does it feel to have just drunk a year off your life. Least that's what it feels like."

"Oh, you," Constance says, her voice fond. "You're no better than Shauna. Why, I made her a drink with some of my homemade limoncello the other night, and she accused me of putting Pledge in it."

I feel like a light's been flicked on inside of me. I guess I was looking for an excuse to talk about her, not just the wedding game.

"She didn't want to come tonight, huh?" I'd hoped. I'd even asked Delia to give her a little push.

Constance sighs, looking off into the night. "That girl's deep in her doldrums again. All of this fuss about the wedding and Bianca is bringing back some bad memories."

"Oh?" I ask, angling my head for a better look at her.

Danny takes out his phone and starts messing with it. Knowing him, he's clocking out of the conversation because he knows it's semi-private.

Constance turns her gaze on me, her eyes searching. "You may have noticed she's a bit prickly."

"Like a damn cactus," I say with a grin. "I'm not opposed."

"Because you like a challenge. Same as I do. You know the

people who are most worth knowing don't always make it easy for you."

I nod.

"It's hard for her to trust people," she continues, her gaze intent. "Because when she does, she gives them everything. So, Bianca turning on her like that is the worst thing that could have happened to her."

There's a warning there, and I nod to acknowledge that the message has been received. I know I'll be thinking about it later. Reminding myself of it when I find myself noticing Shauna's tits. The gleam of muted mischief in her eyes.

"Which is why we need to help her feel like she's still in control," I say pointedly. Then I reach around and poke Danny. "And that's where this talented bastard comes in."

"I appreciate the compliment," he says, "but I'd appreciate it even more if you could go in and get me my laptop and a beer."

"You got it, bud. Let the magic begin."

"Indeed," Constance says, smiling slowly. She looks like she's got something she's plotting, but I'm not going to push her for answers. Not right now, anyway.

When I get home later, there's no sign of Reese, so I text the little tyke and let him know he's welcome to come back. No answer.

In the morning, I come down, my head feeling like it got run over by the stolen Chevy, which then reversed and ran it over again, and there's a dirty dish in the sink.

The little shit ate all of my Fruit Loops, so I have no idea why I'm smiling.

ten

SHAUNA

IT'S FRIDAY MORNING. I'm at The Waiting Place, sitting at my desk with a massive travel cup of coffee and doing my part to make the name of our business accurate. The pompom party is tonight, and I can practically feel the minutes ticking toward it.

I stayed up late watching *Time to Settle Down* with Bertie last night. Hate-watching that TV show is addictive. Delia texted me while the male star was on a swimming pool date—his knees are knobbly, which brought me great pleasure—and asked me if I was really attending a pre-wedding pompom-making session with Leonard. I confirmed my insanity. When she followed up with an invitation to join them at her boyfriend's place, I took a selfie with Bertie and insisted I was too busy being his emotional support pillow to leave the house.

I remained busy until midnight, shouting expletives at the TV.

Of course, Bianca saw fit to text me as well:

I can't WAIT to meet your man tomorrow.

I'll bet she can't. With a grin that would make a tiger proud, I wrote back:

> We're SO excited. When I told him you make pompoms for a living, he couldn't believe it! You know, he asked me about the functionality, but I told him he was missing the point.

> Exactly! I told Colt the same thing about that monster figurine you made him for his birthday last year.

> It's wonderful to feel so understood.

I'm not usually a passive aggressive person. My nana is an ace at telling it like it is, and she raised me to be the same way. With one exception. Like me, Nana has crocodile-hide pride. She doesn't enjoy letting people know they've wounded her. I'd rather go on pretending—badly—to be Bianca and Colter's ally in marital bliss, than let Bianca win this game she started.

Sighing, I take another sip of coffee and kick back in my chair. I might have told Leonard not to do it, but it feels good.

My phone buzzes with a text. I catch Leonard's name, so I lower my chair and click through the link he sent.

Then gawk at the website on my phone.

Dr. Leonard Smith is a saver of pediatric lives, a maestro of medicine, a true hero in this modern era. His philosophy is that laughter truly is the best medicine—along with penicillin, of course. He was going to be named bachelor of the year by the local blog, Ashevillains, but sorry, ladies, he's taken.

Next to his bio, if it could be called that, is a headshot of Leonard wearing scrubs. I'm pretty sure it must be his head glued onto someone's body, unless he bought scrubs for Halloween one year, but if so, it's a good fake.

He really *is* photogenic. The camera caught the glimmer of mischief in his eyes, the long eyelashes that don't belong on a man like him, or a man at all, and the laughter lines around his eyes.

Ignoring the little dip in my stomach, I text him back.

> Were you drunk when you did this?

I might still be drunk. Good, huh?

Not really, but it looks shiny and slick, so I'm guessing Danny's as good with "computer shit" as Leonard said. Still, no doctor who's not a phony would have a website bio like that.

> It doesn't say where you work.

Because that's the kind of lie that could get us caught. I'll just say I'm not allowed to give details because of HIPAA.

> Isn't that just for protecting patients' privacy?

Maybe. I don't know shit about that. Neither do most people. You say HIPAA to a non-medical person, and they're just gonna nod. That's what Danny said.

> What happens if we meet a medical person?

(Running emoji)

> And if someone contacts the blog?

It's run by someone Delia's sister knows.

> (High five emoji)

87

Yeah, give it to me, Tiger.

Don't make me feel more regret. I already have plenty.

I'm pumped for tonight. Are you?

Maybe. Do you realize we don't have a plan other than the obviously fake website?

Like I said, I do my best when I don't have one. Plans can go wrong. If you don't have one, you can pretend everything you're doing is successful.

Sounds a lot like lying to yourself.

That's exactly what it is. I highly recommend it. Still...I guess I do have an angle.

Sounds like Leonard-speak for a plan. What's your angle?

Wouldn't you like to know.

I figure tonight's mostly about getting the lay of the land. We'll have more time to create chaos at Camp Nightmare.

Say, what do you think about bringing a box of crickets to release in the marital cabin?

As long as I don't have to touch them.

Even though I'm still a hot mess with nothing to wear to a party I'm dreading, I'm smiling as I set the phone down.

"Knock, knock," someone says. I glance over at the open doorway and reflexively smile. It's Delia. She's wearing an emerald-green dress, and her long red-gold hair is loose around her shoulders.

Mira's with her, and the well-hidden circles under her eyes suggest the situation with Byron is still a bummer. I catch her eyeing my coffee and draw it closer to my chest. "This coffee is mine, and I will kill without remorse to protect it."

She laughs good-naturedly. "I'm not a morning person, or even an early afternoon person, but Delia and I agreed we couldn't let you go to the pompom party like this."

"Like what?" I ask, although of course I know what she means. My roots aren't any better than they were a week ago, and I can't remember the last time I bothered to put on makeup. The zit has decided it likes me and would enjoy hanging around.

Mira shrugs. "Like shit. We discussed this the other day."

"She doesn't mean that," Delia insists.

Her sister smirks at her. "I really do."

"I can tell she does," I agree. I find Mira's honesty refreshing, actually. It's nice to be around people who actually say what they mean.

Ignoring us, Delia says, "We just want you to go there feeling confident, like you can take on the world, because you *can*. We're here to build you up."

"And give you a makeover."

Mira makes a grab for my coffee. I thwack her hand, then remember she's here to help me. Sighing, I say, "There's a coffee machine in the staff lounge to the left of me." I wave toward the display cases that I finally finished arranging. "Feel free to pick a mug. You can keep it if you can figure out how to cover up this zit without making me look like I have a lesion on my face."

"Sweet," she says. "You're on."

"Don't worry," Delia says reassuringly. "You're going to look fantastic tonight. We'll take care of everything."

Her offer gives me a shocking sense of relief. When was the last time I let someone else take care of everything?

When was the last time I let someone else take care of *anything*?

eleven

SHAUNA

Text conversation with Leonard:

> Can you grab some Fruit Loops and bring them over when you pick me up?

> I'll pay you back. Buy generic.

> Are you high?

> Not yet. I'm more of a nighttime smoker, but if you feel like some 420, just say the word. ;-)

> Fine.

> Fine, you want to smoke with me?

> I'll get you the Fruit Loops, douchebag.

I BRING the Fruit Loops to the door of the little purple house, feeling a prickle of interest. I know this isn't Leonard's house, just a place he's been living, but I'm curious about *how* he's been living.

Is it a pigsty, full of open pizza boxes and flies drunk on possibility?

The house is tidy on the outside, freshly painted and with windows that look like they haven't been waging a losing battle against the elements for forty years like the ones in my grandmother's house.

I knock on the door. Leonard tugs it open, and I almost drop the cereal. He's wearing a white button-up shirt with the sleeves rolled up to show just a few of his tattoos—the dog, the scar, and the funny fungi are hidden away. The pot leaf too, thankfully. His hair is still a little too long for him to pull off the doctor look, but I'm glad for it. He's wearing a pair of khakis—*khakis!*—and dress shoes.

Dr. Leonard, indeed.

He looks sexy...but not really like himself, and part of me wishes he were in one of his band T-shirts and I was in the coveralls I like to wear in my studio.

"You got brand name," he comments with a sigh, as if I just kicked a baby chick. "It's such a racket."

"That's okay," I say numbly, handing over the box. "My treat."

His mouth hitches up as he looks me over, pausing on the top of my gold sundress in a way that makes me feel his perusal. Mira dyed my roots and trimmed my hair, and I'll be damned if Delia didn't magic that zit out of existence, at least for the night. Maybe I'm like Cinderella, and it'll grow the size of a pumpkin at midnight, but if so, it's worth it—until tomorrow.

"*You're* a treat," he says.

I roll my eyes, but I can't help but smile. It feels nice to be appreciated, even if it is by a man who may or may not get busy in fast food bathrooms.

He whistles, his lips forming a shape that makes me feel hot behind my ears. "I'm guessing they got to you too?"

I laugh, because surely this means he also got the Mira and Delia treatment. The Evans sisters to the rescue. "They caught me at a weak moment," I say. "Now, what do you say we go make some balls?"

"Just a second," he says. "I got something we need to bring."

My eyebrows have probably met my hairline by now. I want into that house, though, and this is my big opportunity. I take a big step forward.

"Eager to get inside, Tiger?" he asks, giving me another glance. It's almost...hungry, and heat settles inside of me. "So am I."

I poke him in the chest, annoyed with myself *and* him. It doesn't help that his chest is solid and warm. "There will be no hooking up of any kind, Dr. Leonard. This is a *professional* arrangement."

"I know," he says with a grin, still holding that box of cereal. "You teach me how to make a clay dick, and I help you screw with your ex. Even trade."

"Don't forget the cereal."

He lifts the box and nods. "Thanks for that. That's what we can call a bonus."

"You're welcome, but there will be no other bonuses. At least not of the sort I suspect you're interested in."

He lifts his eyebrows, his hazel eyes boring into me. "But if I'm not allowed to touch you, how are we going to make everyone else insane with jealousy?"

Crap, he has a point. I'd never considered that he'd have to put his hands on me to make the ruse seem real. The thought of him touching me, running his hands over my body, sends a burst of heat through me.

His lips lift up, revealing a flash of teeth whiter than they probably should be given he doesn't seem like a paragon of self-care. "And shouldn't we have a little fun?"

"That's not the kind of fun I'm looking for," I say with a firmness I don't feel. I step past him into the house, giving myself a moment to think. The interior is...a surprise. Mostly because there aren't dirty dishes sitting out, band shirts slung over the banister, or ash trays full of half-smoked joints. It's *tidy*, and it smells like lemons.

I say that out loud, and Leonard snorts. "You thought I lived like a pig, huh?"

"It was a favored theory of mine."

"Rookie mistake. You want to make a mess, you do it at someone else's place. That way you don't have to live in it."

"Sounds like you," I say, mostly teasing.

"Besides, you clearly haven't meant Mrs. Ruiz, the old broad who owns this place. She'd make your grandmother look like a kitten." His mouth lifts up as he follows me in and shuts the front door behind him. "Speaking of which..."

I don't know what the hell he's talking about, but I don't comment as he leaves me in the main room and goes off to stow the cereal and grab whatever it is he wants to bring.

Condoms, my mind supplies.

Stupid mind.

To ignore the intrusive thoughts, I look around. It really is very orderly, with a place for everything and everything in its place. There's a little framed photo sitting on a side table, and I'm surprised to see it's very clearly *Leonard's* little framed photo. He's in it with four guys. One of the others is Burke, Delia's boyfriend, who was probably born with a chiseled jaw and five-o-clock shadow. Another is Drew Jones, Sinclair's brother.

It's...surprising that Leonard put this photo out. He comes off as a guy who doesn't give a shit about anything, but I guess he does care about his friends. Then again, there are serial killers who are fond of their mommies.

Tell that to the feeling inside of me, like I accidentally swallowed a firefly.

"You ready for this?" Leonard calls out from the other room, laughter in his voice.

"Something tells me I'm not and could never be."

He comes out with a fuzzy black kitten cuddled in the crook of his arm and a pleased-with-himself smile on his face. "Meet Tiger, Jr. Actually, I was thinking we should call her Bean. Colter will hate that."

"What the hell?" I blurt. "You're bringing a cat?"

"To a pompom craft night, yes," he says with a grin that's more sly than not. "I'm sure Bianca and Colter will understand. Bean needs constant supervision. We'll take her crate too, but something tells me she'll want to get some air." His grin stretches wider, his eyes sparkling, his whole face lit up with chaotic glee. "You'll want to check this out."

He goes to the coffee table and pulls a pompom out from a shelf built beneath it. The pompom goes on the couch, followed by the little kitten. She immediately launches herself at it, attacking with teeth and claws. Yarn flies around like confetti.

Grinning at me, he says, "I taught her to go after them by putting catnip in the middle."

"Diabolical," I admit, impressed. How long has he had this cat anyway? "But I'm not sure how I feel about bringing an animal into the situation. What are you going to do with her after tonight?"

He shrugs, looking a little self-conscious, and picks her up again. "I figured maybe I'd keep her."

"You like cats?"

"Sure. I've heard they're more self-sufficient than dogs."

I remember the look on his face when he told me that Gidget was dead and it was his fault. There's a swelling feeling inside of me. I put a hand on his arm, but Bean bats it as if to say he's her man.

You can keep him, Cat.

"Tell me about your friends," I say on impulse.

His eyes find the photo that I was shamelessly checking out a couple of minutes ago. He steps closer, standing by my side so he can look down at it too. He's close enough that I can feel his heat in every inch of my body. "But those are *my* friends, Tiger, not Dr. Leonard's."

"And we agreed it's best to stay truth adjacent in our over-the-top lies."

He pets Bean, who leans into his hand, her little eyes squeezing shut as she purrs. Does he know how sexy that is?

Judging from the crafty look in his eyes, yes, he does. He's trying to get me to bend on the whole no-touching thing. Not because he likes me, I'm sure, but because he's the kind of man who likes to fuck.

I'll bet he's good at it.

I bet he could make me the delicious kind of sore.

I deliver myself a mental slap. It's been too long. Long enough to make me forget why it's a mistake to sleep with unsuitable men.

"I met them at a bar when we were dumb kids. Twenty-one, maybe twenty-two. I let Burke think I had a college degree, and he helped me land a job with his folks before we realized they were assholes. I don't have a degree, though, so it was a lie from the get-go." He pauses, a vein in his neck pulsing. I have the impulse to lick it, so my libido is definitely out of control. "What do you think about that?"

I snort. "I'm not going to judge you for it. My grandmother may have started this lie without my permission, but I'm the idiot who's leaning into it. We've both lied to our friends."

His gaze is pointed. "Those people aren't your friends, Tiger."

"No," I agree. "That's the biggest lie of all, isn't it? You know, I did think some of the people who'll be there tonight were my friends, but that was bullshit too."

"Still, I don't think your not-friends would be impressed with my GED."

"Probably not. Maybe that's why they chose Bianca over me. She'll tell anyone who listens that she went to the College of William and Mary."

"Is that made up?" he asks with a puff of air. "Sounds made up."
I have to smile. My face demands it. "No. I looked it up. It's
about as self-important as you'd expect. *I didn't go to college.*"
He smirks at me, one corner of his mouth inching up above the
other, his eyes crinkling with mirth. It's hard to look away from him,
but I do, lowering my gaze to the kitten. "Are you telling me you
learned how to create clay dicks all on your own?"
"Sure. I knew what I wanted to do." I smile at him. "The clay
part, not the dicks specifically. I didn't see any point in waiting."
No, at the time, I thought the future was spread out before me,
waiting to be staked with a flag with my name on it. It didn't take
long for me to realize I was a dumb kid—that "making it" is nearly
impossible as an artist, and even harder when you make things
people figure they should be able to get in a discount bin, but I
haven't let that stop me.
"What made you want to sculpt with clay?" he asks, watching
me intently, as if he actually cares how I answer the question.
"The same old cliché answers you'll get from any artist, I'm
guessing. Making something out of nothing. It's like being a god of
small things."
There's laughter in his eyes, but none of it escapes, so I have no
reason to shove him. "I like being a god too."
I give him that shove then, careful to avoid the kitten. "If a
woman calls that out in the bedroom, she's probably faking."
His expression turns positively lecherous. "I can tell when
someone's pretending."
"Everyone thinks they know," I scoff.
"Most people aren't natural liars," he says pointedly. "I'm not
most people. You don't get good at playing cards if you can't pick up
on other people's tells without giving up your own."
"Are you good at cards?"
He laughs a little, his eyes crinkling. "You know what? Maybe
I'm not so hot at it after all. I've won a lot of money. Lost more."

"I knew you were trouble." I poke him in the chest again.

"Don't try to hide it."

No, he doesn't. It's one of the things I like about him. Most people try to conceal their flaws. He hangs his over himself like a sandwich board.

"You know," he adds, "Burke's parents gave me a pay-off years ago to keep quiet about their shitty business practices. I pissed all the money away."

"Too bad you didn't invest it instead, huh?"

He laughs harder this time. "Nah, then I would have lost it anyway, but I wouldn't have had any fun."

There's a look in his eyes that's not so amused though. It suggests that he wasn't having all that much fun, and that's just a story he tells himself.

"What'd you buy?" I ask out of curiosity. "I'm guessing you didn't gamble it *all* away."

"Nothing I could keep." He clears his throat. "I changed my name a few times too. That's expensive, if you do it the right way."

"Is your name even Leonard?" I blurt.

"I mostly stuck with changing my last name. There are a lot of last names out there to choose from. I guess I got lazy with this last one. There are a lot of Smiths."

I can't believe he's telling me all of this. He's usually a man who plays his cards close to the chest. So why open up like this?

At the same time, what has he really told me? He's revealing bits and pieces of himself, but not enough that I can join them together into anything meaningful. All I know is that he's more complicated than I expected. Beneath his charm there's a history that's as full of patches as a quilt.

Maybe he's trying to scare me away or give me an out. Either way, I don't want him to stop talking. I'm fascinated despite myself. "Is this not the first time you pretended to be a pediatric surgeon?"

"Oh, that's a first, all right." He pauses, then adds, "I did it because of the Burkes in the beginning."

"Then why did you come back here?" I ask, pointedly.

His mouth hitches up again. "Burke can be very persuasive. Besides, his parents are in legal trouble now. He played hero, the way he does best, and turned them in."

He doesn't say it darkly or with any menace. He thinks Lucas Burke is a hero and deserves to be.

He swallows. "They'd be stupid to mess with me. No point. They arranged for me to leave because they were worried about what I knew, but it got out anyway. I'm irrelevant."

I don't like the way he says that, like he believes it's true in a way that goes beyond the Burkes.

"Not to Bean you're not," I say as she snuggles into his arm.

He smiles at me. For a second he's quiet, then he says, "I know what drew you to clay. It made you feel like you had control over something." I don't like that he's right about me, when I know so little about him.

"Maybe." I shrug as if I don't care. "Maybe I just had a Play-Doh fetish as a toddler and never got over it."

"You know, I think that's why I like fixing old houses," he says, catching me off guard. The kitten has squirmed upward and is batting her little paw at the side of his face, as if she too would like to feel his scruff.

"Why," I ask, my voice raw and strange, "because you had a thing for Pick Up Sticks?"

"Nah, I spent so much time breaking things—and watching other people do it—and I wanted to put them back together for a change." It's another real thing, and it feels like I'm finally getting to know him. Which is probably why he instantly launches into something that's not real. "Must be why I decided to become a doctor."

I shrug. "I guess the best school is the school of life."

"There were a few classes I probably should have skipped," he says, giving Bean another pet.

"And a few others you shouldn't have slept through."

Bean snuggles up under his chin, making a little noise of contentment, and it's so damn cute to see them together, I can barely stand it. Maybe he's hoping Bean will sabotage the yarn—and piss Colter off because of her name—but I'm starting to realize my real secret weapon is Leonard himself.

Dr. Leonard, Ruler of Pussies.

Damn it, mind.

I clear my throat. "Shall we?"

"Let me get her crate. Walk with me? It's in my bedroom."

"I said no funny business," I all but growl. Still, he's already walking, and I find myself following him.

"Gotcha loud and clear," he says. "No fun will be had. This is where her crate is. Besides, I figured I'd show you the way in case you change your mind."

I give him a flat look that he doesn't see because his back is too me. "You can't help yourself, can you?"

"Not really, no. Can't say I have a mind to, either. But we should settle on some ground rules. I'm going to need to touch you in front of them. Otherwise they'll never believe we're together—no man who has you with him would keep his hands to himself. You don't let me touch you, they'll know something's up."

Colter never had his hands all over me like that, even in the beginning, but something keeps me from saying so.

"There will be no ass-grabbing of any kind," I say, then swallow, my mouth dry. "You can hold my hand."

He turns to face me, his mouth in that ever-present grin, as we reach the landing at the top of the stairs. "So, it's a summer camp kind of love. Got it. What about kissing? Can I kiss you, Tiger, or will you scratch?"

"We're going to be in public. No one wants to watch us make out, but you can kiss my cheek."

His grin widens. "Sure. But again, if you were my woman, I'd do a hell of a lot more than kiss your cheek. I'd want to let everyone know you're mine, especially the chucklehead who let you go."

I avoid rolling my eyes. Barely. "I doubt you've ever had a girlfriend."

He shrugs, his smile devious now. "Never say never. Say, how'd you meet this guy, anyway?"

Embarrassment grips at me, squishy and cloying. "I don't want to tell you."

He makes a sound of amusement and turns down the hall and then into the first door to the right. Bean peeks at me over his shoulder as I follow him in.

To my shock, the bed is made, the navy comforter folded back to give me a peek of a pillow with the indentation of a head on it. There's something strangely intimate about it, and there's the fleeting thought that I'd like to lie my head down on it, where his goes.

I'm losing my mind. Or maybe I've already lost it, and this is the leftover mush I've been left with.

I avert my eyes, taking notice of the glass of water on the side table, along with that ashtray I was expecting. I lift my eyebrows and point to it.

"Wouldn't Mrs. Ruiz object to that?"

"I'm counting on Drew giving me at least twenty-four hours warning if they get a hair in their ass about coming back," he says, putting Bean in a cloth-sided crate and setting it on the bed. She yowls her disapproval, then retreats to the back to curl up sulkily in the corner.

I've never related so much to an animal.

"Why don't you want to tell me how you met Colton?"

I sigh. "Because you're going to make fun of me. And you *know* his name's Colter."

"Now I have to know how you met," he says, his eyes bright as he picks up Bean's crate.

"I met his mom at a craft show."

He whistles. "Sounds like a lot of bad shit go down at those. Maybe you should rethink your career."

I have to smile, but I keep going. "Anyway, she and I got talking. She runs a craft shop in town, the one Colter manages, and she said she was interested in stocking some of my monster mugs. Then she told me a bit about her 'single son' and asked if she could give him my number."

He gives me a wide-eyed look. "And you gave it to her? What if he was a mutant?"

"She showed his picture to me," I say, but my voice is defensive.

"But why'd he call you?"

"I took a photo with her," I say, fighting the impulse to look away. It *is* sort of embarrassing, to be honest. It makes me sound like I was desperate, but the truth is that I really liked his mother. I wanted to please her, and not just to make a sale.

Truth be told, I *didn't* make a sale. A few months after we met, Colter told me it wasn't the right season for my mugs—they were more of a fall item. Later, they had too much stock. No room. Eventually, he'd asked me not to talk to his mother about it anymore because he didn't want me to put her on the spot. It took me a while to realize the truth—he was stringing me along. So was his mother. They needed to sell things that were more mainstream and universally pleasing.

Like pompoms.

After Colter and his mom made an order of five hundred pompoms, Bianca took me out for drinks and said, "Now, don't say I told you so, but Mrs. Rogers was never seriously interested in your monster mugs. She and Colt think they're a bit too niche for a store like that."

That went down just before Colter and I broke up. By then, Queen Bee Pompoms were a big deal anyway, so it made sense, I guess. A sound business decision. Still, it made me feel like she'd sliced me open.

The messed-up thing is that I felt more betrayed by Mrs. Rogers than I did by Colter. It seemed like it had all been a lie from the beginning, breadcrumbs to draw me in. She'd never really appreciated or loved me. She'd never seen me as anything other than a nice girl, maybe a little troubled, who makes crafts.

It made me hate her a little, or at least hate the story of how Colter and I had met. Because there's a part of me that still wants to be drawn into one of Mrs. Rogers's hugs, which always smell like fresh-baked cookies.

A sigh escapes me. A defeated sigh, which makes me pissed at myself.

"Our story is going to be much better than that," Leonard says as he leaves the room with the cat.

"Wait, what?" I try to catch up, but let's be real, his legs are several inches longer than mine. "I thought we were going with the gym thing."

"Nah, it's too boring. We should give them something to remember. Something that blows *my mommy matchmade us* out of the water."

"I don't like this," I say as I follow him down the stairs.

He turns to me at the foot of them, a grin on his face. I'm still a couple of stairs above him, putting our heads level with each other. "You sure, Tiger? Because I'm having fun."

I realize, with something like surprise, that I am too.

twelve

LEONARD

WE WALK into the events space at Buchanan Brewery, past a sign that says,

Add Bianca and Colter,
and get Happily Ever After! #theABCsofLove

I'm not sure whether I want to laugh so I hard I piss myself or change my name and move to a different state. Maybe one and then the other.

I immediately peg Colter as the guy who's standing by the open doors and eyeing up Shauna in that sexy-ass dress. He's wearing white pants and a shirt that looks like a cut of salmon, collar popped. His hair is blond, and his eyes are the sad blue of a baby seal who's about to see the business end of a club.

I immediately nickname him Champ in my head, because he looks like the kind of all-American guy you'd see in a commercial where they're playing softball and eating shitty hotdogs.

If we weren't so close to him, I'd lean down and ask Shauna why she fucked this guy but won't fuck me. I can guarantee I'd show her a better time. He looks like he could only have an accidental acquaintance with the female orgasm.

"Bean," Colter says with a grin, taking a step toward Shauna. I put my left arm around her hip, holding the cat carrier with the other hand. My fingers brush the firm swell of her ass as I loop it around her, and I feel something jump to attention inside of me. It's not just my cock, which took plenty of notice of her when she was in my bedroom earlier.

"She tell you we repurposed that name for our foster kitten?" I ask.

His frown is like a shot of whiskey after the worst day of your life. I suck it up and savor it.

"You brought a cat?" His gaze shoots to the animal carrier.

"Tiger here thought you'd understand," I say, giving her hip a squeeze. She steps on my foot. I grin. "This here is Bean. We were told she's not supposed to be left alone for more than half an hour at a time."

"Uh, I think there's a no-animal policy," he says tightly.

"Not to worry, Champ," I say, unwinding my arm from Shauna so I can slap him on the back. "One of the owners is married to the woman who runs the animal shelter where we got our precious baby."

True, actually. I read it on the website. The panicked look on Shauna's face says she thinks I'm lying, but I did my research.

It's always best to know the lay of the land when you're going into enemy territory.

"Huh," Colter says, trying to recover. "Wait a sec. Bee," he calls.

A woman with dark hair and the eyes of a parole officer turns around, and from the surprised expressions of the people in her group, she's clearly abandoned them mid-sentence. Huh. Not a blond then. She has on a sleek black dress, and there's a look of cunning in her eyes as she studies us.

Shauna got it in one. This woman may not even know it, but

she's playing a game. She's probably always playing a game—the kind that she can win, to her mind.

I catch Shauna staring at me, and there's a pout around her lips, like she's not happy with me for scoping out the competition. I slide my arm around her again, letting her know that I'm not drawn in by this uppity woman or her airs. My assessment was purely about being prepared.

I think I already have a read on the situation. Colter's nothing. A patsy. As easily played as a guitar with one string. This woman's the real brains in the joint.

"*Darling?*" she says, joining Champ and leaning into him.

I shoot Shauna a significant glance. Champ mimics me. Finally, she clears her throat and says, "Sorry." Her gaze turns to me, burning, and she layers her hand over the one I have on her hip. Her hand is small and smooth, and I like the feeling of it. Even if she's only touching me out of spite for another man. Actually, it's better this way. No expectations. "This is Leonard. Leonard, meet the happy couple, Bianca and Colter."

"You can call me Doc," I tell them with a grin. Maybe I'm imagining it, but I think Shauna's holding back a laugh. I edge a little closer to her. She pinches the hand I have on her hip.

"So great to finally meet you," Champ says, holding out his hand. I release Shauna's hip and transfer Bean's crate to my left hand so I can give him a shake. I figure he'll try to crush my hand into submission like the big guy at The Waiting Place. Rafe was protective of Shauna, which I respect. But Colter's shake is limp and lacks any conviction. I transfer Bean back over after his hand drops.

Bianca surprises me by leaning in to kiss my cheek, her lips dry and cool.

When she pulls back, I catch Shauna giving her death eyes, which was obviously the intention behind the cheek-kiss.

"We've *really* been looking forward to meeting you," Bianca says. "The man who finally cracked Shauna's shell."

The look on her face saying she's very much enjoying this game.

"Same," I say. "I've heard *so much* about you both."

"You know, when she said she had a Plus One, we figured she was bringing Rafe until Constance spilled the beans. You've met Rafe, of course. Who'd guess someone who looks like a meathead could paint, huh? But he's not bad."

I can feel Shauna getting pissed off next to me, so I grin at Bianca and say, "Well, no one could say that to you. You look exactly like the kind of woman who'd professionally make pompoms."

She gives me a smile so coldly assessing my balls almost shrivel. We both know it wasn't a compliment, but she says, "Thank you."

A couple of people pass us, greeted by Champ, who's watching us from the corners of his eyes, like he sees that club coming down.

"Like I said, Shauna here has told me all about you two," I continue, "but you know what? She didn't mention the ABC hashtag," I wave in the direction of the sign. "Love it. People will be talking about it for months. Years. Who came up with that *brilliant* idea?"

Shauna makes a sound that could be laughter or choking. Too bad I'm not a real doctor. If she's choking, she's screwed.

"Colt and I came up with it together," Bianca says, but I'm guessing she was the one who put it to paper. She probably doesn't want to take credit without knowing whether we genuinely like it. How anyone could genuinely like such a stupid thing is beyond me. Then again, weddings in general are beyond me. And hashtags.

"And who's this?" Bianca says tightly, nodding to the cat carrier.

"This is our little buddy, Bean," I say. I can't deny it—I enjoy the reflexive stare she gives Shauna, who smiles back at her.

"That's Shauna's nickname," Bianca says sweetly.

"That's what I said," Champ adds to feel important. He sidles up to Bianca, ignoring the next couple of people who come through the door. They look around like lost dogs hoping someone will pull bacon out of their pocket. I follow their gaze to the long tables set up with crafting supplies and yarn. People are gathered around them, drinking beer and shooting the shit. Some of them already have strips of yarn laid out.

Once the new people accept no introduction is coming, they walk timidly toward one of the tables.

I'm guessing they belong to Champ.

I smile at the happy couple with my teeth showing. "It's not Shauna's nickname anymore. Seems more fitting for a cat, don't you think? Sorry to bring the kitten along without asking first, but my girl here said you wouldn't mind. Told me you were a real bleeding heart for animals."

"Well, as long as you keep her in her crate," Bianca says tightly. It's obvious she isn't thrilled about the situation, but we've already attracted attention from the other guests, and a couple of women from the back of the room are moving in on the zippered crate, wanting to say hello to my fuzzy friend.

That's the other reason I brought the cat. Bean's going to bring us good will.

That's also why I kept Gidget when I found her sleeping in an alleyway, beaten and starved. I told myself she'd be good for getting some female attention, and she was. I didn't think I'd love her like I did. If I'd known, I might have brought her to a shelter and left it at that.

Maybe both of us would have been better off if I had.

"How'd you two meet?" Champ asks, patting me on the back.

Shauna looks like she's about to launch into her gym explanation, so I bust in with, "Funny story. She was choking at a restaurant, and I stepped in with the—" Fuck, what is that called? "—hug of life." Good enough. "She told me she'd do anything for me for saving her life, and I said the only earthly thing I wanted was a date with her. We've been glued together ever since."

Shauna grinds her heel into my foot, and I grin at the happy couple.

"Wow, that's some story!" Champ says, and he seems to mean it, the rube.

"Yeah, it sure is," Bianca says with more suspicion. "Well, feel free to grab a seat at one of the workstations. We're about to get started."

"Looks like forced labor," Shauna says. "Do you have an order to fill?"

I have to laugh because she's right. It certainly doesn't look like much of a party.

"You're too funny," Bianca says flatly. "I've always loved your sense of humor. Remember that time you—"

"Is there beer?" I put in. "Because I'll do anything if there's beer."

"Even karaoke?" Bianca asks in challenge.

"I'd do that stone cold sober, honey."

"Good," she says flatly. "Because that's an organized activity for the campground tomorrow."

"We look forward to it," Shauna says, reclaiming my free hand. I like the feel of it in mine—soft but with a grip that's firm as hell.

Bianca titters. "Really, Bean? Because you've always said you're tone deaf."

An older woman approaches Colter, and he shifts his attention to her.

"Better to throw out that old nickname, huh?" I say, pulling Shauna's hand around my waist. "It'll be too confusing if there's more than one of them."

"You might not want to bring the cat tomorrow," Bianca adds, her gaze dipping to little Bean, who's poking her head at the mesh front of the crate. "Wouldn't want it to get lost in the woods."

"Why?" I ask. "We gonna play hide and seek?"

"Maybe," Bianca says with a wink that's meant to upset rather than excite.

Champ is still standing next to her, making small talk about peach cobbler with an old woman who looks like she stuck cotton balls all over her head. He completely misses the wink. Or maybe he's just used to his woman trying to sidle up on strange men. If it were me, I wouldn't take it.

Then again, I've never claimed a woman as my own. I've avoided it. Other than Constance, the only woman I've ever tried to keep happy was Gidget, and look how that turned out.

I bury the dark thought as Shauna pulls me away—toward the bar, thank all that's unholy.

"*That woman,*" she says in an undertone that's half growl. Her hand is still clutching mine, squeezing, and I don't mind one bit. It makes me wonder what it would feel like if it were angrily wrapped around my dick—painful and a good bit pleasurable too.

"I think all of this is for you," I say as we join the back of the line. There's a couple in front of us who look like brother and sister, both with dark hair and brown eyes, having an argument about toothpaste that they're trying to soften by aggressively calling each other *dear*.

"As much as I'd like thinking everything's about me, I doubt it," Shauna says with a huff.

"Champ back there is too easy for the pompom queen. Messing with him is like trying to get a bee to land in a flower. But you... you're more interesting to play with."

She gapes at me for a second, then her mouth works into a smile as the dude in front of us tells his woman, "Fluoride is important, *dear*. You crunch enough granola, you're going to get cavities. I don't give a shit how much charcoal you use."

That's going downhill fast. On the plus side, maybe they'll adios on the line and we'll get our beers sooner.

"You think Bianca's some kind of narcissist?" Shauna whispers close to my ear, the air from her voice tickling my neck. If only she were whispering something dirty.

I edge a little closer, pretending it's so we can whisper and not because I want to feel her words. "I don't know about that psychobabble, but that woman wants something from you. Or maybe she's jealous."

Her eyes dance with humor. "Of *you*?"

Well, damn. Way to javelin me in the chest, Tiger.

"She should be. But no. She hasn't had time to realize how desirable I am."

She rolls her eyes, and I add, "I mean she's jealous of who you *are*."

This time she looks off in the distance, or maybe she's eying the yarn, putting together a strategy for how big she wants to make her balls. "I doubt that, Leonard. She's got everything she wants."

"I don't think so," I say, thinking of Bianca's calculating gaze as we mosey forward a few steps with the line. "A person like that won't ever have everything she wants."

"You're a pig," the woman in front of us says. For a second, I think she's talking to me. It's an accusation that's gotten slung around a time or two, but she's talking to Fluoride Guy. "You don't even brush your teeth half the time. At least I try."

I decide to step in. "What's the problem, friends?"

"Do you mind?" Fluoride Guy says, whirling around to look at us. There's surprise in his eyes when he sees Shauna. "Oh, I wasn't sure you were going to come. It's good to see you, Bean."

Well, shit, she knows them, although from the look on her face, she wishes she didn't.

"Yeah, you too," Shauna mutters unconvincingly. "It's been a while."

The woman plays with one of her curls. They look fake, but I'm no expert. "I thought about reaching out," she continues, "but I figured it would be best to give you some space...you know? And then I heard that you were going to be in the wedding, and I figured you were doing okay if you accepted, so..."

Shauna's annoyance has slipped into something else—she's... hurt. I left Asheville for eight years, and my friends took me back with open arms, but these people have clearly abandoned her. Admittedly, they seem shitty—the kind of people you'd be better off not knowing—but it still makes me feel like pounding my fist to something.

I don't like the thought of her feeling alone. Of her being stuck in those doldrums Constance told me about. Bean must feel it too, because she gives a sad little yowl from behind her mesh.

"Well, anyway," the woman says, "I'm hoping—"

"What were you arguing about just now?" I ask, cocking my head. "Seemed pretty heated."

"Gus doesn't believe fluoride is bad for us," she blurts. "He says it's in the drinking water."

I grunt. "No offense, my friend, but that's not the best argument I've ever heard. Why, just last week, the water coming out of my sink was as red as Satan's taint."

"Red?" he asks, edging slightly closer. "I've heard of water being brown before, but never red. Is there rust in your pipes?" He glances back and forth between me and Shauna, silently asking her if I'm for real. She gives a half shrug.

"How would I know if there's rust in 'em, Gus? I don't have one of those tiny cameras outside of the office. All I can tell you is that it tasted funny."

"You *drank* it?" the woman asks, horrified. I can feel Shauna watching me, amused now, and I'm grateful that I was able to chase away that other look—one that doesn't belong on a tiger's face.

"Wouldn't you feel the need to take a sip if your water came out red?" I waggle my brows and nod for them to move forward with the line. We're almost there. "That's not the kind of thing that happens every day."

The two of them exchange a look as they step up behind the couple giving their order.

"I needed to make sure I didn't have a haunting on my hands, but don't worry, friends, it wasn't blood." I bump Shauna with my shoulder. "Shauna here thought it tasted like Kool-Aid."

"You tried it too?" the woman asks breathlessly.

"Sure," I put in. "No harm, no foul. I'm a doctor, so I'd know." They don't seem to find this comforting, so I go for broke and add, "I treat children."

"Where do you work?" the woman blurts.

"I try not to say." I give her a wink, then turn a grin on Shauna. "HIPAA."

The woman's lips part. "But—"

"What would you like, ma'am?" asks the bartender. He's a big guy with a beard, like about half to three-quarters of the men in Asheville.

"Is it made with tap water?" she asks. Fluoride Guy rolls his eyes at her, forgetting the red water and diving back into their argument. I give them a month, or maybe a lifetime, of unhappiness—it could go either way.

"You're incorrigible," Shauna says to me in an undertone.

"There you go with another of those five-dollar words," I say, even though I know this one. I've been called it enough times.

"You're an ass," she replies, her eyes sparkling. "Is that better?"

"Yes," I say, then release her hand and put my arm around her waist, resting it over the top of her ass. "Might as well earn it."

I'm surprised, and a damn sight pleased, when she doesn't brush my hand away. "Thank you," she whispers under her breath, and suddenly I feel like the King of England.

Fluoride and his woman nod to Shauna but are quick to move off, bickering about possible fluoride run-off in the beer now. We make our order and grab our drinks before walking off to find a table.

"You were really friends with those people?" I whisper.

She gives a shrug-nod. "They're okay. Misty's a pretty good painter, but she's kind of—"

"Dumb?" I suggest, lifting my eyebrows.

Another shrug-nod. Her mouth lifts up slightly, one of her near-miss smiles. "I'm the one who got her on the fluoride train. I had a few women over to my house for a crafting night, and she was being a real bitch about these drinks Nana made us—"

"Didn't have Kahlua in them, did they?" I ask.

"No," she says, giving me the look of someone who has not yet been subjected to her grandmother's Kahlua.

I nod. "Carry on."

"Anyway, I told her the reason it tasted strange was because Nana had used tap water as the base, and fluoride carries a flavor because it's slightly toxic."

"No shit," I say, impressed.

She frees her smile, nodding to another couple who quickly look away. A woman calls her name and waves, pointing excitedly to the empty station next to her. Shauna waves back, then goes for an abandoned table in the corner. Cold. I like her that way, but I steer her away from the empty table. I look around until I find an open craft station next to a couple of giggling women who're acting like they've already sucked their way through a couple of high-gravity beers. One of them's got long blond hair, and the other's a brunette.

They might be just the ticket. We have to be "persuaded" to let our little friend, Bean, out to play. If we get very lucky, these tipsy ladies might even do the deed for us.

When I beeline for them, Shauna shoots me a dagger gaze, like she thinks I'm moving us because I'm hoping one of these chicks will get drunk enough to give me a blow job in the bathroom.

"Amateur," I whisper to her. "It's all part of the plan." I give her a quick rundown of my idea as we mosey toward the table.

"You said you don't make plans."

"I'm a good liar," I told her. "You should know that."

I said it in a teasing way, but I also meant it. Mostly. Based on her tight-lipped expression, she seems to get that.

It was a stupid move given I want to get on Shauna's good side... except I'm very aware that I like her more than I should. It's a good idea to give both of us a reality check.

"You know these women?" I whisper.

"No. They're probably a couple of Bianca's replacement friends."

As if anyone could replace her.

We reach our destination, and I set Bean's crate and my beer down on the table. Shauna does the same with her drink but pauses to take a gulp first.

"Oh. Em. Gee," the brunette says, turning to her friend and then the crate. "Is that a *kitten?*"

I give Shauna a pointed look. She shakes her head slightly, the smallest of smiles on her face.

"Yes, this is Bean," I tell the woman. "But we made a promise not to let her out, you get me?"

"Oh, I get you," her blond friend says, giving me *that look.*

"This is my boyfriend," Shauna says pointedly. "*And* my kitten."

I give her the big, shit-eating grin that's gotten me into plenty of trouble, then bend my lips to her ear and ask in an undertone meant only for her, "You don't want anyone else to touch your pussy?"

She shoves me so hard I nearly bump into the brunette.

Someone clears her throat over a microphone, and then Bianca, the Queen Bee of Pompoms and this here party, says, "Who's ready to make some balls?"

"This girl," I call out, pointing at Shauna.

thirteen

LEONARD and I are in a competition over who can make the biggest pompom. Mine looks like a basketball, so I think I'm winning. In contrast, the one Bianca made up front looked more like a grape, or maybe a shriveled raisin—big compared to your conventional pompom, sure, but it's got nothing on ours.

She didn't know the rules of the game we were playing, so it shouldn't make me feel as victorious as it does.

The two women next to us stopped working on their pompoms several minutes ago in favor of another round of beers. One of them seems to have her eye on the bartender, who keeps pointedly flashing his wedding ring at her, and the other is obviously into Leonard.

I don't know why that pisses me off, other than that she knows he's supposed to be mine.

My phone buzzes, and I check it. It's a text from Rafe.

> Is Leonard behaving himself?

> No, thank the lord. What are you up to?

> At some frou-frou cocktail thing.

> So I'd obviously love an excuse to leave.

> If you two need backup, let me know. I'm good at intimidation.

> Yes, I know. It's your favorite.

Leonard glances at the screen of my phone, and I scowl at him, hiding it.

"There are no secrets between us, Tiger," he says with a grin. "So your Viking friend wants to break my face?"

"Only if I tell him to," I say.

"I'll be as sweet as a peach."

"Please don't," I say as the girl who's been checking him out giggles and flutters her fake lashes. I grit my teeth and add more yarn to my pompom. It looks like it could be used to bludgeon someone.

Bianca comes over, her eyebrows raised. "Did you have trouble following the tutorial?"

"Not at all," Leonard said, wrapping an arm around my waist again. He does it so confidently, like his arm belongs around me. Then again, he's probably used to having his arm around a woman. "My girl prefers for her balls to be supersized." He cocks his head. "You'll understand why she needed to move on."

I want to suck up Bianca's surprise like it's soda, but then a crafty look enters her eyes. "I can understand Shauna would want to remember things that way."

She pats my hand, and I remember the way she looked at me in the bar that night—the night when Carter supposedly broke up with her. Her tear-streaked eyes. The way she told me, *You're the only one who would understand what it feels like to be alone.*

She knew. She knew my parents had basically abandoned me in

life before they did in death. She knew how much it still hurt, and she turned that knowledge against me like a knife.

I turn her hand over, then slap the basketball pompom onto it. It's so big it barely stays on her palm. "I made it for you."

"I have plenty of pompoms. I don't need another. Besides, I don't know what I'd do with it."

"The same thing people do with any pompom," Leonard says with a laugh. "Keep it for a while and then throw it away before it can gather too much dust."

I smile sweetly at her. "Really, I want you to have it."

"It's yours," she says through her teeth. "You've clearly spent a lot of time and effort on it. I don't *actually* want it."

I lean my head into Leonard's shoulder. It's warm, and his chest is hard beneath the button-up shirt. He strokes a hand through my hair, and I feel the glow of having backup, of not being here alone. "But I don't need it. I've got *him*, and you've heard how he feels about pompoms."

Her face stretches into a fake smile. "A bit like how Colt and his mom feel about your monster things."

Maybe we'll go on debating this for the rest of the night, or possibly until Bianca and Colter celebrate their fiftieth anniversary. What's the wedding gift for that? Arthritis?

"Say, speaking of monster bowls," Bianca says slyly. She's obviously about to say something bitchy, but there's a loud yowl next to us, and I know it's finally happened. One of the drunk women gave into the lure of the cute kitten and unzipped Bean's crate.

The kitten pounces on the pompom in Bianca's hand, and Bianca shrieks bloody murder before throwing it like it's her wedding bouquet. My heart thumps with panic for Bean—cats might be known for landing on their feet, but she's so tiny, such a baby, but Leonard catches both her and the pompom she's still mauling. Yarn starts flying down. Leonard doesn't take any notice of it—he's too busy giving Bianca a stern look.

"Don't hurt my cat." He's intimidating, his brow lowered, his smile gone. Usually, he's all easy laughter and sex jokes, but this is a different side of him.

Like this, he's not a man to be laughed at or with. He's...magnificent.

"It scratched me," Bianca says vindictively, lifting her hand to his face. There's maybe a quarter-inch long pink spot, so small it can barely be seen. Her hand is shaking a little, though, as if she knows how pissed Leonard is.

"I'm *so* sorry," says the blond woman next to us. "I just wanted to pet her. I didn't mean for anything bad to happen. I—"

"You're the one who unzipped that thing's crate?" Bianca says. Her death gaze suggests that this woman, whoever she is, might just be lucky enough to get disinvited to the wedding.

"Yes?"

Bianca walks off without another word, and the woman laughs shakily. "I'm so sorry about your kitten. Can I get you a beer to make up for it?"

Another piece of yarn flies off the basketball pompom and hits her in the forehead.

Thank you, Bean.

"I need to get her out of here," Leonard says to me. His voice is still dark. His whole demeanor is dark, like a switch has been flipped.

I don't want to stay either—we made an appearance, played the game. So I nod and gather the kitten's crate. But Leonard doesn't put her inside, even though I see a couple of bleeding scratches on *his* hand. His knuckles are scarred, I notice.

He heads straight for the door, not giving our neighbors the jovial goodbye he usually throws at complete strangers. My heart thumps erratically. I don't know what to do with him when he's like this. It's uncharted territory.

We pass Bianca, who's complaining about us to Colter, and I wave at them as we go.

"You're leaving?" Colt asks. We haven't exchanged more than a few words the whole night, but he has this puppy dog face that makes him look crestfallen over everything. It used to be something I liked about him...until it wasn't. Because that crestfallen look was always directed at me.

Don't want to make brunch for me and ten of my best friends? Puppy dog look.

Don't feel like watching football with me? Puppy dog look.

At least Bertie has the soft puppy dog floof to go along with the expression.

"That's what it looks like," I say.

"Are you still coming tomorrow?" Bianca asks.

I don't know how to answer that. Suddenly, it seems ludicrous for us to be here, for me to be involved in this charade with them. Pride never helped my grandmother—why should it be any different for me?

True, I'll have to run into them. I'll have to listen to Bianca whisper to other people about poor Shauna, who couldn't handle the sight of true love when it dick-slapped her in the face.

Yack.

"Wouldn't miss it for the world," Leonard says flatly over his shoulder.

I hurry to catch up with him, the empty crate in my hand, nodding to a few other people I know as we leave. Colter's mother, Shelly, is sitting at a table by the door. Leave it to Bianca to invite her future mother-in-law to what's supposed to be a bachelorette weekend. I was lucky enough to miss eye contact with Shelly earlier, but this time she catches my gaze. Her blond hair is perfectly curled, and she's in the same dress as Bianca, in a different shade. It's a bit of a gut punch, seeing that. I'll bet they get manicures together too. Shelly was forever after me to get manicures with her, but I never did because of my clay.

Her eyes light up, and she starts to get to her feet, probably because she's so eager to meet Doc.

Nope. Nuh-uh. No way.

I hate that I still want this woman's approval. It's just...she's the kind of mother who squeezes cheeks, bakes apple pies, and hums with disapproving fondness when people curse. My mother is a cloud of smoke and perfume in my memory, an *absence*, and Nana, God love her, isn't soft. Neither am I, but it's nice to have someone treat you like that now and then, like you're the kind of person who deserves to have plush pillows and pancakes on Saturdays and umbrellas held over your head.

I blow a kiss and put on a burst of speed.

Leonard and I are in the parking lot before either of us say anything. He's still radiating this hard energy—dark and brooding, his arms wrapped around the kitten. We've probably left a path of yarn confetti leading directly to my car. Maybe someone will follow it later, only to be disappointed when it leads them nowhere.

"You should probably put her in the crate," I tell him, because we've almost reached my old station wagon, and there's no way I want the kitten bouncing around inside like a pinball. She's clearly on a yarn high.

He turns to me, looking at me for almost the first time since we left that table, and I'm floored by the his expression—at once devastated and angry. Bean has a wild-eyed look as she digs her paws into the yarn, probably pissed that the catnip hasn't materialized. Beneath the streetlights at the edge of the lot, I can see there are little red marks on Leonard's shirt from where she's scratched the skin beneath it, but it's obvious he hasn't noticed.

"I need to bring her back to the shelter," he blurts.

"Tonight?!"

He swallows, his arms flexing slightly, as if he wants to create a cage with them to keep Bean safe. "I'm too irresponsible to have a cat. I don't know what the hell I was thinking. Bianca could have hurled her across the room."

Oh. He's thinking about Gidget and whatever happened to her. It tugs at my heart to see this big, tattooed man cradling a kitten and fretting about her.

"It's time to give her to me, Leonard," I say firmly.

He delicately detaches Bean and the decimated pompom and hands her over.

I put her and the pompom—she deserves to have a little fun—into the crate, earning myself a bite and a yowl before I get her zipped up. He doesn't say anything as he gets into the car, but I hand Bean in to him, and he takes her with that same gentleness.

I feel an uncharacteristic urge to comfort him. Uncharacteristic with him, to be clear.

I slide behind the wheel and start the drive back to his place.

"You didn't know Bianca was going to throw her," I say.

"Does that woman look like an animal lover to you?" he asks with a wry look.

I laugh, so clearly I am terrible at comforting people.

"Sorry, sorry."

"No," he says, shaking his head moodily. "I'm the one who's sorry. I wanted to help you, but I fucked everything up."

"You didn't mess anything up. Bean seems incredibly happy when she's destroying things. This is probably the best day of her life. I mean, don't let that give you a big head, she's probably only sixty days old, so she's not working with a great sample size, but still..."

I glance over slightly, and he's smiling, or at least half smiling— the other side of his face is hidden from me—so at least I've said something right.

"Look at you, trying to be nice to me. I must be coming off as really pathetic."

"A bit," I admit, "but I like seeing you this way."

He makes a sound that's half snort and half laughter. "I'll bet."

"I like seeing you let your guard down. It's always up."

It's only as I'm saying it that I realize it's true. Most people's walls look like walls. His look more like Jell-o studded with Taco Bell roll-ups and Beavis and Butthead posters, but it's stronger than it looks. Stronger than any concrete. I'd like to reach inside and tug him out.

"And yours?" he asks, giving me a sidelong look I feel everywhere. My whole body wakes up this time. It's pure lust, but that doesn't mean it's not powerful.

It's just...it's been so long. So incredibly, pathetically long since a man has touched me with anything like need. I don't want to be needed for my mind or personality, even, or at least that's how I feel right now. I want him to touch me like he did in my dream—to fuck me in a way that's not tender or gentle but powered by raw, coursing need.

I need that eleven out of ten sex.

I need to feel like I'm alive.

I swallow. "You're right, of course."

"Whaddya say you let your wall down for a moment so we're square?" he asks, because of course everything is transactional with him.

With you, too, a voice in my head says.

"Maybe," I hedge. "What do you want to know?"

"Why a tiger like you would want a man like him. Constance got it right with the whole milk toast thing. The guy's like a whole gallon soaked a loaf of white bread. Knock-off Wonder Bread at that."

Surprised laughter snorts through my nose. "The word's not milk toast, it's milquetoast." I spell it out.

"Ten dollar word," he mutters.

"I just know because my grandpa Frank is the king of useless information." I feel a little flutter of missing him, which I stow away. "He always lets people know within five minutes of meeting them that he'd slay on Jeopardy. Anyway, Milquetoast was the last name of some 1930s cartoon character. That's where the word comes from."

I can feel him studying me again. "I bet you fifteen bucks that cartoon guy was named after milky toast."

I tap the wheel, taking the final turn. "Probably."

"What about my question?"

Sighing, I say, "I probably stayed with him because of his mother. She's nice, and I let myself get drawn in by her, in the beginning. By the thought of having a mother who wants to bake cookies with me and do normal shit like that."

"You have Constance," he says, a bit of defensiveness in his tone.

I like him for it. And for caring about Bean. And for recognizing Bianca is a narcissist.

Of course, he's still an overgrown man child who lives for causing trouble. Nothing's going to change *that*.

"Yes," I agree. "I love Nana. There's no one like her. But there's part of me that still wanted one of those moms they have in jelly commercials. Someone sweet and soft and kind who'd tell me everything's going to be okay even if it's bullshit."

"Your mom wasn't like that."

It's not a question, not that I'm surprised. It seems Nana's told him every other goddamn thing, so why not that?

"Or my dad."

"Me either," he says. I don't pretend to be surprised. He's already told me his father's in jail and his mother was his enabler. That's not exactly the kind of family you see in commercials for family-friendly TV shows.

"So you know exactly why I'd look for someone..." I wave my hand as I pull up to the little purple house and park the car.

"Who resembles a piece of soggy-ass toast?"

"Sure, let's go with that." I shrug as I park the car. "For all the good it did me. I wanted solid and reliable, but there's nothing solid or reliable about getting dumped for your friend."

When I turn to him, he's staring at me, his eyes glittering in the dark. I can see the strong line of his jaw, the way his shirt flares out to accommodate his biceps and hide the ink that fascinates me.

Tattoos tell a story, and I'd like to know his.

I'd like to know everything about him, truthfully. Despite myself, I'm fascinated by him.

I swallow and tell myself to look away. I don't.

"Bianca was never really your friend," he says, his voice rough.

"So you've said."

"She saw your claws and wanted to steal them for herself."

"And my milky toast," I say with a partial smile. "She can have him. I... It was never right, obviously. It's probably not a great sign when your favorite thing about someone is their mother." I lift my eyebrows. "Or their grandmother, as the case may be."

He gives his head a shake, eyes still glued to mine. There's a ferocity in them, and there's hunger there too. *Appreciation.* I feel an answering throb between my legs, so strong it makes me squirm a little.

"Constance is one in a million," he says. "But she's not my favorite thing about you, Tiger. Not even close."

My breath hitches. Tension hangs in the air between us, like we're both waiting for a roulette wheel to stop.

"What about my ass?" I ask, because I caught him looking. I also can't help myself. Call it morbid curiosity or sexual starvation, either will do.

"Top three," he says with a wicked grin. Then shrugs as if I called him out on lying. "Okay, top two."

Maybe it wouldn't be the worst idea to have sex with him. He's made it clear he wouldn't be opposed. Besides, wouldn't it make our chemistry more believable if we've touched each other?

I want—

Bean meows.

"What are you going to do with her?" I ask softly as I look at her little face pressed to the mesh door of the crate.

"I'll take her back in the morning," he says, his jaw flexing, and I can tell how badly he doesn't want to do that.

Then he forces a grin that's as fake as Bianca. "If you'll give me a ride. Burke's buying me a new truck for the business, but we can't do that until all of the paperwork goes through."

I almost smile at the way he says it, like someone who's trusting his best friend to set everything up because he doesn't know dick about paperwork. I'm a little like that too. My soul wants to create things, but it doesn't know its way around a spreadsheet any more than Colter knows how to find a clitoris. That softens me toward Leonard too. Maybe that's why I find myself saying, "I'll walk you in."

His eyes hood as he studies me. "You don't need to walk me in, Tiger. I may not have a black belt in taekwondo, but I think I can handle myself."

I'll bet he can. I'll bet he has no trouble handling himself. Those big, scarred hands stroking, pulling, cupping, and squeezing unmercifully. The thought of him doing that, and the possibility of him thinking of me while his hand works his hard cock, has my blood pumping faster, the bass of my pulse drowning out every other noise around us.

I lean in toward him, needing to, and smile. My wicked thoughts must show in my eyes, in the way my body is arcing toward him. "I was thinking it might make our chemistry seem a little more realistic, if..."

My words halt, because he's not looking at me the way I thought he would. There's something like regret on his face. Horror grips me with clawed hands, as if I've been enfolded into one of my monster vases. What if all the flirting and innuendo is just Leonard's default mode? What if this man who I was convinced would sleep with anyone isn't interested in having some fun with me?

From the expression on his face, I'm clearly the last woman he wants to sleep with. I ignore the burning shame in my chest, my hands reaching up to grip the steering wheel so they have something to do other than grab him.

"Forget it," I blurt, shifting my gaze to the windshield. "But you should keep the cat. She should be yours."

"Because she likes to cut me with her claws?" he asks.

"Because she's a little terror." My eyes are still out the windshield. "I don't know what happened with your dog, but it's not easy thinking you're at fault for something terrible. Living with the guilt. Maybe you should let yourself—"

Suddenly he reaches over, his hand weaving into the back of my short hair and pulling slightly, turning my head toward him.

"You're right about one thing. I like little terrors," he says, his voice low and raspy. "Were you trying to tell me you want to fuck, Shauna? Because I won't say no. Even though we both know I should. I'd promised myself I wouldn't touch you."

There's a razor-sharp second of relief—cutting, because when did I become this person who needs approval like it's air?

Leonard's hand is still in my hair, tugging, lighting up the nerve endings, and in the dim light from the roof of the parked car, he looks like a fallen god, so delicious and damned that I want to sink my teeth into him.

He tugs me toward him, my belt digging into my chest, and I release the buckle one handed as his mouth lowers to mine with purpose. His lips are softer than they look, but they're demanding. His tongue licks along my bottom lip, and when I open for him, it winds with mine. His hands tighten in my hair, and he moves my head to make the angle deeper so he can take more from me. I grip a hand in his hair too, because I've been imagining it. Wanting it and pull him in closer, swallowing the sound of amusement and need he makes.

No one's ever kissed me like this before—like kissing me is their sole reason for existing. Like they want to suck me down and savor me. Even though I know it means nothing to him, it's impossible not to fall into it, to want those lips to travel north and south and consume me. He tugs my bottom lip into his mouth and bites it, then pulls away with mischief gleaming in his eyes, making them more green than hazel, almost as luminescent as the cat's.

Speaking of whom, Bean makes an aggrieved sound as if she wants to fight me for making the moves on her man.

"So, what happens next, Tiger?" Leonard says, studying me. "Are you going to take me for a test drive?"

I roll my eyes, which is significantly harder now that every nerve ending in my body is begging for his touch.

"This doesn't mean anything," I say.

He nods firmly. "It can't."

I don't ask why. Like I said, *trouble* might as well be tattooed across his forehead. Maybe *baggage* should be tattooed across mine.

"It's not a good idea," I say.

His eyes dancing, he reaches over and traces my lips, his finger callused from the work he does at those flip houses and God knows what else. I wonder what his hands would feel like on my chest, grazing across my bare flesh. His finger pauses on my bottom lip, which fell open for him, and he slips it inside just slightly. When I bite his finger, his smile spreads wider, filling his eyes, his face, all of him.

"Fuck no, but I can't see myself regretting it."

He gets out, cat carrier in hand, and shuts his door behind him. Bean gives a plaintive wail, but he waits, giving me the choice.

A dry spell long enough to turn my body into the Sahara makes it for me.

fourteen

LEONARD

SHE'S CONSTANCE'S GRANDDAUGHTER.

You already like her too much.

She's fucking gorgeous, dressed in gold like a gift that's meant for someone else. A gift I'd very much like to steal. And her lips are soft but firm, just the way I knew they would be, because this isn't a woman who coasts through things—she's take-charge, a fighter. A *tiger*.

She's—

She's getting out of the damn car is what she's doing, and even though this is one more shitty idea in a lifetime of them, I meant what I said. I won't regret it.

I smirk at her as she joins me in the driveway.

"Stop looking at me like that," she snaps, making for the door. She doesn't try to hold my hand or touch me, and part of me is amused by it. Still, I don't want to wait to have my hands on her again.

So I reach out and lightly smack her ass. It fills my hand perfectly, the feel of her warm flesh under that dress making me hard. Hell, I was already hard. I got that way the second she started talking about making things *a little more realistic*.

She jumps and then glares at me.

"You're a dick."

"I thought that's what you wanted from me," I say, giving my eyebrows a waggle.

She sighs and veers back toward the door and keeps walking. I'm happy she's jonesing for my dick so much she's in a hurry, although I'm not sure how she thinks she's getting in there without the key.

"You that eager for me, Tiger?" I ask, earning my arm a punch. It's obvious she threw it—Tiger has muscles and then some. I'd like to watch her use them someday. Maybe on Colter. Maybe in a cat fight with Bianca. It'd be a helluva show if they threw cake at each other at the wedding.

"What are you thinking about?" she asks suspiciously.

"You and Bianca getting into a cake fight at the wedding. I never thought anything about a wedding could be a turn-on for me, but I might have been short-sighted."

"You really are a pig," she breathes out. The way she's looking at me says she doesn't mind. At least not right now.

She doesn't think much of me, but she wants me anyway.

I'll take it. It's a pretty good description of every single...well, relationship would be an exaggeration...I've been in.

I grab the short hem of her dress and tug her closer, liking the way she licks her lips, like she's wetting them for me.

"Damn right," I tell her. "You know, thinking about all that cake made me hungry, Tiger. What do you say we get Bean settled and head into the kitchen for a little snack?"

Her eyes flash with defiance. "Fruit Loops?"

"Maybe afterward. I was thinking I'd sit you up on the counter and have a taste of that sweet pussy."

I earn a swear from her pink lips, and I lean forward and kiss her again. Because she told me I could, for tonight. Because I want to, and whenever possible, I like taking what I want.

She ends the kiss by biting my bottom lip, same as I did to her, and I'm grinning as she pulls away.

"Don't be the kind of man who overpromises and underdelivers," she says, nodding to the door. "That's a disappointment for everyone involved."

"Was Champ like that?"

Her lips tip up, her eyes mischievous the way I like them. "I think you already know the answer."

I make a pact with myself to blow Champ out of the water, not that it should be difficult. I want to give her something to remember —and if I do, maybe she'll be game to make the rest of these wedding-related events more fun for both of us.

I open that door quick as I can, then lower Bean to the ground before shutting us inside and locking it. Shauna tugs me to her for another kiss. My Tiger's hungry, and I like it. I like it a lot more than I should, but that's a thought I shut down quickly, because I don't want to let anything take away from my enjoyment. Or hers. I lift her up because she's short, and she wraps her legs around my waist.

It really has been too long since I've had a woman, because the feel of her pressed up against my dick makes me see stars. It must be doing it for her, too, because she kisses me so hard our teeth clink, her nails digging into my back like she remembers what I said to her earlier. Excitement beats through my blood as it all drains down to my cock.

I carry her to the kitchen like that, barely able to see, but I have my hand wrapped around her, so if we bump into something, I'll feel it first. She makes a little humming noise in the back of her throat, and it's so sexy I feel like a teenager again.

By the time we stumble into the kitchen, I'm panting into her mouth, her nails still digging into my back. When I set her down on the granite counter, she pulls back, her eyes bright. The look of hunger on her face is the best thing I've ever seen—so I decide I'd like to see something even better and pull off one of the straps of her dress so I can get an eyeful of her tits. A bra is no barrier to a determined man.

But there's some strange gluey pinkish tan thing sticking to each of them, as if she dipped them into glue at that craft prison we just left.

"What the fuck is this?" I ask in horror.

She bursts out laughing, running a hand back through her hair, leaving it messed up in that sexy way of hers. Her tits are bobbing with her laughter, and if I weren't worried about touching that glue shit, my hands would be all over them.

"It's a bra, you ignoramus."

"Going for gold and pulling out a twenty dollar word this time, huh? I've seen a lot of bras, and I've never seen one that looks like that."

She takes down the other strap of her dress, then puts her hands on her tits, bringing life back to my cock. I watch, riveted, as she peels off the bra thing, setting it on the counter. She does a doubletake—maybe she disapproves of the way I store bananas—but I can't spare much attention for anything other than her chest. She has the most perfect nipples I've ever seen in my life, small and budded and dark pink. The sight of her on Mrs. Ruiz's kitchen counter, tits out, dress hanging down to her waist, is unbelievably hot. God help me if the old broad ever finds out—it was rule one in the literal book I was given when I moved in here—but regret doesn't exist in my vocabulary tonight.

"Did she put glue on you?" I ask her tits, lifting my hands up to cup them. "She won't say it, but she's sorry. I'll treat you real nice."

"Are you talking to my tits?" she asks, laughing again, and I can feel them bouncing in my hands, which makes my cock even harder.

"Yes, and they're talking back to me, baby."

I catch her rolling her eyes as I lower my head to take her nipple in my mouth, sucking and working it with my tongue. I glance up at her as she leans her head back, her throat long and slender, and I want to kiss and bite it. It's at times like this that one mouth, two hands, and a dick doesn't seem like enough for the work a man needs to do. I want to touch her everywhere, to show her that there are some things I'm good at.

As I move to the second nipple, I slide her legs open for me and reach in with one hand to trace her panties. They're damp, which makes me think I'm not doing my job, because I want them soaking. I run my fingers over her while I suck, then start pulling the panties down her legs. She lifts her body weight up with her arms, letting me tug them off. When they fall onto the floor, I pull off her nipple, leaving it shining slightly in the dim light.

A satisfied sound escapes her, and she slides her hand into my hair and grips it, making me grin.

"You can talk to my tits anytime you'd like if you suck them like that," she says in a voice that makes me feel like a king among men again.

"Don't think I won't. In a couple of minutes you'll be begging me to sing lullabies to your pussy."

She laughs, even though there's a different kind of light in her eyes—a hunger that I very much feel too. "I don't want you to put it to sleep, Leonard. I'm kind of looking for the opposite."

"Good." I lean in to kiss her, because she's the kind of gorgeous you want to touch and taste at every opportunity available to you. She's especially gorgeous now, set out for me on the counter like a feast, her legs parted in a tease, her nipples on display and wet from my mouth. Then I get on my knees, because I need to taste her elsewhere too.

"I like the sight of you on your knees in front of me," she says, while I spread her legs open wider.

"And I like the sight of your legs spread wide, your pussy bared for me. You should try that look more often."

She swears, and I smile as I trace along her open thighs with the

133

tips of my fingers, loving the feel of her soft skin and the way it gets softer as it leads in to the promised land.

"Take off your shirt," she says. I like that it's not phrased as a question, so I do it, shrugging it off as I kneel there at her feet. Her eyes are hungry as they move over me, pausing at my scar, at Gidget. I don't want to think about any of that right now, so I lean in and kiss her thigh. Moving in toward the goal like I'm the real champ, I use my other hand to give her clit a tease, letting it know it can't hide from me. Her little moan makes me grin against her skin, and then she's weaving a hand through my hair again and gripping. My cock is uncomfortably hard, but I want to start by giving her a taste of what I want to do for her—and to her.

I keep moving toward my goal, my heart racing, the scent of her making me dizzy because I want her so fucking bad, I can barely handle myself. Then I finally get there, and I bury my face between her legs, hoisting her thighs onto my shoulders. Her hand flexes in my hair as I learn the territory and her taste. She's so wet for me. So wet and soft and delicious. I want to move into this pussy. To set up camp here. To raise up a Leonard flag and let everyone know this pussy belongs to me.

My thoughts don't make any sense, but then again, all I can think about is right now, of having the slick heat of her against my face, about dipping my tongue inside of her so I can feel her pulsing around me before I move up to her little budded clit and take it in my mouth. Her hands grip my hair, probably ripping it out. It just makes me smile against her, because she wants this too, she wants what I can give her, and she wants it bad.

I move my fingers into the game, because she made a point of telling me that she didn't just come from attention to her clit. I trace her wetness before I slide them home, one and then two, keeping at her clit with my tongue and mouth. I need to find her spot—the place that drives her mad—so I can set up camp there too.

"Oh. My. God," I hear her through the blood thrumming in my

ears, and her legs flex against my shoulders. She's giving more of herself to me, pressing her pussy into my face, her hands gripping me, and my dick is so hard that I can't think about anything but giving it to her. My mouth and my hand and then my dick. I want her to come more than twice. Three times. Four. Five.

I suck a little harder, moving my fingers slightly as I rub at her front walls, searching. I know when I find it because I feel her clench harder around me. Bingo. I keep up the friction while I suck on her, tasting her. Enjoying her. I look up as I do it. Tiger stays behind her walls too, and I want to see her face as they fall down and pleasure takes over everything.

She looks unspeakably good, her tits spilling out over that gold dress, her thighs spread for me, her head arced back to show that long neck. I wish I could bottle this up, because there are plenty of times when I need something good to get me through the night, and it doesn't get better than this.

Her eyes meet mine, almost golden in the low light of the kitchen, and I feel her pulse around me, her mouth falling open.

"Leonard—"

I know, baby. I know. I'm going to give you what you need.

I double down with my hand and my mouth, and I feel it as she falls apart, her hands on me, my hand in her, and it's the most beautiful thing I've seen or tasted, and I don't care to ask myself why. I just want to stay here in this moment. Maybe all night. Maybe all year. Maybe for the rest of my miserable life.

I watch her as she comes down, her hand releasing my hair, and when I'm sure she's ridden the wave for all it's worth, I stand up next to her.

She's staring at me, eyes wide, so I make a show of licking my lips.

"You taste delicious, Tiger. Just like I knew you would."

"God, of course you're good at this," she says, and something inside of me deflates, just a little. Then she tugs me closer. "Let me look at you."

My dick likes that suggestion and is hopeful she wants to look at all of me.

Her small, smooth hands run over my shoulders and down my arms, then explore my chest. "You had to be beautiful, too," she murmurs like she doesn't even know she's saying it.

"Can't blame that one on me. We're born with what we're born with."

"But you've worked with it, too," she says, tracing my muscles, then one of my tattoos—this one another five buck job—a little devil woman with a pitchfork.

"Looks like you, don't it?" I ask, lifting her up off the counter. Her tits press against my chest in a soft tease as I set her down, and she must feel how much I need her. Maybe I'll take her against the wall. I'd have to hold her up because she's short, but—

"Is that my mug?" she asks, her voice more alert and less of a moan. "I noticed it earlier."

"Uh, yeah," I say, glancing at it on the counter next to her. It's sitting there in all its super-glued glory. She'd offered to help me fix it, but something inside of me didn't like seeing it broken. It felt like one more thing I'd screwed up, even though she was the one who'd dropped it. It's been nice, having it in here. A piece of this house that feels like mine, when almost everything else is borrowed.

"You really do like it."

She sounded surprised, so even though she's still got her tits out, I don't grab any of the things I'd like to touch and tease. I lift her chin with my hand pressed to her neck. "Of course I like it. I hope you didn't take anything Queen Bee said to heart. You're talented as hell. She sees something in you she wants to steal. Talent. Heart."

"I don't think..."

I guide her away from the counter and push her into the wall. Then I kiss her, my hand still beneath her chin, holding her there.

She looks up at me as she kisses me back hard, and there's a flutter in my chest, almost like the beginning of a panic attack. I pull back, release her. Breathe in deep, feeling shaky, like I do when I wake up from one of my dreams. Except when I take a deep breath in this time, all I can smell is Shauna. Her skin on me. Her subtle perfume. Her pussy. "She's fucking jealous, and she should be."

"*Leonard*," she begins, and the light in her eyes has me wanting to know what comes next. But then there's a mechanical sound, followed by a pop, and the back door swings open. We both swivel around to look at the same time. Shauna's chest is still exposed, her perfect nipples pearled in the cooler air in the kitchen.

It's Reese with one S.

He pauses in the doorway for a second, his eyes wide, probably because he's looking at Shauna's tits. Shit. I reach out to fix her dress, feeling an almost primal need to hide it from him, and he takes the opportunity to turn and run. I'm about to follow him, but Shauna beats me to it.

She's out the door and on Reese in an instant, before I can get a single word out.

fifteen

LEONARD

"SHAUNA," I shout, just as she knees him in the balls right outside the door. *Damn.* I don't want to get on her bad side. My own throbbing cock gives a sympathy wince as the hard-on starts to subside. "It's okay. I know him."

She turns and gapes at me, and I guess I understand her surprise. He *did* just break into my house.

"Come in," I say and he does. He's got his hand cupped over his business, and I feel another jab of pain for him. Shauna comes in after him, shutting the door, and he shrinks away from her.

"What the fuck, Leonard?" she asks.

"It's okay," I say, although whether I'm trying to comfort him or her, I've got no clue. I mean, it probably doesn't feel okay to Reese. He *did* just get kicked in the nuts after witnessing something he shouldn't have seen. I pick my shirt up off the floor and shrug it on.

Everything's spun out of control so quickly I have whiplash, like that time I had to stop my car right quick on the I-4 in Florida because, I shit you not, an alligator was crossing. I can still taste Shauna, still hear her breathy little moans. I'd much rather be in that moment than this one, but what can you do? Time has a way of

taking away good things. Bad ones, too, because sometimes—rarely
—it has mercy.

"You know him?" she asks, turning on me.

One of her tits looks like it's in danger of popping out of her
dress and giving Reese a show—something he'll notice as soon as he
gets over the shooting pain in his balls. I'm surprised by another
pulse of protectiveness as I reach over and fix it.

"Yeah, I know the kid," I tell her in an undertone.

That word gets another gasp, her eyes flying to Reese.

"He's a kid?"

"Does he look like he'd qualify for an AARP card?"

"Oh my God," she says, taking a step toward Reese. "I'm so
sorry. I didn't... I mean, you *were* breaking into Leonard's house."
She pauses, then adds, "Are you the one who stole his truck?"

"No," the kid says, hands up. He seems absolutely terrified of
Tiger. "I never even saw the truck. Leonard said I could crash here."
Then, turning to me, he continues, "I didn't know you were
bringing your girlfriend back. I swear."

Now, he seems terrified of *me*. My father once beat me blue for
walking in on him with one of his side chicks. Then he told me what
would happen if I breathed a word to my mother.

I didn't. And she didn't ask me who'd given me the bruises. She
never did.

Maybe this kid's foster father is the same way.

I lift my hands, trying to give off what Danny would call
calming energy, even though I'm so worked up I'm probably putting
out the opposite. "I'm not upset with you, man, but why'd you break
in? I told you to text me next time."

"I did, but you didn't answer, so I figured I'd try the door. You
didn't fix the deadbolt like you said you were going to the last time I
broke in."

Shauna looks at me with wide eyes that say I'm an idiot. "The
last time he broke in?"

"Who'd you think the cereal was for?" I ask with a shrug.

"*You*, you man child," she says. "I need to talk to you in the other room. *Now*."

I rub the back of my neck.

"You better go, man," Reese tells me, his hand still over his balls like he's worried Shauna might go in for another jab if he lifts it. "When my grandmother used that tone, she meant business." I want to ask what happened to her, but it's clear enough. She must be dead or gone, like his mother. He doesn't have anybody on his side except for me, or else he wouldn't be here.

That's not a good situation to be in—for him or for me.

The back of my neck feels like it's burning, and not in a good way. There are too many people relying on me. Burke, for the flip jobs. Shauna, to pose as Doc. Reese, to help him out with whatever shit he has going on. And then there's Bean...

Bean.

I need to feed her and get her upstairs to my room. That I haven't is further proof that I can't take care of myself, let alone another person or cat.

"Don't leave," I tell Reese. "You can crash on the couch again, but first have some cereal. I got it special for you."

He spots the box on the table and lights up like a slot machine that's about to give someone some sugar. "Brand name."

"I know, right?" I say, patting him on the back. "How those stitches treating you, Reese with one S?"

I'm getting a death glare from Shauna. I can feel it as surely as that knock to the head I got the other day.

"They hurt like hell. Is that normal?"

"As long as the wound's not puffy or full of pus, you should be good."

"Are those underwear?" he asks, his eyes wide as he points at the floor.

"Thanks for looking out, man," I say as I stoop to grab them, then stuff them in my pocket. I have no intention of giving them back. "We'd lost these."

He looks impressed.

Then Shauna's dragging me out into the living room. She stops in front of the couch, glances at the open doorway to the kitchen, then apparently decides it's not far enough because she tugs me into the damn bathroom and closes the door behind us. There's nothing in here but a can, a sink, and a mirror, and all of a few feet for us to fill together.

"Good thinking. It'll be a tight squeeze, but we can make it work." I reach a hand up the skirt of her dress. She slaps it away, which is fine. It was a joke anyway, or maybe a fourth of one.

"Who is this kid?" she asks. "How old is he? Did you stitch him up?"

I sigh and run a hand through my hair. "He's a runaway, like you're probably thinking. Says he's gonna be eighteen in a few weeks."

"Have you checked?" she asks.

I have to admit that I haven't, and from the expression on her face, she's not surprised.

"Why'd he run?"

"His foster father's been beating him."

She flinches. "Is he the one who made him need stitches?"

"I don't think so, but the kid might have lied."

"Could he have lied about the foster father too?" she asks, studying me.

I can feel myself raising a wall. "I believe him. I checked with Mrs. Ruiz too, the lady who owns this house. She said the foster father's no good. Besides, I don't see why he'd lie to me about that when he was upfront about fleecing supplies from a couple of stores."

"So he's been living off stolen goods," she says flatly.

"Most likely." I flex my hands. "Don't you think he needs somewhere safe to stay, someone he can go to if he needs help?"

"He needs someone to get him out of trouble, Leonard," she hisses in an undertone, as if she's suddenly worried Reese is listening at the door. "He doesn't need an adult enabling him."

I have to laugh, maybe at myself, for having made such a bad impression on her. It stings more than it should, like stepping on a nail last week at the flip house. You'd think by now I'd be used to people thinking little of me. "I'm not teaching him the tricks of the trade. I could, though, if that's what you're getting at. I'm not good at a lot of things, but I do have a couple of special talents." I fake a smile. "You already know what one of them is. I'm also good at freeing fools from their money. Have been since I was a good bit younger than him."

My mouth wants to lift into a real smile, maybe at the surprised look on her face. She's been calling me trouble for weeks, but she wasn't expecting me to flat-out admit it, I guess. "I'm less good at keeping the money, obviously. But no. I wasn't planning on leading the kid into a life of crime. I figured I'd be here for him if he needs help or a place to crash."

"It's not enough," she insists, and no bullshit, she stomps her foot. "He could get in trouble out there. Killed."

"You think he's going to listen to a single thing you say if you march out there telling him how it's gonna be? He'll be on the first bus out of town. I know I would've been." I pause, looking away. Then I shift my gaze back to her. Suddenly, I have a new awareness of how small the room is, how close she is to me, and the taste of her still on my tongue. I swallow, tracking her eyes as they follow my throat. "I can't let you call the cops on him, Shauna."

"What are you going to do?" she asks, leaning forward, her voice and eyes full of challenge. "Tie me up?"

"I think I'd like that," I say, feeling the blood pulse hot to my cock. "But not tonight. I'm telling you it would be the wrong move.

That kid's got no one. You think he'd be here, relying on me, if he had any other choice?"

A corner of her mouth twitches, and I'm sure she's going to tell me I'm right—Reese must really have shit luck if he's relying on me. But she gives her head a small shake, then says, "Maybe. You're going to bat for him. So, you really stitched him up?"

I lift a finger to my lips. "I can't answer that. HIPAA."

To my surprise, she starts laughing.

"Does this mean you're not going to tell?" I ask.

Her laughter cuts short, which sucks, but I still need an answer. I don't want to throw Reese into the giant's mouth. "No, I'm not going to say anything to the authorities. But telling him he can break in if he needs a place to stay is not a solution. What about giving him a key?"

"You think Mrs. Ruiz would thank me for giving a petty thief the key to her crib?"

Her brow creases. "How's that different from letting him break in whenever he wants?"

"I told him I'd let him in if he texts, but I guess I see your point."

"What about giving him a job?" she says, leaning back against the sink. "Something to keep him out of trouble."

I've thought of that—and gotten about as far as a brick wall. I could get the kid a new ID, I guess, but that seems like the nuclear option. Once you go that road, trying on names and personalities like they're suits, it's hard to go back to being a person. Or to remember who you were beneath all the layers you've put on. "He's got no papers. He's not eighteen."

"He's old enough to ask for emancipation."

"Takes thirty days. He'll be eighteen by then."

"You looked up the timeline," she says, something like approval in her voice.

"I did," I concede.

"You could take him to your flip house," she suggests. "Put him to work unofficially."

I'd thought of it. I don't want to bring my problems to Burke's door, though, and besides...

"Burke's parents are all about finding a way to get him into some shit. If they found out we had an underage runaway working with us, that'd be just the ticket. Besides, I don't think he's a bad kid, but he's desperate. Desperate is dangerous."

She surprises me by reaching out and taking my wrist. Her eyes are bright under the lights, and fuck, are those *tears* in them?

"You don't think I understand," she says. "But I do. My mom used to lock me out of the house for hours. She said it was character building, but it was because she didn't want to have a kid around. After my parents moved us away from Asheville, I used to dream that I'd have to go live with Nana and Grandpa Frank. I ran away five times. One time, I took the Greyhound, and I got all the way to their house. I cried so hard I almost passed out when Grandpa Frank said I had to go home. Nana was crying too."

Five times? No wonder Tiger's got some claws.

Constance has told me a thing or two about Shauna's folks, enough to have made me realize they weren't gold-star parents, but I hadn't realized it was this bad.

"And then it happened," Shauna adds softly. "My dream came true. They died in that car wreck, and I *had* to go live with Nana and Grandpa Frank."

Well, shit.

Her eyes are still shining with tears, but she wouldn't thank me if I brought attention to them, which is just as well, because I have no clue how to stop someone from crying. I'm much better at making people cry in the first place. But suddenly I really wish I knew.

"You didn't make it happen," I offer, lifting a hand to touch her chin. It's pointed like a fairy's, and it's such a stupid fucking thought that I can hardly believe it. Clearly a woman's tears are enough to drive a man crazy.

"Obviously not," she says with a huff. "I don't have psychic powers, Leonard. But it sure felt like it was my fault." She gives me a pointed look that reaches into my guts and twists. "Maybe the same way you blame yourself for Gidget."

Guilt wraps around my chest. "Let's not dip shit in sugar and call it candy."

"Gross," she says, her nose wrinkling.

"Exactly. What happened to her was my fault, and don't try to tell yourself otherwise. I own it. Just like I'm gonna own this problem. The cops are looking for the kid."

Her eyes narrow. "What do you know that I don't?"

I lift my hands in the 'I'm an innocent man' gesture that's probably only made by guilty people. "Not what you're thinking." Or at least I don't think it is. "I'm pretty sure it's the foster father who's behind it. Reese with one S said this guy's brother is a boy in blue."

She swears under her breath, because this is obviously not good news, then says, "We can work around it. We have to."

Something softens inside of me. I expected Tiger to want to go running for the cops, but she gets it. She actually gets it. That means *everything*.

"Let's go talk to him," I say with a nod.

We reach for the door at the same time, our hands overlapping, and a zip of heat shoots straight to my dick. Damn it. I hope she'll still be in the mood for making bad decisions tomorrow night. One taste wasn't enough.

In a fit of crazy, driven by my dick, I take her hand in mine and open the door with her, my fingers layered over hers. She gives me a weird look, but we step out together.

I swear under my breath as we enter the kitchen.

So much for nowhere to go.

There's an empty bowl with a lining of pink cereal milk in the

145

sink, and a note on the table, written on a ripped-out page from the book I was reading. Thanks, Reese.

> *I can't believe you convinced her to go into the bathroom with you. Legendary. Be careful, man, she's stronger than she looks.*
>
> *Thanks for the cereal. It's better with milk, but I'm gonna take the box with me.*
>
> *Fix the back door, man. I don't want someone else to break into Mrs. Ruiz's house, and I've heard there are bad people hanging around. There've been two different robberies in the past two days. (Don't worry. I had nothing to do with either of them, but word gets around.)*
>
> *I'll text if I need to get in, but I've been thinking of taking off for a while to lose the heat.*

There's a little doodle at the bottom of Shauna with an oversized knee.

For half a second, I'm amused—he doesn't want "someone else" to break in, huh?—then I run to the back door and look out, hoping he didn't get far.

There's nothing but me and the moon.

It's those damn shoes. They let me run like the wind too.

I rub the place where Gidget's inked into my arm, because I have a feeling I fucked this up too. Hopefully it comes off better for the kid.

When I come back inside, Shauna's holding the note, her bottom lip between her teeth.

"I scared him off, didn't I?" she asks softly, sounding sad about it.

Maybe. But it's not her fault; it's mine.

I knew in my gut that he was jumpy, and I gave him an excuse to run when I left with her instead of sitting down with him.

I text Reese, asking him to come back so we can talk, but I'm not surprised when he doesn't answer.

"You don't have to come tomorrow," Shauna blurts.

"What?"

"To the stupid camping sleepover thing. In fact, this whole—" she waves her hands around, "—thing was a bad idea. I'll just tell them we decided not to go. Bianca can ask someone she actually likes to be her maid of honor."

"But then she'll win," I say slowly, not liking the idea one bit. "You can't let her win."

"It's not a competition."

But it is. It obviously is, and if Shauna backs down, Queen Bee will lord it over her every damn time she sees her at a trade show or around town. I can't let that happen.

That's not the only reason, though. I don't want this to be over—and it's not for the pompoms or even the excuse to own a whole roomful of people at karaoke. I want to spend more time with Shauna.

That's not surprising. I know what she tastes like, what she feels like when she's coming. And I'm not going to be satisfied, or anything like it, until I'm buried inside her. But it's not just that either. I want to get to know her better, to learn more about her *from* her, not from Constance being loose of the lips when she's had too much to drink.

That's bad news. I can't get hung up on this woman—even if I'm pretty confident she won't get hung up on me. So I should tell her she's right, that we'll back off and let Champ and Bianca destroy themselves, something that'll obviously happen whether we have a hand in it or not. But I don't.

"It *is* a competition," I say instead, taking her hand and squeezing it. Something in her face lifts, like maybe she likes what I said. "And we're going to crush it."

Then I let her go, because she's not mine, and if I've learned anything it's that you shouldn't take what's not yours if you don't know how to keep it.

sixteen

SHAUNA

AT MY SUGGESTION, we take my station wagon around the neighborhood, looking for Reese, but we only find a family of pissed-off possums and a man so drunk he can't operate the key to his front door. Eventually we give up, because it has all the stench of a hopeless cause.

"He'll come back," I say as I pull up to the purple house. I'm saying it for myself as much as him, definitely not because I believe it.

"Sure he will," he offers, and it's obvious he believes it even less.

I pull the car to a stop, and he turns in the passenger seat to look at me. "Thanks for trying. A lot of people wouldn't bother."

"We could look for his foster father," I say. "Maybe use a private investigator."

"You want to hire a dick?" he asks.

I'm ninety percent sure he just said it that way so he'd have an excuse to say dick, but it's not the time to call him on it. "Maybe. If we know his full legal name, it might be easier to look for him."

He shakes his head slowly. "Burke has someone on retainer, but I don't think it's a good idea. If the kid hears someone's asking around after him, it'll only make him run farther. Besides, I'm not so sure a P.I. would agree to look for a boy we're not related to. We don't even know his real name. I tried doing a search for missing kids called Reese, and I didn't find squat." He cracks his knuckles in obvious frustration. "Checked all the photos too. His foster parents mustn't have reported him missing."

"Burke's guy might know someone on the police force. I'll bet he does."

"And for all we know, it might be the foster father's brother. Or one of his buddies. They cover for each other, Shauna. Don't fool yourself into thinking otherwise."

The look on his face reminds me of his expression when we left the pompom party, dark and brooding and broken. My heart thumps faster, and I'm suddenly aware that I want to kiss him. *Need* it. Not just because he's sexy and I'm desperate for a taste of him, or because I feel an aching need to finish what we started—but because I want to comfort him and let him comfort me.

Maybe he knows I'm feeling that way, because he turns to open his door and gets out without saying anything else.

I feel a little crestfallen, even though I shouldn't be. He's not my real boyfriend, and he's made it clear that I shouldn't get attached to him.

"Are you going to fix the lock on your back door?" I call out to him.

He turns to look at me, his face unreadable. "No, Tiger, but I'd prefer it if you wouldn't shout it to the moon. If he needs to come back, I'm not going to make it any harder on him."

I think about that a lot, on the way home, and once I'm lying in my bed. It's what prompts me to text him.

> Did he come back?

> No. Didn't think he would. I sent him a few texts.

I don't like this.

Neither do I.

At least you didn't knee a seventeen-year-old in the balls.

There is that.

You know, there aren't many latchkey kids anymore. You were one, I was one, Reese has made himself one. We should form a club.

You, me, and the seventeen-year-old I kneed in the balls?

Sure, sounds like a good time.

Get some sleep, Tiger.

Do you still want to bring Bean back in the morning?

It's not about what I want. It's about what she deserves. It ain't me.

You should give it more thought.

Nope. I've given it the maximum amount of thought I'm capable of.

Are you going to be able to sleep?

Sleep never comes easy. That's what the ganja's for.

Does it work?

We'll see.

I'm going to bring over some more Fruit Loops in the morning.

Maybe Reese will come back for the night if you tell him they're there and we're not.

Like luring a kid into a white van by promising him candy.

Very funny.

I can still taste you, Tiger. That's not funny. It's driving me crazy.

I'll bet there's only one bed in our cabin at sleepaway camp.

Who needs a bed?

You make a good point.

5 minutes later

Hey, if you can't sleep, you want to watch The Sopranos with me? We could text or talk while we watch it.

You're going dark with this revenge shit, aren't you?

No, it's just a good show.

Likely story.

Which episode? If you can't think of the name, just tell me who died in the last one you watched, and I can figure it out.

The one where Christopher and that other guy almost freeze to death. You want me to call you?

Yeah, that sounds mighty nice.

I call him up, and he answers on the first ring. "Doc, here," he says, his voice a low rumble.

"Very funny. You ready for this?"

"I was born ready, Tiger. You got it pulled up?"

We make sure that our videos are perfectly in sync before we start the show. Most of the time we're quiet, watching what's on our screens, but I'm almost painfully aware of him—of his breathing over the phone, the rumble of his voice when he says "oh, shit" or "that's the way you do it, son," the sound of his soft laughter in my ear. I keep imagining him lying in his bed with his shirt off, Bean snuggled up next to him. I suspect his shirt will always be off in my imagination now that I've seen the goods. I'm turned on by that image, by him, but I'm also comforted. It feels good to be awake with someone, rather than awake alone. So when the closing credits roll around, I suggest, "One more?"

"Oh, most definitely."

By the time the second episode ends, I'm yawning. Even though I'm pretty sure Leonard will go another hour or more without finding sleep, he says, "You go off to bed, Tiger. I'll see you in the morning."

By then, it's late. Seriously late, verging on being too early. But I end up tossing and turning for a long time before sleep comes. My mind is fixed on Reese, who's spending the night who knows where.

There are plenty of homeless people in Asheville, but that doesn't make me feel better, because it means he'll be sleeping out there on the streets with other people who could potentially hurt him or steal his Fruit Loops.

And then there's Leonard.

Leonard, who made me come so hard I saw stars on the edges of my vision.

Leonard, who loves cats and hangs out with grandmothers and tries to take care of runaways.

Leonard, who fixed that broken mug I gave him the other day and left it out on his kitchen counter, like it was something worth saving.

Leonard, who can't sleep at night for reasons I'd like to know.

Leonard, who watched *The Sopranos* with me.

What it comes down to is that he's not who I thought he was—or at least he's not *only* who I thought he was.

I'll be honest, I *wanted* to think badly of him. It was so much safer to think badly of him. Because whatever else he has going for him, he's also a self-admitted thief, gambler, and ladies' man. It would be absurd of me to get attached to him.

It's exactly the sort of thing I'm contrary enough to do, so I have to steel myself against it.

That's not to say I intend to stay away from him. Because I've realized why Nana enjoys spending time with him. He makes me feel more alive. I think he does it for everyone he's around, without even meaning to, maybe without even realizing it.

Finally, I go to sleep, only to have a reprisal of the sex dream. The neighbor lifts up her sign again, and again it's a two point five. I give her the finger and she lifts up her sharpie and crosses out the point five.

When I get up on Saturday morning, Nana's already made coffee, thank all that's holy. Its scent fills the air like the promise of spring at the end of a brutal winter.

I check my phone. There are a couple of hungry messages from Delia and Mira, who want details I'm not ready to give them, and another check-in message from Rafe, who demands confirmation that I'm not dead. I give it. The last message is from Grandpa Fruckface:

It's been thirty-three days.

When I come out, Nana's sitting at the little round table in our yellow kitchen, doing a crossword puzzle. Bertie is lying at her feet on his ham and eggs bed.

A warm feeling fills me as I approach her. I have her—always have—and she saved me from making any big mistakes that would be difficult to walk back from. Leonard and Reese had only the wrong people, it sounds like.

My mind shifts to Grandpa Frank. I'm not ready to forgive and forget, but I have to admit that at least he's trying. Trying with annoying-as-hell phishing messages, sure, but it's something.

Nana looks up, sniffs, and says, "Good morning, dear. You look like one of the zombies in Leonard's video game."

So much for the warm fuzzies.

"You've been playing video games with him?" I ask.

She makes an affirmative noise, watching me as I get out my biggest monster mug. I feel a sort of reflexive fondness of them after Bianca spent all night bad-mouthing them.

For Leonard too. It's sweet that he's been introducing my eighty-two-year-old grandmother to the glories of gaming. I could have done that—I like gaming too, when the mood strikes. But it never occurred to me that it might be something she'd enjoy, probably because she never would have tried prior to my grandfather leaving.

I fix my coffee and join her at the table.

"Have fun at the Sten thing last night?" she asks.

"Sort of," I admit. I pause, then say, "Nana, will you help me convince Leonard not to do something stupid?"

She jostles the mug she'd lifted for a sip, nearly soaking her crossword puzzle with coffee. My grandmother is and always has been very serious about her crossword puzzles, so I know I've rattled her. "What thing would that be? Has he challenged Colter to a duel? Because I'd very much like to see that. In fact, I'd invite all my friends. That boy never appreciated you, and there's not a doubt in my mind that Leonard will make mincemeat of him."

I roll my eyes, because she's expecting it and I don't want to disappoint her. "Nope, not happening." I take a sip of my coffee, trying to decide what to say next. "He adopted this cat, and now he's got it in his head that he can't take care of her. I'm supposed to pick him up so he can bring her back to the shelter this morning, but I think it would be a huge mistake."

She leans forward and gives me the same intense look I got a time or two when I was a teenager. "He *can't* bring her back."

"Oh. My. God," I say, feeling like I watched seven seasons of *Lost*, only to find out it was all a dream. "You're the one who brought him to adopt her."

"Well, of course," she says. "Someone stole his truck. He had no other way of getting around. We made quite a lot of stops on Thursday before we brought you lunch." She gives her head a shake. "Why anyone would want to steal that fool truck is beyond me."

I lift my hands, leaning back in my chair, and just barely crush the desire to kick back in it. "I can't believe this. You encouraged him to adopt a cat so he could screw up Bianca's pompoms?"

She gives a dramatic shrug, head to shoulder. "Pompoms are useless, and Bianca's a little homewrecker, just like your grandfather's water strumpet."

"You told me you were relieved that I wasn't with Colter."

"I am, but it doesn't make her any less of a homewrecker," she says primly. "We invited her to our home God knows how many times, and this is how she chose to repay us?"

"How much time do you and Leonard spend together, anyway?"

She ignores that question and asks, "Did the pompom trick work?"

"Sort of," I say, scrunching up my face.

"Good. By the way, I didn't just encourage him because I thought it might upset Bianca," she says loftily. "Although I *do* love the thought. That boy's been through a lot. I figured it would be good for him, especially..."

"Let me guess," I grumble. "Especially after what happened to Gidget."

"Well, yes."

"He told you what happened?" I ask, sounding a little more confrontational than I meant to. It's just, shit, I got the sense that Gidget's fate was an upper-level confidence—it's certainly one he hasn't shared with me. If I'd known they were this close, I would have thought twice before letting him go down on me.

Actually, no, because I can still feel the way he absolutely buried his face between my legs, licking and sucking like he liked what he was doing. Like he *loved* it. Colter went down on me when we were together, but it always felt like it was out of duty—if you do me, I'll do you. This...this was something else. I shift a little in my seat, because it's not a good look to be turned on in front of your grandmother.

"Not as such," she says, and I feel a twinge of relief, because this is her roundabout way of saying she doesn't know jack. "But I know it still hurts him."

She's right about that.

"So what are we going to do to stop him?" I ask. "He wanted me to swing by this morning to bring him to the animal shelter."

"Car trouble seems to be going around," she says archly, pausing for a sip of her coffee.

"What if he calls one of his friends for a ride?"

She taps her pen over top of the crossword puzzle, prompting Bertie to look up. I reach my leg over and pet him with my foot. "It would be an easy thing to persuade them to have some car trouble too," she says. "Or..." She looks up at me. "I have another idea, but it involves some dishonesty."

What doesn't lately?

"Nana, can you tell me something truthfully?" Maybe it's foolish to ask, given what she just said.

"Maybe," she answers, so at least she's being honest about the possibility that she might be dishonest.

"Are you trying to set me up with Leonard?"

She tuts her tongue and glances down at the puzzle, filling in a square. "Whatever gave you that idea? I love the boy like he was mine, but he's hardly suitable."

It's a mark of my own absurdity that I'm disappointed.

"I'm still so fucking pissed," Leonard says, rubbing his jaw. It's hours later, after our trip to the animal shelter, and we're on our way to Camp Smileshine for the adult sleepover. "Can you believe it? Who would hurt a kitten? I've never heard of such a ridiculous thing."

I *can* believe it, actually.

My grandmother made a call, because she is a freaking consigliere. When we showed up at the animal shelter earlier with Bean, Leonard was quiet and withdrawn, his mouth a flat slash in his face and his eyes flinty. The closed-off look is also sexy as hell on him, although maybe that's just the flutter between my legs talking. Being around him is a constant reminder of what he did to me last night. A promise of what he might do to me tonight.

The attendant at the desk told him they only had room for so many cats, and a hoarder had turned in her stash of animals last night. If he left the kitten there, she said, Bean would almost certainly be euthanized within the day.

A flat-out lie.

But for someone schooled in lies, Leonard didn't pick up on that. I think it's because he wants to keep her, because for all his bitching to me—and *at* the attendant, who took it stoically—he hasn't once complained about the need to keep Bean. Nor has he suggested bringing her to another shelter or putting up an ad. In fact, he took her out of her crate and cuddled her to his chest after we left the shelter, as if he was worried she might have heard us discussing her impending doom.

She's staying with my grandmother tonight. You'd think Bertie would be the boss in this particular game, but he took one sniff at Bean, she swiped at him with her tiny paw, and now he runs to the nearest soft surface whenever she looks at him.

Before Leonard and I left, we put out some things for Reese on the kitchen table in the little purple house: non-perishable food, fruits and vegetables, wet wipes, toothpaste and a toothbrush, and some other things he might need if he's been sleeping outside or in shelters. Leonard texted him to let him know. There was a hopeful look on his face while he did it that made something hurt inside of me. So does the way he's acting now—infuriated on behalf of a kitten.

"Yeah," I say, trying not to smile, "it's unreal."

A chirp resonates from the backseat. We paid a little visit to the pet store after leaving the shelter, because Leonard needed some additional supplies for Bean.

Among other things.

My smile breaks out of captivity. I haven't decided if we're going to go full cricket on Colter and Bianca, but I don't mind having the contingency plan. Call me cruel, but I love the thought of a cricket landing on Bianca's face in the middle of the night. Maybe she'll see the beauty in monsters after she's had a few sleepless nights of her own.

Leonard says he's got another surprise up his sleeve, but he refuses to elaborate. According to him, he ran it by Colter, of all things. When I asked him where he got Colter's number, he gave me a wry glance until I answered my own question. My grandmother.

Of course she was involved.

"What's got you smiling, Tiger?" Leonard asks now, giving me a sidelong look. It's a warm day, and he dressed down in a dark green short-sleeve T-shirt and gray athletic shorts, both of them giving pops of color, because he has a leg tattoo too. Truthfully, he looks better like this. Nothing like a doctor, mind you, but then again, I've never wanted to fuck a doctor.

That look he's giving me makes me shiver with more remembered pleasure.

"Are you thinking about midnight snacks?" he presses, his tone making it clear he's not talking about Fruit Loops.

"It wasn't midnight," I insist, looking pointedly out of the windshield. The mountains stare back at me. It's a windy road to Camp Smileshine, so I have to pay attention to the road. I also can't look at him right now without feeling the need to pull over and climb on top of him...and without experiencing a strange ache in my chest that I can't pinpoint. "But sure. I'm the kind of person who likes to finish what I start."

"In front of an audience?"

"Not a juvenile one."

"Oh, I'll finish what we started," he says, running his hand up my leg from my knee to the bottom of my cut-off shorts. Pleasure pulses across my skin, because it feels just as good as it did last night, a little rough but soft too. "That was just the appetizer," he adds, his voice seductive, "you're always supposed to leave people wanting more."

I know he's looking at me, not because I've glanced over, but because I can feel his gaze pounding into me, like other parts of him should be doing.

I suck in a breath. "Appetizer's long enough to be a five-dollar word."

"Everyone who's worked at a restaurant knows what an appetizer is," he says softly.

"So, you've worked at a restaurant?"

I do glance at him then, because he's telling me things, even if they're small ones. Enough pieces, and maybe I'll be able to make that picture I want.

He gives me a half grin, his eyes crinkled with laughter. "A few. I killed at getting tips."

I'll bet he did. My mind skips to what he told me last night, about having a talent for liberating fools from their money.

"Did you get fired because you added extra zeroes to the receipts to up your tips?"

"No, that'd be a good way to get caught. I got fired from one of them because the hostess and I fucked on a table in the dining room after closing, and we got caught."

"So you *are* into public displays," I say flippantly, ignoring the little ping of jealousy. I really am losing my mind. If I start being jealous of other woman who've gotten the whole Leonard Smith experience, I'll never be able to stop.

"And I got fired from another place because I punched a customer."

"Why'd you do that?"

From the corner of my eye, I can see his jaw working. "He didn't give my buddy a tip on a big table because he was Mexican. Called him a shitty name on the receipt like a coward, but I saw what he wrote before he got out of the lot. Got in a couple of hits, but he had a knife on him and got me good in the arm. Still got fired."

So that's how he got his scar.

Leonard stands up for people, too.

Dammit.

"Couldn't you have pressed charges?"

"I'm the one who started it."

I pause, then ask, "What other jobs have you done?"

"Photographer's assistant. Checkout clerk. Bartender. Muscle."

"Muscle for who?"

"You don't want to know," he says. "Second time I changed my name was when I left that one." I feel him watching me again. Waiting for a reaction.

"And you were a thief?"

"Since before I was old enough to know what I was doing, but I left that behind a long time ago. Mostly. I walked off with a hat from the movie set last month. The costume guy gave me the go-ahead, but I would have taken it anyway. Took an old book from the estate we were filming at too. And I saw Burke's parent's car parked at the Grove Park Inn, so I nabbed the key from the valet stand and took the old broad's purse. I kept the cash, but I had a fun little fire with the rest of it. I liked thinking about them having to call in and cancel everything. Everyone knows that's a pain in the ass. I figured it was the least I could do after they drove me out of town." He pauses, then adds, "I didn't tell Burke."

"Why were you at the Grove Park Inn?" I ask, latching on to the detail for reasons I can't wrap my head around. It's a fancy hotel that looks like a gingerbread house turned to stone, and it has overpriced restaurants with admittedly fantastic views.

From my peripheral vision, I can see Leonard giving a little *oh, Shauna* shake of his head. "My weed dealer works as a valet there."

Huh. "Who would've thought?"

"It's the people who stay there who're rich, Tiger. Not the staff."

My mind shifts back to Burke's parents. "You're the one who figured out that they were responsible for that building collapse."

"Yeah, and I ran away instead of taking them on. Burke's the hero in that story."

"Why'd you run?" I ask, because I've been wondering. This was the part of the story that played along with him being a sleaze and not caring about other people, but I've gotten to know him well enough to know it doesn't fit. Not quite. There must be more to it.

"Because *that's what I do*. After I told them what I knew, they dug up dirt on me. They told me no one would believe someone like me, and they were right. So I took their hush money. But they couldn't just leave it at that—they hired someone to keep an eye on me. Do you know how paranoid you get when you have someone following you around after you've nearly been killed half a dozen times?"

"How'd you find out they did it?"

"I told you. I'm good at telling when people are lying. I knew they were up to something, so I listened where I shouldn't've. I poked around. I went to see the guy they pinned it on in jail, and after I talked to him, I was damn sure he didn't know anything but the inside of a bottle. That's why they hired him. Perfect patsy. I have a thing against people who pin their sins on patsies." He huffs air. "But not enough of a thing to take a stand against them. You want to know something?"

"Maybe not."

I can feel him smiling, although it's not the kind of smile that has any happiness behind it. "I lied about how I met Burke and the other guys."

"Oh?" I glance at him, but he's staring straight out the windshield now, like it's the only way he can say this.

"I knew Burke was rich. He was a mark. I wasn't planning on sticking around in Asheville. I was gonna get some money out of him and move on."

"But you didn't."

I steal a glimpse of him again as he reaches up and rubs a hand along his stubbled jaw. "I liked him." He swears under his breath. "I liked all of them. And then he got me a job, and I figured why not? Maybe I'd found somewhere I could stay."

"You ever tell him that?"

He throws a wry glance my way. "What do you think?"

For a second I'm stunned silent. Why would he tell me something he hasn't even told his best friend? Of course, it's not exactly the kind of thing you'd want to tell a friend, but he has even less of a reason to share it with me.

"Maybe you *should* tell him."

A grunt is my only answer.

"Why are you telling me all of this, anyway?"

He shrugs. "It's an hour-long drive. Figured it would go faster if we made conversation."

But I suspect there's more to it. He's worried that I'm softening toward him, become less tiger and more kitty cat, and he's warning me not to. I wonder if he shares his rap sheet with all of his girls, but I don't ask. I'm afraid the answer will be no—and also that it might be yes.

"Sure," I tell him. "Why don't we ask each other some getting-to-know-you questions?"

"Don't you think we're past that?" he asks, his voice low and throaty, almost a growl, and I feel it quake through me. Just like it was meant to.

"No, I don't," I tell him through clenched teeth. "What am I going to say if someone asks me what your favorite color is?"

"You can tell them it's a stupid fucking question."

"I probably would," I agree, "but you're right. It's a long drive, and I don't think we need to spend the whole time talking about how much you suck. I agree, it's been a favorite topic of mine in the past, but after a while it starts feeling repetitive."

A laugh escapes him, and I feel a sense of...relief, or maybe victory that I managed to lift him out of his mood, even if it's just for a while. "Well, I wouldn't want to bore you. Should we sing 'Ninety-Nine Bottles of Beer on the Wall'?"

"Stop it with the good ideas, already," I say, reaching out to give his arm a shove. It feels perfect, solid and hot, and my fingers start to wrap around it on reflex, like they don't want to let go. I remember in short order that I'm driving a car and will be for the next thirty-five minutes. When we get there, though, we'll be in a cabin all to ourselves, a cabin that will almost certainly only have one bed.

I know we're both thinking about it.

I steal a glance at him and find him watching me with those hazel eyes full of mischief.

"Blue," he says.

"What?" I glance back out the windshield. Both because I don't want to kill us and his gaze has rattled me.

"My favorite color. It reminds me of the Blue Ridge Mountains. It's the color of home."

"But you're not originally from here, are you?"

Part of me hoped he'd offer up that information willingly, but he gives his head a little shake that I see in my peripheral vision. "No, Tiger, but where you're from isn't the same thing as home. I think you know that."

Suddenly, I feel like crying.

I tell myself it's only because he's right—I didn't feel like I had a home when I was a kid either, not until something horrible happened. It's awful to only have found happiness because of something so horrible. So final.

I tell myself it's not because this impossible man is the only one who seems to really understand me.

Then, because he's Leonard, he really does start singing "Ninety-Nine Bottles of Beer on the Wall."

Damn him, he has the voice of an angel.

seventeen

LEONARD

I'M A MESS INSIDE. Reese hasn't answered any of my messages, and he could be who-knows-where. He could be *dead*.

I don't know the kid well, and he's now stolen both my cereal and my shoes, possibly my truck if he's more wily than I've given him credit for, but it's very important for him to be all right. I guess I see myself in him, a kid who's lost and lonely and doesn't know his ass from his elbow. When I was that age, I needed someone to step in, and no one did. I want to be that person for him, but I don't know how.

Then there's Bean. I'm still in knots over what happened at the shelter. Whoever heard of killing kittens?

I've told myself it's okay, that maybe Constance will want to keep her and the problem will resolve itself. But there's an aching inside of me—a sense of wanting.

I've been feeling more of that lately, and that kitten is just the tip of the iceberg that's going to sink me. Because Shauna, sitting beside me, has brought on a whole different kind of wanting—one that feels dangerous as hell. If I have no business keeping a kitten, I have even less business doing whatever it is I'm doing with her.

Fucking around, sure, but it's not that simple. I'm...protective of her, and I want her to be happy. That's become more important than doing Constance a favor and having fun while doing it. Maybe it was always more important.

She glances at me as she pulls into Camp Smileshine, beneath a huge-ass sign of a bear smiling like it's high on mushrooms. It looks like the kind of place a mass murder would go down in a slasher flick, and I say so. "I think we need to rename it from Camp Nightmare to Murderland."

She takes a look around as she pulls in, and says, "That tracks. But I heard there's a gazebo on the lake. There was one near our house in Raleigh, and it was my favorite place in the world." Her gaze darts to me before returning to the windshield. "You know, the people who have sex always die first in horror movies."

"But they die happy, sweetheart," I say, letting myself touch her leg again. Her skin is soft, but not as soft as it gets farther up. I inch my fingers higher, seeing how high she'll let me go before she shuts it down. We pass a big cabin with a banner reading,

#ABC Headquarters

"They've really got an alphabet fetish, huh? You think they're hinting that he already knocked her up?"

She flinches, and I realize I've got no idea whether Shauna wants kids. Hell, maybe she talked about having two point five children with Champ before he decided to trade her in for a downgrade.

I pull my hand away. "Shit, I didn't mean to upset you, I—"

Giving her head a shake, she reaches for my hand and puts it back on her leg, as bossy as you please. "You didn't. I was flinching at the thought of their future children."

"You think they'd name their son Champ?"

She laughs. "You know what? Probably."

We're cruising slowly through the camp, heading to the address Shauna was given for our cabin. We pass a few smaller cabins, a couple of them with people outside doing some porch sitting with beers. It's kind of nice, actually, a definite upgrade from forced crafting.

An older blond woman with big curls and a dress that looks as out of place in this dump as a diamond studded collar on a pug waves to us, giving Shauna a big-eyed stare through the windshield that makes it clear she wants us to stop. Shauna mows on past but gives her a fake grin and a wave as she goes.

"Who's that?" I ask.

"Colter's mother."

"I thought you liked her? Isn't she the jelly lady?"

She snorts through her nose this time. I feel the high of having made her do it. Her snort-laughs are harder to earn than the others. "Sure, I thought so at one point."

Then, as she glides past more cabins, she tells me about Champ's mom passing her up for the craft store but buying five hundred of Bianca's poofballs.

"Sounds like an idiot if you ask me," I say as she finally pulls up in front of the tiny cabin we've been assigned and parks the car. No joke, it's the last of the buildings and in the worst shape. It looks like Jason Voorhees has been hanging out in it. Actually, scratch that. Even Jason had his standards. I nod toward it. "Looks like they really appreciate us coming."

"Yeah, right?" Her mouth ticks up as she undoes her belt. I do the same. "Well, we did bring a hundred crickets and whatever your mysterious surprise is, so maybe they're right not to want us."

"That's where you're wrong, Tiger. We're bringing the fun."

Turning in her seat, she grins at me, and I'm gut-punched by the sight. She's always caught my eye, but today she's gorgeous. There's something glowing inside of her. She's got on a V-neck T-shirt that shows off the goods and a hot little pair of cut-off shorts, but it's less what she's wearing and more *her*. There's a bit of naughtiness in her eyes, like those doldrums are starting to lose their grip.

"You bring the fun everywhere you go, don't you?" she asks, eyes amused.

Not everywhere, no.

But that's not the answer she needs right now. "Yes, ma'am."

She shoves my shoulder with her little hand. "You did *not* just ma'am me."

I tug her into my lap, and before a squawk of righteous fury can escape her, I start tickling her.

She laughs as she bucks on top of me, and goddamn, my dick is all about this game.

"Stop! Stop!"

As soon as I do, she turns in my lap and starts tickling *me*, so I resume my tickle torture, and soon we're both laughing like idiots, our arms smacking the window. Then she stops the game in an instant by grabbing my dick through my shorts.

"Fuck, you win," I say as she starts rubbing. Not that she needs to do anything to get my boy to stand to attention. Feeling her squirming around in my lap was enough for that.

"That's what I like to hear." Her voice is low and breathy, and I'll be damned if it doesn't make me harder. She leans in and kisses me, her hand still on my dick. Her lips are soft but she presses them against mine firmly, like she means business. I hope to hell she does, because I've been wound up over her for weeks now, and I need a release that doesn't come from my own hand. When she leans back, her eyes are full of victory.

"What would you like your prize to be?" I ask, catching her wrist. I move it up to the top of my shorts, because I need to feel her hand on my skin, not through two layers of fabric.

"I think you know the answer to that," she says as she plays with the drawstring, giving me a saucy-ass look.

I glance out the window, but there's no one around. Maybe they did us a favor by sticking us in the Jason cabin. More privacy.

Then Shauna surprises me by slipping back over to the driver's seat.

"Not into public displays of affection?" I ask, giving my dick a token rub through my pants because it's feeling the loss of her. "I'll be sure to add that to my list of relationship shit to remember."

"My favorite color's purple. You can add that one too."

"I already know that," I say as I reach over to ruffle her hair. "You know, you're not supposed to make your tells so obvious."

"There's a reason I don't mess around with poker." She's smiling as she goes for the drawstring again, and a sigh escapes me as she slips her hand under the band around the top. I lift slightly and push down my shorts and boxer briefs.

"Well, hello," she says, wrapping her hand around my cock. She glances up at me with those ever-changing eyes of hers and smirks. "If you get to talk to my tits, it's only fair."

"Oh, feel free to chat him up, baby. In fact, you can get up real close and personal. He won't bite."

"You're such an ass," she says, "but it just so happens that I *would* like to get closer."

My heart thumps in my chest as she glides her hand up and down, squeezing.

Then she leans all the way over and takes the head of my cock in her mouth, just the head, sucking on it like it's a lollipop. The soft, wet suction sends darts of pleasure to the base of my spine, making me feel like a teenager again—like I'm a kid who can't take another second before blowing my load.

I put my hand in her hair like she did with me, weaving my fingers through the light purple strands as she bobs her head down to take in more of me, her tongue circling me. Down and then up. Down and then up. My hips thrust up slightly, because I can't take it.

"Yeah, just like that, Tiger. Fuck, that feels so good. You can put your mouth on me anytime you like." It feels even better because she's doing it in here, in the car outside of our cabin, where anyone could come along and see us. There's a thrill to it, and I'm all about chasing thrills. Anything to pull me away from the void.

I watch her as she lifts up again, licking at the head of my dick, her eyes meeting mine as she does it, and I feel it again—that almost panicky sensation in my chest.

It still feels fantastic. Better than fantastic actually, like I won the lottery, and someone handed me a stack of bucks on a gold platter, but there's a razor edge of panic. Of *what the fuck am I doing?*

I've already told her too much, more than I've told anyone in I don't know how long. Maybe I've held on to the words so long they burst out like soda from a shaken can the first time someone cracked me open.

She reaches down and touches my balls while she gives me another pass with that sweet little mouth, and the panic is buried under pleasure. I'm close. I open my mouth to say so, because even though I'd love nothing better than for her to swallow me down, I won't surprise her with it, when I hear someone shouting "Yoo-hoo" from beyond the car window.

Well, ho-ly shit.

I glance out and see the blond lady with the curls. Jelly Lady. She's several feet away, and because of the way the car's parked, on a little upward tilt of the gravel road, she can't see Shauna.

She can't see her *yet*. If I let her get too close to the car, that'll change.

Shauna pops off my dick, and I let go of her hair. I feel the big oh backing off, but she doesn't pull up my shorts.

She swears as I roll down the window.

"Hello," I call out cheerfully as I fumble for my phone in the cupholder beneath the radio. Shauna, who's stretched over it, figures out what I want and hands it to me. I lift it out toward Jelly

Lady, who has stopped in her tracks. "I was just about to make a work call out here while Shauna gets changed inside. Beautiful day for camping, isn't it?"

The woman starts wringing her hands and glances at the cabin.

"Oh, I was hoping for a private word with her."

"I'll be sure to let her know," I say, biting my lip when I feel Shauna's mouth descend on me again, her tongue circling the head of my cock. I want to look down at her—I'm desperate for it—but I keep my gaze on Jelly Lady.

"You must be Doctor Smith," the woman says with a warm smile.

Shauna's hot, wet mouth is on my dick, and I'm supposed to make small talk? It's like having hell and heaven thrown at you all at once and being asked to juggle them for the devil. If that doesn't make sense, that's because, again, *my dick is in Shauna's mouth.*

"You can call me Doc," I choke out.

"Doc," Jelly Lady repeats. "I was so happy to hear that Shauna had met someone new. She's such a lovely girl. But of course you already know that." Then she takes a few steps closer, like she wants to come up to the window and shake my hand. No way can I let that happen, but what can I say to get her to step off?

My mind's not working right, so I blurt out the first idea that surfaces. "Ma'am, I'm sorry to be crude, but you'd better stay back. We stopped at Taco Bell for lunch, and it's like a hotbox in here."

Shauna laughs a little against my dick, and it feels out-of-this-world good.

Fuck. I'm about to come in front of Jelly Lady, aren't I?

"Oh," the woman says, her expression as startled as if a bird just shit on her head. At a guess, nobody's ever talked to her like that before in her whole life. "Oh, yes. Well, maybe I'll go in and say hello to Shauna."

"I wouldn't go in there if I were you," I say, my voice low. My face is probably all twisted up, because I can feel it—I'm right at the peak. Shauna stopped moving for a second, probably because she's still fighting laughter, but one more suck or lick is all it's going to take to get me there. "I'm not the only one who was having some stomach trouble, if you know what I mean. She might be in there for a while."

That's when it happens, Shauna pinches my thigh while she moves her mouth down, and I'm gone. I'm toast. I come in her mouth, and even though I didn't mean to do it, I can't regret this either, because it feels so damn good.

My face must look janked up, because Jelly Lady looks both worried and disgusted. She probably thinks I shit my pants.

"Oh dear," she says, taking a step forward and then back. "Are you okay? Should I send over some Tums or Pepto? Or...I guess you are a doctor, but we can find someone else in the party who's a doctor, I'm sure."

I'm tempted to ask for their name so I can stay the hell away from them.

"That's swell of you to offer," I say, my voice probably coming out strained. I feel Shauna pulling off my dick and then tugging up my underwear, but she keeps her face down in my lap, her breath fluttering off my still-sensitive cock, even though it's covered. "But, you know, I always carry that stuff with me. Being a doctor and all. We'll see you down at the shindig."

She seems uncertain, like if she goes now, she'd be leaving us to die in this remote cabin, so I say, "Everyone knows the price of Taco Bell, am I right? But it feels so good going down, it's worth it."

Jelly Lady gives a nervous laugh. "Oh, yes. Well." She checks her watch, hopefully because she's got the hint and is finally going to leave, and says, "Looks like there's just fifteen minutes before the opening reception. I'll have to find some time with Shauna later tonight. *Thank you*, Doc."

"And your name?" I ask.

"Oh dear," she says with a tittering laugh, then takes another step closer.

"Hotbox," I remind her.

"Yes, that's right." She comes to a stop, thank all that's unholy. "I'm Shelly. I look forward to getting to know you better."

A lot of fuss for one of her son's ex-squeezes if you ask me, but maybe she has a guilty conscience. Guilt can be a powerful motivator.

"Okay, I'd better make this call, Shelly. It's about this kid with a really jacked-up leg. I'm gonna make him run again, you mark my words."

"What's wrong with him?" She looks like she wants to run over to the hospital and give him a hug. I'm starting to get what Shauna meant about the whole jelly thing.

"HIPAA," I say, patting the side of my nose. "Can't tell you, unfortunately."

"Of course," she says. It really is the magic word, because she turns and leaves. I wait until her back is far enough in the distance that I know she's actually leaving before I pull Shauna up off my lap.

"You're a naughty girl," I tell her, my voice gruff, because she looks hot as hell with her hair mussed up from my hands, her lips swollen. My cum down her throat.

"You like it."

I kiss her hard. "Damn right."

Her eyes are shining when I pull away. "Hotbox?"

I have to laugh as I lift my shorts up. "I couldn't think with your lips around my cock. It's your fault."

"Now I'm going to have to pretend to have a stomach ache all night."

"Nah, eat everything you want, and prove to her you're a fighter. Now let's go check out our digs."

We pile out of the car and head inside. There's not much in

there. Just a small bed that my feet are going to hang off of, plus a little table that looks like it's made of matchsticks and a couple of chairs to match. If one of them doesn't fall apart by the time we leave tomorrow, it'll be a miracle.

On the table is a little wicker basket—the kind of thing that's useless for anything but giving gifts people probably don't want—filled with different pompoms. The one at the center is enormous, bigger even than the one Shauna gave Bianca last night.

"Looks like someone's enjoying this game, Tiger." I throw the central pompom to her. "But she won't be enjoying it for much longer."

eighteen

SHAUNA

Group text: *The Evans Sisters Want the Goods*
Mira: *You've been shortchanging us.*
Delia: *Leonard hasn't told Burke anything. Are you at the sleepover camp? Is there only one bed?*
Me: *Yes, and we plan to make use of it.*
Mira: *I hope you don't only mean for sleeping. It would be a real tease if you're just talking about sleeping.*
Me: *Nope. Sleep is the last thing on my mind.*
Delia: *Have fun! ;-)*
Mira: *Remember, let him rock your body but DON'T fall for him.*
Delia: *She can if she wants to, Mira. Stop being bossy.*
Mira: *Trust me. The first time I saw Byron with his guitar, I knew I wanted to fuck him. If I'd left it at that, I wouldn't have had to pour bleach in his laundry this morning.*
Me: *I'm pretty sure no one made you do that.*
Mira: *He brought a woman home last night.*
Mira: *It's a one-bedroom apartment, and he forgot that it was my turn to sleep in the bed. They literally fell on me while I was sleeping.*
Me: *Okay, maybe he DID make you do that.*

THIS PARTY SHOULD BE BORING. It should be *outrageously* dull. Dinner is a buffet of food, the courses alphabetically arranged, on the picnic tables lined up against the back wall of the big front cabin. The soft jazz Colter—and probably no one else —loves is playing softly over the speaker. The collection of beer is subpar since Bianca made a point of saying not all beer is camping beer, whatever that means. But it isn't boring...because of *him*.

People have been gravitating toward Leonard from the moment we walked in, me still in my cutoffs, him in those shorts I pulled down to have my way with him. Some of them were probably sent over to us as Bianca's spies but not all of them. Leonard has this gift that I didn't let myself fully acknowledge before now—an unreal ability to draw people out and get them to cut loose.

He's the one who issued the ABC food challenge after Bianca rang the bell to announce dinner—trying one food for every letter, including X, Y, and Z, which have the fewest offerings.

"Won't you get sick?" Shelly asked with genuine horror. She's obviously scarred from the whole hotboxing incident, but much less scarred than she would have been if she'd known what I was doing in that car.

I hadn't planned on taking him into my mouth again. I don't know what possessed me, other than that it turned me on to listen to him carry on a conversation while I was driving him crazy with my mouth. I liked the feeling of his hand in my hair, of his dick rising up to meet me because he couldn't completely control himself.

"Oh no," Leonard told her with a wink. "That's all been sorted."

Ten of the thirty or so people present took him up on the challenge, one of them Melly, the blond woman who was eying him up at the pompom party last night. She finally introduced herself. Leonard and I are making our way down the alphabetical buffet, followed by her. The first few people have ravaged the buffet, knocking a few of the cutesy signs over. Bianca's muttering under her breath to Colter in the corner closest to the buffet. They look like Barbie and Ken in the camping set my mother refused to buy me when I was kid, him wearing a flannel shirt and her in cut-offs and a checkered shirt that ties above the waist.

"Is your kitten okay after last night?" Melly asks Leonard. Her gaze darts toward Bianca, then she adds in a hushed undertone, "I felt so bad about what happened. It looked like Bee was going to throw her clear across the room."

Salt meet wound.

Her friend is trailing after her, looking bored and holding a Bud Light like it's the only thing that will save her from falling asleep. It's obvious she's not that into the Bianca show.

"Yeah," Leonard says, but I notice the way his jaw is flexing. When I checked my phone earlier and answered the Evans sisters' texts, I noticed that my grandmother had already sent us at least ten photos of Bean. In one of them, the kitten's wearing a hideous dayglo yellow sweater.

Leonard said Nana did it to taunt him, since he and Burke like to make fun of her animal sweaters. Knowing my grandmother, she's trying to convince Leonard he needs to take Bean back for her own good.

"She's being spoiled by her great-grandmother, actually," I say and pointedly pluck a cookie for C off Leonard's plate.

"Your grandmother lives in town, then," she asks him as if I didn't exist.

"No, she's talking about her grandmother," he said, leaning down to take a bite of the chocolate chip cookie in my hand. Chocolate smears on his lip. Deciding to give them both a show, I put the cookie down so I can wipe the chocolate off his mouth with my finger, and then I slowly suck on it.

Leonard's throat bobs as he watches me, and I feel the rush of having affected him again. Maybe this is a game too, but if so, it's more dangerous than the one I'm playing with Bianca.

Turning back toward Melly, who looks annoyed by my refusal

to disappear, he clears his throat and says, "If I called that woman granny, she'd shoot me. But you never know..." he adds with sparkling eyes. "If these two crazy kids can make it work after eight months of dating, then maybe we'll chase 'em down the aisle."

I pinch his thigh, and he drops his plate. It shatters, spraying ABC food everywhere—including onto Bianca, who was standing close enough to get some on her shirt.

"Well, shucks," he says as if his vocabulary weren't half-swears. "Don't I just have butter fingers."

"It's fine," Bianca says tightly, in a tone that makes it clear it's not. "Our cabin's close. I'll go change."

Colter follows her out, and Leonard says, "Ain't that nice. They can't keep away from each other for even a minute. We're a little like that, aren't we, Tiger?"

I notice the way he watches through the side windows as Colter and Bianca head to their cabin. I know without asking that he's keeping track in case I want to bring out those crickets. Maybe he plans on doing it anyway.

We offer to clean up the mess from Leonard's food mishap, but Shelly, who's been orbiting us, steps in. I feel something catch in my throat, because at moments like this, when she's so kind and sweet, it's hard to remember that she pulled a bait and switch on me. She hasn't tried to pull me aside yet, probably because Leonard has stuck to me like that adhesive bra, but I know it'll happen sometime tonight.

Maybe it's time for me to actually confront her about the shop.

Maybe I need to have a come-to-Jesus moment with all of them.

It's what Tony Soprano would have done.

Nah, he probably would have popped them off and hidden the bodies somewhere.

Leonard leans in and presses a kiss to my neck. "That was right where you pinched me in the car, Tiger," he whispers into my ear. "Right before you made me come. You're driving me *wild*."

His voice shudders through me, his words amping me up, because I still haven't had him all the way.

I remind myself of what Mira said: *Don't fall for him.*

I'm too sensible to do something so dumb, but I can't deny that I feel his gravitational pull—or that his hands on me feel different than anyone else's. Of course, I know he's had plenty of practice to get good with those hands. I need to remind myself it's nothing personal.

When we bring our plates outside to sit at an empty picnic table, a few of Colter's friends join us, as well as Melly, who's impressively dedicated to hitting on my fake boyfriend. Her friend's there, too, but her attention is focused on Colt's best friend—a CPA named Grayson, who's helpfully wearing a gray shirt. He's Colt's best man, my counterpart.

Leonard makes a show of trying to feed me from his plate.

"Oh, aren't you sweet," Melly says with a breathy sigh. "I wish I could find someone who'd treat me so nice."

The guy next to her, another one of Colter's buddies, nearly spills his plate in his lap in his hurry to offer her a cookie. The thing is, Leonard's not actually being nice. I'm pretty sure he's choosing the nastiest things on purpose to torment me because he thinks it's funny. I've held back so much laughter that I might explode from it. The crinkling around his eyes tells me I'm not alone in that.

It feels like we're alone in a bubble, just the two of us, and I'm actually having *fun*. If I'd come here alone, I'd probably want to gouge my eyes out right about now.

I put my hand on Leonard's leg, just below where those shorts end, and rub slightly.

I tell myself it's part of the act—and that he only puts his hand over mine for the same reason.

After everyone finishes eating, Bianca, who's wearing a different button-up shirt tied above the waist, rings her bell from the doorway of the front cabin and announces it's time for us to go inside and "enjoy" the karaoke machine.

"Now, you all know I can be a little Type A," she adds from the doorway, getting a round of half-hearted laughter, "so I've gone ahead and chosen a song for everyone. Colt and I are going to pop your cherry, but the list for the rest of you is posted on the bulletin board just inside the cabin door. The songs are all significant to Colt and me in some way."

I exchange a look with Leonard. Leaning in, I whisper in his ear, "I really am tone-deaf. She probably picked something horrible for us."

"Sure, but who cares?" he says back brightly, with the confidence of someone who has a beautiful voice.

We file inside with everyone else, and the whole group huddles around the bulletin board next to the door as if it's the list of who made varsity basketball. Bianca and Colter's names are at the top, singing "At Last" by Etta James. They doubled down with the stupid alphabet theme, because our names are listed next. She assigned us "Bohemian Rhapsody."

I don't have to ask why. For one thing, the song is significant to Colt and *me*. We watched *Wayne's World* on our first date, because I couldn't believe he'd never seen it. When I asked him what he'd liked about it, the only thing he could come up with was that song. Later, he admitted he'd been distracted because he was trying to figure out how to make a move.

I'll bet it didn't hurt the song selection process that "Bohemian Rhapsody" mixes multiple different styles of music into one song, giving me a variety of ways to embarrass myself.

"Well, that's it," I say in an undertone. "We're fucked."

Colt and Bianca don't hear me—they're at the back getting set up for their performance, which I'm sure they've practiced at least thirty times. Hell, they probably even choreographed a dance. But Melly turns to face us. "I'm screwed too," she says, stricken. "She assigned me a rap song. I've never rapped before in my life. I knew she was pissed at me for letting your kitten out last night."

Leonard whistles. "Brutal."

Melly's friend is happier with her pick—a Britney Spears song that apparently speaks to Bianca and Colter's souls.

Other guests murmur around us as they check out their songs, and then Bianca makes an announcement that the fun is about to begin. People settle into chairs or lean against the wall to take in their highly staged performance. Leonard and I are wall-leaners, and he draws me close. My heart flutters as he presses my back up against him, his arms clasped in front of me. Colter never held me like this around other people—he was always embarrassed by physical affection, as if touching his girlfriend was the same as carrying around a teddy bear.

He's only pretending.

Then Leonard whispers in my ear as the song starts up, "Why'd she choose that song for you?"

I tell him in an undertone, and he listens, rocking me against him a little as if he's a secret Etta James fan.

"We're about to blow them out of the water, Tiger," he tells me in my ear, his words a pleasant tickle. "Don't you fret."

"We should have unleashed the crickets in here," I whisper back, just as Bianca launches into her part of the song. It would be fantastic if she were pitchy, but she's not the kind of person who would host a karaoke night unless she was damn sure she could pull it off.

As predicted, they have a whole little dance number prepared. They've obviously been pouring time into it for weeks. It's no accident that she scheduled us to go next.

Then again, I remind myself of Leonard's rendition of "Ninety-Nine Bottles of Beer" in the car. Maybe I have a secret weapon.

The happy couple finishes by exploding heart confetti into the crowd, no joke. Bianca gives me a pointed smile as she leaves the mike and walks over, "Your turn, Bean."

"Maybe you missed the first few times we told you," Leonard tells her in a jovial voice that's got metal beneath it, his arms still around me. "That's not a nickname she answers to anymore."

Something burns in my chest, because he's standing up for me again. He comes off as a joker most of the time, closed-off and mysterious the rest, but he keeps standing up for me.

"Old habits die hard," Colter says with a smile. His eyes land on me, a bit sad suddenly. "We picked a song we know you like."

It hurts a little, but only in the way that old wounds do if they're poked.

"Now, go on up there and show us what you're made of," Bianca says, patting me on the ass. It's the kind of thing she would have done when we were actually friends, and that hurts too.

"Oh, we will," Leonard tells her.

He pulls a chair up toward the karaoke machine, the feet screeching against the floor. Then he signals for Colter, who's playing DJ, to get us going.

"Is that for me?" I ask in a whisper as the opening strains start. "Because I might need to sit down. You can gyrate around me."

"I'll give you a lap dance later, if you ask nicely. I have plans for that chair."

If I doubted him, I didn't for long. He jumps on top of the chair while he's singing about Scaramouche, doing a Freddie Mercury act that has everyone in the cabin shouting and tapping their feet. In the beginning, I do my best to stay as silent as possible, because I don't want my crappy voice to screw things up. But Leonard's having so much fun, it's impossible not to join in. After a minute or so, I'm belting out the lyrics right along with him, getting lost in the fun of it. Both of us beat our chests dramatically as we tell our mamas we've just killed a man.

When we finish, everyone cheers, and several people slap

Leonard on the back and call him doc. I take great satisfaction in the sour look on Bianca's face as she whispers furiously to Colter. Thirty seconds later, he announces over the microphone that there will be no more karaoke because the machine is broken. He immediately unplugs it and starts to carry it out of the cabin, probably to avoid the possibility that someone will inspect it and realize it's just fine.

Leonard has obviously figured out that the best way to mess with Bianca is by taking attention away from her. We won this round, and from the look on her face, she can't stand it.

I'm watching Colter return when Leonard takes my hand. The jolt it sends through me catches me off guard.

He's got his phone in his other hand, and he's grinning. "My surprise is almost here, Tiger. It's for them, obviously, but it's also for you."

"Oh yeah?"

"Yeah, I think you're gonna like it."

"Which means you think I'm going to hate it."

His grin widens, his eyes crinkling at the corners, and he's so beautiful it's like a gut punch. "I guess you're just gonna have to wait and see."

nineteen

LEONARD

"A PSYCHIC?" Shauna asks, lifting her brows so they almost touch her purple bangs.

We're standing at the outskirts of a circle that's formed behind Josie the Great's setup—a card table with a crystal ball on it, surrounded by a dozen candles. Champ and Queen Bee are sitting in a couple of chairs they pulled up to it while Josie stands behind the crystal ball, wearing a black veil and black-frame glasses and holding a chunk of crystal. She called it a tuning rod, but it looks like a dick if you ask me.

When Josie rolled in with her setup, Colter took Bianca's hands and said, "I hope you don't mind, honey, but I put together a little surprise for you." Then the sucker threw a wink my way.

I'd encouraged him to take credit for my idea as another way to poison the well and avoid getting caught.

Was it kind of me to give Champ the runaround? No, but the more I hear about his and Bianca's past with Shauna, the more I think they've been screwing around for longer than eight months. I'd be lying if I said I've never told a fib to get laid, but one thing I've never done is commit myself to a woman and then bend her best friend over a table.

"She's not just any psychic," I tell Shauna in an undertone, putting my arm around her back. "She's the worst psychic in all of Asheville. She has a reputation for telling people they're going to die alone. Burke told me about her. I figured she'd have something fun for our happy couple."

She gives me that snort-laugh, her expression delighted. "You mean you paid her to say something horrible."

"I plead the fifth."

She smiles at me, but there's something nervous about it, like she's wondering how many times I've *actually* pled the fifth. She's remembering what I told her earlier. That's good. She *should* remember.

So should I.

We've been spending too much time together, and I've liked it too much. In a weird way, it reminds me of hanging out with Burke and the guys back when I first met them. I had very different intentions toward him in the beginning, but I let myself start to think things could be different. That I'd found somewhere I could belong.

But I had to leave anyway. Sure, I came back. But it'll never be the same as if I'd held my ground. Shane won't talk to me really, on account of he doesn't want to get dirty, and Drew lives hundreds of miles away.

A soft light fills the crystal ball on the table. Neat trick. Josie's entire focus seems to be on the ball, but I'm guessing she has a remote of some sort wrapped up in her hand. Either that, or it's on a timer.

Champ looks like he just watched the Easter Bunny hop into the room, but Bianca's a tougher customer. It's obvious she thinks this is bullshit, and from the look on her face, she doesn't like that she wasn't consulted.

"I'm connected to the other side," Josie says.

"Do you see my Great-Aunt Mabel?" someone asks from the peanut gallery. It's the blond woman from earlier. I don't remember her name other than that it ends in a 'y,' but she cornered me in the line to the can and asked how serious I was about Shauna.

Under normal circumstances, I'm not one to turn down attention from a pretty woman. But I told her I was as serious as a heart attack.

Josie's brow wrinkles while she stares into the surface of that glowing hunk of stone. "Did she look like Jack Nicholson?"

"Yes!" Blondie says, taking a step forward.

Bianca gives her a look that should turn her to salt, but Blondie's not too good at playing games. Something tells me she won't be in the inner circle for much longer.

Josie blows out a breath, making the black veil puff out. "Huh. That's unexpected."

"What is it?" Blondie asks, leaning in.

"She says she loves you."

I barely swallow a laugh as Blondie stares at her in confusion.

"Oh, and she says she really enjoyed the reading of—" Josie makes a gagging sound and then shrugs. "I guess there's no disputing taste, but she enjoyed the Mitch Album reading you did at her funeral."

"Oh my God!" Blondie says loudly, glancing around the small crowd. "That's true, and only twenty people came to Mabel's funeral, so she'd have no way of knowing that was my great-aunt's favorite author. She really *is* psychic."

Shauna nudges me, and I crowd in closer so I can whisper to her without being overheard. "I know what you're thinking, Tiger. But I didn't have a damn thing to do with that. She must've done her own research."

She looks up at me, her eyes shining. "She's going to give Burke a run for his money if he decides to open that call center."

I swallow a laugh. My buddy's not the kind of guy to buy into the supernatural, but his girl is into crystals and flowers and good vibes, so who knows. Love does strange things to a man.

"She's supposed to be doing a reading for *us*, Melly," Bianca says, her voice sharp-edged.

"Sorry," Blondie aka Melly says, her eyes wide. She's probably wondering what Bianca's going to do to her next, if the first punishment was that song she didn't have to sing.

Josie peers back into the crystal, pushing her lips to the side.

"Okay, happy couple," she says in a flat voice. "Twelve months together, huh? A lot of people would say that's not a big enough foundation for marriage, but I can see you're perfect for each other."

"But we've only been together eight months," Bianca snaps.

"No, what I'm seeing is very clear," Josie argues. "Twelve months."

"You're wrong," Queen Bee repeats, but there's something off about her tone, and Colt looks like someone shoved a hot poker up his back door.

Shauna goes rigid beside me.

Shit. Damn. Fuck.

What if she thinks I found out Colt's a cheater and decided to let her know in the worst way possible? It's not true. I've got no idea what game Josie the Great is playing, but Shauna doesn't know that.

"Sure, whatever," Josie says as a few people start whispering. She leans in closer to the glowing ball, then whistles and leans back. "I see a broken wedding cake. Oops. Oh, and some violence. Make sure you don't get steak, because if you do, about half the guests are going to get food poisoning. But the good news is you *do* get married. Yay for you, and then...yeah. Hey, make sure to watch out for scissors. Can't tell when they'll be a problem, but you're going to want to listen to me on that one."

"I'm a crafter," Bianca says, sounding like she's pissed and then some.

"Might want to change fields." She shifts her gaze to Colter, who's staring at her like a fish gazing into the face of the fisherman who hooked him. "You too, actually. But you know what? It's not gonna rain on your wedding day, so that's pretty sweet. Oh, and a mourning dove is going to fly over you on your way out to the car. There's a chance it'll release waste onto you, the image isn't clear enough for me to tell, but that's pretty nice, huh?"

"What the fuck?" Bianca asks, popping up out of her chair. "Is this supposed to be funny?"

Whether or not it's supposed to be, it is, but I'm still at a loss about the twelve months thing. How did she know?

I decide that she couldn't have known. She was testing them, and they failed the test. I glance at Shauna, but her expression is unreadable.

Josie lifts up her hands, palms facing out. "I don't know if you're the type of people who read the fine print, but there are no discounts or refunds for people who aren't happy with their futures. That's why our slogan is *don't shoot the messenger*. I don't make the future. I'm just the person you paid to tell you about it. Now, does anyone else want a fortune while I'm here?"

"You'll be leaving," Bianca says tightly.

I squeeze Shauna's hip, hoping she'll laugh, but she steps away from me. Her eyes are shiny with tears, and panic tightens its hold on me.

There's more fuss behind us, something about broken cake and making wishes come true, but all I can see is the hurt on Shauna's face.

"Shauna..."

She turns and runs for the door. I'm about to go after her when Champ grabs my shoulder. Pulling away would cause a scene. I'm tempted to do it anyway, but I don't want other people to notice Shauna ran out like that. Not after Josie's twelve months bombshell.

They'll draw conclusions.

"That didn't go down well, man," Champ says in an undertone, as if there was a chance I hadn't noticed. Shouting breaks out behind him.

189

Bianca has Josie's crystal ball, and it looks like she's about to hurl it against the wall.

"You think a broken mirror causes bad luck? Just wait!" Josie shouts. "Just wait and see what happens if you break my precious."

Dammit, I have to do something about this, don't I?

I might not care if Bianca makes a fool of herself in front of everyone, but I'm the one who brought Josie here. It's on me to make sure she's safe.

"Let's get her out of here," I say.

So we do. Champ gets the crystal ball from Bianca after whispering in her ear, probably reminding her that their dearest friends are all watching, and then we escort Josie to her car with her things while the party resets for a third time.

Apparently, they're going to play charades, so I'm sorry to miss that, obviously. Champ also poured everyone a round of "emergency whiskey" that he had the foresight to bring, so I guess he's not all the way stupid.

All three of us are silent as we make the trip to Josie's car—I'm thinking about Shauna, and I'm guessing Champ is plotting an exit plan so he doesn't have to marry that shrew.

At least that's what I'd be doing.

Who knows what Josie's thinking, but she's cradling her crystal ball like it's a baby. I'm hauling the table for her.

When we get to the car, a VW Beetle so old it looks like it's held together with masking tape and a hallelujah, we help her stow her things.

Before she gets in, Champ toes the ground and says, "Sorry again about the..." He obviously doesn't know how to finish that remark, because he turns to *me*.

"I guess that must happen to you a lot," I finish. "If you tell people things they don't want to hear."

"Yeah," Champ says, feeling bolder. "Why didn't you make up, you know, happy shit? The kind of things women want to know about their wedding day."

She gives a long-suffering sigh and flips the veil over. She's younger than I thought—maybe late twenties—but she looks tired. I feel that down to my bones. Sometimes I wonder if I was born tired, or if it's the dreams that have made me this way—like I'm never more than half awake unless I stick my finger in a socket.

"If you wanted someone to tell you what you want to hear instead of what's true, you shouldn't have hired a psychic. You could have just looked at yourself in the mirror and said those things. It would have been cheaper and more convenient for both of us."

Then she jolts slightly, as if a bug bit her in the ass, and turns to me. "You're going to jail."

Now I'm the one flinching like a bug bit my ass. I guess she doesn't appreciate that I brought her here to put up with Bianca's bullshit, but she couldn't have said anything more certain to wig me out. It's been my fear my whole life, that I'll end up where the old man is. That the last of my shitty luck will finally run out.

"Thank you," I say. "I hope you have a glorious evening too."

She shrugs. "Don't shoot the messenger."

Then she gets in and drives away, leaving Champ and me standing together in the dark, warm September night, stars shining above us.

It would be the perfect evening for a porch sit with a beer, but I sure as shit won't be doing it with him. I need to find Shauna.

Except it hits me that this is my chance to get the goods from him—if there are any goods to be gotten.

"Sorry, man," I say, rubbing my jaw, putting on my best *aw shucks* look. "I had no idea it would go down like that. My friend told me she was the best, and I figured...hell, I thought she'd bring some tarot cards, show people a good time."

"It's not your fault," he says with a thump to my back. The car has already disappeared into the night, but he's still watching the road out of Camp Smileshine as if he'd like to run away.

"But it's not a big deal," I add. "Maybe she just woke up on the wrong side of the bed this morning. I mean, everything she said was bullshit, right? I know she was wrong about the whole twelve months thing."

He scrubs a hand over his face, looking as miserable as a Ken doll someone melted in a campfire.

"That's the thing," he says. "It wasn't bullshit."

I can't believe he'd be stupid enough to confess *to me* that he cheated on Shauna, but I've learned there's no limit on stupid, so I lean in and say, "You need to get something off your chest, man? You want to take a walk, maybe?"

I don't think he'll go for it, but maybe he's had more Bud Lights than I thought, because he agrees. "Yeah, that'd be good." He nods toward a small, pebbled path leading through the trees in the other direction. We walk a ways in silence, and then we reach a big pond. There's a wooden bench facing the water.

"Want to sit a minute?" I ask.

He heads toward it and sits down. It strikes me that it would be a pretty romantic spot if I weren't sitting next to Champ. Trees block our view of most of the lake, but it looks like the path goes all the way around.

"I didn't mean for it to go down like this, Doc," he says, sounding like he's near tears. "Shauna's important to me."

I don't say anything, because when a man's on the cusp of a confession, it's best to leave him to tumble over the edge by himself.

"It just happened...We were all at a party. Bianca spilled something on my shirt, and then she said I'd better take it off so she could work on the stain, and—"

"Whoa, now." I tap a hand on his arm to stop him. "I don't need a play by play, friend. Was Shauna there?"

He mumbles something under his breath.

"What's that, now?"

"It was her birthday party," he says louder, sounding miserable. "It happened at my house."

He's not miserable enough. Anger pounds through my veins, but I keep my voice even. "You fucked Bianca for the first time at your girlfriend's birthday party?"

"It was like you said!" He rises to his feet. "I realized she was the one. That she'd always been the one. We have more in common, you know?"

That's for damn sure.

"How long ago was that?"

"Almost twelve months, like that woman said. I didn't want to tell Shauna on her birthday, obviously, and there were some other things to work out, so..."

Champ keeps on babbling while my mind chews on that one...

I get to my feet too, blood rushing through my veins, sending adrenaline shooting through me. Fight or flight. Story of my life, but I already know what choice I'll be making tonight.

"When's her birthday?" I ask, my voice no longer even.

"You don't know?" he chokes out.

"When's her birthday?"

"September 30th."

The day of the wedding.

That's it. I don't warn him, I just round up and punch him in his stupid fucking Ken face.

twenty

SHAUNA

TWELVE MONTHS.

That should be what I care about. I've wondered, obviously. I didn't want to believe it, but it's become pretty obvious there's not a lot they wouldn't do. Bianca's been scratching at me for months, trying to get me to show that I'm upset. That I hate her for going for Colter. Or maybe she's worried I'm still in love with him. I don't know what she wants from me, but it feels very important not to give it to her.

It started when they announced they were getting married on my birthday, but when I sent her a "so excited" gif instead of calling her up sobbing, she doubled down by asking me to be her de facto maid of honor.

I sat with that one for a while before agreeing. Ultimately, I told her yes because of my mother.

The only times I'd ever seen my mother truly happy were when she'd brought someone down. She'd done it with me over and over again, because my father wasn't easy to bait. One of the things Bianca and I had bonded over, in the beginning, was that her mother had been the same way. Except Bianca has become just like both of our mothers.

Still, I'm not wandering down the path by the pond because of Bianca and Colt. I'm not crying because of them either. I'm upset because Leonard must have learned the truth from someone, either tonight or last night, and this was how he chose to tell me. Maybe he figured it would be more dramatic if my fears were confirmed in front of thirty of Bianca and Colter's friends. In front of *Shelly*.

If so, he was right.

"Shauna," someone calls.

It's a woman's voice, and I hate myself for being disappointed.

I turn on the path to see Shelly. I must be the biggest idiot alive, because a sob bursts out of me, and I walk right into her arms.

"Oh, my dear girl," she says into my hair, rubbing my back.

I settle into her and take in her cookie smell like it's mine. Leave it to me to waste two years of my life on a man because I've always wanted a mother.

"Come with me," she says, and I let her lead me down the path like she's the pied piper and I'm a braindead mouse. I gasp because the path leads past a grouping of trees to the edge of the pond, where a little gazebo waits like something out of a fairytale, vines grasping the wooden surfaces. There's a dim solar light affixed to the top.

It's much more beautiful than the one I went to for comfort as a child, and I know at once that I'd like to make it out of clay. Maybe with a tentacle gripping the bottom slats of wood, because monsters are everywhere, even in the water lapping beneath lovely places.

We walk inside silently, then sit on the bench, looking out at the water.

"I like your boyfriend," she says kindly, and I laugh as I cry harder.

"No, you don't."

She tuts her tongue as she wipes under my eyes, clearing up the mascara, hopefully. "Maybe I don't know him well enough to have an impression, but I *do* like the way he's been looking at you all night."

I can't take any comfort in that. Leonard's told me on multiple occasions that he's a good liar.

But I don't want to think about him right now, so I just nod.

"Bianca isn't my choice," she says to me pointedly, meeting my eyes. "There's something spiteful and small about that girl. I thought so from the first time you brought her around."

I nearly choke on my own spit.

"But it isn't my choice to make."

"No," I agree. I pause, my heart thumping. Then I figure I might as well hash everything out. "Why'd you act so interested in my art if you didn't really want it in your shop? Colt kept putting me off, and then he asked me not to talk to you about it anymore."

Her hand lifts to her heart, a sorrowful look on her face. "Oh, Shauna. Colt and I went back and forth on it several times, but he... he didn't see what I did. And then he said you'd changed your mind and didn't want your art in Craft Me. He told me not to ask you about it because it would make you uncomfortable."

Which was exactly what he'd told me.

Anger floods me, burning away the tears, and I'm glad for it, because when I'm angry I want to break things. When I'm angry, I don't feel so broken.

At the same time, I'm...relieved. Because even though I don't get to keep Shelly—even though she'll never be *my* Jelly Mom, at least she didn't reject me the way I'd thought.

"Oh..." I say. "I see."

She pats my hand, her face tight. "I swear, sometimes that boy acts just like his father."

It's not a compliment. Colt's father left her two months after she gave birth to him.

"What can I do for you, honey?" she asks. "Can I bring you a beer? A snack? Get your man for you?"

"No," I say, sounding harsher than intended. "I need some time alone. I think I'll sit out here for a while."

"In the dark?"

"It's not dark," I say, gesturing to the solar light on top of the gazebo and the stars and full moon over the lake.

"You got your phone?"

I lift it from the pocket of my cutoffs.

It's obvious she doesn't want to leave me here by myself, but after another tight hug that I soak in as if I'm thirsty dirt, she walks off, giving me a backward glance full of sweetness.

I soak that in too—I'm going to need it.

After she's gone, I step out of my sandals to feel the wood under my feet, something that's always grounded me. Then I sit stewing for several minutes, my mind full of fire and brimstone. I want to decimate Bianca and Colter. A plague of crickets isn't enough. I want...I need...

There's the sound of footsteps approaching on the path, moving fast—running—and a shiver shakes through me. Because, Christ, Leonard had something going with the whole Jason thing. The gazebo is isolated and quiet but for the chorus of crickets and the occasional bird swooping down. It's a place good or bad things could happen without being noticed by anyone but nature.

Then Leonard steps out of the opening in the trees. He's sweating and his hair's a mess, sticking to his forehead in places. His tattoos are muted in the low light from the gazebo and the stars. He looks good enough to eat, and I can't deny I'm relieved to see him. Then again, I befriended Bianca. Maybe I have poor judgment.

"Oh, it's you," I say as coldly as I can muster. "How'd you find me?"

"I ran into Shelly on the path," he said, breathing hard as if he's trying to catch his breath. "She told me where to go. And I remembered what you said about that gazebo near your folks' place." He takes a few steps closer, then leans against one of the wooden supports of the gazebo.

His gaze meets mine, and even though I want to look away, I can't.

"I didn't know about the cheating," he says, huffing the words out. "Not until half an hour ago. I didn't tell the psychic to say that. She was free-balling."

Relief wants to wrap me up like a blanket, but I don't let it. Not yet. "How do I know you're telling the truth?"

He swears. "You don't. I'm...asking you to believe me. Also, you should probably know that we might have some trouble on our hands. There's a chance we're gonna get kicked out of Murderland."

"What kind of trouble are we talking about?" I ask, immediately on high alert.

"I punched Colter in the face."

"You *what?*" I ask, pushing toward him. He meets me halfway, standing on the floor of the gazebo, and I take his hand and lift it into the dim light. Sure enough, the scarred knuckles of his right hand are bleeding. I sweep my fingers softly over his knuckles.

"I'm sorry," he says, looking like he thinks I might throw him in the pond. "I fucked up. But I guess the psychic lady was right about the twelve months thing. Sorry about that too. He admitted to it, and then he told me about your birthday, and I just...snapped."

Tears fill my eyes again, and I lift his hand to my mouth, pressing a kiss in the center, and then hold it to my chest. "You did that for me?"

Rafe would have hit Colter for me, of course, and I could have hit him myself—hard enough for his balls to retract—but for some reason this feels different. It feels like some sort of declaration.

He studies me in the dark, then he reaches his other hand up and thumbs away my tears. "I sure as shit didn't do it for me. I've been trying to stay out of trouble. Which you probably won't believe after tonight."

Another thought pummels into me. "Does Shelly know?"

"I'm sure she does now. He was farther down the path from where I saw her."

"Did you knock him out?" I ask, my heart racing. Not because I'm worried about Colt, but because Leonard could get into trouble for this. Colt's not a litigious guy, but Bianca has been looking for ways to screw me over lately. She'd probably delight in the opportunity.

"No. I told him he could punch me back, but he didn't." He shrugs and looks off. There's an expression in his eyes I can't read, something I've become used to with him. "He said he didn't blame me."

"Leonard, what are you doing out here?"

He meets my gaze again, and his eyes are warm. "I needed to see you. I know you don't think much of me, but I couldn't let you think I'd do something like that."

My heart expands and breaks at the same time. I pull the top of his shirt down and kiss him. He makes a sound of surprise, then kisses me back like he's desperate for it. Within seconds we're tearing into each other in the fairytale gazebo, our hands in each other's hair, our bodies pressed together, our mouths clashing like it's a battle each of us wants to win. He pulls his hand from my hair and reaches under my shirt, and the feeling of his hot, callused hands on my flesh unleashes something wild in me—maybe that tiger he's always talking about.

I break our kiss with a bite to his bottom lip. Trailing my hand down to touch his hardness through his shorts, I say, "You know, I had a dream about you once."

"Only once?" he says, moving his hand up to the bottom of my bra. His fingers skate across it, sending tingles cascading through my body.

"Let's call it a recurrent dream." I rub as I talk, feeling him get harder under my hand. The fact that we're out here in the breeze, just off that path anyone could come down, is an unexpected turn on. Even more so than earlier.

"That's my tiger." His other hand moves around to my back, and within seconds my bra falls to the slats.

"You have a gift," I say, the words turning into a moan as he cups my tits. "You can take my shirt off."

"No," he practically growls. "If someone comes down here, I don't want them to see you. Tell me what happened next in your dream." He leans in and kisses my neck and then grazes his teeth down it.

I swear before continuing, "We were out on my front porch, and you bent me over the railing—"

"I like where this dream's going," he murmurs against me.

"Do you have a condom, Leonard?"

He leans back to look at me, a corner of his mouth hitching up. "I'm a hopeful man. I've been carrying one around since I met you."

"A delusional man then."

"Not so delusional, it turns out." He finds my nipple, and a happy sigh escapes me as he rolls it between his fingers. It's the hand he punched Colt with for disrespecting me. I'm uncomfortably turned on, my panties wet from it.

He reaches for the button of my cutoffs.

"But you said—"

"That we're keeping most of our clothes on. Not that I'm not going to fuck you. They won't be able to see much of you beneath the waist, and we'll hear them before they come out of the woods."

I'm not so sure of that. I'm so attuned to him, I probably wouldn't notice if the rest of the guests stampeded the gazebo. There's a light breeze, and feeling it against my arms and legs is a reminder that we're out here in the open.

"Keep talking, Tiger," he says, pushing my jean shorts down. I step out of them, and he sucks in a breath when he sees my green lace thong. "You wear that for me?"

"That depends. Do you appreciate it?"

He cups my ass, then slaps it, the edges of fingers so close to where I need them—the slight pain radiating hotter need through me. "Oh, hell yes, I appreciate it. You're going to keep that on while I sink into you. But first I want to hear about the rest of your dream."

He shifts his hand to the front, toying with me, while his other hand dips back beneath my shirt to play with my nipple. It's only fair that I get to play, too, so I push his shorts down and grab his thick cock around the base, pumping with my hand.

"You miss it?" he asks as he steps out of the shorts and his sandals.

"Yes," I admit.

He grunts and says, "You were saying?"

"So you bent me over the railing—"

"Like this?" he asks, turning me and pinning me against one of the sides of the gazebo, my torso bent over the broad railing.

"Just like that," I manage, my body so attuned to his hand on my back, the other palming my ass again. "And you started to fuck me like that while the neighbor watched us from her porch."

He leans in close, his body layered over mine, and whispers into my ear, "I knew you were a dirty girl."

Then he pulls away, and even though I know it'll just be for a few seconds, I have to fight the impulse to tug him back.

"Can you step up onto the supports between the slats?" he says. "I need to reach that pretty pussy."

I do, my heart pounding. I stand with my feet between the slats, my body bowed over the railing toward him.

I hear him take something out, then the ripping of a wrapper. My whole body is an ache. "She only rated us a two-point-five out of ten, Leonard," I say. "She lifted up a placard and everything. It was an insult."

"We can do better than that." He leans over me again and kisses my neck, his hand reaching around and under the lace of my under-

201

wear, circling my clit. I can feel him behind me, hard and close. It's the sweetest torture I've ever endured. "You're so wet for me, Tiger. Does it turn you on to be out here with me like this? To be doing something bad with someone bad?"

He's *not* bad. But I can't say that now. I won't say anything that might make him stop. It's been so long since I've had anything but a silicone dick between my legs, and it was *never* like this with Colter. Who am I kidding? It's never been like this with any of the men I've slept with.

I can't seem to help myself with Leonard. Right from the beginning, I couldn't look away from him. Even in his raggedy old band shirts and ripped jeans, maybe especially in them, he looks like a hot fudge sundae I'd like to gorge myself on. I've tried fighting it, but I'm sick of fighting this, because it feels so good. So very good.

"*Yes*," I say, turning my head and capturing his mouth. I bite his bottom lip, and he grins against me. I feel him reaching back, adjusting himself. The anticipation has my whole body on edge, every molecule waiting for him. His eyes flutter shut as his cock slowly sinks into me, the sensation so perfect, so fucking magical, that I nearly come on the spot. I settle for kissing him again.

"You fit me so well," he says, running a hand up my back and into my hair as he pulls out and thrusts back in, the movement pushing my body against the slats. My knees are shaking from the onslaught of sensation. It seems like I should fall, like I *will*, but he's holding me in place. A sound I don't recognize as my voice escapes me as he reaches his other hand around for my clit.

"She was lying if she didn't rank us a ten, Tiger."

"That's what...I...was thinking," I say, the words coming out in spurts as I push back into his thrusts. "More like an eleven."

"Your pussy is an eleven."

I laugh, but it turns into a moan when he lifts off me and thrusts in harder, one hand still on my back, in my hair, and the other circling my clit while he works me with his cock. He changes the angle as if he's experimenting, and when I moan, he says, "That's it, Tiger. That's the spot," and he stays there, stroking me slowly and then faster. The breeze touches my skin where I'm bared to it, to him. I can feel the old wood beneath my chest, see the water beneath us, that hint of woods. Anyone could come around that bend. Anyone. I wouldn't hear them; I wouldn't notice if a fire siren started blasting through the woods.

The pleasure is working through me, boiling my blood, and I know it won't take me long now.

"Leonard, I'm close," I say, and he leans down so his head is close to mine again.

"Thank the Christ," he whispers in my ear, "because I don't know how much longer I can go for."

His face and hair are sweaty from the effort of fucking me, and somehow that turns me on too. So does the sight of a bird landing on the water thirty feet from us and the view of the trail that leads back to the cabins.

I feel myself teetering on the edge, and he swears gutturally as his fingers circle my clit and he buries his cock down deep. "That's it baby. Grip my cock just like that."

And that's it. That's all it takes. I push back against him hard as I come, needing as much of him as possible, and he gathers me up in his arm and holds me to him as he comes too, saying my name in my ear.

The last thought I have before someone screams is that I'm in danger of doing something truly stupid, like falling for him.

twenty-one

LEONARD

"I TOLD you this looked like Jason's hangout," I say with a groan as I pull out of the best place I've ever been allowed to visit.

I've always liked sex, what's not to like? For however long it takes, you don't need to think about anything but feeling good and making someone else feel good. But sinking into Shauna was...

I don't have words for it.

I take off the condom and knot it before stuffing it back into the package. Let it never be said that I corrupt youth, because I pull on my shorts and underwear and stuff it back into my pocket rather than leaving it on the gazebo floor.

Shauna has lifted up from the railing, still in that shirt but with nothing else on but that little tease of a thong. I like the look. I palm her ass because it really is one of my favorite things, shapely and strong, perfectly rounded for my hand.

"Do you think something bad happened?" she asks, looking startled. I'd like to think it's because of what we did, because eleven out of ten, I would do it again. And again. *And again.* Maybe it's the last couple of months of no sex that's done it, but I think I'm already addicted to this woman. To the feeling of her around me, to the taste of her pussy, to her kisses and her bites, and her claws.

I don't know what I'm doing.

"Nah," I say. It was a single scream, no follow-up, and there's at least thirty people here. If something truly bad happened, we'd be hearing about it. "I'm guessing Bianca just got a look at Champ's face. There's a pretty good chance we're going to get thrown out on our asses. He's gonna have a shiner for those photographs next week. No way she'll forgive me for that."

Shauna snorts, making me smile. "He can hold a flower over it. Anyway, I don't care. I hope they *do* throw us out."

"Really?" I ask, getting in another good feel of her perfectly round ass as she reaches for her shorts and bra.

I should have pocketed the bra when I had a chance.

"Really." She slides the shorts on. The sight of her putting them on is sexy, even though I prefer the view when there's nothing but a piece of lace keeping me from where I want to go.

"Well, I guess we'd better go face the music, Tiger."

She surprises me by reaching up and cupping my face in her soft hand. Then she gets on her toes and kisses me. Something warm fills my chest, and the feeling of panic comes back—just the razor's edge of it for now.

"Thank you for that."

I laugh. "You know, two days ago, you told me you'd never fuck me, and now you're thanking me for orgasms. You're making my head spin."

"Maybe you're making my head spin too."

I don't mean to, but I kiss her again, then lift my face to look at her. There's barely an inch between us, maybe two. I can see a few freckles across the top of her nose and a small scar, barely a half inch, above her eyebrow.

I'd like to know what it's from so I could punch whoever did that to her too. Even if it was a header into a coffee table.

"That was incredible," I say. "Hell, I'll even roll out a five-dollar word. It was stupendous."

Her nose wrinkles, making those freckles dance. "Look at you, being generous."

"You bring it out in me."

She smiles up at me. "I don't know if it's because it's been so long, but I'm thinking we might need a ten-dollar word for it."

"How long?" I ask.

"Nine months."

"Nine months?"

She laughs at the look on my face. "Yes, I know. Might as well be a century for you. It's a surprise I wasn't re-virginized."

"No," I say as I reach up and trace those freckles. "It's been some time for me too."

"A week?"

"A couple of months. Maybe three."

Her look of surprise makes me laugh. "You think I bang women in fast food bathrooms. Your grandmother told me."

"Was I wrong?"

"It may have happened before, but that don't mean it's a habit."

She shoves my arm, but I wrap it around her. "I've been trying to do things differently. I don't want that life anymore."

The look she gives me settles in deep. It feels as good as a double shot of whiskey on a cold winter's day—and as bad as the hangover you'd get after downing too many of them. Because I really don't know what I'm doing, and she may be the one to pay the price.

Shoving those thoughts down, I say, "Now, let's go get run out by some pitchforks."

She laughs, and we slide on our sandals and start walking toward the opening of the gazebo. I'm fond of this gazebo. I'm tempted to burn it down so no one else can ever use it for anything, or maybe move in with my toothbrush and pillow.

As we head back toward the main cabin, she tells me about the other lie Champ told—how he'd convinced her it was his mother who wasn't interested in stocking her art when it was him all along. If I'd felt some respect for him for admitting he'd deserved a punch for messing around on my tiger, it dies a quick death. I want to hit him again.

"We can't let them uninvite us," I blurt, grabbing her hand. "No way is this done."

Shauna stops in her tracks but doesn't release my hand. "What do you mean? You just punched the groom in the face. You were right. There's no way Bianca will let that slide, even if she wants to keep messing with me."

"We're gonna make those psychic's predictions come true. Bianca will think she's cursed or some shit." Somehow it feels important, like this is what was meant to happen. Not in a fated way, but in a *we're going to make our own fate* way.

"Bianca doesn't believe in that kind of thing," Shauna says. "She's a cynic." But I can tell I have her attention.

"Let's make her believe."

"She's not going to let *you* come to the wedding."

"So? Tell her you've dumped me. You can make it happen on your own. I'll help from the outside."

She watches me for a moment before saying, "I'm not saying I can't do this without you, but I'd rather not."

I get that tickle in my chest again. "I want to see it through too," I say, but I let go of her hand. I can't allow myself to get used to this. "We'll see what we can work out."

When we get within view of the main cabin, there's a small group of people gathered around the porch with lanterns. No pitchforks yet, but unless they're out there whispering ghost stories to each other, they got all the makings of a problem.

As we get closer, Bianca steps to the front of the gathering. "It's them," she shouts.

Fuck, are we about to get murdered? Because if so, I would have preferred to go out while I was still inside of Shauna. I've always thought that's the way I'd like to die—balls deep in a beautiful woman.

But no one tries to run us down. They stick where they are as we get closer, like they're afraid to go near the woods.

"Where *were* you?" Bianca asks, her voice shrill. Champ's next to her with a hangdog smile, his eye swollen. "Don't you know there's a psychopath on the loose? Someone wandered into the camp and punched Colter in the face and tried to steal his wallet. Everyone else has already left. We've been looking for you and trying to call. We even went to your cabin to warn you, and there was a horde of grasshoppers in there." She says this last part with a shudder. "One of them..." She pauses and swallows, as if she needs to scrape up the bravery to continue. "One of them got stuck in my *hair*. Another one..." She takes in a deep breath. "Another one almost jumped in my mouth when I was screaming. This place is a *horror* show."

Well, shit, I guess those little suckers found a way out of their box. I swallow down the rest of what she said and glance at Champ, who gives me a slight nod. I don't know what his game is, but he had my back. Either so he'll get a future chance to screw me over in a different, worse way, or because he really knows he deserved the punch. Given my knowledge of the world, I'm guessing it's the first.

His mother's standing with them, along with a couple of meat-heads. Shelly clearly didn't say a word to Bianca about having seen us in the woods. I feel like we did Jelly Lady dirty, because she's apparently cool as shit.

"Grasshoppers?" Shauna repeats, and damn, she's a good liar when she needs to be, because there's not a bead of sweat on her face.

"I'll be complaining to management," Bianca says. "What a fucking disaster." She glances around. "We don't even know if that psycho's still here, hiding in the woods somewhere."

Shauna has an *oh shit* look, probably because she didn't put two and two together to make four. Of course, Bianca's the sort of person to complain. If Shauna feels the need to make this right for Murderland, I'll help her, although I'll bet it won't hurt them to have a review like that. It'll make the place sound like more fun than it is, that's for sure.

A glance inside the main cabin suggests it's still full of ABC crap, like an abandoned baby shower. That'll be fun for the Smileshine people.

"Well, shit," I say. "Sounds like we'd better grab our bags and get a move on, huh?"

"We'll come with you," Bianca insists. "We should all travel as a group. In those slasher movies, it's only when they break off that he comes for them."

She's being awful dramatic seeing as she's the one who chose to party down in Murderland.

"Really, it's okay," I say, wrapping an arm around Tiger. "My girl here's got a black belt in taekwondo. The psycho will think twice before messing with us."

They must be in a hurry to bounce, because we only a get a few weak objections before they peel off, leaving the mess in the cabin behind, and we head down the long gravel road to our place.

We've made it about halfway before laughter explodes out of Shauna. It's the kind of laughter that catches, and soon it's rumbling through me too. The image of Queen Bee opening the door to that cabin and getting a face full of crickets is fucking funny—even if we're going to have to brave our own horde to reclaim our shit. I grab Shauna up and swoop her around in a circle, hooting, and she laughs harder, her whole body shaking with it. Then I capture the rest of her laugh with a kiss before setting her down on the gravel.

She grins up at me. "You know what, this has been fun. I think it's the most fun I've had in a long time."

"Me too, Tiger. Me too."

I'm not blowing smoke. I feel more alive when I'm with her,

even when we're not causing trouble. There's this...connection, I guess you call it, that I sensed from the beginning, and it's gotten stronger.

She turns to look at me while we walk. "You know, Nana's not expecting me until tomorrow. Maybe we can still have an adult sleepover?"

There's that clutching feeling in my chest again, panic trying to grab me down, but I fight it. Because I want this. I want to take her back to the purple house and explore more of her. Make her forget that Champ or anyone who came before him ever touched her. I want to watch *The Sopranos* with her head in my lap instead of on the other side of the phone. I might not know what it means, but I want it.

"Way ahead of you. I downloaded the entire series of *The Sopranos* after we watched that episode last night."

"Something tells me you torrented them."

"Why waste good money on a show that's been out for twenty years?"

She nudges me with her arm but doesn't give me a hard time about it.

When we get to the cabin, she turns to me again, my arms still around her, and looks up. "Thank you, Leonard."

"You already said that."

"Thank you for having my back. You didn't need to."

I'm about to tell her that I enjoyed fucking her that way, seeing her bent over the gazebo railing, her perfect ass lifted to me like an offering, but she's being genuine. Even though it makes me uncomfortable, I say, "It's easy to have your back, Sugar. And not just because you promised me that clay lesson this week." I run a hand along her jaw, ending at her pointed, fairy chin. "Now, let me run in there and grab the bags. If I scream, don't mind me none. I don't like grasshoppers."

"What if Jason jumps out at you with a knife?" she asks with a smirk.

"Then step in, for the love of God. I don't have your fancy taekwondo moves."

We spend the whole car ride talking, and we nearly get into a wreck when a cricket jumps out of my pocket. Going into that cabin, I felt like Indiana Jones, but I got all of our stuff out, and Shauna kissed me like I was her hero.

It was worth it, is what I'm saying, although I'll think twice before I pull that particular trick again.

When we get to the little purple house, my pulse amps up. Reese hasn't messaged, but maybe he's here. Or maybe he was here. But it takes all of a minute to figure out no one's touched the stuff in the kitchen.

I'm tempted to hit the wall, but I've already fucked up my knuckles, and the only thing it'd get me is a sore hand and a talking-to from Mrs. Ruiz. Still, there's something sour in my throat. There's an old need to destroy something and make a fire from the ruins.

"He'll be back," Shauna says, rubbing my back as I stare at the stuff on the table, taking a tally in case something is missing. It's all there, though. Every last thing we bought for him. "You just keep letting him know he has somewhere to come back to. That's what mattered most when I was a kid."

I glance back at her. "You ever run anywhere except to Constance?"

She gives a shrug. "Sure. I tried to go to the beach one time. I like the beach."

"Did they ever hurt you?" I ask, the words escaping in a grumble. I know they're dead, have been for almost twenty years, but I'd be tempted to light fire to their bones if her answer is yes.

"Not like that," she says, shaking her head. "They were more... absent. I didn't understand why they wouldn't just let me leave. My mom had post-partum depression, but it never seemed to go away. My dad worked around the clock, and she stayed home and smoked and watched TV all day. She didn't like having me in the house most of the time. It wasn't a problem when I was little, because we lived near Nana and Grandpa Frank, but then my dad got a new job in Raleigh and moved us away."

"And that's when you started running."

"Yeah...I figured they'd let me go if I made enough of a nuisance of myself. I just...I needed to be with someone who loved me." She watches me for a second, her throat working with something she wants to say, then asks, "How about you?"

Laughter huffs out of me. "Took me a while to realize I *should* run. When I was little, I thought my old man was cool as shit, always bringing back gaming systems and new TVs and jewelry for my mom. Always moving us to new places. I got wise before I was smart enough to get away from him. The second time I tried to run, he nearly killed me, so I stopped trying until I knew I could make it."

In my head, he's chasing me, my old Little League bat in his hand. He broke it on me, then kept on with his fists. That's an old favorite that keeps coming back to me at night.

She lifts a hand to her throat but doesn't touch me. Somehow she knows she shouldn't touch me right now. "And your mother?"

"She let him do whatever the fuck he wanted. Didn't matter to her where it was coming from or how we got it. And she figured a boy needed to learn to take a few knocks. All she cared about was herself."

"So he's the one who—"

She cuts herself off, her eyes on my white knuckles. I'm

squeezing the edge of the table, consumed with the need to destroy something. I don't want to do it in front of her, though. I don't want to keep talking either, but I've already gone this far. The words keep flowing out. "Yes, Tiger. He's the one who taught me to take things that weren't mine. It helped him and his crew to have someone small with him. Someone who could run fast. Someone who could be a part of their cons. My father figured if he could teach me young enough, I'd be able to help him with other stuff by the time I got old enough." I pause, swallow. "But one day, he and his pal broke into a place that wasn't empty. I watched them beat a guy until he couldn't lift his head anymore. So I ran. My old man wouldn't let me leave, though. The first time he found me, he beat me and told me to mind myself. The next time, he took to me with a baseball bat until I couldn't move. After that, I got smarter. I stuck around until I knew I could outsmart him."

"Shit, Leonard." She reaches for my hand, the one that's gripping the table, and runs her finger across the back.

I pull back from the comfort and from the look in her eyes, which isn't pity but feels like it anyway. "You don't have to feel bad for me. I liked it, in the beginning. It felt like a game. And I'm the one who had the pleasure of turning that fucker in so he could rot in jail."

"Maybe you're more like Burke than you think," she says, looking at me with a pointed stare. "You're not a bad man."

I feel a surge of something. Rage. Self-hatred. *Need.* Need most of all. I didn't ask for it. But it's there, and I can't deny it. I reach out and sweep all that shit off the table with my arm, boxes bouncing off the floor. Something cracks. It's a bigger mess than all that ABC crap in the cabin from earlier, and I'm the dumbass who'll have to clean it up, but it feels good.

Shauna looks startled. "Why'd you—"

"I'm no hero. It's best if you understand that now. I'm no one's good news, Shauna."

213

Her eyes get wider as I open the button of her shorts and shove down both them and that thong I like. She helps me by pulling them off. Then I lift her up off her feet and sit her on the table, spreading her legs and stepping between them.

"I'm going to fuck you now. If you don't want that, you should leave."

"I'm not going anywhere," she says, spreading her legs wider.

"I'm trying to warn you that you *should* leave." But even as I say it, I'm grabbing a second condom from my pocket. Always be prepared for the best and the worst.

"Aren't you listening?" She reaches for me and pushes down my shorts. Just like that, she's wrapping her hand around my cock and pumping. "I *want* you to fuck me."

I don't try to prime her this time. I put on the condom and shove myself home because I need it. *I need her.*

The table moves back a few inches with the thrust, and Shauna wraps her arms around me so she doesn't lose her balance, her nails digging into my back as I thrust into her again, needing to lose myself in her wet warmth.

I pull away, my cock still inside her, so I can take off her shirt and bra. She looks like a dream, sitting there on my table, my cock inside of her, her gorgeous tits bared to me, her hair bright violet under the harsh lighting. It's the kind of dream I'd like to have someday.

"You're so fucking beautiful." I pull out and then thrust in again, lowering my head to suck her nipple.

"So are you," she says, panting as she grinds against me.

"You didn't seem to think so when I first met you."

She moans as I grab her thighs and hike them up, going in deeper. "Of course I did."

Smiling, I press her down onto the table, her head against the wood, and lean in to kiss her. Her hands circle my back and find their way under my shirt, pulling me closer, so maybe I'm not the only one who feels like nothing could be enough. I feel a deep need to be buried inside of her, to soak her in. To let her help me beat back the void.

And that scares the ever-loving shit out of me.

I kiss her neck and then stand up, telling myself it's so I can see her lying back, taking my dick, and not because I'm a coward.

"I want you to watch me fuck you," I tell her.

"There's nothing wrong with my eyes."

The table bangs against the wall, and I laugh as I thrust again, making it bang a second time. "What do you say we leave a mark on the wall?" I pant out.

"Sounds a lot like a challenge."

"You know how I feel about challenges."

But I forget all about the table and challenges, because she grabs my hand and tugs me down to her again. I lean in close and kiss her. Of course I do.

"I'm close, Leonard," she says.

"I want you to run your nails down my back when you come, Tiger," I say in her ear. "Screw the wall, I want you to mark *me*."

She slides her hands up into my shirt, and as she clenches around me, she digs her nails into my back and scratches. The pleasure and the pain twine together, instantly shoving me over the edge with her. It's a long one, and it echoes through me as I prop my elbows on the table on either side of us.

"Twelve," she says in a husky, sexy-ass voice.

It takes me a second to figure out what she means, but then I start laughing.

She smooths a hand down my back, her touch gentle now. "Did I hurt you?"

"Yes, and it felt damn good."

She laughs and then kisses my scruffy cheek, her lips soft. It hits me that it feels good to have her here, in my space. That's not something I do. I've gone over to women's apartments or hotel rooms. I've fucked them in semi-public locations. But I haven't brought anyone to my place. It's partly because of the dreams, and partly because if you let people enter your private space it becomes harder to keep them at a distance.

I don't want her at a distance.

I also can't let her get too close.

But when she asks, "Do you want to watch *The Sopranos?*" My answer is immediate. Thoughtless.

"Yeah, Tiger. I do."

So that's exactly what we do. She holds me, and even though I know she's doing it because of what I told her, because of the things I unloaded on her that I should have kept buried deep, I let her.

twenty-two

SHAUNA

Group text: *The Evans Sisters Want the Goods*
Mira: *Well???????? Was it an eleven out of ten or what?*
Me: *Twelve.*
Mira: *Fuck. I feel like I should have a cigarette in honor of you.*
Delia: *You stopped smoking six months ago.*
Mira: *You try sticking to your new year's resolutions under these conditions. Byron practiced Free Bird on his guitar until three a.m. last night.*
Delia: *Lucas is moving out of his apartment in a few weeks. Maybe you could live there? Do you want me to talk to him?*
Mira: *Doesn't he have a roommate?*
Delia: *You'd barely see him. Danny keeps to himself, and he's a really nice guy.*
Mira: *Have you met him, Shauna?*
Me: *I think so? I don't remember, honestly.*
Delia: *Um. You've met him too, Mira. More than once.*
Mira: *Huh. There's something to be said for forgettable.*

Message from Grandpa Fruckface:

It's been thirty-four days since you last responded to me.

LEONARD and I fall asleep in his room after watching a couple of episodes of *The Sopranos*, but when I wake up, he isn't next to me. My heart feels like a stupid rabbit, lost in my chest, because all I can think is that he ran off after opening up to me last night. But when I go downstairs, he's curled up on the couch, which is much too small for him, dressed only in his underwear. The sight of him like that—vulnerable, his scar and his tattoos revealed to me—makes my throat tight.

So does the fact that he left me to sleep down here in a much less comfortable place. He's trying to put space between us again, and the intelligent thing to do would be to listen. A couple of weeks ago, having space from him sounded like a fantastic idea, but now left is right and right is left.

Hearing Leonard talk about his past broke something in me, because I hurt for that little boy. My parents were neglectful jerks who shouldn't have been allowed to procreate, but they didn't use or harm me. What I've learned explains a lot about Leonard, but there are still so many secrets I want to know and don't.

Gidget.

His time as muscle.

The way he changed his name more than once after leaving Asheville, when once would have probably done it.

I could probably think of five thousand questions for him.

He groans and looks up at me, squinting. "What time is it?"

"Ten o'clock," I say with a snort.

"It's a Sunday. What are you doing awake, devil woman?"

He surprises me by pulling me down onto the couch with him, snuggling me up to him.

"What are you doing down here?" I ask. "You wanted to sleep

in a less comfortable bed?" I don't want to sound needy, but I hear it in my voice.

He runs a hand up my back. "I woke up and couldn't get back to sleep. Didn't want to disturb you."

"We need to pick up Bean," I say, making no move to get up. It feels...*nice.*

"Bean's a creature of the night like we are," he says, running a hand down my back and settling it on my butt. "She'll be asleep."

I notice he doesn't say anything about bringing her to another shelter or trying to adopt her out. I shouldn't push him, but I do a lot of things I shouldn't. "You're going to keep her, aren't you? I think what happened at the shelter yesterday was what Josie the Great would call a sign."

He makes an amused sound. "Not a sign. More like you and your grandmother setting me up."

I gasp and turn in his arms. "How'd you know?"

He grins and bops me on the nose. "Caught you, Tiger. I figured it out this morning when I was trying to get back to sleep. I Googled the shelter's policy for taking back pets. Turns out it's a no-kill shelter. I'm pretty proud of you and Constance, actually, you conned me good."

"We both think you want her." I place my palms on his bare chest. "We think she's meant to be with you."

"I'll try." He stares at me as he says it, and maybe I'm just believing what I want to believe, but it sounds like maybe he's talking about me too.

"Wouldn't want to disappoint my girls," he adds with a glimmer in his eyes.

When we get to the house, my neighbor Mrs. Applebaum is outside in her Adirondack chair, very pointedly watching us.

I give Leonard a significant look. "That her?" he asks under his breath, his eyes dancing with amusement.

"Yes. Doesn't she look like a low scorer?"

He waves to her before I can grab his hand. "Howdy, over there. It's a mighty fine day, is it not?"

She pouts, her mouth turning down. "I would say not, young man. The humidity is sixty-five percent."

"You're right about that," he says, "but you know what? I'd still give it a ten out of ten. Then again, *I'm* a generous scorer."

I bite back a laugh as she buries her head in the book she brought out with her. A prop, because she spends most of her time sitting out there and people watching.

Taking Leonard's hand, I lead him to the door but drop it so I can unlock and open it.

I figured Bean would react to our presence the way cats usually do—like she can't tell the difference between Leonard and the mailman, but she immediately runs up and does figure eights around his legs. The look of delight on his face as he crouches to pet her is something I'd like to capture. My hands itch for my clay and tools, and for the second time in weeks, I don't want to make only hideous and misshapen things.

There's a feeling of thank goodness in my heart, because it's been so long since I've made something I love, or the kind of monster that I'd like to be my friend.

"Well, hello, sugar," Leonard tells Bean in a soft, warm voice. "It's good to see you too."

"I'm going to assume you're talking to me," my grandmother says, prompting him to laugh. She's holding Bertie, who's squirming to get away, probably because he wants to nip at Leonard's heels the way he usually does.

"You know I wasn't, you old boot."

She gives him a wicked smile. "Just for that, I'm going to put you to work."

And she means it.

We spend the afternoon helping her move furniture around the house. Nana has decided feng shuing her bedroom was the best thing that ever happened to our house, and now the rest of the place has to be done to match. Since she supposedly has back pain, she's the director and we're her puppets.

Leonard's a good sport, but he doesn't touch me around Nana, so I'm guessing he doesn't want her to know what we're doing.

Whatever it is we're doing.

Bertie's a little stinker with Leonard, but he takes it with good grace. I'm starting to think my little man is jealous, so I make a point of fussing over him and giving him plenty of pets. Later tonight, there's some vanilla ice cream with his name on it.

We order a pizza after all of our sweaty work, and eat it outside in fold-up chairs in the back garden. Maybe Nana and I should add gardening to our bucket list, because it's more weeds than plants.

Leonard entertains us with stories about the two weeks he spent making pizzas in Tennessee, and how one of his co-workers accidentally baked a fingernail into one. Not exactly the kind of thing you want to hear while eating pizza, but he has us laughing anyway. Nana asks us about last night, and by unspoken mutual agreement, we leave out all of the sex, Colt's black eye, and the horde of crickets.

If we told her, she'd ask where I'd stayed last night, and that's a conversation I don't think either of us is ready to have with her. We can't exactly tell anyone what's going on between us if we don't know ourselves, can we?

When my grandmother excuses herself to use the bathroom, Leonard lifts his eyebrows at me and puts a hand on my thigh. "When do I get to play with clay?"

"When can you come by the studio?" I ask.

"When can you pick me up, Sweet Cheeks?" He grins, then adds, "I'll talk to Burke and text you. Maybe I can get out of doing something horrible at the flip house. Flooring's a bitch on my knees."

"Speaking of something horrible, what should we wear for the photoshoot next weekend?"

Bianca sent an email this morning to everyone who'd gone to the campground, apologizing for the "disaster" on Saturday night. It also assigned us colors to wear to the photoshoot.

"I've always wanted to try parachute pants," he says. "Think I could pull it off?"

"Maybe we should just skip it and save our ideas for the wedding. I figure we already ruined the photos because Colter's going to have to wear layers of makeup to hide that black eye."

"Black eye, you say?" my grandmother says, stepping out of the house. Damn it, for someone who claimed she couldn't move any furniture because of back pain, she can move like a ninja when she feels like it. Then again, that's one of the perks of aging—getting other people to do tedious shit for you.

Leonard pulls his hand back, but I know she noticed.

"Sure," he says, leaning back in his chair. "They said some psychopath broke into camp and punched him in the eye. Crying shame."

Nana reaches her fist out for a bump, and he laughs and gives it to her.

"I will say this for Colter," he adds. "He's not a snitch."

"Because he's afraid of that woman of his," she retorts. "And he *should* be. We had her over here dozens of times, didn't we, Shauna? For tea. For crafting. To cry her crocodile tears about her mama. And then what did she go and do?"

"Her mama?" Leonard asks, glancing at me.

"Was as difficult as mine," I say. "Nothing was ever good enough for her."

"Sometimes the apple don't fall far, huh?"

Maybe I'm reading too much into it, but it feels like there's a challenge layered into his words. Like he's saying his apple didn't fall far from the poisoned tree either, and Nana and I had better remember that before we go expecting things from him.

Nana leans over and shoves his arm. "You'd take that back, young man. My mother had a hairy chin and warts."

He grins at her, then me. "I said what I said, Constance, although I expect you own a tweezer."

"Maybe I should make you young people tweeze my chin."

"No offense, Nana," I say, "but I'd put you in a nursing home first."

"Hallelujah," Leonard says, leaning over to nudge me with his shoulder.

After he takes an Uber back to the little purple house with Bean, my grandmother and I relocate to our newly feng-shuied living room, which *does* feel more open with the couch in its new spot. She settles onto it with a sigh and says, "Shauna, be a dear and fix me some tea."

Bertie wags his tail, as if telling me he's ready for that ice cream, and climbs into one of his plush beds.

I'm happy to oblige them, mostly because I need a minute to collect myself before what's sure to be an interrogation.

When Nana and I are settled on the couch with our tea, our identically shaped feet propped up next to each other, I sigh and say, "Oh, out with it. I know you have something to say."

Bertie's on the floor, nose deep in the little dish of ice cream I set out for him, and he won't be coming up for air anytime soon.

She lifts her eyebrow and says, "You think I'm surprised you didn't listen to me about Leonard? What better way to get you to do something than to tell you to do the opposite? It's been like that since you were a little girl. If your bull-headed grandfather knew his ass from his elbow, he'd stop texting you altogether. Within a week, you'd be dropping by that harlot's pool to see if he'd had a heart attack."

I nearly drop the hot tea into my lap. "So, you *were* trying to set me up with Leonard?"

She lifts her shoulder and dips her head. "Not as such. You're an adult now, and you do what you want. But I wasn't opposed to the idea. From the first time I met him, he reminded me of you. Stubborn and funny. Quick."

Wounded, she means but won't say.

"I wouldn't say we're together." I set the tea down on the coffee table since I don't trust my hands. "He's made it pretty clear he sees himself as a bad bet."

"Then it's on us to prove otherwise to him. Don't you think?"

"He's not open to the idea of having a girlfriend, Nana. I'm not sure I want to go there with him either. The last thing I want..."

Is for my heart to get broken again. Is to let in someone who's going to reject me. Leonard calls me a tiger, but I've only become that way because when the people you love keep turning you away, you grow claws.

I cough, then continue, "We're just having a good time. There's no reason to make it any more or less than that."

"So you agree with him then?" she asks, giving me her best *Shauna, I'm disappointed with you* look.

"No," I argue, "but—"

"I think he's going to surprise everyone, himself most of all. There may be some setbacks, but he's headed in the right direction." She pauses, sipping her tea, and then sets it down. "And you're going to surprise yourself, too. Because you're nothing like your mama, Shauna May. Your grandfather and I tried our best, but she was missing a piece, and there was no one on this earth who could give it to her. Every time we had to bring you back to her, we cried together. That's the closest I've ever felt to that infernal man."

Pain radiates through my chest, because my secret fear is that I'm as twisted and ugly inside as the monsters I've been making for the last several weeks. It also hurts to think about my grandfather crying for me.

Maybe Rafe's right.

Maybe I don't need to cut Grandpa Frank off altogether.

My grandmother reaches for my hand and squeezes it, and when she meets my gaze, I'm alarmed to see there are tears in her eyes. "There's no end to the love inside of you, my sweet girl."

And before I know what's happening, I'm crying too.

twenty-three

LEONARD

BY FRIDAY, I've convinced myself that Reese has moved on. There's been no sign of him, and I've done about a dozen walk-throughs of the neighborhood over the last few nights—enough that one old bird yelled at me about casing her place. She has about five hundred bird baths outside, so you'd think she'd be grateful to anyone who'd take some off her hands. My next-door neighbor saw me walking around last night and warned me that there've been another couple of robberies.

I hope to hell Reese wasn't involved in them, but judging by his note, that's exactly what scared him off.

I've checked the missing person's list about a dozen times, and while a couple of new photos have popped up, his picture still isn't on there.

It doesn't mean he's dead, I keep telling myself.

It doesn't mean he's in trouble.

I'd moved on plenty, starting when I was just sixteen.

"What's on your mind?" Burke asks, giving me a sharp look. The weather's mighty fine today—even Shauna's sour neighbor would give it a five out of ten—so we're out back, working on replacing a few pieces of rotten siding. The paperwork for the business still hasn't gone through, so Burke's been picking me up every day, dropping me off every afternoon. Danny gave me a ride to the grocery store the other day, too, although I'm shit at planning meals, so I'm already out of nearly everything.

I want to tell Burke about Reese.

I want to tell him other shit too.

I want to tell him that I've avoided Shauna since last Sunday, even though seeing her is the only thing I really want to do. We texted a little on Monday and Tuesday—mostly photos of terrible clothes we could wear to the photoshoot to piss Bianca off. But then she told me Bianca had up and moved the photoshoot to next weekend because she still felt "psychological distress" over what went down at the campground. We agreed it was Champ's black eye that had done the deed, especially since she'd texted Shauna previously asking if "Doc" had any hints for getting rid of a black eye. I'd told her to use a raw steak, not because I thought it would work but because it would be another crappy experience for my old buddy old pal.

We don't have any more wedding stuff to show up for until the photoshoot and the rehearsal dinner, followed by the wedding itself. Then it'll all be over.

I haven't set a date for my clay lesson. Shauna's asked; I haven't answered. I also put her off when she asked if I wanted her to come over, even though the house feels empty and wrong with just me and the little terror cat running around.

It didn't used to feel empty. I used to like the quiet.

I've pulled up Shauna's number half a dozen times without calling or texting. Something has always stopped me. Maybe it's that I still have no idea what I'm doing, or how to do it—and if I mess up, she's the one who'll pay the price. The thought of being the one who takes away her smiles is more painful to me than the knife wound that left that scar.

Maybe it's also what Josie said. It's stupid, because I don't believe in psychics or airy-fairy shit, but it slid under my skin in the way a person's deepest fears do.

You're going to go to jail.

Bean's been scratching up the stair rails, but it's not in me to feel sorry for keeping her. Without her, there'd be nothing but the void, which has become wider. Because I haven't let myself see Shauna. Because Reese is out there somewhere, alone and probably scared. And because I can't bring myself to ask Constance out to lunch or for a drink because I'm avoiding her granddaughter like a coward and she probably knows it.

I keep watching *The Sopranos* because it helps me imagine Shauna watching it. Lying in her bed, her hair mussed, her ass cupped by pajama bottoms that are probably several inches shorter in my imagination than in reality. I think about slipping my hand into those shorts and making her come with my fingers again and again while we pretend to watch the show.

I want to tell Burke all of those things, except for obsessing about her sweet pussy, but I can't seem to open my mouth.

With Shauna, I can't stop talking, but it's different with him. Maybe it's because I've always felt like a problem for other people to fix, and I especially feel that way with Burke.

Or maybe it's because I've never forgotten the way we met.

I saw him as a target, a con. I feel the need to make up for that —even if it's not the kind of thing a person can hope to make up for.

I can still see Burke and the other guys in my mind's eye, sitting in that bar in their outdoor gear, shooting the shit. They looked comfortable as hell with each other, because even then they were like brothers. I was wearing hiking shit not because I enjoy scaling mountainsides but because I knew all of them did. So I took a seat at the bar near them, waiting for an in to their conversation. I felt like I did when I was a teenager who was homeless in the winter, walking past restaurants with fireplaces, groups of people who had scarves and sweaters and coats. I wanted to get closer, and not because of what it might get for me.

In the back of my head, I hear Shauna saying I should tell him about that too. She'd be right. She's right about a lot of things, but there are a few hits I know I'd never be able to recover from.

One of them is Burke turning his back on me and telling me I'm a lost cause.

Sighing, I run a hand through my hair.

"Not a damn thing's on my mind, brother. Just enjoying the sun. It feels good to work outside."

"It feels damn hot, is what it feels," he says. Then, "Nothing else weird has happened, huh? I mean after the truck getting jacked."

"Nope. There've been some other robberies in the neighborhood, so I'm guessing those guys are the ones who lifted the truck. No one's bothered with me or Mrs. Ruiz's place. It's been quiet as a church mouse." I feel the heaviness of that in my chest. If anyone had told me a few months ago that I'd be sad because no one had broken into my place, I'd have called them a lunatic. There goes life again, making a liar of me.

"Good." He nods, then slugs some water down from his bottle. "Our accountant said the paperwork should go through next week. We won't have to wait much longer to get you a new one."

I laugh at this. "We have an accountant?"

He grins back at me. "Sure do. He's called Danny."

"Danny did this shit for you?" I whistle. "I knew he was an ace with computers, but I didn't know he messed around with spreadsheets."

"You know Danny. He's always looking for ways to do shit for me because of the apartment." He gives me a sidelong look. "Hey, you know Delia's sister might be interested in moving in with him. She's in a bad situation right now, living with her ex. Do you think Danny would go for that?"

I hoot, because even though I don't know Mira well, she's obviously a live wire. "You just got done saying he wants to do you favors, so I'm guessing he won't complain, but I tell you what, it'll be fun as hell to see that go down. Couldn't think of two more different people."

He laughs and rests a hand against the siding of the house, then pulls it back quickly, because it probably feels like a hot plate. It might be nice out with the breeze, but the sun's still brutal back here.

"Maybe we need to put up a tarp over the deck," I say. "Make it a bit nicer for porch sitting back here."

"That's a good idea," he agrees, smiling.

I have to laugh, because he's giving me the kind of approving look I never got from any of my teachers. "Do I get a gold star?"

"Maybe a lunch beer."

"Even better," I say, following him in through the plastic sheet we got hanging where the sliding door will go once it comes in.

He grabs two from the cooler we brought over, and we clink bottles before he opens his with a bottle opener from the cooler. I pop mine with my teeth.

"Show off."

"What can I say? I got a wealth of useless knowledge."

"Want to sit for a minute?" he asks, nodding to the two folding chairs we have set up in the living room.

We get seated and he leans back a little and sighs, then sets his beer on the floor. "I'm going to ask Delia to marry me."

"For real?" I ask, even though it's not exactly a shock. They're the real deal, no question. I might give him shit about the whole thing, but I'm happy for him, even if he's agreeing to be with only one woman for the rest of his life—to stay with her, no matter how many times either of them screw up. To be steady and reliable. To be her rock.

All the things I'm pretty sure I can't do or be.

"For real," he says with a smile, and I'm glad I didn't tell him about Reese yet. My buddy needs this. I watch as he picks the bottle back and up and turns it around in his hand, pretending to be interested in the label.

"So, what's the other part you don't want to tell me?"

"I know you're going to give me shit," he finally says, meeting my eyes with a smile, "but I need your help with something."

I can already tell it's gonna be good.

"Give it to me."

He pauses, still playing with the beer bottle. "You know how Delia does those readings for kids in her mermaid costume?"

"Yes, buddy," I say slowly. "That's not the kind of thing you forget." I already have visions of Burke dressing up like a fish. No, a merman. Holy shit. This is going to give me material for years. I'm going to have to tell—

Except I haven't been talking to Shauna, really.

There's a tightness in my chest that I rub away, because this is Burke's moment, and it shouldn't be ruined by my bullshit.

"I thought..." He pauses, his cheeks flushing.

"Are you blushing?" I ask with a grin. "I'll be. Never thought I'd see the day."

"Oh, come on. I figured I'd dress up like that prince in *The Little Mermaid*. You know she'd like it."

My grin broadens. "Would she ever. You're some guy, Burke. So what do you need me for? To hold the video camera? Because there's no way we're not getting this on tape and showing all the guys." I snap. "We'll have a group viewing. We can even call up Drew in Puerto Rico."

"Negotiable," he says. "I was thinking you could help me get dressed."

"Oh, so I'm your hair and makeup?"

"I knew you were going to give me a hard time about this."

"It's basically my job. But sure, bud. You got it. Of course I'll help. I feel privileged you asked. I'm really into wedding shit these days."

He gives me a *you're full of crap, Leonard* look, but I'm being serious. About the feeling privileged part anyway.

I don't deserve his friendship.

I'll *never* deserve it.

But I'll take it anyway.

Hell, maybe I can offer to snap some engagement photos for them after the proposal, since I'm apparently the maestro of love. We can make a whole day of it.

You're avoiding Shauna, the voice in my head says.

That voice is fucking correct, however Doc hasn't been entirely asleep on the fake boyfriend gig. Last night, I did some research on where to buy mourning doves. It's apparently illegal, and since I'm pretty sure my pot dealer doesn't have a line on illegal birds, I spent half an hour researching how to catch myself some. That's frowned upon too, obviously, but there's no end to the messed-up stuff you can find on the internet.

Screwing with the cake is easier. I can give it a donkey kick as they pull me away from the reception. The thought makes me smile, but there's a burn in my chest when I think about seeing Shauna again. She must be disappointed in me. She's probably already realized it was a mistake to let me in. That she was right about me all along.

"Hey," Burke says again.

I take a sip of beer. "Hey."

He rolls his eyes. "There's something else I've been meaning to talk to you about."

"The weather? The Carolina Panthers? Because I'm gonna be straight with you, man. I've done some sports betting back in the day, but I honestly couldn't give a shit. That right there is a good way to lose money if you don't know what you're doing."

"I've been seeing this therapist. Only for a couple of weeks now, but it's really helping me. I was wondering if you'd ever think—"

"No," I say, already shaking my head. "No, man. I don't want to relive all of that. I can't."

"All of what?" he says, raising his eyebrows. There's a bead of sweat traveling down his forehead because we've got no air on in here, only a couple of lousy box fans. We won't have the air conditioning on until the door's delivered.

"You know there's some bad stuff I left behind."

We've danced around this conversation before. In the past, he hasn't pushed me. I'm hoping today's not the day he decides to put in his heels.

"I know. But you're not avoiding it by hanging on to it, buddy."

"That something the shrink told you?"

"Sure." He takes a swig of beer. "And she was right. I didn't even realize how much this stuff with my parents was still weighing on me and holding me back. It's hard to unteach yourself the lessons life's taught you. You have to work at it."

I take a sip of my beer too, my heart hammering, panic gripping me. "There're some things I could tell you that might make you turn your back on me. I don't think I could handle that."

Burke sets his beer down and leans over. He claps a hand on my shoulder, squeezing it. "There's not a thing in this world you could tell me that would make me turn my back on you. You're my brother. You need to bury a body, I'll show up with a shovel." His mouth quirks to one side. "I'm only hoping we don't need to make that literal."

I'm shocked to feel tears in my eyes, so I take a minute to choke the emotion down, because I can't cry. I *don't* cry. The last time I remember crying was when I found Gidget dead. There's not a damn thing you can do to rewind the clock when it comes to death. Not a damn thing.

"I don't want to burden you, man," I say thickly. "You're getting married. We should be celebrating, not talking about dark, depressing shit. Why don't we blow the house for the day and go bother Danny? Go out on the town."

Another excuse to avoid Shauna.

Another excuse to avoid saying what needs to be said.

"Delia hasn't said yes yet." He squeezes my shoulder once more before letting go.

"She will. I can see it on her face when you're together. Yours too."

"Thanks, man. You're not burdening me, by the way. I want to know what happened to you, because I want to share your burden... same way you've been sharing mine."

My laughter has an ugly edge to it. "I'm probably the cause of half your problems, bud. If I'd told you everything eight years ago, then—"

"Then I never would have met Delia," he says pointedly, his blue eyes flashing. "Maybe everything's happening just the way it was supposed to."

I force a smile. "She's got you believing in fate, huh?"

"Maybe. There are worse things than admitting you're not always the one at the wheel. What happened with your father, Leonard? You've told me he was bad news but not much else. What did he do to you?"

I take a deep pull of the beer, my mind torn between two possibilities, two paths.

Tell him. Don't.

Shauna's one smart lady, and she thought I should. Ultimately, that's the thought that makes me sit back with my beer. I will abso-fucking-lutely be draining all of it.

"Well, Burke, it's some story..."

"Don't I bet," he says, but his smile is strained. So is mine, I'm sure.

And I tell him all of it. I tell him about my dad making me into a thief, about turning him in and changing my name for the first time. I tell him about struggling to find a job as a high school dropout with no skills except for sticky fingers, and how it turned me back to thieving and working for thieves, right up until Gidget died and I left that life behind. Changed my name again.

I wanted to get out, but I still didn't know how, so I decided I'd pull a few big con jobs to save money to start over somewhere. My second stop was in Asheville, where I tried to con *him*.

"And this is why you thought I'd turn my back on you?" he asks slowly. He's been watching me through all of it, quiet mostly, and even though I started out slowly, I've been babbling like a damn fool.

"That's about the shape of it," I say lightly, acting like panic's not still clawing at my chest like one of Shauna's monster mugs.

Maybe that's part of why I'm so drawn to her.

Shauna understands panic. Unease. Anxiety. The feeling of being too big and small for your skin. The wriggling worms that fill your head and body and tell you it's all going to end, and it's going to be because of you.

And you're trying to turn your back on her.

"Leonard," he says, leaning forward and clasping his hands. We both finished our lunch beers at least ten minutes ago. "I don't know how to tell you this, but I'd already figured that bit out. I would have told you if I'd known it was weighing on you. I didn't think I could bring it up without sounding like a dick."

Relief pats me on the back and offers to buy me a cigar. Still... "Are you fucking with me?"

"No. I mean, I didn't realize that was what was going on at the time, obviously. But thinking back on it, it just made sense. I mean, you were never as into the outdoor stuff as you said. The day we met at the bar; you said you wanted to do the Pacific Crest Trail. That's serious."

"I never would have made it. I'm allergic to pollen."

He laughs, and suddenly I'm laughing too, the relief making me as dizzy as when I went on the Scrambler five times in a row at the fair when I was a kid.

Giving me an amused look, he says, "You think I haven't had other people come at me for my money?"

"No, but I was hoping I was the smoothest."

"Yeah, because you never went through with it."

"It would have been too hard to rip you off after I took a job with your folks. That's how a guy gets caught."

"I'm sure that's what you told yourself," he says, trying to hold back a smile. "For years. When did you accept that we were just your friends?"

I rub my chest, where there's still some tightness. "It took a while," I admit. "It wasn't easy for me to let anyone in."

"For me either. There's a reason why all of my other friends are people I've known for decades."

"Thank you," I say, even though it's such a small thing to say for everything's he done for me—for everything he and the other guys have been to me. They saved what little was left of me back then, and then they did it again a few months ago.

"You left Asheville because my parents threatened you?"

"They found out who my father is. I guess they hunted my mom down too. She's always happy to tell anyone who'll listen that I'm the one who took him down even though I'd been doing jobs with him since I was six."

He winces. "Fuck, I'm sorry."

It's easier to shrug now, to pretend it doesn't matter. "We both have shitty parents. It's not your fault. But I figured if they told you you'd put two and two together and make four. I thought you'd side with them over me. I should've known better."

"So you ran."

"I figured I had to, but I couldn't seem to make myself do it.

Until they hired that guy to follow me around. It made me jumpy. I've always been a little jumpy since—"

Since I got all the way to Atlanta from where we were living in Greensborough, North Carolina and my father broke into my motel room at night and beat me with my own baseball bat until I pissed myself and passed out, then threw me in the back of the car. My best guess is that the people at the front desk didn't buy my ID—*his* ID—and ran a check. I was fourteen, so even though I looked like the old man, I wasn't a man.

My leg and arm were broken. He'd wanted to prove he was still stronger, and back then, he had been. For a couple of months, I was too fucked up to do anything for him. It had happened during summer vacation, and he had a buddy who'd set my bones, so no one asked any questions.

I spent the next two years working out every chance I got. Getting into scraps so I learned how to fight better. Getting ready to take him on.

But in the end, I didn't have to. He got himself caught by the cops, and the stupid fucker told them I was his cover. I saw my opportunity, and I took it. I went in and told them everything.

My mother threw me out of the house for being a snitch, but I was sixteen, old enough to take care of myself.

Or so I thought.

My mind turns to Reese.

He's okay. He's got to be okay.

"I get it," he says. "Were you...is there a chance he has friends who'd come after you for turning him in?"

"I don't think so. He'd burned all his bridges by then. I didn't like thinking about it, though, or about my mom knowing where to find me. Still don't, but I imagine she's too strung out to do anything about it."

"And this is why you kept running after you left. Changed your name a few more times?"

I scratched my head and looked away. "I guess I was always chasing that fresh start—the way I felt when I got here and met all of you. But I never found it." Then I grin at him. "Besides, I won't lie. I got myself into trouble a time or two."

"Wouldn't be Leonard if you didn't," he says, "but that's one of the things we love about you, man."

I lift my eyebrows, trying to act cool. "Delia's really getting to you, huh?"

"Yes, thank God." He pins me with an intense look. "She's the best thing that ever happened to me. Maybe you should be more open to new things."

The panicky feeling crawls back. He's talking about Shauna. I know he is. Still, I say, "Like that therapy b.s.?"

"Not b.s. If you find the right person, it could really help. When you're ready, I'm going to help you."

Just like Burke to say *when I'm ready*, as if it's going to happen and isn't just something he'd like to happen. He believes in me. He has no reason to, but he does.

"But I was talking about Shauna," he says, just when I figured I was safe. "There's no way you nearly crashed a Rolls Royce because you were that excited about posing as a pediatric surgeon in front of a bunch of assholes."

"Think about it. I'm a former con artist who's trying to behave. It felt like someone had just handed me a present."

"Sure," he says with a half-smile. "But don't con me, Leonard. I know you wouldn't have been half as into the idea if it weren't for her."

"Sure," I admit. "I like her." He's still waiting, so I add, "A lot. Which is why I know she deserves someone who's going to treat her right."

"Why can't you treat her right?"

I prop my elbows on my knees and put my head in my hands. "I don't know how."

"Is that true, man, or is that just something you've been telling yourself so long you don't know the difference? Because from where I'm sitting, you know how to be good to people. You're going to help me dress up like Prince Eric for fuck's sake. That's some favor."

"Again." I look up at him. "It's something I'm going to take great enjoyment in doing."

He angles his head, studying me. "And you don't take enjoyment from being good to her?"

I pause, caught off guard. "Of course I do. But I'm going to make mistakes and screw everything up. That's a given. She'll be better off if I leave her alone."

A little late for that, but surely late is better than never.

"Why's it a given that you making mistakes is going to screw everything up? We all make mistakes."

He's right and he's wrong. Because there's something inside of me that feeds off bad decisions, that wants to turn left because everyone else is going right. Sometimes it sleeps, but when it wakes up it's a real bitch. It's hard to believe that I could have this life, that I could live here and run L&L Restoration with him and have a girlfriend who doesn't want to kill me after a week. It's not something I can wrap my head around.

I say so, and he smirks and says, "You don't think Delia ever wants to kill me?"

"No, it hadn't occurred to me," I say. "That woman would cry if she stepped on a spider."

"Don't let her fool you. She gets mad just like anyone. And, sure, I'm betting you'll piss Shauna off a time or two—sounds like you already have—but that's part of what keeps life interesting. You can't make up if you haven't had a fight."

I laugh, but it dies a quick death. "I'm trying to be unselfish here. I...I don't know if I can pull this off. I've never been in a real relationship before."

He turns a little in his chair, facing me more, "You don't think you're being selfish? You're making the choice for her, bub. Doesn't she strike you as the kind of woman who'd like to make her own calls?"

"Fuck, you're right." I get up from the chair, sit down, and then get back up again. "But I still don't know what I'm doing."

He laughs and gets to his feet. "That's what the therapy's for."

I tell him I'll think about it. I'm pretty sure I mean it this time.

twenty-four

SHAUNA

Group text: *The Evans Sisters Want the Goods*
Delia: *We miss you. We need a rundown on everything.*
Mira: *We want to hear about the sexxxxxx.*
Delia: *Mira, really.*
Mira: *What can I say? I'm a horndog. I hate Byron, but he's still kind of hot. I've thought about hate-banging him.*
Delia: *Seriously don't. Lucas says he's going to talk to Danny about you moving in. You only have a few weeks left. Maybe a month. The end is in sight.*
Delia: *Shauna, are you there?*
Mira: *Do we need to stalk you like a morally grey hero?*
Delia: *You've switched to dark romance?*
Mira: *What can I say? It's where my head's at.*

5 hours later...

Group text: *The Evans Sisters Want the Goods*
Delia: *Shauna, we need to know you're okay. Say something.*
Shauna: *Something.*
Delia: *Will you come to the bar for drinks?*

Shauna: *Not tonight, sorry. I'm exhausted.*

Delia: *Tomorrow?*

Shauna: *I have a feeling I'll be exhausted then too. It's been one of those weeks.*

Mira: *Monday. My day off. No ifs, ands, or buts. We're exercising tough love here. And don't underestimate what will happen if you don't come. I really have been bingeing dark romance. ITS BEEN GIVING ME IDEAS.*

Shauna: *I agree with Delia. No hate-banging. At least wait until after you move out. You don't want to have to live with someone you had a bad hate-bang with. That would be like finding out your shitty one-night stand is your new next-door neighbor.*

Mira: *You two are killing my vibe.*

Message from Grandpa Fruckface:

> It's been thirty-nine days since you last responded to my messages.

"FUCK. Why didn't you tell me it was this bad?"

Rafe's in my studio at The Waiting Place, looking at my ugly babies. I've been on a monster-making spree this week, and each is uglier than the last. My latest creation, which took me most of the last two days, is a foot-high basilisk with a woman's face, a forked tongue, and scales shaped like razor blades.

She looks a bit like Bianca, which wasn't intentional.

Inspiration's had me in a literal chokehold. When Rafe showed up to check on me, nearly giving me a heart attack, I glanced out the window and nearly did a doubletake when I realized it was getting dark. I'd meant to take fifteen minutes off for lunch, but that must have been hours ago.

"Shauna?" Rafe says, his brow knitted with worry.

I run a hand back through my hair. "I didn't want you to worry, which is exactly what you're doing right now. I've got to work through it—you know that. You're the same way when you're on tear with something. I mean, you must've painted five thousand portraits of Sinclair."

"Sure," he says, "but this is disturbing, Shauna. I'm going to have nightmares."

"Want to bring one home to Sinclair?"

He pretends to laugh. Shit, he really *is* worried. Should I be more worried?

I started out the week strong. The piece I made on Monday is the exception to the monster rule. It's a mug with a man's arms holding a kitten as the handle. His eyes are Leonard's eyes. Full of wonder and love and fear.

I made it in two hours, my hands moving constantly, inspiration a sticky flame inside of me, and for the first time in weeks, I was proud of something I'd molded with my hands. I wanted to make the gazebo next. But on Monday night I offered to drive Leonard around his neighborhood to look for Reese since he'd said he planned on canvassing it on foot, and he refused, saying he needed the exercise.

And when I asked if he felt like watching *The Sopranos* on Tuesday night, he claimed he was going to bed early.

My ass. I doubt he's ever been to bed before midnight.

Sure, he did send me photos of hideous outfits we could wear to the photoshoot before Bianca moved it, but I know when someone's avoiding me. My stomach's felt like it's an hourglass full of sinking sand all week. I keep telling myself that it's okay, that he was never mine to lose, but it had sure as hell felt like he was last weekend. And the connection we'd formed wasn't so easy to shake loose.

He's avoiding Nana, too, because last night she poured each of us a stiff drink and said, "You haven't heard from our boy, have you?"

"I don't think he's *our* anything," I scoffed, because I felt burning in my eyes, and it pissed me off.

"This is the storm before the calm, Shauna May," she said, pouring a little more liquor into the glasses. "But it might be a longer storm than we'd like."

"I think you got that saying wrong," I told her.

"I said what I said. Have you texted your grandfather back? The old fool's resorted to texting *me*."

No, I haven't.

I've meant to, actually.

What Nana told me last Sunday has stuck with me—the image of Grandpa Frank crying because he had to send me back home with people who didn't love me.

But something's held me back.

"I'm not sure I can forgive him for hurting you," I admitted. Then took a sip of my drink before pushing it back.

Of all her hobbies, the home-mixed liqueurs are the worst.

"Why not?" she asked, raising her eyebrows and waving a hand as if to encompass our newly feng-shuied home and Bertie's crocheted collar. "If he hadn't gone and left, I never would have discovered what I'm capable of. What I had sleeping inside of me."

"So you've forgiven him?" I asked in disbelief.

She threw her head back and laughed. "Of course I haven't. I'll resent that old boot until he's six feet under, and I'll throw vinegar on his grave. But there's no reason for you to resent him for my sake. I *am* happier. Bad things happen to everyone, honey, and even if it hurts so much you can't breathe, you can come out the other side and find unicorns shitting rainbows. It's okay to still hurt. And it's okay to enjoy the view."

I had to smile, because Nana really has a way with words when she's worked up. "Unicorns shitting rainbows, huh?"

"If you make a piece like that, I want it dedicated to me."

"You got it."

I sketched out a design for a unicorn-shitting-rainbows-mug when I got to The Waiting Place this morning, before I jumped back in with Snake Lady. I haven't put her in the kiln yet, but I look forward to baking her.

"Anyway," I tell Rafe, "I didn't bring you back here because I need an intervention. I had an idea. You think Sinclair would want to hold a big Halloween event at the end of October? Maybe we can get each of the artists to come up with spooky shit to sell, and we could hold special classes for making something..."

"Terrifying?"

"Halloweeny."

He glances at the Bianca snake monster, frowning, then concedes my victory with a nod.

"It's a good idea. A *really* good idea."

I grin, running with it, because Halloween's always been my favorite holiday. There's something heady about pretending to be someone else, letting your base impulses roll out. Courting fear for the fun of it.

I'll bet Leonard likes it too.

I put a pillow over the thought's mouth and asphyxiate it.

Maybe I've been watching too much of *The Sopranos.*

I clear my throat and wave a hand to the curtain separating my workshop from the front room. "We could have a reception in the floorspace in the atrium with bobbing for apples—"

"Hard pass." He crosses his muscle-man arms. "I'm not sticking my face in other people's spit water."

I roll my eyes. "So don't do it. But I reluctantly admit you might have a point. We don't want to spread the plague. How about..." I snap my fingers. "A caramel apple decorating station. You can lead it since you're the painter."

"Yes," he says dryly. "So much skill goes into creating a caramel apple."

"I knew you'd see things my way."

"So what are you going to teach them?" He takes a good long gander at my ugly babies. "How to terrify their visitors with snake statues?"

"Nah, I was thinking I'd go simple—have them coil clay into a snake bowl or something like that."

He leans in closer to study Bianca's face, then turns toward me with a raised brow. "Is this a wedding present?"

I hadn't planned on it, but I start laughing, because it's perfect. I'll have to make some sort of Colter statue too. Maybe a troll with a bent back and a nose the size of an heirloom tomato. His and hers monsters.

I tell Rafe, and he starts laughing right along with me.

"Give him a big forehead," he says through his laughter. "He's always had a punchable forehead."

"And a receding hairline," I add, tears coursing down my cheeks. About a year ago, Colter got a bug in his bread about having a receding hairline. He kept doing mirror checks and even took photographs every morning so he could compare them.

"You should put them in a really pretty box when you're finished," Rafe says. "Becca in The Paper Place is a master wrapper."

"That's a thing?" I ask, laughing harder.

"I didn't think so," he says, wiping his eyes, "but then I saw what she can do. I shit you not, she's a miracle worker. A bit too nice, though. Every time I talk to her, I get dragged in for twenty minutes, but she can wrap one hell of a gift."

"Oh, it's on. And if they call me up and ask why I made my monsters look like them, I'm going to gaslight them into thinking it's all in their heads."

He grins at me, and I feel grateful for having such good friends.

Him. Delia and Mira. The other artists here at The Waiting Place. Maybe this is the something good that was waiting for me on the other side of Shit Mountain.

But my mind is a traitorous bitch, because it flashes to Leonard.

"Look at us," I say, sobering. "We're really rolling with the good ideas tonight, huh?"

"I'll talk to Sinclair about the Halloween event, but I know she's going to go for it," Rafe says. "She has a thing for Halloween."

"It's the actress in her," I say.

His gaze sharpens. "You may have spun a good idea out of this —" He waves at the children of my despair. "—but you haven't made me forget about what's behind it. Did the conman do something?"

He cracks his knuckles, and it really is very threatening. Or it would be if I didn't know he's ninety percent teddy bear, five percent piss and vinegar, and five percent actually dangerous. That five percent is reserved for the people who piss off or threaten the people he loves, though, and I'm lucky enough to be one of them.

"So you're back to calling him a conman?" I ask, lifting my eyebrows.

"I'll call him worse if he hurt you."

"He didn't do anything wrong," I say, feigning interest in another of my creations—a mug with five eyes, a mouth with two rows of teeth, and a sixth eye sculpted into the bottom of the interior. I don't think anyone will be drinking from that.

"He did if he hurt you."

"Where's this attitude when it comes to Grandpa Frank?" I ask, mostly because I feel like being ornery.

He lifts his hands in the universal sign of *don't shoot.*

"Okay, fine, that was unfair. I'm going to answer Grandpa. Eventually. I don't mind making him sweat, though. He was a real jerk."

"I'm happy to hear you say that," Rafe says, letting his hands drop. His eyebrows lift. "But don't think I don't realize you're changing the subject."

That's what you get for letting people know you too well.

"Leonard really hasn't done anything wrong," I insist. "He gave Colt a black eye."

Rafe looks somewhere between amused and annoyed, probably because he was hoping to claim that pleasure for himself. "Did Bianca shit herself?"

"Yes, but somehow we're still invited to pictures next weekend and then to the wedding. I don't know how he did it, but Leonard convinced Colter to lie for him. Colt pretended some psychopath wandered into the woods and punched him in the eye."

Of course, Bianca wrote a scathing one-star review of the campground, complaining about the "psychotic drifter" and the crickets in our cabin. I spent an hour combing through internet groups, trying to find a society of cricket enthusiasts who might want to meet there and study whether it was a special breeding ground. But cricket the sport is apparently more popular then crickets the bugs, so it was a waste of time. I settled for writing two glowing reviews and sending the owners a box of "happy" danishes from a local bakery.

Rafe pushes his lips out. "So, the guy's got skills."

My mind flashes to Leonard, fucking me on that table and in that gazebo. Leonard, on his knees with his mouth between my legs.

"Yeah," I say through a dry mouth. "He's got skills."

"Why'd he hit him?"

I'm about to let it all spill. Colt cheating. Him and Bianca conniving to make sure my monster mugs never made it into the store. But then the curtain ripples and a throat is cleared on the other side. "There's no good way to knock on a piece of cloth," a voice says.

It's *his* voice.

twenty-five

SHAUNA

I'M annoyed by the way my whole body lights up.

"Come on back," I say, my lips suddenly dry.

I watch as Leonard pushes through the curtain.

"The front door should be locked. Who let you in?" Rafe asks with accusation, his eyes more onyx than dark brown as he studies Leonard. Maybe it's because Leonard is covered in sweat. He has on an AC/DC T-shirt and athletic shorts. His hair is damp, and there are sweat spots beneath both of his arms and under his chin. Did he *run* here? It's got to be at least five miles from his place, across some major roads without streetlights.

My heart does strange things in my chest, trying to grow and break at the same time. *I want him.* I want to hold him close and press my face into his sweaty neck, and I want to push him down onto my worktable so I can ride him in here, where I'm queen of the monsters. And I also want to throttle him for staying away from me, for making me feel like one more person I value has left me.

"A lady down the way," he says, pointing. "Said she was Becca of The Paper Place."

Rafe mutters something about The Paper Place being the weak link, and Leonard shuffles a little on his feet, his eyes darting to me.

He looks like Bertie does after he's relieved himself on the floor or mangled one of Nana's slippers.

"You punched Colter, huh?" Rafe asks.

"That I did," Leonard confirms. He runs his right hand back through his sweaty hair, the knuckles scabbed over. The sight of his bicep, sliced through with that scar he got while defending someone, makes my heart even more confused.

Rafe grunts, looking torn between being a dick to Leonard and patting him on the back and getting him a beer. I understand that.

"I was going to do that someday," my friend says after a second.

"Nothing's stopping you," Leonard tells him. "He's got another eye that's as perfectly punchable as the one I got to."

Rafe laughs, but it fades after a second, as if he's remembering there's more he'd like to say. Probably some sort of not-so-cryptic warning about Leonard having two perfectly punchable eyes too, so he'd better mind himself. But Leonard came here, possibly *ran* here, and I need to know why.

Rafe starts to say something, but I grab his arm and usher him toward the curtain. "So have a talk with Sinclair, and maybe we can have a meeting about the Halloween event in the next day or two, huh?"

"Sure," he says, lifting a hand to rub his mouth. "But are you certain—"

I give him a little *out you go* push toward the curtain. "I'll text you."

"Tonight," he insists, looking back with a somewhat dark expression.

"*Tonight.*"

"See you," Leonard says, throwing him a salute.

Rafe gives him a severe nod but doesn't give voice to any of the things running through his head. I'm guessing Leonard's not going to get a free pass forever though.

I don't have siblings—my parents looked at me and said no

thanks—but Rafe is like a brother. Has been since we met at the first craft fair either of us had ever participated in, exchanged a look, and agreed we had no idea what we were doing.

Rafe passes through the curtain with another grunt. Some people might linger and listen by the curtain—Bianca would—but I know he's not some people.

I turn back to Leonard, watch his throat bob, take in the sweat on his forehead.

"Did you run here?"

"Yes," he says, his eyes on mine.

"*Why*, Leonard?"

He swallows again, and I want to bite his Adam's apple and then lick it. I want to do bad, bad things to him.

"I had to be with you," he says after a moment, his voice pitched low. "I couldn't make myself stay away anymore."

With one sentence he lifts me up, and the other he brings me down. Because he wanted to be with me but was making himself stay away.

"If you'd called me, I would have picked you up. And you wouldn't have been in danger of getting flattened by a truck."

"I didn't want to ask you to do something for me when I've been a dick. And I needed the run. I had to work through some shit on my feet."

I itch to go to him, to soothe him. To reassure myself that he's really here. But I don't move. "Why'd you make yourself stay away?"

He laughs and scuffs a foot against the floor. The expression in his eyes says he thinks I might kick him or send him outside. "I don't know how to do any of this, Tiger. Maybe I'm not cut out for it. But I talked to Burke, and he got me thinking that maybe it's something I can learn."

"What is?" I ask, my eyes glued to him as I wait.

He takes in a deep breath and says, "I like you, Shauna. Truth is, I've got it bad for you. It's been that way since we first met. When Constance told me about her lie, the honest-to-god first thing that came to mind was, 'Here's my chance.' But I've never been in a relationship with a woman. Never. I don't want to fuck everything up. Seems to me you've been hurt enough."

Everything in me feels like it's quaking. I hadn't thought it was possible that I'd hear him say these words, and until this moment, I didn't realize how much I wanted it.

"So have you," I say softly, my mind bringing up a picture of that little boy, forced to do things he didn't understand. Beaten and twisted by his own father.

"You deserve a man who's not afraid of his own shadow."

He may be afraid of his shadow—of the darkness within him— but he's fearless when it comes to everything else. It's obvious he doesn't see it that way, though.

"I don't want you to stay away," I say. "If you stay away, that's what's going to hurt me." Then I let myself span the distance between us, running to him like he ran to me.

"I'm sweaty as fuck," he says as I reach him and wrap my arms around him. I bury my face in his neck and kiss him there, tasting the salt, snuggling in close so I can feel him against me. His heart is thumping fast in his chest.

"I don't care," I say into his neck. "I've missed you. And I've got it bad for you too, Doc. Really bad."

He wraps his arms around me, holding me tightly to him, like he's worried I'm the one who might run away. "I'm sorry," he says softly into my ear.

We stand like that for a long moment, wrapped around each other, soaking each other in. "I told Burke about my father and about what I meant to do when I first came to Asheville," he says then. "Just like you told me I should."

"What did he say?"

He tightens his hold on me slightly and speaks into my hair.

"He said I was his brother, and nothing could make him push me away."

He sounds incredulous, like he can't believe a person would ever feel that way about him, and a sense of shame envelops me. I used to think the worst of Leonard—I used to *bask* in thinking the worst of him. It was wrong, even if I did it because I knew I could fall for him, and it would be a long, dangerous tumble into fire.

"Of course he did," I say, kissing him again and tightening my hold on him.

He kisses the top of my head, then pulls back slightly and lifts me up by the hips. I wrap my legs around his waist as he kisses my mouth, his lips needy, his teeth tugging on my bottom lip.

Then he ends the kiss and smiles at me, my legs still wrapped around him, his hand on my ass. "I've been meaning to ask, Tiger. Is this here a new line? They don't look much like the pieces you've got out front."

I groan and bury my head back in his neck. "It's a problem is what it is. Sometimes, when I'm upset, my monsters have more teeth and claws."

"My little hellcat," he says. Then, sobering, "Was it because of me? Because I stayed away this week?"

"A bit," I admit. "But I've had trouble making anything else lately. I've been on a bit of a dark jag."

"That's why you didn't want me to come back here the other week."

"Yes. But I did make a different kind of piece on Monday…"

"I don't want to set you down," he tells me. "So you're just going to have to point."

I do, to the piece sitting on the rack in the corner, and he goes to look at it. I'm close to his face, so I can see his jaw working and the emotion filling his eyes.

I trace his cheek with my finger, ending at the slight lines around his eyes—the laugh lines that he managed to form despite going through hell. My heart aches for the boy he was. For the man he's becoming. For the fact that he's kept his sense of humor and joy intact through all of it. "It was the look in your eyes when you saw Bean again. That's what made me want to make it."

His gaze burns into me. "I want to be a better man for you."

I don't even realize I'm crying until he traces the tears from my face and then kisses my wet cheeks. "I need you inside of me," I say.

"That's not something a man would say no to." He kisses my cheek again, then my mouth, groaning a little before he pulls away, his hand caressing my butt. "But I don't have any condoms."

"I'm on birth control."

He stares at me for a second. "I've never—" He swallows. "I've always used one."

I'm about to tell him it doesn't matter, but then I realize there's something like fear behind his words.

"What's wrong?" I ask.

He swallows. "Being careful is important to me. I can't bring a kid into this world. I guess I should tell you that too. My parents fucked me up but good. I won't do that to someone else."

I know he'd never treat another human being the way his parents treated him, certainly not a child. But right now he needs levity. He needs something sweet in his coffee.

"Aren't you getting ahead of yourself?" I ask, and he barks a laugh.

"I suppose I am." He's still holding me to him, cradling me like he can't bear to let me go. "I told you I don't know what I'm doing."

"I get why you feel that way." I squeeze my legs around his hips so he knows I'm not going anywhere. "But I'm in no hurry to pop out kids. So I don't think that's something we have to worry about. If you want, we can get in my car and speed all the way to the pharmacy to get some condoms."

He doesn't speak for a long moment, his gaze locked on the back wall as if it's got answers to all the big questions in the universe.

Then he says, "No. I need you like this." He carries me toward the worktable. "I want to feel you clench against my cock with nothing between us."

"Thank God, because I was going to feel really impatient in that car."

He sets me down on the edge of the table.

"Take off your shoes," I say.

His eyes are dancing. I've heard that expression plenty of times before, but I'd never really seen it happen before I met him. "You gonna boss me around tonight?"

"*Yes.*"

He leans down to unlace his shoes, which is when I realize he's got on work boots.

"You ran in boots?"

"Reese stole my sneakers. Haven't had time to get new ones," he says as he takes them off and then removes his socks. I wince at the sight of the raw spots.

"Didn't that hurt?"

A harsh laugh escapes him. "They feel like ground beef."

This man is so maddening, so childish, so *endearing.* "You didn't have to do that, Leonard. You didn't need to hurt yourself to make a point."

"I did." He takes a step toward me in his T-shirt, shorts, and bare feet. His hair is messy, the wave brought out by the humidity. He looks like every fantasy I've ever had poured into a cocktail glass and shaken up, and I want to suck him down.

"Now, what do you want me to do, Tiger?" he asks, his voice low and husky. "I'm yours to command."

He says it with an expression that's half challenge.

Neither of us can back down from challenges. Maybe it's because we're used to them. For me, it was being the girl with parents who didn't care and then parents who were dead. For him...

God, everything was a challenge.

We need something lighthearted, something fun, so I take out my phone and turn on "Pony" from *Magic Mike XXL*, streaming it to my Bluetooth speakers. "Why don't you give me a little show?"

His smile expands to fill his whole face. "All you had to do was ask."

He starts moving to the music. I meant it mostly as a joke, but he's good enough that he could have been an understudy for one of the actors in the movie.

He dances closer, pulling off his shirt in a sexy tease before throwing it into my lap. I hold onto it as I watch his muscles shift with his movements and take in his thick, tattooed arms. He's slightly sweaty still, and the overhead lights glisten off it, making him look golden. I'm uncomfortably turned on, squirming on the hard table. "Be honest. You were an exotic dancer in one of your lives."

"Nah. But I do like to dance."

And sing. And drive women insane with need—and also just plain insane.

He swings up onto the table and starts dancing on top of it, so I bring my feet up and turn toward him, laughing. He stalks across the table like a beast—and even though the table is also a beast, made out of a thick, heavy slab of wood designed to hold weight, it creaks under him. When he starts thrusting in time with the music, his dick inches away from my face, I laugh at first. I'm not laughing for very long, though, because raw need unspools inside of me. The next time he does it, I reach for the band of his shorts.

"No touching the talent, pretty lady," he says, his arms clasped behind his head, showing off his biceps.

"Isn't touching the fun part?"

"It's *all* fun, Tiger."

"I promise it'll be more fun if you take them off."

He starts swaying his hips, his arms moving through the air, and it truly is more than one woman's ovaries can take.

"I'll take my shorts off if you do the same."

"I like it when you're impatient for me," he says with a smirk. But he must be feeling it too, because he adds. "Your shorts and your shirt.

"Deal."

"You can leave your apron on, though."

I laugh, because it's about as unsexy as an apron can get. Long and wide and made of a fabric that might as well be burlap.

"You've got yourself a bargain."

I stand up on the table too, earning another creak, and shake my ass as I shimmy out of my shorts. Might as well prove to him that he's not the only one who can conquer at this game. It's not easy taking off my shirt while leaving on the apron, but he threw it down, and I'm going to rise up to the challenge.

He swears under his breath as he takes off his shorts and underwear. He's hard and thick, and *I want him.* Pulling me to him by the pocket of my apron, he kisses me. "You're sexy in burlap," he says into my lips. "I like the way it just barely covers your nipples."

The song shifts to "Never Gonna Give You Up." Getting Rick-rolled isn't exactly sexy, but neither of us care enough to change it.

His lips find my neck, followed by his teeth, and one of his hands dips between my legs and then starts playing with my clit.

"What do you say? We gonna break this table, Tiger?"

"Let's give it the old college try. Lie down for me."

He looks up from my neck, his eyes flashing. "You're finally gonna take me for a ride, huh?"

Heat floods my body, centering between my legs. "That's exactly what I'm going to do."

He lowers down, his eyes on me, and lies back. He looks like an offering on my table—a sacrifice. That thought sends worry through my veins before need chases it out, because his dick is pointing at me, just asking me to lower down onto it.

I straddle him right below it, teasing him—and myself—by rolling my hips.

He takes it for a minute or so, his hands caressing me under the apron, but then puts his hands on my hips and lifts me up.

I laugh, the sound gusty. "Now who's impatient?"

"Both of us," he says, grunting when I position him and then slowly lower down, taking him inch by delicious inch. The feeling ripples through me. My lips part, and he reaches up and touches them. I suck in his finger as I move against him, taking him at my speed.

"You feel so impossibly good," he says, panting slightly. "You do whatever you want to me. Take your pleasure from me, baby."

It's maybe the sexiest thing anyone's ever said to me, so of course he has to follow it up with, "I always dreamed about getting ridden by a woman in a burlap sack."

"No...you haven't."

"I didn't know what to dream about. We can blame my lack of imagination."

Then he lifts up, his mouth reaching for mine, and I lower on top of him, kissing him while I keep moving against him. And he's right, it should be impossible to experience these sensations. I feel some of my darkness easing, the monsters slipping further into their cave.

My need for more of him—quicker—kicks in, and I lift my upper body up again, moving my hips faster. He groans and reaches toward where we're joined, making sure I get enough attention where I need it. I push down harder as he thrusts up, and then I know it's happening—I feel it sliding over me like a tidal wave that's powerful enough to pull us both under.

"Give it to me, Tiger," he says. "I can feel it coming."

And with another thrust, it does. The pulsing pleasure grips me again and again. I must be gripping *him*, because he groans and comes inside of me, the look on his face one of pure bliss. I lower down, both of us sweaty now, and kiss him.

He rolls me over, still inside of me, making me laugh, so he can pin my arms and kiss me deeper. His shorts go flying over the edge of the table, kicked by his leg, and there's a crack as they hit the floor. He lifts his head to look, swearing.

"You left your phone in your pocket?" I ask laughing. "Don't they cover that in Stripper 101?"

"I guess I wouldn't have graduated," he says, then pulls out of me with a regretful look.

"You wanted to stay in there."

"As long as possible. Always."

I reach down to grab his shorts and take out the phone to check the screen. I nearly do a doubletake, because the screen, while intact, has a lock picture of us. It's a selfie we took last week at Murderland. We're squinting because the sun's in our eyes, but we look almost deliriously happy.

He shrugs when he sees me looking at it. "I figured Champ and Bianca would expect it, but I also don't mind looking at it."

We order pizza to the studio, confusing the poor deliveryman, who can't seem to decide whether we have a right to be here. To be fair, Leonard's dressed in his workout clothes, and I refused to let him put those boots back on his feet. Ultimately, the pizza guy decides it's not his problem and takes off with his tip.

We set up at a table in the atrium, which was designed so people can bring in their orders from the food trucks we've contracted to set up outside.

Leonard gives a whistle as he checks out the space. It's lovely, with a gold-rimmed skylight embedded in the roof and indoor trees all around us. The gathering of wrought iron two-top tables and chairs look like they belong in a French cafe. Although I had my own tiny art studio before Sinclair got it into her head to start this place, it was a shitty little box of a room, and I was barely breaking even. This is a whole different playing field.

"Some place you got here," he says.

Is this the kind of place he would have cased back in the day?

Probably. Sinclair's a millionaire many times over. There's discomfort attached to the thought, because even though I trust him, it occurs to me I'm trusting him not just for me, but for Sinclair. For Rafe. For Becca in The Paper Place and all the others.

Is it worth the risk?

I look at him, taking in the way his hair is curling at the nape of his neck, his bright hazel eyes, always mischievous but so often kind too, and I have my answer.

"You look mighty serious," Leonard says.

"I take my pizza seriously," I hedge as I open the box. We don't have any plates and didn't think to ask for any, so we eat it like that, right out of the box.

I tell Leonard about my idea for the Halloween event. He grins, saying he thinks we should dress as a tiger and her trainer. I counter that we should be a tiger and her prey, but my heart's happy that he still intends to be here by Halloween.

And Leonard tells me about his talk with Burke, sharing more pieces of his past. I hate to think about him going through so much of his life alone, without anyone to have his back or tell him he matters.

He watches me as I close the pizza box. "You know, I intend to collect on that clay lesson I was promised."

I lift my eyebrows. "Now?"

"What better time? Seems like I gave you a pretty good lesson on the male anatomy."

I give his arm a shove, and he pantomimes falling out of his chair. "You really want to give your friend a clay rendering of your dick for his birthday?"

"What better gift, baby? He can mount it on the wall and hang his earphones on it. If you're a good teacher, I'll even make you one for *your* birthday." His jaw tics. "And present it to you in front of everyone at the wedding, because hell, it's your birthday."

The corners of my mouth lift, and I lean in to press a kiss to his tight jaw. "Wait until you hear what we're going to be giving them."

I tell him as we dispose of our trash.

"Wicked of you," he says as we head back to The Clay Place. "I approve."

"I thought you would."

We duck through the curtain to the back, and he watches as I get the wheel out and then retrieve a wrapped block of clay from the metal storage container beneath my worktable.

"Rafe's important to you, isn't he? I can tell when people are close."

"Sure. He's the best friend who hasn't screwed me over yet." I glance up from what I'm doing. "You know, I think he likes you despite himself."

"That's something I'm familiar with," he says with a wry laugh. "I'm going to do my damnedest to make sure he keeps liking me despite himself."

"So you won't be making him any clay dicks?"

"I don't have a death wish, no."

When I get done laughing, I direct him to sit on the chair I've set up beside the wheel. When I lower into his lap, he says into my ear, "I think I'm gonna like this lesson."

"Hopefully we won't break your dick in half. That would be hard for you to see on a psychological level."

"You're right," he says. "I'm already fucked up enough."

I elbow him in the ribs. "I'm the only one who gets to be mean to you."

He laughs softly and kisses the back of my neck, sending hot shivers through me.

I guide him in placing the clay in the center of the wheel and show him how to move his hands, supporting his elbows on his legs. It's sensual in a way I hadn't anticipated, feeling our fingers locked together around the clay, his body surrounding me, his lips on my neck and his breath in my ear.

He insists on adding veins after we've finished turning it for 'heightened realism.'

When we're done, we stand back to study our masterpiece.

I nudge him with my shoulder. "It is, as advertised, a foot-tall clay dick. *Your* foot-tall clay dick."

"Is it supposed to be lopsided?" he asks, angling his head to study it from a different direction.

"Your dick does have a slight curve to it," I tease. "So we we're just being accurate."

"Hey, now." He bumps me with his shoulder. "Don't be sassing me about something like that."

"Didn't say I didn't like it," I tell him, wrapping my arms around him. "It hits all the right places."

I reach up and touch those laughter lines around his eyes as he says, "Damn right it does."

He leans in to kiss me, but then his phone goes off in the pocket of his shorts.

He shrugs as he takes it out. "I kept the ringer on just in case—"

He doesn't need to finish that sentence for two reasons—one, I know how it ends—*in case Reese calls*—and two, I see the name on his screen.

He looks up at me, and I can see the fear layered under the excitement in his eyes. I don't have to ask why. There's a possibility it's not Reese on the other end of the phone. It could be a person who found him and called the last number he'd dialed. It could be his foster father, trying to figure out where he's been and what he's done.

Reese could be hurt, or dead.

I give Leonard a squeeze as he reaches to answer the call, his hand shaking.

twenty-six

LEONARD

IT FEELS like everything is hanging in the balance. It's been one hell of a day. Highs in the clouds, lows dancing down with the devil.

At least I'm with her.

After Burke and I got done talking, he dropped me off home. I walked through the house five times, going room to room like I was looking for something, Bean following me because she probably hoped that something was food—and then I realized why I felt restless. Because I was looking for her, and she wasn't there.

I don't know if I have it in me to be the man for Shauna, but I realized then that I had to try. So, I put on my boots and ran six miles like an idiot, nearly getting creamed crossing the road.

It was worth it.

I tell myself that if I could find it within myself to do that rather than hiding or running, then I can do this too. All it will take is pressing the button. Answering the call.

He's dead.

He's alive.

He's—

I press it.

"Leonard?" Reese's voice comes over the phone, and I nearly

drop it. Until this second, I didn't realize how worried I was about this kid—a kid I barely even know. In the back of my mind, I was certain he'd bit it. That he was dead, and it was my fault for being such a deadbeat dumbass that I didn't do more to stop it.

"Thank the Christ, kid. I've been flipping out, wondering what happened to you. Where are you?"

"I'm at your place. I decided I was going to take a bus out of town, get as far away as I could. I like the beach, so I went to Wilmington. But there was some trouble at the shelter I was staying at, and—"

I flash back to that hotel room—the sound of the door opening, ripped so hard the chain broke. My father, coming at me with that bat, his eyes cold. I didn't start crying until the fourth time he hit me, because that one broke my arm.

Shauna puts a hand on that same arm, squeezing. She's saying my name, I realize, and so is Reese.

Shit. Reese.

"Stay put, kid. I'm coming."

"Can you get some cereal and milk? The only food here is mustard and bread and a box of mac and cheese. But there's no milk. Don't you eat adult food?"

"Not when I can help it. There's some fruit rollups in the cupboard over the sink. You should've seen what all we had for you last week. How's them stitches?"

He pauses, which isn't good. "It's puffy...and it smells a bit."

I swear under my breath.

"You been taking care of it?"

"Not as good as I should have."

I look up at Shauna, my mind working at the problem.

Constance. Constance was a nurse. Sure, she stopped being a nurse twenty odd years ago, but I'll bet it's like riding a bike. Someone who's been a nurse will know if it's infected.

"We might have someone who can help us with that."

"I can't go to the doctor, man. He'll find me."

"I'm not talking about the doctor. I'm talking about someone better than the doctor. Don't leave, Reese. We're gonna help you."

"Who's we?" he asks, an edge in his voice. I'm pissed at myself for using the "we"—it didn't go down great the last time he met Shauna. What's done is done, though, and she's a part of this as much as I am.

"My girl. I'm with her now."

He's quiet for a second, and worry presses in on me. I'm sure the back door will be swinging in the breeze by the time we get back. I grab my socks and boots, but midway through pulling the first sock on, I decided my bare feet will do just fine.

So I grab them, motioning for Shauna to come with me. Way ahead of me as always, she already has her car key out, shoes on. "She gonna knee me in the balls again?" Reese finally asks.

"Not if you behave," I insist as we hurry out of The Clay Place, through the halls to where her station wagon is parked outside. "We both had bad situations when we were your age. We get it. We're gonna make sure you get through it."

"How do I know I can trust you?" he says.

"You don't," I admit, feeling the weight of it. It's not easy trying to find your way in the world when the only examples you were given were crap ones. "Just like I don't know if I can trust that all the shit you told me is true. This here's what you'd call a leap of faith. I hope you'll take it with me."

We bust out of the front doors as the phone clicks. Either he's got shit manners or he's leaving. I say as much to Shauna, because I know she's waiting to hear what was said.

She swears loudly, then unlocks her car. We pile in. My feet are plenty fucked up from the run and the gravel in the lot, and every step hurts.

Shauna doesn't hesitate—she backs out and then pushes the pedal to the metal.

"You're a speed demon like your grandmother." I try to smile, but it won't take.

"Learned from the best." She darts me a quick glance before staring out through the front window. "You were thinking we'd bring Nana in on this?"

"So you picked up on that, huh?" I ask, grabbing the handle over the door because I need something to squeeze.

"I'll bet the only other nurses you know are strippers."

"You're right. It came as a real disappointment when I asked one of 'em to stitch me up."

"You're trying to make me laugh."

"It's not working."

She reaches a yellow light, darts another look at me, then guns it, getting over the line just in time.

"Hellcat." I release the handle over the door and put a hand on her leg, because touching her helped ease my panic earlier, and right now it's a high-pitched ringing in my ears. I keep imagining that door, open. Reese, gone who knows where. With my luck, Bean will probably pull a runner too, and then it'll all be gone...

No, not everything.

I move my fingers over her leg, needing to feel her beneath my hands—because if you're not touching something, it might slip away from you.

"It's going to be okay, Leonard," she says, but I know she's only saying it because that's what we both need to believe.

She parks in the drive of the house, and we hurry around to the back. Something sinks in my stomach when the knob turns. He left. It might not be swinging in the breeze, but it might as well be. I freaked him out but good and he took off.

I walk into the kitchen and find it empty except for a bag that used to have bread in it, sitting on the table. The little shit didn't even clean up after himself, a thought that almost makes me laugh.

Shauna follows me in. She doesn't say anything, but she takes my hand. It's only her grip on my fingers that keeps me from shutting down.

Then there's a rustling from the living room, and Reese steps into the doorway. He's wearing a different pair of clothes, probably a "gift" he lifted for himself from Walmart. He smells like he hasn't had a bath in a week, but he's alive—and he stayed. He's holding Bean in his arms.

"You didn't lock the door?" I ask in disbelief.

He shrugs. "You said you'd be here any minute." His gaze shifts to Shauna, and he takes a step back.

"She scares me too," I quip, earning a light shove from her.

"Did you bring any food?"

"Nah, man, we didn't know if you were going to stick around. But it's like I said—we're gonna bring you to someone who can look at your stitches. There's food there, too."

"Yes," Shauna says. "Unlike Leonard, we have real food."

I can't argue with that.

"We're going to your place?" the kid asks her.

"Yeah," I say, "and the woman who's going to look at your stitches is Shauna here's grandmother. She's gonna get you sorted."

"What'd you do to your feet?" he asks with a whistle.

"Someone took my sneakers, so I had to run in boots," I say, but I can't find it in myself to sound pissed about it. I'm too relieved he's okay—or will be if he doesn't have gangrene of the arm.

I glance down at his feet, but he doesn't have my kickers. He's in some cheap shoes that look like they have holes in the soles. "What gives?"

He grimaces. "I needed money for the ticket. They were nice shoes. I'm sorry, man. I had this plan to earn money in Wilmington. I was going to sketch those big head pictures of people on the beach. You know the ones."

"Caricatures," Shauna supplies.

"Yeah, those." He rubs Bean under the chin. "I was gonna earn the money and send it back to you. But it turns out you need a license to sell things, even shit like that, and someone ratted me out. The cop gave me a talking-to. And then there was a fight in the shelter, and a kid got knifed. That's when I decided to come back."

"It's okay. Next time ask."

He nods, lifting Bean a little so she's tucked under his chin. He's holding her gently, like he knows she should be protected. That's good. "What's the cat' name?"

"Bean." He looks like he thinks I'm fucking with him, so I add, "No bullshit."

"That's a dumb name." A pause. "But I like her."

"I agree on both counts. Why haven't you been reported as a missing person, kid?"

He sighs, shuffling his feet like he wishes he'd run. "You checked?"

"Like I said, we were worried."

"My foster father likes dealing with things himself. Like *I* said, his brother's on the force."

I nod at him and then look to Shauna. "Should we call Constance and warn her?"

She snorts. "Are you kidding? The excitement's going to add five years to her life."

Constance tuts her tongue as she finishes wrapping Reese's arm in a fresh bandage. "You did your damnedest to lose your arm, but you'll live."

"I could have lost it?" His eyes widen and skate to the scar slicing across my bicep.

"You're right," I tell him. "I didn't take care of it, and now I'm scarred for life. You'd do well to learn from my mistakes."

We're sitting in Constance and Shauna's living room, Reese in an armchair next to Constance, who's set up in a dining room chair next to him with her First Aid bag. Shauna and I on the couch, next to a dog bed from which the little gremlin's giving me a stink stare. A better acquaintance isn't doing the trick with him, so I'm going to have to start carrying bacon around in my pockets.

"Are you really almost eighteen?" Shauna asks pointedly, straight for the balls as always.

"I am," Reese says, "swear to Christ."

"Your birthday?" I ask.

"September 25."

Which puts it just before Shauna's.

"So we need to keep you hidden for another week or so. The cops want you for anything other than being a runaway?"

"I haven't gotten caught doing anything," he says with the stiff upper lip of someone who has a right to be offended.

"Do you have any skills?" Shauna asks. "Anything you enjoy doing?"

I give her a sidelong look, because I don't know where she's going with this.

"I flipped burgers at Wendy's for a while." He gives Bertie a hopeful look. The little gremlin wags his tail. "I like animals."

"That's good," I say. "We have an in at an animal shelter where they pretend to euthanize kittens. They'd probably let you volunteer. Just don't get too attached to any of the animals."

His mouth drops open, but before any words can escape, Shauna shoves my arm and says, "You said you were planning on sketching people on the beach. Do you like art?"

He looks away. "Drawing's a waste of time."

"Says who?" Shauna says, letting a bit of her tiger out, because I'm sure we both know who said it.

Reese wiggles a little in his chair, his hands worrying at the edge of his new bandage. "My foster parents."

"Do you know how to push around a broom better than you know how to clean a wound?" she asks.

He huffs air. "I said I worked at a Wendy's, didn't I?"

Shauna touches my arm but keeps her eyes on Reese. "We're going to have to hire a janitor at The Waiting Place before we open. So if you want an honest job, I might be able to give you one. But if you steal anything from anyone, I'll be the first one to turn you into the cops. Got it?"

"What's The Waiting Place?" he asks, his eyes wide.

"It's a collective of artists. We're going to sell art and teach people to make it. My best friend is a painter. If you want to learn, he'll teach you, but you'll find he doesn't take bullshit either. He's also a former personal trainer, same as me. And Leonard and his friends are all big guys. No one's going to bother you with us around."

A sense of wonder fills me as I look at my girl. Because she's sticking out her neck for him, same as she's done for me. She's... magnificent. Except that word doesn't seem big enough for her. She's the kind of woman you need a ten-dollar word to describe.

The kid's quiet for a moment, staring at Bertie, his throat working.

"Well, out with it," Constance says. "Either way, I imagine we can keep you hidden until your birthday."

When he looks up, his eyes are glassy. "You don't know me. Why would you do that for someone you don't know?"

I meet his gaze, then get up and lift my fist out to him. He bumps it. I can tell he's being careful not to cry in front of us—that he'll think less of himself if he does. "Because it's like I said, kid, we've been there. Sometimes you need a helping hand, and sometimes you are the helping hand."

"You said you'd been in a bad situation when you were my age," he says. "Did someone help you out?"

"Not then," I say. "It was later I found help, but by then I'd been through hell and back enough times to make a map. You take your out when you're given it."

He nods slowly. "Yeah. Okay." Then he glances at Shauna and says, "Thank you."

"I've tried to be polite about the smell," Constance says, which makes me snort, "but really, young man, I think it's past time you washed. A bath will be best, keeping that shoulder out of the water, but I'm going to tape plastic over it anyway."

"Is there any food here?" he asks.

"I'll fix you something while you're in the bath."

He gets up but glances doubtfully at his dirty backpack. "I don't have anything better to change into, so I'm probably still going to smell, ma'am."

She tuts her tongue again. "Do you have any objection to wearing clothing left behind by an odious man?"

"Depends on what odious means," he says, slouching a little.

"Well, my dear boy, it's a long story involving a water aerobics instructor. Why don't you come with me, and we'll find you some dismal but clean clothes to wear, then get that shoulder squared away so you can wash."

He goes with her willingly enough, because that's the power of Constance. I defy anyone not to trust her if she orders them to.

I go back to the couch, back to *her*, and Bertie gives a yip of objection. Shauna pats his belly with her foot before pulling me closer and draping her legs over mine.

"You didn't need to do that, Tiger." I place a hand over her thigh, but I'm well aware that it's not a big house, and Constance is just a hallway away. If she doesn't approve...

I don't want to disappoint her, is all. I don't want her to look at me differently.

"I think we can trust him," I continue, "but—"

"This is how he'll become the kind of person who's worthy of trust." She turns slightly, her lips close enough for me to claim them if I had a mind to. "Isn't that how you became a person who's worthy of trust? It changed things for you, when Burke and the others accepted you as one of them. Maybe it's time for us to pay it forward."

"You've taken ownership of my bullshit," I say, tracing my hand along her leg. "I shouldn't like that."

"Feel free to." She kisses the side of my face, and I close my eyes, feeling a ball of emotion jammed in my throat. Because hot damn...

I know I haven't done anything to deserve this. Then again, maybe Reese feels the same way. Maybe we get more than we deserve sometimes, to make up for all the times we got less.

"Besides," she adds, "you said Mrs. Ruiz told you he's a good kid. And Bertie likes him. Bertie's an excellent judge of character."

"I see what you did there."

There's the sound of footsteps from the hall, and Constance emerges alone. Her eyes take in everything, same as I knew they would, but Shauna doesn't move her legs and I don't move my hand.

"It's about time," she says, propping a hand on her hip. "You really tried to make me sweat with all this will they or won't they mumbo jumbo, didn't you?"

Relieved laughter rumbles out of me, and Shauna laughs too.

Then I shift her legs and get up, because Constance deserves to hear this part face to face. I walk over to her, holding her gaze, then say, "I'm not good enough for her, we both know that. But I'm going to do my best to make up for it. I'm going to treat her right and walk on the straight and narrow."

She's laughing as she pulls me into a hug. "If you walk on it all the time, we won't have any more fun."

"So, I'll do it most of the time," I say with a grin as she pulls away.

Reese shows up in a pair of tweed pants, a polo shirt with white buttons and a sour look on his face. "I look like someone's grandfather."

"Someone's shitty grandfather," Shauna pipes up from the couch.

And I feel lucky, so damn lucky, that I just know the other shoe is going to drop. Or maybe a couple of concrete blocks, right on my chest. But I'm going to live like it won't, because I'm sick of living in fear.

Been there, done that, lost the damn T-shirt.

twenty-seven

SHAUNA

"*STOP, STOP.*"

I stir, woken by the sound of someone's voice. I groan, because it has to be the middle of the night. It's pitch-black in my room, and sleep's still making my eyelids heavy.

It takes me a minute to remember that Leonard's in bed beside me.

Last night, Reese fell asleep on the couch in my grandfather's clothes. We all agreed we shouldn't move him, and Leonard said he didn't feel right about leaving us alone with him in the house. Obviously, I can defend myself against a kid who's maybe a hundred and twenty pounds soaking wet, but I didn't fight him on it. Besides, I don't think he's ready to be separated from Reese.

So he stayed with me in my bedroom.

But now...he's thrashing. Saying that word over and over again. Something clogs my throat, and I remember the way he went downstairs last weekend, spending most of the night on the too-small couch. He's made comments about not being able to sleep...

I shake his arm, and he flinches away from me before opening his eyes. They're full of...fear, and it takes a second for recognition to filter in.

"Fuck," he says soundly. "Are you okay?" He sits up and runs a hand over my face, my shoulders. "Did I hurt you? I shouldn't have..."

"I'm fine. Are *you* fine?"

He swears again, then slumps back onto the pillows. "Yeah. Shit. I'm sorry. I told you I'm not a good sleeper."

"You bring any of your ganja?" I ask, using his word.

He smiles and shakes his head. "And risk the wrath of Constance? No thank you."

"She'd probably ask to smoke some with you." I touch his cheek, knowing he's sensitive about this and anything I say might make him pull back. Retreat. "What are the dreams about?"

He's quiet for a minute, and I don't think he's going to answer me.

"It's my father. When he found me..."

"You dream of him hurting you," I ask, my hand still on his face.

"Yes." He swallows. "And I'm always a kid again. I can't fight back."

A sadness comes over me, so thick and choking I can barely breathe. "Leonard, I think Burke's right. You should talk to someone about all of this. A therapist. You've been through so much..."

"I'll think about it," he says. "But maybe I should find somewhere else to bring my pillow. I don't want to wake you up with my bullshit. Or hurt you. I couldn't stand it if I hurt you."

"I want you in here with me," I insist. Then I lean in and kiss him softly.

He kisses me back like a man who's desperate. We're naked under the covers, so there's nothing separating us when he rolls on top of me. This time it's slower, softer, and full of a different kind of need.

After I clean up, I fall asleep in his arms, and he doesn't wake up again. Neither do I. Until his alarm goes off.

He seems as displeased about it as I am, mostly because it's way too early for anyone to willingly wake up on a Saturday.

"Oh, shit," he says, after he gets it shut off. "I have somewhere to be. Burke's proposing to Delia this morning, and he needs my help."

"He's doing what?" I ask, nearly falling out of bed. "Why didn't you say anything about this last night?"

He grins at me, sitting up in bed. "I'm guessing he didn't want me saying anything at all. We know how you girls talk."

"Girls?" I say, raising an eyebrow. He reaches out and traces it, sending a flutter through me. One corner of his mouth lifts in an amused expression.

"Women. Queens. Goddesses. That better?"

"Moderately."

He grabs his T-shirt from where it landed on the floor and pulls it on, which makes me want to pout. Then his underwear and shorts go on too.

"You're going in your sweaty clothes?" I ask.

"What else would I wear? Grandpa Fruckface's chinos?"

Laughter bursts out of me, then I remember he has no car and no shoes.

"Do you need me to drive you to your house? You have a shoe problem."

"You're telling me," he says with an aggravated *I haven't had any coffee* sigh. "My feet don't like me much. I've got some sandals at Mrs. Ruiz's house."

Sighing, I get up and pull on some clean clothes from my bureau. "I don't mind playing uber, but we should take Reese with us."

"What do you think Constance would do to him?" he asks. "Teach him how to badly crochet?"

"Very funny. No, I was actually thinking about this last night. I'm going to ask Rafe if he can come by The Waiting Place this morning so we can give Reese a tour and maybe an art lesson. I figure he needs something good."

"That's mighty fine of you," he says, pulling me in for a kiss. "I'm going to tell Burke about Reese," he says in an undertone. "I don't like keeping something like this from him. He's got a right to know, especially since this is the kind of thing his parents could use against him. Plus, he's smarter than I am. A problem solver. He'll have ideas for—"

"Do I have to knee you in the nuts? Because you know I'm capable of it."

"What'd I do this time?" he asks, his lips quirking slightly. I run my finger over them, and he sucks it in. It's distracting, but I'm not going to let him distract me from this.

"Quit acting like you think you're stupid." I pull my finger back. "You're not. You're one of the most non-stupid people I know."

"Careful, Tiger. That was almost a compliment."

"You're smart, Leonard. You're capable. There's your compliment."

He's grinning now. "If you want to puff me up, you could just tell me I have a big dick and be done with it."

"But you *know* you have a big dick," I say. "And this is the kind of stuff you need someone else to tell you."

He kisses me, which is satisfying but also not satisfying, because I know he still doesn't believe me. It'll take a while, probably, but I'm nothing if not persistent.

We leave the room, and my heart takes on a nervous rhythm as we step into the hall. There's the possibility Reese left and we didn't hear him, but he's there on the couch, nestled up in a blanket my grandmother crocheted. She may not be talented with her hook, but she *is* prolific. Bertie is curled up right beneath him.

Reese looks so innocent, so young, and I feel my inner tiger flex her claws. I'd like to tear them through his foster father.

A smile settles on Leonard's face, telling me he was worried too.

"I'm going to go wash up and text Rafe," I say.

Leonard pats me on the butt as I go by him. Once I'm in the bathroom, I brush my teeth and poke out a message to Rafe.

Bless him, he's not thrown.

But he does complain that I forgot to text him last night.

> I was busy.

Gross. Don't want to think about that.

> Not with that, you ignoramus. With the kid showing up.

Fine. You get a pass.

> With sex too, obviously, but that came first. You may not want to touch the worktable in The Clay Place anytime soon.

I hate you.

> I just texted Sinclair. She's good with offering the kid the job once he's eighteen. I'll meet you at The Waiting Place in an hour and a half. I'm still at the gym.

When I come out, Reese is up, and it takes everything in me not to laugh at the sight of him in my grandfather's clothes. They're both too short and too wide.

"I washed your clothes," I tell him. "They're in the dryer."

"Oh, thank God. I thought we were going to have to be seen with him like this," Leonard teases—and Reese is smiling as he goes off to retrieve them. Nana gave him the grand tour last night, and the house isn't large enough that he's forgotten where things go.

"You have a gift," I tell Leonard in an undertone.

He lifts his eyebrows. "Are you still hyping up my bra trick?"

279

"No," I say, leaning into him. "You have a gift for making people laugh. For making them comfortable."

"That there's what they call ill-gotten gains."

He means he's flexed that muscle by charming people into giving him what he wants. I imagine that's true, but it's not the whole story.

Nana's already gone, off to some class or another, but I text her with our plans.

We stop at the house so Leonard can change, grab some shoes, and feed Bean, and then I drop him off at the community center where Burke is going to pop the question. I'd love nothing better than to hide behind a potted plant so I can witness the big moment. But it's *their* moment, and Leonard's promised to get it all on video. I'm sure Delia will tell me about it too.

Reese is mostly quiet on the way to The Waiting Place, but his eyes widen when I pull into the parking lot.

"It's really big," he observes. "I'd have to clean all of it?"

"Sure," I say, "but you could listen to podcasts or whatever while you work. I'm not saying it's a dream job, but it's a way for you to earn money while you figure your shit out. Plus, it's an opportunity to learn, if that's something you want."

We get out of the car and approach the building, but I can tell there's still something on his mind. It's there in the way he's picking at the bottom of his shirt. My gaze catches on the shoes he swapped for a bus ticket. We're going to have to pick up some replacements.

"What's up?" I ask. "You worried about tripping over the broom?"

He glances at me as we walk. "What if I'm no good at it?"

"It's something you can *get* good at. We're not going to throw you out on your ass if you miss a spot when you're mopping the floor."

"What if someone pukes?"

"Then you'll have fun cleaning it up. But most of the time you'll be cleaning up after the artists." I pat him on the back as we reach the door. "I'll be making lots of work for you, kid. Clay is messy."

I open it, and we step inside, Reese looking around like he's a toddler at Disneyland, overwhelmed and excited. Last night, I could tell the art bug had bitten him harder than he was willing to let on. It's there again today. A spark he's tried and failed to smother.

Before I discovered clay, I used to make origami creatures out of school papers, the Thank You cards my mother bought but never sent, and the sales postcards that seemed to come in the mail every day, anything I could get my hands on without being cursed out by my mother. I had this drive to make the things I imagined real—to bring them into being as if they could become an army of monsters who'd save me. I recognize that same need in Reese. There are a million images in his head, I'll bet, and maybe we can help him figure out how they need to come out.

"The Paint Place is this way," I say, gesturing to the right side of the hall. The building spans out in either direction from the atrium.

There's a grin on my face as I watch Reese glance around, soaking it all in as he walks. Then Rafe steps out of The Paint Place at the end of the hall and waves to us. It's a big hallway, but my friend's built like a Viking, a solid tank of a man with dark hair and eyes. Reese stops in his tracks; his Disneyland look gives way to fear.

"Holy shit," he says, practically tearing at his hem now. "I thought you said this guy was a painter?"

"He is," I confirm, feeling a tugging at my heart. "He's good. A good guy too. You can trust him. Just like you trust Leonard."

Reese considers this for a second, then nods and starts forward again. There's something muted about him, though, like a sunbeam through frosted glass, and I hate whoever did this to him. I want to send them a box of crickets. I want to show them that a small woman can take a man down if she knows what she's doing.

"You look moody as usual," Rafe tells me as we get close.

"Good morning to you too." I nod to the kid. "Reese, this is Rafe.

Rafe, this is Reese. He has talent, but he needs a teacher. Think you can handle it, or are your arms too sore from lifting?" We always give each other shit about our workouts, a holdover from when we worked at the gym.

"I can handle it if the kid can keep up. So, what do you like to sketch with?"

"I don't...I haven't..." Reese sputters to a stop, but I can tell Rafe gets it. The kid hasn't had a chance to use anything but what he's found lying around.

"You ever paint?"

"In school some." He glances around as if he's worried who might be listening, then adds, "A bit with some cans."

"Right on," Rafe says. "Maybe we can do a mural together on one of the outside walls."

"Really?" Reese asks, and I'm happy to see that Disneyland look spark back to life.

"Sure, man. Come on in, and let's see what we can get into."

Reese heads into the opening to The Painting Place, passing Rafe, who winks at me.

I wink back.

For the first time in a long time, I don't feel anything but good.

"Can I be your peanut gallery?" I ask as my friend follows the kid inside. Rafe set out a bunch of paper, charcoal and pencils, plus acrylic paints, brushes, and a couple of canvases and tabletop easels. Judging by the look on the kid's face, it might as well be Christmas morning. I feel a contact high, remembered from when my grandmother decided one of the rooms in the basement should be an art room. She's the one who bought me that first big hunk of clay—and as I worked with it, I cried for the first time since my parents had died. I cried for everything they hadn't been to me—and for everything they were. For those few moments when my mother had hugged me, and my father had said he was proud of something I'd done.

I still have the monster I made that afternoon.

I'll *always* have that monster.

Maybe Reese needs that too—a way to let everything that's bitten at him from the inside out.

"If you want to stick around, it's up to my man Reese here," Rafe says, nearly giving me a jump-scare I was so lost in thought.

Reese nods quickly enough that I suspect he's still a bit intimidated by Rafe, but the intimidation doesn't last long, because soon they're sketching together. Reese is *good*. Rafe and I exchange a glance—the kind of giddy look of two people who love art who've found a third person to indoctrinate into their cult.

The time goes by quickly, and I'm surprised so much of it has come and gone by the time Leonard texts me. I fumble to get my phone out of my pocket, then snort-laugh at his message.

She said no.

Liar, liar pants on fire.

OK, she said yes, but Burke looked like a tool in his outfit. I would've said no.

Did you tell him about Reese?

Yes. He's going to meet us at your house after he fucks Delia.

He said this to you?

In so many words.

So, how much time are we talking here?

For his sake, I'm hoping a couple of hours.

For her sake, I hope so too.

> I'll be there soon. Just got in an Uber.

> Text me when you get here so I can open the door.

A few minutes later, my phone buzzes again.
Leonard:

> I'm here. Look how well I listen.

I go to open the door for him, and he comes in and instantly lifts me off my feet, sweeping me around in a circle.

"Put me down," I cry out.

"I'm in a good mood, Tiger," he says as he sets me on my feet. He leans in to kiss me, I grab the top of his shirt to pull him closer. When he breaks away, he says, "I got a feeling today's going to be a good day."

"All that romance go to your head?"

"It only seems right to help out with one wedding if I have it in my mind to destroy another."

It's funny, but I haven't been thinking about Bianca and Colter and their war against my monster mugs. They've barely blipped on my mind after Bianca sent the message cancelling today's photo-shoot. A couple of weeks ago, it seemed incredibly important to show her that she couldn't get to me, but now...

Do I really care what she thinks of me?

"Maybe we shouldn't bother destroying them," I say.

"Quit your crazy talk." He takes my hand and starts walking in the wrong direction with a confidence that makes me laugh.

I swivel him around. "I think you'll find they're this way. Why's it crazy talk? I honestly couldn't give a shit about either of them or their wedding."

"But if we make Josie's predictions come true, we'll be cementing that woman's career as a psychic. People will talk about her predictions of the future for years to come. We'll be modern-day heroes. Besides, we'll also teach Bianca and Champ a valuable lesson."

"And what's that?" I say as we get close to The Paint Place.

"Fuck around and find out, that's what."

He whistles as he steps in and catches sight of the piece Reese is working on. They started off sketching, then sketched on the canvases and took out the paint. He's painting a little black cat. Bean, to be specific.

"Well, dip me in chocolate and call me a sundae."

Reese turns and grins. "This place is the shit, Leonard."

"It sure is," he agrees, nodding to Rafe.

There's a smile playing on Rafe's lips, and even though he looks like he wants to pull some macho bullshit, he's too pumped up to go for it. "This kid is something else," he says.

Reese looks embarrassed, but Leonard says, "I got the sense that a future Picasso stole my shoes."

"Don't you know anything about art, man?" Reese says. "Picasso drew messed-up faces and shit."

Leonard puts his arm around my back as he laughs. "No, my friend. I don't know jack about art. Maybe y'all can teach me."

"I was waiting for you to ask," I tell him.

twenty-eight

LEONARD

I'M A SHIT PAINTER, but it's fun. Rafe's a good guy, but he does pull me aside, as predicted, to tell me that if *I* fuck around, I'm gonna find out. I'd have thought less of him if he hadn't.

"I have a feeling you're not the only one who'd teach me a lesson," I say, nodding in Tiger's direction. She's talking to Reese with a hand on her hip, her gaze on his canvas. Maybe painting isn't the poison she's picked, but she's still in her element in this place, and it's sexy as hell. "She's not the kind of woman you screw over. Colter's about to learn that."

He raises his eyebrows. "Because of her, or because of you?"

"Both of us. They did her dirty, and they deserve to be reminded of it."

"I'm with you on that. You're the one who helped the kid?"

"Shauna did too," I say, because he's staying at her house, and she has a much clearer sense of what she's doing than I probably ever will.

"You did good," he says. And even though I've only known him for a couple of weeks, it means something, hearing that.

We spend another hour or so messing around in The Paint Place, and then Shauna takes us over to The Clay Place to give us a clay demo. Of course, my giant dick is sitting out in the middle of the work room. Damn, I forgot what a veiny bastard we made. It's a masterpiece.

Reese notices it immediately, of course. "Is that—"

"Probably exactly what you think it is, kid. My woman here agreed to help me put together a little birthday present for a friend."

"Seems like a big present," Rafe says, his mouth twitching.

"He's a good friend," I reply. "So naturally I want to embarrass him."

"Can you teach us how to make more of those?" Reese asks Shauna hopefully.

"No, absolutely not," she says. "I'm surrounded by enough testosterone as it is. No more dicks in this house."

That's when my phone buzzes with a text from Burke. Apparently, it took him and Delia about three hours to get it out of their system.

> Meet at Constance's place? I'm bringing Delia.

> Affirmative. We'll head over now.

I tell the others that play time is over. Rafe doesn't ask to join us, but he tells me to keep him updated on the plan. I understand that the kid is his concern now, too, and I appreciate it. The more friends Reese has in his corner, the better.

Half an hour later, Burke and Delia, Shauna, the kid, Constance, and me are all gathered in Constance's house. Burke and Delia are on a loveseat, and Shauna, the kid, and Constance are gathered on the couch. The dog's lying next to them, giving me a dirty look. I'm sitting in an armchair. We're all drinking sweet tea and pretending to eat some raw cookies Constance made. They're a worse flop than the homemade Kahlua, but I'm not about to tell her. Negative feedback only makes her double down. If I told her they taste like rotten fruit mixed with sawdust, she'd probably buy a raw food cookbook and make it her personality just to spite me. It's one of the things I love about her.

Shauna too, which is why she surprised me by saying she doesn't care about going to the wedding anymore. *I* do. This is how it all started—how *we* started—and it seems important to see it through. I'll talk her around if need be.

But there's something I have to do first. Something that's been itching at me ever since the kid showed up in my house. I've got to do it alone. And the information I need is about to be shared. Last night, I was too happy he'd returned to ask, but now...

"Who is he?" Burke asks for the second time, giving Reese a look that's firm but also sympathetic. He's good at that. "We have to know, Reese. Not because we're going to send you back but because we need to be ready in case he tries anything." He pauses, takes a bite of one of the raw cookies before I can shove it on the floor to save him, and then frowns before adding, "I have a private investigator on retainer, and he can look into your foster father. See if there's anything we can bring to the authorities' attention."

"His brother's a cop," Reese says, his face pale. "And he's a teacher. His wife says he's not doing anything wrong. She thinks he just takes obedience seriously."

"Does he hit the other kids?" I ask, my hands in fists. I can feel the nails cutting into my flesh, but it's not enough. I need to sink my fist into that bastard's face. I want him to feel what it is to be afraid.

Shauna's giving me a look from the couch that says she knows it, so I flatten my hands and set them on my thighs. There, that's what a calm person would look like.

"Sometimes." Reese sighs and messes with the hem of his shirt. "But with me the most. He says it's because my dad's a bad man. He...he's in prison for aggravated assault and robbery. Joel says he needs to beat it out of me so I'm not the same way."

"Bullshit," I say. My voice is louder than I meant it to be. I clear my throat and say, "That's bullshit, kid. You're in charge of who you are. Not your father. Not this Joel asshole."

Shauna gives me a significant look, and I can practically hear her whispering in my ear, *Listen to yourself, Leonard. You have surprisingly good advice sometimes.*

I take in the rest of the room. Delia looks like someone just drop-kicked a puppy in front of her. Everyone else is good and pissed.

"I guarantee you that someone who pulls this kind of crap has done something else," Burke says, pretty confident considering there's only a few charges out on his parents despite them being certified shitty people. "He'll find something else. He's good."

Reese looks off into the distance and sighs again. "His name's Joel Edwards. He lives in West Asheville. A few streets down from Mrs. Ruiz."

Constance putters off to the kitchen and returns with a notepad she probably swiped from somewhere and a promotional pen from a teashop. "Here," she says, handing it over. "Write it down for them."

Reese bites his lip, then looks from Burke to me. I nod at him, feeling the knot in my throat and that burning need to break my fists. "You can trust Burke. I'd trust him with my life."

"Feels like that's what I'm doing."

But he writes down the address. I get up from my chair to grab a glass of water from the kitchen, and on my way back, I see the address, clear as day. I commit it to memory, because I'll be paying old Joel a visit, come sunset.

I don't have a car, so I have no idea how it'll happen, but maybe I can take an uber to a location a couple of blocks away, and then...

I lower into my seat, my mind working.

Reese tears off the paper and hands it to Burke, who pockets it.

"Thank you. I'll get him working on this. I've got a good feeling that we'll be able to bring this guy down."

But if they rely on the legal system, on the right way of doing things, it'll take months. Maybe longer. How many kids is he going to hit before then? How many kids is he going to convince that they're garbage?

I swallow, feeling a tightness in my gut.

There are eyes on me, and when I glance at the couch, I notice Shauna's watching me.

Something tells me she knows exactly what I'm planning.

Damn it. She's going to try and stop me, isn't she?

Burke clears his throat. "I think it would be best if you stay with me and Danny," he tells the kid.

"Why?" I ask.

My voice sounds strangled. I liked it, being over here with him and Shauna and Constance last night. It felt like maybe I had...

It felt good, is all.

"He can't stay in your neighborhood," he says, giving me a significant look. "The cops are already looking for him there. And he can't stay here, in case this asshole does figure out—"

"I'll be staying with them," I blurt. Then I glance at Shauna and Constance. "If my ladies agree with it, of course. I'd need to bring Bean."

"*Of course* Reese is staying here," Constance says. "And you're welcome too, Leonard. I've never minded having a house of sin. Frank might have had something to say about it, but he can go—"

Shauna grabs Constance's hand, her eyes on mine. "Yes. Both of you should stay." Her gaze floats down to Bertie, who looks pissed off, like he's suddenly learned English and wishes he could forget it. "Bertie could use a little competition."

"What can we do to make you more comfortable, Reese?" Delia asks, sweet as can be. She keeps reaching for her engagement ring, touching and twisting it like she can't believe it's there.

"Shoes," Shauna says. "He needs new shoes." She gives him a sidelong look, taking in his outfit. "Actually, a whole new wardrobe.

Maybe you, Mira, and me can go pick up some stuff tomorrow afternoon instead of meeting at the bar?"

"I don't get a say in this?" Reese asks, sulky.

"Nope, bub," I say. "You don't want to run into ole Joel at Target a week before you get your wings. It's a miracle it hasn't happened before now. You're on house arrest unless Shauna takes pity on you and brings you to The Waiting Place."

It's not open yet, so there's little to no chance someone he knows will see him and report it back to his foster father.

Reese swears, earning a shoulder swat from Constance. His flinch is the flinch of someone who's seen violence, and I feel my fists balling again.

Constance's face shifts from fond annoyance to horror. "You should know that no one will ever hit you here. *Ever.*"

"Yeah, I got that," he says, looking embarrassed.

She must be able to tell, because she shifts gears again. "But no swearing until next week."

"Seriously?" he squawks.

"Unfortunately, she means the vast majority of what she says," Shauna tells him.

We all eat dinner together—pizza again, because Delia insisted that Reese be allowed to choose—and then Burke and Delia say they need to head off to continue their bonkfest. Or at least that's what they mean. Before they go, Shauna pulls Delia aside, probably to plan their shopping trip or discuss the rock on Delia's finger.

Constance is grabbing more of Grandpa Fruckface's clothes for the kid and cleaning up the guest room, which has been taken over by her new hobbies. A little pile of crochet here, a couple of bottles of shitty Kahlua there. The kid might be tempted to try them, but I have a feeling even a seventeen-year-old will have better taste than to want to get drunk off of it.

I nod to Burke. "Thank you for letting me hijack your day."

"I'd have been pissed if you didn't tell me. I'm going to put

Danny on this too. If there's anything online about this guy, he'll find it, no matter how deeply it's buried."

I nod, because it's a good idea. This is what I rely on Burke for—to be my steadying force. To know how to make it through the world the *right* way.

"Be careful, brother," he says, delivering the words with a cautioning look.

So Shauna's not the only one who's guessed what I'm thinking. Maybe my poker face could use some work.

"You know what they say about old dogs."

Bertie lifts his head from his dog bed by the couch, giving a token growl to let me know he's still not pleased with the way I've moved in on his girl.

I lift my hands to him. "I wasn't talking about you."

"I mean it," Burke says as he stares a hole into my head.

"I know you do."

"You've got something to lose now," he adds, because he's the kind of man who likes to make a point and is good at it.

He's right.

I've got a lot to lose all of the sudden, and I'm not used to it.

I nod slowly and watch as Delia joins him and they head off into the night.

As I close the door behind him, I feel Shauna's arms circle my waist, and I turn to face her. She's looking up at me with a flat mouth and the same kind of disapproval that she threw my way in the beginning.

"I know what you're planning, and you don't have a car. If you get caught, you'll lead him right back to Reese. You know that, right?"

I reach down and smooth her hair. "Look at you, getting right to the point."

"I mean it, Leonard."

"Someone's gotta give this guy a talking-to, Tiger."

She glances back, making sure that Constance is still gabbing Reese's ear off elsewhere in the house.

"And is that all you're planning? You really think conversation is going to make him see the light?"

"I can be mighty persuasive."

"So can I," she says, grabbing my hand and guiding it down the front of her shorts.

Fuck me, I'm right there, and I can't not cop a feel. I rub slightly, then dip a finger into her.

"Shauna."

"You're going to go no matter what I say to you, aren't you?"

I lift my finger out and suck on it. Her sigh heats my blood, but she's right...

"I'm going for a walk."

"It's miles away. Do you even have a mask? A getaway plan?"

No. I was going to think about that as I went along, but she's got a good point about the mask. I'd be dumber than a Thanksgiving turkey if I showed up without one. Still, when I think about the way Reese shrank away from Constance's little love tap, I want to crack the world open like it's an egg and fry it.

I have to stop this guy. I *need* to. I don't know if I can go on existing if I don't do anything.

In my head, that hotel door is opening. "*Found you,*" my old man says. "*And I'm gonna make damn sure you never run again, you little shit.*"

And then the pain starts—bright at first, like looking into the heart of an eclipse, and then dull, like it's happening to someone else.

I take a step toward the front door, but she stops me with her hand on my arm.

"We're going to wait until dark, and we're going together. We're only going to talk to him if we can get him alone, away from the kids."

293

The thought of putting her in danger is a non-starter. I don't want her or Reese or Constance anywhere near this guy.

"I'm not putting you in the middle—"

She squeezes my arm. "I'm already in the middle of it. We do it together or not at all."

I raise my eyebrows. "You're going to stop me?"

"I've flipped men bigger than you. I can and will stop you."

It's obvious from the look in her eyes that my tiger means business. Dammit, I *like* that she wants to do this with me. That she'd risk everything to stand up for the kid...and for me.

I glance back at the hallway, and bless Constance, she's still chatting away like there's no tomorrow.

"I need this, Shauna."

Something sad passes through her eyes, and I hate that it's because of me.

"You never got to confront him," she says. "You turned him in, but you never got to tell him what he did to you. You didn't get your moment of reckoning."

She's thought this through more than I have, not that I'm surprised. "It's not just that, dammit. I can't sit back and wait for Burke's private dick to put together paperwork. I need to do something. This man's a foster father. A teacher. He's around kids all day."

"Wait until it's dark. I have ski masks we can wear."

"You're not going anywhere near him."

"Fine," she says, although I'm not sure I believe her. "But I'm bringing you. You don't have a car, or any way to get there. For God's sake, you haven't even looked up his picture so you know you're going for the right dude."

She's right about that too.

"And we may not have an opportunity to talk to him today. Or tomorrow. Or the next day. We don't step in until we find him alone, and you will *not* seriously hurt him. If you do, you're no better than he is."

I feel like hanging my head. "You should know I've done bad things before, Shauna. I've shaken people down for money."

"When you were muscle."

"Yeah."

I hated myself then. My life was hollow and small, and even though I'd broken free from my father I didn't *feel* free. It was like I'd gone from one shitty prison to another. I only did it for a for a little while before...

Well, I don't want to think about that either.

"Which is all the more reason you're not going to go back to that life." She lifts out her little hand. "Either you shake on it, or it doesn't happen at all."

I pause, my mind working, while she watches me with her hand extended. "We're going to the wedding," I say. "I'm setting that as a condition."

She snort-laughs. "Seriously? What's the wedding compared to this?"

I don't know, but it seems important. I'm not backing down. "Seriously."

"Okay."

So I shake on it.

We case the place for three nights, driving by the house and then parking a few blocks away. After Shauna sees the property is a good size and overgrown, next to a greenway that makes getaway a cinch, she agrees to let me scope it out on foot alone. It's on the third night that I get my opportunity. Joel's out back on his phone, talking in the shadows of the trees like he's asking for someone to give him trouble. He's got a wholesome look—short hair, buzzed on the sides, and pleated trousers secured with a braided belt. Then again, bad people aren't given a dress code they have to abide by.

I slide up behind him from the trees where I've been hunkering and get him in a headlock, his arms twisted behind his back. His phone goes flying.

He gasps before kicking out at me. He's a big enough guy, but he's let himself get out of shape.

Danny's done some research on this joker over the last few days and shared it with all of us—he's the teacher of the year at his school, a deacon at his church, poster boy for doing the wrong things and getting patted on the back for it.

My adrenaline skyrockets, and buzzing fills my ears. "I know what you've been doing, you piece of shit. You come off as some local hero, but you beat those kids you're supposed to be helping." I ease up on his windpipe enough so he can answer for his crimes. He might holler for help, of course, but if he does, I'll have time to run.

"Reese," he says, trying to turn back to get a look at me. I'm wearing a mask, but I still hold him steady. I don't want him looking at me. I don't want to get a good look at his face right now either, because then I'll want to punch it. "I've been worried, is he—"

"You stay away from him. If you touch one of your foster kids again, I'll come back here, and we won't have such a pleasant conversation. You feel me? I'm going to keep an eye on you. I'm gonna know it if you didn't eat enough fiber and can't shit right."

"The boy lied to you," he says, and it's obvious from his tone that he's trying to work this around to his advantage, even here in a headlock with his phone on the ground. "There's a difference between discipline and—"

"There's no reason for you to hit a kid, you piece of shit." My fist itches to make close contact with his face, but I remember what Shauna and Burke told me. I have a lot to lose. "No fucking reason. You want someone smaller and weaker than you to live in terror of you?" I amp up the pressure on his neck. "Remember what it is to feel afraid."

I loosen my grip, and he gasps for air.

I want to hit him once.

I want to break his nose.

I want to hear him cry out in pain.

My father probably felt that way when he busted into that room, looking for me.

And it's that thought that makes me push him away instead.

He staggers from me and falls to the ground.

I back up. I'm about to peace out and run when he charges toward me like a bull.

"You don't tell me how to run my house, you piece of shit," he shouts.

I sidestep him, and he charges headfirst into a tree, the thump as loud as a drumbeat, then falls to the side in what has every appearance of a dead faint.

Well, shit.

Someone steps out of the trees, and I flinch, ready to take off, but it's Shauna wearing her mask.

"What'd you do?" she whispers furiously.

"I didn't do shit!" I swear in an undertone, lifting my hands. "I had him in a headlock, sure, but it was only so I could talk to him. Then he charged at me, and the tree did the dirty work."

For a second, I'm sure she won't believe me, then her shoulders start heaving up and down. It takes me a solid second to realize she's laughing. "You think this is funny?"

"Yes," she says through silent laughter. I almost laugh too, because it's a ridiculous fucking story, but I'm too hung up on the fact that she believes me. "We need to get out of here."

"Should we leave a note?" I whisper back.

"What would it say? Next time, we'll get you with the maple?"

I bite back laughter, then pick up his phone. The screen is shattered. Good. Whoever was on the other line ended the call, but I type in YOU'VE BEEN WARNED and send it from him, to him. Then I wipe down the phone and set it on his chest. It's moving up and down regularly.

From the look of him, he got a good knock to the noggin, but not in a place that will give him any permanent damage.

"Or should we take the phone and give it to Danny so he can mine it for info?" I ask, second-guessing myself.

"Let's keep our crimes to a minimum," she whispers.

We step off, and before we leave the woods and brush at the edge of the property, we pocket our masks. Then we make our way back to the car, which we parked a few blocks away, and Shauna drives us back toward the house as casual as you please.

Giving me a quick look, she asks, "How do you feel?"

I take a moment to consider it. "I don't know if it'll do any good, but I'm glad I did something. You're right, though." I run a hand across my mouth. "I'm glad I didn't hurt him."

She glances at me again. "Do you regret punching Colt?"

I snort. "Hell, no. He deserved it, and I'll give him this much, he took it like a man. If I'd punched this asshole, though, I don't know if I would have been able to stop. That's not something..." I flex my hand, feeling the ache from earlier—the need to break him. "That's not a test I want to fail, Shauna. Why'd you follow me?"

She tips her head back and laughs. "You think I haven't been following you back there every single night? Amateur."

Fuck me. I'm pretty sure I'm in love with her.

twenty-nine

SHAUNA

Message from Grandpa Fruckface:

> It's been forty-four days since you last responded
> to my messages.

"RESCHEDULING on us was in bad form," Mira tells me, her lips painted red and pouty.

"I was busy."

It's Wednesday night, and I'm at Glitterati with Delia, sitting at the end of the bar next to the old-fashioned jukebox spraypainted with glitter. It's buzzing with life even though it's in the middle of the week, after eight.

Mira, Delia, and I went clothes shopping for Reese on Sunday afternoon. We also stopped at a vintage store and picked out a couple of hideous his and hers outfits for Leonard and me to wear to the photoshoot this weekend.

Mira took particular delight in choosing a boy band shirt for Reese. I'm pretty sure she was being ironic, but then again, she's bedazzled her bar and covered it in glitter, so I can't be sure. We also talked about Burke's proposal, which Leonard had already showed me on video, and they wanted to know all about Leonard and me. In fact, Mira loudly asked me what twelve out of ten sex felt like while we were in line at the Starbucks in Target. I told them a bit about what happened last weekend, but they didn't get all the details.

Now, sitting at the bar, Delia asks me, "You're not going to tell us what you were busy with on Monday night?"

What I was busy with was scouting Joel's house with Leonard.

There's no way of knowing whether Leonard freaked him out enough that he'll behave—but in the meantime Danny and Burke's private investigator are on the case, trying to unearth some of the dirt we're all hoping is there.

Reese's birthday is also coming up in less than a week, so soon he'll be legally free of the jerk.

I consider how to answer for a moment and then figure, screw it, they both already know about Reese. It feels good to have friends I can trust enough to confide in.

"We paid a visit to the a-hole who was terrorizing Reese."

Delia's eyes pop wide. "Does Lucas know about this?"

"No, but don't worry. The guy didn't see our faces, and a tree did all the work for us."

"Explain," Mira says, pointedly ignoring a man who's clearing his throat a few spaces down at the bar, waiting for service. On the weekends she has another bartender, but tonight it's just her.

I do, and Mira slaps the bar with a wide, toothy grin. "Sometimes life really does deliver."

The guy who could use a throat lozenge says, "And sometimes it doesn't," giving her a look that would peel paint off plaster. Then he leaves the bar, doing his damnedest to slam the door. It was built with slow-release hinges, though, so life has handed him another disappointment.

"Take care! Make sure to review us online," she calls after him.

"And you're the one who has business skills," Delia mutters.

"But I don't have people skills, sister dearest," Mira says, reaching across the bar to tap her on her slightly upturned nose. "And most people would say that's what counts."

She steps off to take care of the other, more patient patrons, and Delia gives me a pointed look. "You see it now."

"See what?"

"Leonard. You can see that he's a good man."

I take a sip of my drink, another special blend of who knows what that Mira has named 'A 12 out of 10.' It is. It really is. "Yes," I say simply. "Obviously. If he wasn't, he wouldn't be so invested in helping Reese."

Or in fixing Nana's broken sewing machine, which she pulled out of the basement after God only knows how many years. She's decided crocheting is too tedious, and she'd prefer to sew together fabric someone else had the misfortune of making.

Or in buying paint for the craft room downstairs because Reese told him the only thing he remembers about his mother is the color green. Her favorite. So Leonard wants to paint it for the kid's birthday, make it feel like his.

Or in telling me the story of every tattoo on his body because I wanted to know—even the ones that embarrass him.

I was drunk when I got that one, Tiger.

That there is what a mistake looks like. You'll see a few of them.

Or in taking a photo of a strange bug he saw while he was working on the house he's flipping with Burke because he thought I'd 'like the look of it.'

Delia's still watching me, and I have a feeling she can see right through me or identify the color of my thoughts.

They'd probably be pink, dammit.

"You've fallen for him," she says.

My heart feels like it's thumping around in my chest. She's right. Of course she's right. "Is it that obvious?"

"To me." She leans in a little closer, speaking in an undertone. "But maybe it's easier for one person in love to recognize another."

I glance behind the bar, but Mira is pouring someone a drink on the other side.

"Don't tell Mira yet," I say. "I have a feeling she's not going to let me live this down."

"I won't."

She's smiling at me, which suggests she's not totally horrified by what I just told her. Then again, smiling is her default mode. I'm not ashamed of being in love with Leonard. He's a good man who's had a hard life, up until recently, and I have every intention of continuing to make it better. But I have something I don't want to lose—so naturally I'm worried that's exactly what will happen.

"You're not going to tell me I'm being stupid?"

"I'm not," she says, stirring her drink with the pink flamingo stirrer. Honestly, this place. It's ridiculous, and I absolutely love it. "Lucas and I were kind of hoping this would happen."

"Seriously?"

"What's happening?" Mira asks, flipping a towel over her shoulder and returning to her spot.

"We want to know if you're moving in with Danny," I deflect.

"Yeah, have you talked to him?" Delia asks. Turning to me on her stool, she explains, "She was supposed to talk to him on the phone yesterday."

Mira pulls a frown. "Yeah, so he called me at like nine a.m. I don't think I made the best impression. It was before my first alarm went off, and don't even ask me about coffee."

"She brings new meaning to night owl," Delia tells me.

"He seems kind of..." Her face scrunches more. "I can't think of the word, but he's the kind of guy who'd come in here, with my awesome drink menu, and order a beer."

The suit-type who sat next to Delia with a lot of enthusiasm before he caught sight of her huge rock shrinks a little on his seat. Busted, buddy. There's a draft beer sitting in front of him.

"So?" Delia challenges her. "Maybe you can help him mix things up a bit."

"Like a project?" Mira says, brightening at the prospect.

From what little I know of Danny, I suspect he won't love being seen that way, but he probably could use some help loosening up.

"Remember that movie?" Mira snaps her fingers a few times as if it might get our synapses going.

"Are you talking about *West Side Story*?" I ask. "Because otherwise the snapping isn't helping you get your point across."

"Very funny. No. I mean the one where the cool girl gives the geeky guy a makeover, only it's Patrick Dempsey, so we all know he's going to be a smoke show, and then—"

"Are you the cool girl in this scenario?" I ask.

She gives my shoulder a shove from across the bar.

"Is Danny the smoke show?" Delia asks pointedly.

"Look at you, learning an attitude," I say. "I don't hate it."

Mira starts laughing, then snaps her fingers again.

"Still not helping."

"*Can't Buy Me Love*. That's the movie."

"Are you *attracted* to him?" Delia asks, propping her elbow on the bar, her head cradled in her hand. It's like she's settling in for a long listen.

"What? No! I just talked to him on the phone. And I know you told me I've met him before, but I literally don't remember, so he can't have made much of an impression. I mean, sure, he does have a good voice. Like a low and sexy rumble, but when all that voice does is talk about power bills and gas bills and yada-yada-yada it seems like a damn shame, you know?"

"Interesting," Delia says, then her expression sharpens. "You haven't had hate sex with Byron, have you?"

"Hold that thought." Mira heads off to the other side of the bar to grab someone a drink.

"Classic deflection," I say.

"I don't think she's done it yet." Delia watches her, her head still propped up. "But she's thinking about it. We need to make her unthink it."

I feign shock. "You mean you don't like Byron?"

"He's the kind of guy who writes a song about a generic woman and then tells every girlfriend it's about her."

"Seems like she'd see through that kind of bullshit."

She laughs. "She does, but she says he's hot enough for her to forget it occasionally. Are you still going to the photoshoot this weekend?"

I sigh and take a long sip of the drink. "Yes, Leonard and I made an agreement."

"He wants to go?" she asks, laughing.

"Yes, but God knows why. It's going to be a nightmare."

I meant what I said to Delia. I'm not looking forward to taking photos in a field of flowers with my ex-boyfriend and ex-best friend. But I have to admit, the look on Bianca's face is pretty satisfying when Leonard and I walk into the field on Saturday afternoon.

This is a place I brought Bianca to, ages ago, because I wanted to go flower picking. It's only twenty-five minutes out of town, but it looks like it was plucked from a story about English country life. There are rows and rows of different flowers mixed in together, lifting up as if they want people to breathe them in or stoop and pick them. It sounds silly to say, but it's magical.

If some idiot ever convinces me to marry him, I told her, *I'm going to do it out here.*

It's hard to think it's a coincidence. All the same, I'd be happy to be here with Leonard under different circumstances—say if we'd snuck in here at night with a bottle of wine so we could enjoy each other under the stars. Currently, it's full of uncomfortable-looking people in formal wear, because the high today is an unseasonal eighty degrees, and the men were all told to wear suits.

Leonard is *technically* following the directions. His suit is our assigned color—bright red—and Reese let him borrow Mira's boy-band shirt to go underneath it. It's much too big for Reese, but it's a little tight on Leonard, which only adds to the outfit. He looks like a pimp. It's kind of hot, honestly, although maybe one man in a million could pull it off.

He's doing this for me, and he's having fun doing it. I may not have wanted to say the words out loud to Delia, but I've already fallen good and deep. I'm in love with him. It's exhilarating, and also terrifying.

My hideous poofball of a dress, with puff sleeves and a skirt with a bubble hem, is a matching red. The color clashes perfectly with my hair, just as it was meant to, I'm sure.

Bianca swallows, then approaches us. "I know I assigned colors to everyone, but the other gentleman seemed to understand I was talking about accessories...Doc." She waves to Colter and his friends a few rows over. All of them have tasteful pocket squares. Colter is handing a flask to one of the guys, and he freezes as if he's a deer in Bianca's headlights. But she's so pissed about Leonard's suit she doesn't even notice. There's a photographer standing next to a huge goldenrod plant, her nose twitching like a rabbit's as she takes photos of everyone's natural poses, probably catching the guys with their hooch.

"Well, shucks." Leonard gives me a rueful look, really laying it on thick. "I went and put my foot in it, didn't I, honey? It's just... well, this here suit was given to me by the parents of one of my favorite little tykes. It has sentimental value, and I figured this was an opportunity to wear it."

"It's fine," Colt says, surprising me. He's crossed the rows of flowers to join us, leaving his buddies behind. The last time Leonard saw him, he punched him the face, leaving him with the sickly yellow cast to his eye that hasn't been fully hidden by whatever makeup Bianca's caked over it.

"Colter," Bianca snaps. "It's *red*."

"And you told him to wear red. My buddy here is just doing as you ordered."

Is he...drunk?

He's got no reason to stand up for Leonard, unless he has some weird testosterone-fueled respect for him because he punched him in the face.

Then Colt wraps an arm around Leonard's shoulder and steers him back toward the little circle of bros and their flask. "Come hang out with us, man. There's this hilarious video I have to show you about..."

I tune him out, because I couldn't be less interested—and also because they're leaving me with Bianca.

"Are you sure that guy's really a doctor?" she asks. She's wearing a beautiful lavender dress...probably because it's *my* favorite color. The funny thing is that red is *her* favorite—she's spiting herself just to poke at me. I want to ask her why, to ask what purpose any of this serves for either of us.

Instead, I ask, "Do you want to see his medical license, Bianca? What else would you like, a blood test, maybe? A urine sample?"

She scrunches her nose. "Don't be gross. You have to admit, he doesn't come off as a doctor."

"That's why I like him. He's *unexpected*." I say pointedly, because we both know that Colter isn't exactly a roller coaster of excitement.

She looks away for a second, her eyes twitching as she watches Colter. I can see his mother a few rows back, talking to the woman who has a thing for Leonard.

I wave to Shelly, and she blows me a kiss.

"What's up with you and Colt's mother, anyway?" Bianca says.

"We like each other. I'm not sure why that's so hard for you to understand." I feel a little twinge of sympathy as I say it, because even though she's the very opposite of my friend now, I *do* get why it's hard for her to understand. My grandmother might not be a Jelly Lady, but she's a wonderful woman who's always cared about me and let me know it. Bianca has never had someone like that in her life.

She tightens her lips into a line that she'd never keep there if she had access to a mirror. "She refused to carry your stuff in her store. Doesn't sound like much of a friend."

"You're not the best authority on what a friend does, Bianca. Besides, we both know that Shelly wasn't the one who made that decision."

There's a slight flinch that gives her away—she was hoping I didn't know she'd lied and wouldn't find out.

"I told you Colt didn't like them."

"Yes, you did. Thank you for that."

She opens her mouth, her eyes focused on me, and I think she might be about to break the façade and drop this crazy game. Maybe she'll tell me that I'm not invited to the wedding anymore, or that I can at least be demoted from maid of honor.

Maybe she'll say she's sorry.

Then, from my peripheral vision, I see a woman in an enormous sunhat and a bright orange and yellow kaftan approaching us from the little reception house out front.

I gasp.

It's Josie the psychic.

Did Leonard invite her back without telling me?

"Um, Bianca," I start.

She catches sight of Josie half a second after I do.

I expect her to pitch a fit, but she breathes out a sigh of...relief?

"Oh good, she's here."

"You invited her?" I ask, the words coming out high-pitched.

Her expression tightens. "She's going to do another reading for me, Shauna. She told me her readings become clearer the more time she spends around someone. I need her to change her predictions."

thirty

LEONARD

CHAMP'S ACTING like we're best buds, which isn't how I'd approach the situation if someone had smacked me in the eye. I don't like being cornered over here, leaving Shauna alone with Bianca. She can handle herself, obviously, but I'd prefer to have her back.

Champ offers me a swig from his flask, and since this situation feels like a bad memory in the making, I don't say no.

"That's Macallan—"

"All I care about is the alcohol content."

Champ eyes his friends, who have fallen back into a conversation about some athlete's knee—as if they're sports analysts and not salesmen and bankers. One of them asked me for "a doctor's perspective on the matter," and I told him all high and mighty that it's beneath my professional integrity to make medical guesses.

The look on his face was pure gold.

Champ takes me by the shoulder and leads me behind a big fall sunflower. Maybe he's drunk enough to think plant matter is sound resistant.

"Bianca's been giving me a real hard time about this eye. She made me slap a steak over it last week. Fucking gross."

"Hey, man," I say, "what gives? Thanks for blowing some smoke for Bianca, but I don't get why you're not more pissed about..." I lift my hand toward my eye.

He waves a hand as if getting punched is an everyday thing for him. Which is when I realize something: he'd never been punched before. It was probably some sort of defining experience for him, and now I've gotten roped into it.

"We settled it like men," he tells me. "You're honest, Doc. I like that about you. A lot of people are full of bullshit."

I barely swallow a laugh. I might be honest about some things, but I sure as shit haven't been honest with him. I almost feel bad for the guy, until I remember he's the one who screwed Shauna over. Sure, it left her single and available, but it was the worst mistake he's ever made, and he deserves to feel the burn.

"I get it," I say.

And that's when I notice the woman in the dress that's nearly as loud as my suit.

I whistle. "Are we in for a world of trouble, Champ? Because Josie the Great just joined us, and it didn't go down so well the last time Bianca came across her."

"She's the one who invited her," he says in an undertone, a dark look on his face. "She's convinced she can get her to change her predictions. Hell, she even changed the dinner order for the wedding to chicken instead of steak. I love steak." He frowns. "Cooked steak."

"Is this reading going down before the photos or after?" If there's a chance we might not have to sweat our asses off out here waiting for the photos, I'm all for it.

"After," Champ says, popping my wish like it's a balloon.

"Well, that'll be something."

"It'll be something, all right," he says softly, like a man who already knows regret. I'll bet Bianca's feeling the sting too, because one thing Champ is not is a Grade-A Thinker.

So we pose for an endless stream of photos. Several as a group—arranged in a color gradient—and individual shots of all the couples too. Bianca also insists on taking a whole series with just me and Shauna, her and Champ, as if we're the bestest buds there ever were.

"You need your face angled in the other direction, Colter," Bianca hisses at least half a dozen times. Because that bruise is getting more obvious as the afternoon wears on, the makeup sweating off in the sun.

Champ gets increasingly hostile, too, probably because all of us guys are sweating our balls off in our suits, and he's been chugging Macallan instead of drinking water. Maybe he and Bianca will ruin each other, like Shauna said, and we won't have to do anything but take out the marshmallows.

Throughout it all, Josie lurks at the outskirts of the group, watching us. Maybe it's just because she got so much right on her last reading, but it's creepy as hell. Melly keeps cornering her with questions about the aunt whose funeral she saw, until Josie tells her that her great aunt isn't a clown who can be called out to do party tricks.

By the time Bianca declares that we're done with the photos, I'm more than ready to leave.

"Can we get out of here?" I ask, leaning in to kiss Shauna's neck. It's sweaty.

"Please, for the love of God."

"God's got nothing to do with this, Tiger." Then I break off a flower and tuck it behind her ear. I want to get her out of here and strip her out of that ridiculous balloon dress.

Bianca claps her hands, dramatic as hell, and says, "Let's see what Josie the Great has to say about the wedding, everyone. It was so much fun to hear her predictions last time that I had to invite her back. After she gets done with Colt and me, you can ask her whatever you want, my treat."

311

No one seems that enthusiastic about it, probably because we all remember what happened a couple of weekends ago. Queen Bee has a kind of manic energy tonight, and it don't take a genius to figure out why. She's a Type-A control freak, and Josie's a wild card, not the kind of person anyone can control.

Champ rolls his eyes at me. We're all still standing in a group after our last photo of the four of us. "Here we go again."

Seriously...does he think we're friends? I'll have to disabuse him of that idea before he starts calling me to go to shitty football games, although I'm guessing I could win a pretty penny off him and his buddies in a round of poker.

Josie goes up to Bianca, and my first thought is that she's got no crystal ball. Then she lifts a charm up from her necklace and stares into it for about thirty seconds before lifting it and staring at Bianca through it. We're still out in the field of flowers, and I catch the photographer capturing this gem of a moment.

"Yes, I see it more clearly now," Josie says. "The cake is still broken..."

A sound like an animal's growl escapes Bianca, and Champ openly takes a swig from his flask.

"And he's the one who's going to break it."

She points directly at me.

Well, shit. First her prediction about the slammer, now this. I guess she really does want payback for introducing her to these nutjobs.

"Doc?" Bianca says, her eyes full of accusation. "How *could* you?"

"I haven't." Admittedly, up until thirty minutes ago, I fully intended to make all of Josie's predictions come true. I'm still mighty fond of the idea.

"You can't come to the wedding," she blurts. Then, shifting her gaze to Shauna, she says, "What do you even know about this guy?"

"*Excuse me?*" Shauna's good and riled up, her cheeks flushed from more than the heat. "I know plenty. And are you telling me I can't bring my boyfriend to your wedding because a dime-store psychic told you that he's going to break your wedding cake? I mean, what the actual fuck?"

Josie shrugs. "I've been called worse, but it's still hurtful."

"Whoa now, Tiger." I put a hand on her arm. "Bianca here just wants everything to be perfect on her special day. Who could blame her? Let's have this conversation after we've all had a chance to calm down."

"He's not coming," Bianca blusters, her cheeks red too. "You can bring someone else if you want. But I think you should really look into this guy. Because there's no way he's a doctor."

"We saw his website," Colter interjects.

"It was fishy."

He belches loudly. "Screw this, Bee. He's my friend, and he'll be there. Right, bud?"

There's murmuring from the other guests, and Shelly has the worried look of someone who's going to be hearing a lot of bitching from both of them in the near future.

"Colter, are you *drunk*?" Bianca asks, her voice pitchy.

I lean in close to Tiger, who's still spitting mad and is staring at Bianca like she'd enjoy nothing more than swiping at her. "This isn't going to go down well. Let's get out of here while we still can."

"I can't let her—"

"Tiger," I say, wrapping my arm around her. "Let's go."

"Here," Shelly says, hurrying up to us and pressing a bouquet to my chest. "For Shauna."

"Thanks, Shelly," I say. Bianca and Colter are still loudly bickering. A few other people are starting to filter off the field, but there's a little line forming next to Josie the Great. I guess they think she can peer into that necklace of hers and see the future. I try giving her a dirty look on our way out of the endless field of flowers, but she's not paying us any attention.

Shauna's still pissed off by the time we get to her car.

"That bitch. I can't believe—"

I laugh as we get inside, then I press the flowers to her chest. "For you, my queen."

"Thank you," she says, some of her bluster fading as she turns and sets them on the backseat. "I just—"

I kiss her, and she kisses me back, the flower I tucked behind her ear falling onto the dash between us. I return it to its rightful place. "Shauna, Bianca's right about me. I had every intention of screwing up her wedding. We both did. Maybe you were right the other day too, and we shouldn't go. They're going to be miserable with us or without us."

"Colter seems to think you're his best buddy," she comments.

I laugh and smooth her hair. "He's delusional. But it might be the Macallan talking. Say, let's stop by Mrs. Ruiz's. I need to pick up some clothes."

Some of her bad mood seems to lift. "You mean to say you're not going to wear that suit for the rest of the day?"

I groan. "It may be stuck to my body. I think my balls are glued together."

"Charming." There's a grin on her face, though, and I put it there. That makes me feel like a god after the scene we just exited.

Other people are heading into the parking lot now, talking in undertones, as Shauna backs out of the lot and heads for Mrs. Ruiz's. A glow wraps me up and fills me, making the void I carry around seem smaller. I put my hand on her thigh, below the hem of that dress, and I keep it there for the rest of the drive.

It sounds weird, maybe, but I know something's wrong the minute we get out of the car. The house hasn't changed any, and there's no red note stuck to the door. Still, there's an air of trouble—call it a lifetime of experience cluing me in.

Before I get the door open, the neighbor, an old man who has a collection of seven busboy hats he wears in rotation, calls out to me.

"Mrs. Ruiz's lodger," he calls out, waving his cane in the air. He's never bothered to learn my name, not that I know his. I walk over to his wheezing porch, making a mental note to help him replace a few of the boards. Last thing he needs is to break through it and get caught.

"What's up, man?"

"This neighborhood's going to hell."

"More robberies?" I ask, running a hand over my jaw.

"Not for a few days." His gaze shoots toward Shauna before landing back on me. "You didn't hear it from me, but the police are looking for you. They seem to mean business." He gives me a significant look—a *you better get the fuck out of this city and maybe even this state* look. I barely register it, though, because suddenly that void inside of me is pulsing and expanding outward again.

My first thought is *holy shit, maybe Josie's actually psychic.*

Then my mind starts working overtime. I could do what he's suggesting. I could run. I could send Shauna home with some excuse and then go pack a bag at Mrs. Ruiz's house. Take an uber to the bus station and buy a ticket that'll take me out of state.

I could disappear again.

A couple of months ago, I wouldn't have even paused to consider it. But here's the thing—my old man finds me wherever I go. Even now, after confronting Joel, the dreams still come. Not every night, but almost. Running isn't going to make him go away, but it will take me away from Shauna and the kid. Constance. Bean. Burke. Danny. Drew, if he ever comes back. Shane, if he ever feels like talking to me.

The only family I've ever had.

I run a hand across my jaw and glance at Shauna, standing next to the steps of the little purple house. She looks like everything I've ever wanted but could never have. I'm in love with her, but I destroy the things I love.

Did Joel figure out who I am, somehow? Is he going to have me booked for assault by tree? Kidnapping of a minor?

Dammit. We came so close. Another couple of days, and Reese will be eighteen.

The geezer nods to my threads. "Why you wearing a suit like that, son? You get noticed when you wear a thing like that."

He's not wrong, but I've stopped caring about going through life below other people's notice. I've started to feel like a person again. But here's that other shoe I've been waiting for, dropping on my head.

"Thanks, man," I say, feeling numb inside as I head back toward Shauna.

"Stay safe."

Shauna's watching me as I walk toward her, her forehead lined with worry. With every step I take, I feel like more of a fuckup. A failure.

"Go on inside, honey," I tell her. "I've got to make a call."

"What happened?" she asks in an undertone.

"It's nothing."

It's everything, and she seems to know it.

We enter the house, and after putting the flowers in some water, she sits on the sofa. I can feel her watching me as I head into the kitchen to call Burke. It takes me a second to get my hand steady enough to find his number.

"Hey, buddy," he says, laughing. "How'd those photos go for you?"

And I tell him everything.

He's quiet for a moment, thinking. "He never saw your face?"

"No."

Then he swears. "This isn't about him, but we'll move the kid just in case. Go talk to them. Turn yourself in if they're looking to arrest you. I'm calling Shane."

A disbelieving sound escapes me. "Shane's not going to put his career on the line to help me. He's all but said he's done with me."

"We're family," Burke says. "Shane's...Shane. But he'll come if he knows you're in trouble. I know he will."

I hang up, and I do one of the hardest things I've ever done. I tuck my phone in the pocket of that red suit, then walk into the living room and tell Shauna what's happening. I pace while she sits on the couch, taking it all in.

The color leaks from her face. Her worry hurts worse than my own because all I've ever wanted to do is make her feel good, and here I am doing the opposite.

"He doesn't think it has anything to do with Joel?" she asks.

"He seemed pretty sure of it, but I don't know what the fuck else it could be about."

She lifts her fingers to her lips. "You said you broke into the Burkes' car...that you took Mrs. Burke's bag."

I shake my head. "There weren't any cameras, I checked. And it was weeks ago."

"We should go," she says, getting up off the couch. "We should find out—"

I pull her to me and kiss her like it's going to be the last time. Those 'we's she dropped are still echoing in my brain, proof that she's once again treating my shitty problems as hers. She kisses me back just as hard, sucking in my bottom lip and running her hands under the ugly suit jacket.

I trace my hands up her soft thighs and find her underwear, tugging them off. She steps out of them without missing a beat. Our mouths are still attacking each other as her hands find the belt of my pants and tug it open. I'm already hard, full of need for her. I back her into the wall, hoisting her up by her thighs. My mouth's still on hers, like I have to keep it there to be able to breathe.

I reach down to adjust myself with one hand, and then I thrust in hard to the place I need to be. She makes a sound into my mouth, and I swallow it, because I'm greedy for her. I want all of her that I can take right now, because I think—because in the back of my mind I'm sure—

It's not the last time. It can't be.

I feel her tears against my face. I break our kiss, horrified, and stop thrusting. "Are you okay? Did I fucking hurt you?"

"No," she says. "Keep going. I need you. I'm...I'm scared."

I know what it costs her to say that. Same is it costs me to admit, "I'm scared too." I pause, then add, "Look on the bright side. Maybe it's just unpaid parking tickets."

And I carry her like that, my dick buried inside her, her legs around me, to the couch, so I can make love to her. Something tells me that's what she needs right now.

I take my time, moving into her slowly, deeply as I kiss down her cheek to her neck and then her beautiful tits, pushing down her dress and bra to get access. She wraps her legs around my waist and runs her hands through my hair as I spread kisses across her chest, circling her nipples with my tongue before taking them into my mouth.

I want to remember it all, to remember the way her body lifts up to meet me. The little sounds she makes in her throat when I stroke in deep. The way her eyes flutter shut and then open to find mine. How it feels to meet her gaze while I sink into her—claiming her even though I can't keep her, because there's nothing in this world I want more.

I can feel her starting to tighten around me, her body telling me she's close, but I tell my cock to calm the hell down. This is it. This is our moment—and when it's ripped away, it'll only be a memory. I won't be able to feel her legs wrapped around me or her soft hands in my hair. I won't be able to hold her in my arms.

Still, everything has to end, especially the beautiful things, so I kiss her, feeling her tears between our lips, and thrust in deep. She gasps into my mouth as pleasure rolls through me. Even though it fucking hurts to know this may be it for us, I want to remember all of it. The pain too.

I kiss the last of her tears away, and she buries her head in my neck. We lay like that for a long moment. Then I kiss her neck and her jaw, stealing a little more of her for myself, and make myself say it. "It's time."

"They can't have you," she says softly, fiercely. "We'll fix this."

"Sure we will, sugar." But I don't believe it. I doubt she does either.

We clean up, but I keep on the suit.

"You're going to wear that to the police station?" she asks.

"Might as well give them a thrill."

So that's exactly what I do.

They arrest me, which isn't a big fucking surprise. I saw the writing on the wall the minute my neighbor told me the cops were looking for me.

I always figured I'd go down eventually—I just thought it would be for a crime I'd actually committed.

thirty-one

SHAUNA

"THIS IS BULLSHIT," I say, my voice shaking. "He reported the truck stolen."

I'm still shell-shocked, barely keeping it together. In my head, I still hear the police officer telling Leonard, "Raymond Danvers, you're under arrest."

Raymond? I hadn't even know for sure that Leonard wasn't his original name. I tell myself I'll be able to ask why he chose it for himself, but I'm terrified I won't get the chance.

Yesterday afternoon, my biggest worry was Bianca tap-dancing on my last nerve by trying to disinvite Leonard from the wedding. Now, Leonard's behind bars.

They found his shitty truck, it turns out, and there was evidence in there connected to the burglaries around Mrs. Ruiz's neighborhood. The cops' explanation for accusing Leonard is that he's been arrested for petty theft before, under *other names*. They wouldn't say who'd called in the tip.

I didn't know what was going on until this morning, because they didn't give Leonard his phone call until then. That's against the rules, but no one seems to care about those lately.

I'm pacing in Danny and Burke's apartment. They're with me,

and so is their friend Shane. The only one sitting is Danny, and from what I can tell, he's only doing it so he can turn around and around in his desk chair. Nerves, probably. I can relate.

Reese is staying with Rafe for a few days, until all of this blows over.

I hope to Christ it blows over. I'm numb, but Delia insisted on sitting with me last night. We drank rose and pretended to watch a movie. Mira had to work, but she texted us anecdotes about the bar every five minutes and didn't once tell me I was a dumbass.

Nana's been a nervous wreck too. I'm pretty sure she stayed up all night sewing on that machine Leonard fixed, because this morning she presented me with a lopsided purse. Bertie and Bean already had little bowties affixed beneath their collars. The scratch marks on her hand suggested Bean wasn't a fan.

"Are you sure he didn't have anything to do with this?" Shane asks, which makes me feel a kneejerk dislike for him. His outfit doesn't help his case. It's hot out, even more so than yesterday evening, but Shane's got on a button up shirt and chinos, like he was hoping to get called into the office.

Or to bail out his friend, I remind myself. *He's on your side.*

Burke gives him a dark look, and Shane lifts his hands. "It had to be asked. I need to know what I'm dealing with."

"No, he absolutely did not," I say, my voice rising despite my intention to sound cool and collected. "He's been staying with me and my grandmother for the last week. If any of the crimes happened then, there's no way he was involved."

"Could he have snuck away at night?"

"I have a dog who hates him, so no. Bertie would have woken up the whole house."

"That won't hold," Shane says, grimacing, "but it's fucking weird that they'd think they have a case if he reported the truck stolen."

"The people who made the anonymous report figured he wasn't

going to call it in," Burke says, his jaw tight. His whole body radiates a cold fury I wouldn't have thought him capable of.

"You think it was your parents?" Danny asks from his desk chair.

"Who else?"

"So, they hired someone to commit robberies and plant evidence in Leonard's truck?" he asks, turning in his chair. "That's ballsy."

"They've been stuck behind the doors of that mansion," he says, pacing. "They've had nothing to do but cause trouble. Plus, I know for a fact they're in tight with the chief of police. There's no way they don't have their hand in this."

Shane nods. "Can't think of another reason why they'd bring him in even though he'd reported the truck...unless... What if the cop didn't put in the paperwork? He might not've if he figured they weren't going to find it."

"Wouldn't there be some record of that, though?" I ask. "He said he called the station."

Shane nods again. He paces a few steps, jiggling something in his hand, which he then returns to his pocket. When he looks up at us again, he actually seems excited. "If your parents are behind this, Burke, they may have put their foot in it. This might be what brings them down."

"As long as it gets Leonard out," Burke replies.

"We'll probably be able to bail him out within forty-eight hours," Shane says. "He has no history of violent offenses. I checked." His lips twitch. "All of his names."

At least none he's gotten thrown into jail for, thank God.

If I'm a heathen for thanking God for such a thing, so be it. Leonard's a good man. He's done bad things, but he wants to change. He has been changing, dammit.

"I'll cover his bail, obviously," Burke says.

Shane nods. "Well, I'm gonna go talk to him."

"Can I come?" I ask, relieved and also terrified. Leonard didn't sound like himself on the phone. He sounded broken. Defeated.

"You're his girlfriend, right?"

They're all looking at me as I swallow and nod.

"No, Shauna," Shane says. "Not right now. But I'm going to do everything I can to get him home as soon as possible." He has an air of competency that makes me believe him. Or maybe I just want to. "You're right," he adds. "This *is* bullshit. And I'm not going to stand for it."

I try to tell myself Leonard will be glad to see Shane show up, to know that we're all behind him.

Maybe it will give him the life raft he needs.

Because I'm worried he's already losing himself.

I'm worried that he woke up in a cold sweat from one of his dreams, and found himself in the place he's probably imagined himself for years.

I'm worried he thinks he deserves it.

thirty-two

SHAUNA

Text conversation with Bianca:

> I'm sorry. Colt says I was being irrational.
>
> I just really want everything to go perfectly, you know?
>
> Can I come talk to you?

>> Not everything in the world revolves around you, Bianca.

> Can it revolve around me right now?

>> No.

"YOU'RE GOING to pace a hole through that floor," Nana says.

She's one to talk. It's the kitchen floor that'll probably give way under her feet. I woke up at three a.m. last night because she was making cookies in the kitchen. They weren't even good cookies. It was another version of her raw recipe, which would have made Leonard laugh because of course she made his least favorite cookies out of worry for him. She's got a cake in the oven now, because it's Monday, Reese's birthday.

I went to The Waiting Place for an hour or two this morning, but I couldn't take the sight of Danny's clay dick, still sitting loud and proud on the floor of my workshop. So I came home, and Nana and I painted the craft room green for the kid because Leonard's not here to do it.

We don't even know when—or if—Reese will want to come back. He'll be here later tonight, along with Rafe and Sinclair, Burke and Delia, and Mira, for a small celebration, but we haven't talked about what comes next. There's nothing to stop him from returning to our house now that he's eighteen—*if* that's what he wants. But I know for a fact that Rafe and Sinclair's place is at least ten times nicer and safer. The kid's been shaken by all of this, especially since he stole some supplies before bumping into Leonard. He could have wound up behind bars, and he knows it.

Maybe he doesn't want to be here if Leonard's not. I can understand that.

After Grandpa Frank moved out, the house felt wrong for a while, too big and echoey, but then it shrunk around us again. Now, it's back to feeling empty. Wrong.

Bean seems to have gone half feral without Leonard, spitting or hissing when things aren't to her liking.

After Nana and I finished with the craft room, we exchanged a look.

"They're coming back," she said stubbornly. "Both of our boys."

"They're coming back," I repeated. But I'm not sure how much either of us believed it. I'm not sure how much we believe it now.

The sound of a clearing throat stops my body and brain in their tracks. Nana's standing in the living room, eyeing me. Who knows how long she's been watching me.

"What'd the floor ever do to you?" she asks, raising her eyebrows.

"How long has that cake been in the oven?" I ask. "Did you set a timer?"

"Of course I did," she says, but she turns to check on it quickly enough that I'm guessing it was a lie.

A knock lands on the door, and Bertie bustles over to it, his little butt wiggling.

My heart lifts, but it's too early for Leonard to be out. Besides, if it were him, Bertie would probably be sulking instead of doing his little dance.

Sighing, I head over to the door and look through the peephole.

I nearly stagger back, because *what the hell...*

It's Bianca.

Apparently, my text message kiss-off didn't do it for her.

I consider not answering the door, but she's not the type to give up. I wouldn't put it past her to knock out one of the basement windows and climb in if we ignore her.

"The cake burned a little," Nana calls out from the kitchen, "but I have a plan."

Naturally.

"Bianca's here."

About twenty seconds later, she comes out of the kitchen with a giant knife.

"Jesus, Nana," I say, reaching for the door as Bianca knocks again. "Is murder your plan?"

She shrugs and then laughs. "For the cake, not Bianca. But I'm flexible."

I open the door just as Bianca's rounding up for another knock, and she nearly hits me in the face.

"Good to see you too," I mutter.

Her gaze skates from me to Nana, who's still cackling with the knife in her hand.

"Hi, Constance," Bianca says, unflustered.

"Always a pleasure to see you, *dear*," she says with a grin that clearly says *go fuck yourself*, then disappears into the kitchen.

Bertie paws at Bianca's leg for pets, the little traitor, and she bends and scratches her ear. There's something different about her today—her ponytail is off center, and she's wearing a T-shirt and jean shorts, the kind of outfit I haven't seen her in since her pompom business got big.

"Not for nothing, Bee," I say, "don't you know the meaning of the word 'no'?"

She looks up and gives me a contrite smile. "I think we both know the answer to that."

I'm thrown by this evidence of self-reflection, although I'm pretty sure it'll last only however long this momentary crisis of confidence does.

"Can we sit out on the porch for a minute?" Bianca asks.

"Sure, but I've got plans soon."

She nods, and I follow her out front.

We both sit, but she's in no hurry to speak, and I'm not in the mood to oblige her. "I'm too tired to pretend to be polite. What the fuck do you want?"

She snorts, which is beautifully inelegant and the kind of thing I would do, then says, "I think I let all of this get a little out of hand."

"What? The wedding? Your vendetta against me?"

Surprise flickers in her eyes, probably because we've both been dancing around it, refusing to engage, and I here I am, pulling the rabbit out of the hat.

"It's not..."

"Please, Bee," I say. "You asked me to be your maid of honor. You've arranged most of the events leading up to the wedding at my favorite places and have gone out of your way to make sure I'm as uncomfortable as possible. I mean, you're getting married on my birthday, for Christ's sake, and don't tell me it's just because that was the only date available. We both know it's not true. Now, you're telling me my boyfriend can't come with me." He can't anyway, as he's currently in jail, but that's none of her business. "What's your endgame? What do you get out of making me feel like shit? Do you want me to explode at you? Will that make you feel like you're better than me?"

I catch the neighbor openly watching us, and I wave. She scowls and returns to her sweet tea.

"I..."

To my consternation, Bianca starts crying. I don't want to comfort her—she's been an absolute beast—but I challenge anyone to try not to comfort someone who's sobbing on their porch.

I put a hand on her arm. "It's okay, Bee."

"Is it?"

"No, not really. But everything seems to be going well for you, so I'm not clear on why you're crying."

"I...I've been awful to you. You're the only real friend I've ever had."

I can't help but laugh. "Bianca, I don't know how to break it to you, but we're not friends anymore."

"Because I'm marrying Colter?"

"Because you slept with him while we were still dating and lied about it. Because you and Colter convinced Shelly I didn't want my stuff in her shop. Because you've gone out of your way to make me miserable." I pick a bit of dog fur off my yoga pants. "You changed after your business got successful."

"I..." She swallows. "I was jealous of you."

It's what Leonard told me, but I didn't believe him. I have trouble believing it now.

"Of *what*?" I ask. "Of me living with my grandparents and having to work a second job to support myself?"

"Of Colter."

"And you got him," I say. "He and I weren't right for each other anyway. If you'd talked to me about it, if you'd been honest, then maybe things could have worked out differently."

Her mouth is a quivering line. "The Waiting Place is going to be amazing," she says softly. "Everyone wants a piece of it."

"Bianca, your pompoms were in O *Magazine*, for fuck's sake. What do you want with my granule of success?"

"You're more talented than I am. Shelly likes you better." She gives a sniff. "You're all she ever talks about."

"So I'll stay away from the wedding, and from Shelly. If you can remember how to not be a selfish dick, I'm sure you two will get along great."

"I need you to come to the wedding."

"Why?" I ask, incredulous. "I just got done saying we're not friends anymore. It feels good to admit it out loud, to be honest."

"Because you're the only family I have."

"So why the fuck have you been torturing me?" I ask, pissed now. Leonard's in jail, and I'm sitting here listening to her bullshit. I feel like I've been listening to it for six years.

She's still crying as she says, "I wanted you to confront me. I wanted you to do this. To tell me that I've been an asshole, a selfish jerk. I thought maybe it would make me feel better about everything, but you wouldn't...You never said anything, and you showed up with that sexy doctor, and—"

"He's not a doctor."

"I knew it," she says, and there's a glimmer of the Bianca I've come to know behind this crying woman.

"My grandmother made that part up, and we played along because we thought it was funny."

"But you're really in love with him," she says, which makes me look over at her sharply.

"Why do you say that?"

"The way you look at each other. Colt used to look at me like that."

329

I snort. "What, while he was my boyfriend?"

"I'm sorry," she says.

"Thank you," I tell her, because I don't want to say it's all right. It's not. None of this is. Right now, it feels like nothing will ever be all right.

"I really am sorry," she says again. "I went too far, and I didn't know how to turn it around, and now...Can you ever forgive me?"

A weary sigh escapes me, and I sound like I feel—the tiredest woman alive. I'm guessing that's not even a word, but that's how I feel. Like a thing that's not even a word.

"I don't know, Bee," I tell her. "Our friendship is over. I don't trust you."

"Please tell me you'll come, though," she says. "I want you there. I need to know you're there. I...I love you, Shauna."

"Do you know how toxic this is?" I ask, pissed all over again. "You've been acting just like your mother."

She nods through her tears.

"I don't know," I tell her. "I'll have to think about it."

"And you can bring the hot not-a-doctor, of course." She pauses. "Is his name really Leonard?"

"Yes." It's not technically true, but it's also not a lie. That's the name he's chosen for himself, the one he feels is his.

"Can I hug you?"

"Let's not push it."

She nods, then glances at the door. "Should I say goodbye to Constance?"

"Probably not. I found a voodoo doll with your likeness in her room last month. She's not the forgiving type."

"You are, though," she says with unfounded confidence.

"I'm not the forgetting type."

She gives a final nod and then leaves. I'm left staring after her with a twist in my gut. It's formed around Leonard's original name, the one *they* gave him.

thirty-three

LEONARD

IT'S Wednesday night before they spring me.

I was surprised when Shane showed up at the jail on Sunday, looking like a legal badass in his button down and a pair of pants with creases so perfect they must have been fucking ironed. He even brought a pen and a pad, like he thought I might have something interesting to say. I'd figured he was well and truly done with me, and this mess would just convince him he'd been right all along.

I said as much and he said, "For someone who's smart, you've got a good bit of stupid in you."

"You've stayed away from me for the past couple of months," I challenged him.

"Because I was pissed at you for leaving in the first place instead of coming to us for help. Not because I wanted you in jail." His mouth lifted at the corners. "Besides, I hear you've cleaned yourself up. Got yourself a girl and a kid. That's fast work, man."

My heart started pounding in my chest, because I'd been thinking about her and the kid. Thinking about them and feeling panic wind around and through me. Because everyone around me gets covered in dirt—and I don't want that to happen to Shauna.

I *can't* let that happen to her.

"Are they okay?"

"Worried about you," he said, flipping his pen around in his hand. "We all are. This is some bullshit they're throwing down, but the good news is that we have a good chance of proving it's bullshit. And Burke's going to post bail as soon as they give us a number."

"What if they don't?" I said, because that's the fear that's been growing in my gut ever since that police officer spoke the name I was born with.

"Burke's parents might be big shots, but we're about to show them they're not as all-important as they think they are." He grinned at me, looking every bit like the friend who'd howled at the moon on a camping trip while we were drunk off bottom-shelf whiskey years ago. "You know, buddy, you might have just made my career."

He surprised a laugh out of me. "By being a victim for once in my sorry life?"

"Sure, if that's how you want to swing it."

They did grant me bail, but it took longer than it should've, because even if Burke's parents are no longer the big shots they think they are, they're still more powerful than a criminal. A con man.

While I sat in jail, I did nothing but exercise and think. My mind was an uncomfortable place. Dreaming slipped into waking. My father kept finding me and beating me. Throwing me behind bars instead of the police officer who has a ghost of a mustache over his lip. I saw Gidget's dead body again and again. Felt the weight of her in my arms as I lifted her out of the car, crying, and dug a hole for her in my backyard.

The memories all crowded in, turning the void inside of me into a black hole that's sucking down everything good. The confidence I've felt these last couple of months, building the business with Burke. Being there for Shauna, helping Constance with all of her projects, being a safe place for Reese. The way Burke told me I was as good as his brother. The love I feel for them all, for *her*, has made me happy in a way I'd never experienced before—in a way I hadn't thought was possible for me.

They've claimed me, and I let them. I've wanted to claim them too, but the voice in my head is very clear in its opinions about that.

You bring everyone you love down. You'll destroy them. You'll have to watch it happen and know it's your fault.

Shane told me there's no chance the charges will stick, but I still feel like an animal that's been running for years and finally got torn down. It's easy to imagine how the Burkes might pull it off. I haven't lived the kind of life that's above suspicion.

It's Burke who posted my bail, I know, but Shauna's the one waiting for me in the lobby.

When I see her, that voice in my head starts screaming. I know what I have to do.

She puts her arms around me, and I nearly break, but I can't let that happen. Not yet. I take in the smell and feel of her, the lilac of her hair and the softness of her neck, and I press a kiss to it. Then I pull back.

"You look like shit," she says, and I almost laugh.

"It's the red suit." It was the only thing I had to change into. "I defy anyone to look good in a red suit. You haven't been sleeping."

I lift a hand to one of her eyes. They're puffy, and the circles under them tell me she's been crying because of me.

It only makes me more determined to do what I don't want to do.

She kisses me, and I let myself kiss her back.

One last time.

"Let's go." She takes my arm and pulls me out of the building, and I'm happy to leave. I never want to come back, but part of me is already resigned to it happening. I may not have been caught for some of the things I've done, but a few of them would have landed me with sentences. Maybe a price always has to be paid, and it's finally my turn to pony up.

She packs me into the car and gets behind the wheel. "Let's get the fuck out of here," she says. "I'm afraid they're going to drag you back in."

"Me too."

As she pulls out of the parking lot, she tells me the guys are waiting at Burke's place, if I want to see them. Not yet, I tell her.

"Reese has been back at the house since his birthday party on Monday," she says. "We were worried he wouldn't want to leave Rafe and Sinclair's place since they obviously have a much better situation, but he said he missed us and the animals. Plus, he wanted to be there for when you get home."

My heart swells and breaks, because I fucking want that. I want to go home with Shauna and Reese and Constance. To be there with the little gremlin dog who hates me and the cat who seems to think I'm not a piece of shit. But even if the charges don't stick, they deserve better than me. Someone who's not shattered and patched up with shitty tape.

"He was really touched when he saw the craft room," she adds.

"But I didn't—"

"Nana and I painted it for you," she says, giving me a sidelong glance. "He's worried about you, Leonard. We all are."

"You're not going to call me Ray?" I ask, my voice scratchy, unused.

"Do you want me to?"

"No."

A moment of silence passes between us.

"Why'd you choose Leonard?" she asks.

"Leonard Cohen," I say, deciding to tell her what I've admitted to no one. "It sounds so fucking stupid, but I heard that song 'Hallelujah' when I was feeling really low, and it made me feel something. I hadn't felt anything for a long time, so I let myself think maybe it was a sign. I wanted to be someone different. Someone who could do good things... But that happened before I set out to con Burke, so I guess I was full of shit, huh?"

"Oh, Leonard."

I can tell without looking there are tears in her eyes. I put those there too.

"Please bring me to Mrs. Ruiz's house. I need to talk to you. Just you."

She doesn't say anything, and I'm betting she already knows. But my tiger's not going to make it easy for me.

She parks in the driveway, and the neighbor raises his cane, giving me a look that says *dumbass* more clearly than the word itself. He's in his Wednesday busboy cap.

I salute him, and he laughs to himself.

Appropriate. I unlock the door and walk inside, and it's empty and a bit cold. A void.

It's where I belong.

Shauna follows me in and shuts the door, and I can tell from the set of her jaw that she's ready for an argument. So I take her hand and lead her to the couch. We both sit.

"You're going to try to push me away," she says.

"There's something I need to say." My voice is already strangled, and I feel the emotion sitting inside of me like a ball—dredged up from down deep, where I buried it six feet under.

"So say it," she says, plenty of fire behind the words.

"I told you Gidget died because of me."

She nods, clearly surprised. She didn't expect me to talk about my dead dog, fair enough.

"It happened while I was working as muscle. A few guys were pissed at my boss, so they followed me around. I was going to be his lesson." I swallow. "I'd brought Gidget to the store. I was only going to run in for a minute, pick up a pack of cigarettes. So I rolled the window down a couple of inches and left her in there. But they snatched me, and I never made it inside."

Her eyes have tears in them, and I can feel warmth behind my eyes too.

Your fault. It's all your fault.

"They roughed me up but good. By the time they let me go, it had been hours. She was dead in the backseat of the car, and I know it wasn't easy on her. She'd clawed at the side of the car before she went."

My voice breaks. Shauna tries to take me in her arms, but I pull back.

Your fault.

"Don't," I say. "I don't—"

"Don't you dare say you don't deserve some comfort."

I almost laugh, but I feel the tears falling down my face, and I'm ashamed.

"I don't, though. Don't you see? I didn't mean to hurt Gidget, but she died because of me. The biggest mistake she ever made was trusting me."

"It wasn't your fault."

I do laugh this time, and it's bitter and hard. "It was, Shauna, and I bear the weight of it. I've been a fool, adopting Bean. Spending time with you..."

She takes my hand and squeezes it. Looks me in the eye. "Listen to me. You made some bad decisions, but a hard road led you there. You're not a bad person. The people responsible for what happened to Gidget are the guys who hurt you."

I pull free and get up. Start pacing. My cheeks are wet, and that void inside of me feels like it's pulsing, and some bad shit is about to break free from it.

"I wanted to make them pay, to beat their faces blue. But I didn't because I knew it was my fault. I was the one who was supposed to protect her. Don't you see, Shauna? I'm always going to be broken. And that means everything I touch is going to break too."

She gets to her feet. She's crying too. I don't want her to drive like this, but I also need her to leave, because I feel a crushing need to take her into my arms, to let all of the tears I've trapped inside of me fall. To tell her that I love her more than I've probably loved anyone, and that's why I'm sure I'm going to destroy her.

"That's not true, Leonard," she says. "You don't always have to be broken. If you think that, then it's like saying Reese is always going to be broken. Or me. Bad stuff happens to everyone, and we all have a chance to work through it."

"I blew off my second chance. When shit became real, and I found out what Burke's parents were up to, I turned tail and ran. If I'd stood my ground, I wouldn't be in this position right now. I'm probably going back to jail. You want to write me letters? Flash me your tits over the table?"

"You're not going back to jail. They're bullshit charges, and you know it."

"Since when has that ever mattered?"

She stands there for a moment, watching me, her eyes flashing. "The only way you're a coward is if you step back from us now. If you run from us. Maybe we're your chance."

Haven't I dared to hope it?

But the truth of it is written on the wall. I'm a losing bet.

A *loser*.

"I think it's time for you to leave. Tell the kid..."

I trail off, because I don't know what I want her to tell the kid. Or Constance.

"And Bean?" she asks. "Are you bailing on her too?"

"She's comfortable there," I say woodenly.

"This is what you want?" Tears are still falling down her cheeks, and I want to wipe them away, to kiss her, to lose myself in her.

"Yes," I lie.

She *knows* I'm lying. It's there on her face. "I can't decide for you." Her voice is brave and clear. I'm proud of her, and I adore her. Oh God, how I fucking adore her. "But I love you, Leonard Smith. And I love Raymond Danvers too. But you need to figure out how to love yourself. Both of you."

And with that, she walks out and leaves me with that impossible ache.

I don't know how long I'm alone, draining the bottle of whiskey I'd tucked into the kitchen for a special occasion, but after a while the front door opens. Because I didn't trouble myself to lock it. Burke comes in, followed by Shane and then Danny.

I wave the empty bottle at them. "Are you really here, or am I drunker than I thought?"

"We're here," Burke says as Danny shut the door. "Drew made me promise to FaceTime him so he can be here too."

"I don't feel so good," I say, because it's the only way I can think to describe what it feels like inside of me.

"I know, buddy." He hugs me and has the decency not to pull back even though I've got to smell like the bottom of a bottle.

"First thing's first," Danny says. "We've got to get him out of that suit."

"It's an assault on the eyes and on common decency," Shane agrees.

It's funny, and he's goddamn right, but somehow that's what gets me sobbing. I instantly feel like an idiot, a loser. In my head, my father tells me that real men don't cry. That tears are only for babies who can't hack it.

I'm a baby who can't hack it.

"I've fucked everything up," I say.

"So let's see what we can unfuck," Burke tells me.

"But what if it's my head that's the problem?"

"Like I said," he tells me, "there's something we can do about that."

thirty-four

SHAUNA

Text conversation with Grandpa Fruckface:

> It's been forty-six days since you responded to my last message.

>> You're right. In punishing you for being an asshole, I've become the asshole. That's irony for the ages, huh?

>> Do you want to go to a wedding with me on Saturday?

> Do I have to wear a suit?

>> Why don't you wear a swimsuit? I hear you're partial to those.

> I'll come in a suit, smartass, but I won't like it.

>> There's the Grandpa Fruckface I know and love.

> What?

>> Long story.

IT'S FRIDAY NIGHT. I told Bianca I'd go to the wedding, but I wasn't, under any circumstances, taking part in the rehearsal dinner or the five-hour prep she'd scheduled for us for tomorrow morning. I figured I was giving her an out she'd take, but she surprised me by agreeing. I guess she's really looking forward to the half-baked, bullshit on toast wedding speech I cobbled together with Mira and Delia at the bar last night.

I haven't read it through.

I don't care to.

I haven't heard from Leonard since I left him at Mrs. Ruiz's house on Wednesday, but Delia told me he's been staying with Burke and Danny. I'm glad. I don't want him to be alone. I want him to be with *me*, but he's not ready. Maybe he'll never be ready.

My heart feels like it's been torn out and electrocuted, but I also feel a strange sense of clarity. I love him. Maybe my love isn't enough to help him out of this hole, but combined with his friends' love? Nana's love?

Maybe it'll be enough, someday.

He thinks he'll end up doing jail time for this, but he's wrong.

Shane's theory about the police report panned out. The officer who spoke with Leonard about the truck didn't file the paperwork. But Shane was able to use Leonard's phone records to narrow down which officer had taken his report. The guy actually admitted to flubbing the report, so now they know Leonard reported the car stolen before any of the robberies took place.

It hasn't happened yet, but they're going to drop the charges. Shane seems certain of it, and he doesn't come off as someone who sugarcoats things.

It remains to be seen whether the Burkes will pay for this, but I choose to believe they will. They figured Leonard would be easy to mess with because of his background, but they didn't realize how many people love him.

"You're sure you want to go?" my grandmother asks me from

her rocking chair for what has to be the thirtieth time. "And with *him*? We should do something fun on your birthday. We could go horseback riding, or drive to Carowinds, or get drunk on those terrible wines at the Biltmore."

I sigh and eat a heaping spoonful of ice cream. Those *do* sound like better options than attending Bianca and Colter's wedding.

I've already committed though, and technically we're celebrating my birthday tonight. My grandmother asked me what I wanted to do, and I told her the truth. Well, almost the truth. What I want is to be with Leonard, but I can't have him right now, so I figured I'd settle for watching *Time to Settle Down* and gorging myself on cake and ice cream. Delia's with us, and so is Reese. He told us with a straight face that he couldn't think of anything he'd prefer to do with his Friday night, although I suspect that's because he knew Delia was coming. I think he's got a crush on her, because I caught him sketching a red-headed mermaid the other night, and when I said she looked like Delia, he blushed and said it was *The Little Mermaid*.

I wish I could tell Leonard that.

"You're the one who told me to reach out to Grandpa Frank," I tell my grandmother with a sigh. Then I wave my spoon at the male contestant with the million-dollar teeth. "You think they specifically looked for someone stupid?"

"They must have," Reese mutters. Maybe he's regretting his enthusiasm about spending the evening with us. Bean is sitting on one of his shoulders, and Bertie's curled up in his lap. Before I turned the show on, he told Delia, who's sitting between us on the couch, that Bean would let Delia pet her as long as she was on his shoulder.

He's using Leonard's moves, trying to manipulate women with cute animals.

A sigh escapes me, and Delia pats my leg.

"Reach out to him, sure," Nana says. "Go to the wedding of a woman who hates you with him? No, I don't think I said that."

"Bianca doesn't hate her, Constance," Delia says. "I think she's just confused...and emotionally..."

"Fucked up?" I offer.

Nana hoots. "There's a lot of that going around lately."

"Hey, I get to swear in the house now that I'm eighteen, right?" Reese asks. "You said so."

"Yes," Nana tells him, "You can be as foul-mouthed as the rest of us. Congratulations."

I pause the stupid dating show, because none of us are actually watching it.

"Look, Nana," I say, "I figured it would be a good olive branch between me and Grandpa Frank. And I didn't want to bring Rafe because I think there's a very real chance he'd deck Champ—I mean Colter—in the other eye if I did."

I called him when I was a little tipsy last night and told him everything. He'd wanted to go to the wedding with me—if I *insisted* on going—but I told him I already had a date. He could hardly argue since he's been trying to convince me to talk to my grandfather for months.

"I don't understand why you're going in the first place," she grumbles.

Truthfully, I'm not one hundred percent clear on that either. I definitely don't consider Bianca a friend anymore. Even so, it feels like this is something I have to go through with, maybe because Leonard and I started this together. If it weren't for this stupid wedding, I might never have realized that there was more to him than the sinfully attractive buffoon I'd vowed to stay away from.

"Women are complicated," Reese offers as he pets Bertie.

My grandmother laughs. "Oh, my dear boy. *Men* are complicated. You're told never to express emotions, so when they hit you it's like an atomic bomb going off and everyone has to flee for cover.

Our society has done you a disservice, if you ask me, with all that stiff upper lip nonsense."

"I have emotions," he objects. "And so does Leonard. He texted me happy birthday as soon as he got sober yesterday. It's not easy being thrown in the slammer."

"I imagine not," Nana says.

Delia clears her throat, her gaze flying to me. I eat another, especially large, spoonful of cake and ice cream.

"Lucas says Leonard's doing better. He's..." She purses her mouth to one side.

"It's obvious you feel like you shouldn't say whatever it is you're about to say," Nana tells her. "But you should do it anyway. We all love that fool boy."

Reese rolls his eyes. "I wouldn't say I love him, but he's my bro."

"Your bro, really?" I ask, pointing my ice cream spoon at the little stinker.

He inclines his head. "I guess I love him in a bro way."

God, this kid is special.

"It's just..." Delia meets my gaze. "Burke said he's going to start seeing his therapist. Twice a week."

"Oh, thank God." My bowl drops from my hand and hits the floor, bottom down, and Bertie doesn't even hesitate. He's on the ground in an instant, attacking it. It's some good hustle, and I'm not even mad. I just set my spoon down on the coffee table.

Delia leans her shoulder into me. "He wants to get better," she says softly.

I feel hopeful for the first time in a long while, like I just walked out into a sunny day after a month of rain. I want him to get better. Even if he still doesn't want to be with me—a thought that gives me that sinking sand feeling in my stomach—I *need* him to get better. I'd just wished...

I'd wished we could do it together. That he'd let me help and support him.

"Screw this noise," I say, shutting off the TV. "Let's go to the bar."

"Can I use my fake ID?" Reese asks, his eyes brightening.

"No, but I'm sure Mira has some juice boxes in the back."

We stayed at Glitterati past midnight, because Mira insisted on making us a round of birthday shots. Much to Reese's dissatisfaction, his was non-alcoholic.

Unfortunately, my phone took a dive into a toilet well before we even reached midnight, so now it's living in a bag of rice while I head over to a coffee shop to meet my grandfather. When I get there, he's already sitting at a table in the back, wearing a white suit. What's with all the men in my life dressing like pimps?

I grab a coffee from the kind-faced server and join him.

He stands from his chair and holds out his arms. Even though I haven't forgotten about him being a tool, I walk into his hug. I'm surprised by the tears that form in my eyes as I take in the familiar scent of his Old Spice.

He's a salty old bastard, so it comes as no surprise when the first thing he says to me is, "It's been a hundred and eighteen days since I last saw you."

"Seriously, Grandpa Frank," I say as I lower into the chair across from him. "I don't need a guilt trip about it. You're the one who left us."

"I didn't say it as a guilt trip," he says, adjusting his tie. Red, like Leonard's suit. I feel a pang inside of me because I was supposed to be going to this nightmare of a wedding with him. "I'm saying it because I've noticed. You and your grandmother always say I wouldn't notice if my glasses fell off my face."

"I've missed you too," I admit. "But you were a real asshole for putting Nana through so much shit, and you left a mess for us to clean up."

The present craft room, now green, suffered through an earlier life as a fish room. Before deciding his true love was a water aerobics instructor, Grandpa Frank had decided his second career would be to breed fish, so he'd bought a shit-ton of fish tanks and crammed them into that room in the basement. Only once the damage was done did he remember he didn't like cleaning his ears, let alone his room, and twenty fish tanks was twenty too many. So, he left them all behind when he moved out.

He fidgets with his coffee, so at least he realizes he was a jerk. "I'm not proud of the way I handled that." Then he glances up at me. "I've realized something over the past few months. I never really got over losing your mother. She was an unpleasant sort of person, but she was my daughter. I guess...I never wanted to talk about it with Constance, and then it got to a point where we weren't talking about anything. That's on me, since we both know your grandmother is a talker. If you're not careful in a relationship, it can fall apart without you realizing it."

"So you got it on with someone mom's age because you felt sad about losing mom? I think Freud would have a lot to say about that."

He makes a constipated face. "Your mother would have been sixty this year. Phoenix is in her mid-fifties."

"Yikes, not a great argument, Grandpa Frank."

"We don't need to talk about Phoenix."

"Thank God," I say, pausing to swig some coffee.

If I'm not mistaken, there's a twitch of humor to his pursed lips. "What about you? I've heard you're seeing someone."

"Yup, he's a former criminal, and I'm madly in love with him."

"Very funny."

"I mean it, but we don't have to talk about him either."

His brow is furrowed, and for a second I think I gave him an aneurysm. Then he says, "Your grandmother condones you dating this man?"

"They're best buddies, actually, but he's taking a break from both of us because he's decided he's not good enough for us. What can you do?"

"Are you fucking with me?"

I pause and consider it for a second. "Sort of, but it's also true."

He takes a moment before speaking, probably wondering why he missed me all those a hundred and eighteen days. Then he shocks me by saying, "Well, if your grandmother approves, then I suppose I do too. She's usually a pretty good judge of character."

I'm about to tell him there's one notable exception—*him*—but he's being good to me. Fair to Leonard. So maybe it's time for me to give him a break too.

Sighing, I say, "If you want me to meet Phoenix at some point, I will. But I'm not going to like it."

"Okay." He nods, his expression as readable as a rock's. I know him, though. He's pleased. Phoenix might not be too pleased if he ever takes me up on it, but that's her problem. "And I look forward to meeting your criminal if you can work it out."

I laugh softly, impressed that I still can manage it. "His name's Leonard, and these days he runs a house-flipping business with his friend."

"I like him better already. Now, why are we going to this wedding? Isn't Bianca marrying that potato Colter?"

I laugh harder this time. "Yes, it's going to be horrible, and I'm supposed to make a speech."

"Thanks for the invitation," he says, holding up his coffee cup for a cheers. "It's the most exciting thing to have happened to me since I lost my shorts at water aerobics a couple of months ago."

I bump my coffee cup with his, and something inside of me is healing even as it breaks. "I'm glad I asked."

"What's with the Grandpa Fruckface reference, by the way?" he asks.

"Oh, Nana changed your name on my phone when she was drunk."

He gives an impressive nod-shrug combo. "I suppose I deserved that."

Then he reaches down beside his chair and presents me with a gift bag.

"What's that?" I ask, lifting a hand to my throat.

"Don't think I forgot it's your birthday today."

I had, actually. "This better not be a fish tank."

thirty-five

LEONARD

SHANE SHOWS up at the apartment with a bag of bagels and a look that says he's pretty damn pleased with himself. He's wearing a button down and pants that probably cost more than my entire wardrobe put together. Then again, my entire wardrobe put together is a bunch of shitty T-shirts, worn jeans and shorts, and that one pimp suit I'd like to burn.

"You have news?" I ask before he gets through the door.

He chuckles in that hot-shot way he's probably practiced in front of the mirror as he steps through the opening and closes the door behind him.

Hell, yes, he has news.

"Burke," I call. "Danny."

They emerge from their relative rooms, Burke looking like he's nursing a hangover. Then again, he did go drink for drink with me last night. Danny stayed up late too, but he's more intelligent than either of us and switched to water after the first hour. The bike shorts he's wearing suggest he went out for a ride—and then returned from it—before I rolled off the couch and made coffee. Fair enough: it is past one.

We didn't talk about anything too heavy last night. We just shot the shit about the game Danny and Drew developed. Danny's thinking about selling it to a developer, on account of Drew's still in Puerto Rico with no plans to return anytime soon, and Danny doesn't want to be the front man. It felt good talking about something other than the charges that are still hanging over my head like a meat cleaver. Or the wedding I'm supposed to go to with Shauna today.

I know she's going with her grandfather.

Delia told Burke, and Burke told me. It feels wrong not to be there at her side, stirring up shit. I want to ask her what it felt like, seeing her grandfather again. I want to know if Constance is still making those raw cookies or if she's moved on to another experiment. I want to know if the kid's been painting in that green room. I texted Shauna last night, at midnight:

> Happy birthday, Tiger, knock 'em dead.

And then, because I was already a bit drunk:

> I'm trying.

I don't blame her for not texting back. I didn't make any promises, because I can't, not with that cleaver still in the air.

I did tell my buddies about the dreams. About my girl Gidget. About pushing Shauna away. I told them all of it on Wednesday night, when they showed up at my house like Santa Claus—there to save me from myself.

She sent them to me. She knows what I need better than I do, which is terrifying—and also kind of nice. For most of my life, no one had my back, and now I have a family. I have people who care about me.

I want *her* too.

I want to sweep her off her feet and away from that stupid

wedding so I can treat her the way she deserves. I want to show her that I love her. That I'm going to be there for her.

On Wednesday night, in the front room of the little purple house, Shane assured me that I'm almost certainly not going back to jail. Burke doubled down and said I sure as shit wasn't, because he didn't care about getting the bail money back. He'd drive me to Mexico himself if I needed to make a getaway.

"This isn't something you should be talking about in front of me," Shane had told him, but then he'd shrugged and said, "I'd gas up your car." We all laughed together, and something inside of me began stitching itself back together.

It hurt about as much as that needle probably had, going in and out of Reese's arm, but it felt like a start.

So did going to therapy for the first time yesterday. Burke's a miracle worker, every bit the hero I've told Shauna he is, and he got me in to see his therapist. She didn't say much to me, on account of I spent the whole time telling her about all the shit that's wrong with me, but she ended our session by saying there's a lot for us to 'unpack.'

She's not wrong. I've been carrying my baggage around for too long, and I'm ready to let it go.

Again, it's a start. I'll be going twice a week, presuming I don't get sent back to the slammer.

I've wanted to tell Shauna about the therapist. I've wanted to hear her voice and assure myself that she's okay, because when she left Mrs. Ruiz's house, she definitely did not look okay. But other than sending her that text last night, I've held a hard line with myself—*don't reach out to her until the charges are dropped*. I need to wait until I know I'm not going back.

Because if I am, then all of this is for nothing. I won't let her be with me if she's the only thing I'm hanging on for, and I'm a shackle on her leg. I won't do that. I've done some shit I regret, but I know there would be no greater sin than taking her love like it's a sponge.

If the charges get dropped, I can only hope to hell that Shauna forgives my sorry ass. That she knows I did all of this *because* I love her. I can't bring her down with my drama. I want to stand beside her and help her when she needs it and support her badassery when she doesn't.

"Coffee?" Burke asks, rubbing his head.

"Way ahead of you, bud." I grab the carafe from the machine and a few mugs. My heart's thumping, and I keep sneaking glances at Shane, who's still got that dramatic grin going for him. He's really going to stretch this out, isn't he?

I sit the coffee down on the kitchen island as the guys gather around, all three of them on stools. Adrenaline's pumping through my veins, too much of it for me to park my ass anywhere, so I stay standing but pour myself some coffee because there's nothing adrenaline loves more than caffeine.

Shane opens the bag of bagels, like he's really going to eat his damn brunch before telling us why he's here.

"Nope," I say, grabbing it from him. "Bagels are for closers."

"I bought the damn bagels," he says, but he doesn't seem too upset. He's been waiting for this moment. I try not to hope.

I'm fucking hoping.

"The charges have officially been dropped," he says with a shit-eating grin. "Who's your boy?"

I whoop at the top of my lungs, then slap him on the back and hand over the bag. "You get all of them. You can put yourself in a starch coma, my man."

"Is he getting the truck back though?" Danny asks, reaching around me to sneak a bagel from Shane's bag. "That's what we all really want to know."

He's grinning as he says it, but I can tell he and Burke aren't flying as high as I am. It hits me that they knew this was going to happen or guessed it. Here I was, convinced I was going back to jail, and neither of them thought I'd be in any serious trouble. I guess they had a point. That cop did admit that he'd taken my report but neglected to file the paperwork.

I guess I owe my life to that man's honesty. If that's not a lesson for the ages, I don't know what is. I've lied to plenty of people, but I'm not going to lie anymore.

Well, maybe that's hasty. I won't be lying about anything important anyway.

"Yeah," Shane says, "but I've heard it's in rough shape."

"Good news," Danny says. "I bet it's just the way Leonard left it then."

Burke laughs as he makes a grab for a bagel. "I guess we won't have to get you a new truck then, seeing as this one's so reliable."

Shane starts telling them about the ongoing search for the actual crook, but my mind is on Shauna.

I start pacing while they keep talking and getting into their bagels.

I'm still fucked up, probably enough that I could keep that therapist in business for years, all by myself, but I'm not going to be in jail. And I'm committed to getting better. So maybe...

"You haven't called her yet?" Burke comments. "Get a clue, brother."

Shit, he's right. I grab my phone out and make the call. Crickets.

I glance up at him. "She's not answering. She didn't answer my text last night either."

"Maybe she's getting something done with her hair," Danny says. "When my sister got married, she talked a lot about her hair. She probably should have spent more time questioning the whole marriage thing, because it only lasted four months."

Bianca's definitely the kind of woman who'll spend about ten hours getting ready, so he raises a good point.

"Guess you'll have to wait until she gets out," Burke says.

But waiting an hour to share this news is a non-starter. It's her damn birthday. I have to see her. I have to hear her voice. I've been robbing myself of her these last few days, and it's gotten to a point where it's a physical need worse than any I've ever known, even when I quit smoking cigarettes after Gidget and felt that awful, aching wanting every moment of the day and night.

"No can do," I say as my mind works through different scenarios.

I can't ask Champ for help. He texted me in the clink, saying he was disappointed I'd lied to him about the whole doctor deal and asking me not to go to the wedding because his girl was still worried about the cake.

But maybe I don't need Champ's help. I already know the wedding is at the Arboretum. If it's outside, at a place that's open to the general public, how can they prevent people from crashing the party?

"I'm going to crash the wedding," I say. "Who's giving me a ride?"

"I tell him he's a free man, and his first act is to commit a crime," Shane comments blandly.

"Oh, come on. If it's a crime at all, it's a misdemeanor. I'll bet it's not even an arrestable offense."

"Don't punch anyone." He takes a bite of bagel and washes it down with coffee, obviously not that worried for Champ and Bianca.

"I feel like we should tell you not to ruin the wedding, but do we really care?" Burke asks. "They sound like assholes."

"My objective isn't to ruin the wedding, but I also don't care," I confirm. "They're the ones who decided to get married on Shauna's birthday. I have to go."

His works his jaw. "I can't come," he tells me, actually looking sorry about it. "Delia and I have plans in—" He checks his watch. "Shit. Now, actually." He takes another bite of his bagel, then glances at me before moving his gaze to Shane. "How do I look?"

"I see how it is," I say. "You trust the clean-cut lawyer more than the ex-criminal."

"Ex-alleged criminal," Shane puts in. Giving Burke an assessing look, he lifts his eyebrows. "Go look in a mirror, and you'll have your answer."

"That bad, huh?" Before he gets up, he glances at me. "Do you have a suit? If you're crashing a wedding, you should wear a suit. You can borrow one of mine."

"I can't bring you, Leonard," Shane says, lifting both of his hands. "I'm a partner at a—"

"Very important firm, we know," Danny says with a sigh as he sets down his half-finished bagel. "Fine, I'll go. But do *I* have to wear a suit?"

"You can both borrow suits," Burke says.

"Christ, how many do you have?" I ask.

"More than you want to know," Danny answers for him. "The dry cleaner closest to us closed after he quit the family business."

No shit.

"Let's roll," I tell him, feeling the adrenaline pumping hot again.

Do I have a plan?

Hell, no. But I know the best time to crash a wedding is after the food has been served. People can tell whether there are enough plates, but they give less of a shit if there's another body on the dance floor.

Most importantly: I need to see her now. Because when you realize you have a chance to be with the woman you love after you'd gone and convinced yourself you'd spend the rest of your life in a jail cell, you don't want to wait.

thirty-six

SHAUNA

"WELL, THAT'S DONE AND DUSTED," Grandpa Frank says with a grunt after I join him at the back of the ceremony. I stood up front with Grayson, both of us treated to an up-close-and-personal view of Bianca and Colter saying their vows, exchanging rings, and walking down the aisle with a goat on a leash. Yes, a goat on a leash.

Said goat also walked Bianca up the aisle.

The goat is another sign that the Bianca I loved wasn't totally a lie, because somewhere deep inside, under multiple levels of self-involvement, she thought it was funny to send up a big FU to her parents by having a rented goat walk her up the aisle instead of her mother or father.

"We'll all be able to sleep tonight, knowing Colt folds her socks," Grandpa Frank continued. "Good, that."

He's right, the vows were long enough that I'm guessing they had some kind of competition going to figure out who could say more.

"Don't forget that he's 'wonderfully predictable,'" I say.

He grunts, "Anyone who's met the man could tell you that. You feeling okay about this?"

"Yeah." I mean it, except *Leonard should be here.* He should be laughing with me about all of this. Grandpa Frank is curmudgeon enough for ten men, but it's not the same. "They deserve each other. I hope it's everything they wanted it to be."

Bianca looks gorgeous. It's a fine, sunny day at the Arboretum, the first hint of fall colors are showing but there are still flowers blooming, and the décor is classy. I'm....

I'm not happy for her, per se, but I'm glad that she can go on living her life, independently of mine, and be happy in it. I can be generous because I'm not the one who has to be married to Colter for one to sixty years, however long it lasts.

"Let's get some booze," Grandpa Frank tells me, patting me on the back.

"Hallelujah," I say, then feel another pang because that reminds me of Leonard too.

Fantastic. The next thing I know, I'm going to start crying every time a cricket chirps.

We're following the crowd to the area that's reserved for the reception, a covered veranda next to the Education Center, when I see her. At first I think my eyes have deceived me, because surely Bianca wouldn't have invited *her*, but it *is* Josie the Great. No question about that. And she's wearing a white dress.

Well, holy shit, Bianca won't be happy about that if she's noticed. "Hey," I say, coming up to Josie. "Are you supposed to be here?"

"Are *you*?" She's looking at me warily, like I'm the crasher. "Your boyfriend's going to mess up the cake. I was sure you'd be disinvited for the wellbeing of the wedding." She lifts the charm on her necklace and stares into it the way she did on the flower field last weekend. "Then again, what's seen is seen. There's no preventing it."

"He's not here," I say thickly.

"Oh." She turns slightly, taking in Grandpa Frank. "Yes, I guess you *are* here with someone else. That'll be awkward, when your boyfriend shows up. Do they know about each other?"

"This is my grandfather," I say through my teeth, "and Leonard's not coming." I feel unreasonably annoyed with her for making me acknowledge it out loud.

"We'll see about that," she says in a lofty tone that suggests she knows better. My heart pumps harder for half a second, because I want to believe it. But she's no more psychic than I am.

"Who is this odd woman?" asks Grandpa Frank, never the soul of discretion.

"Her name's Josie. She claims she can see the future."

"Well, I'd better stay away from her then," he says, grabbing my arm and steering me toward the bar. Yes, alcohol is a good idea.

We spend the next hour or so socially shunning people, although I *do* say hello to Shelly. Grandpa Frank flirts with her, the rascal, and when I call him on it, he says that he and Phoenix have an open relationship, so I officially know more than I ever wanted to about my grandfather's sex life.

We give the cake a wide berth. It's a beautiful three-layer behemoth with a design of real, edible flowers and the hackneyed plastic couple on top. It sits on a small table to the side of the dance floor. There's a little child gate spray-painted gold around the table, so apparently Josie's threat has been taken somewhat seriously despite Leonard's absence.

"They should have written *happy birthday, Shauna* on it," Grandpa Frank quips.

"No thanks. I don't want to share my cake with them."

The DJ announces the salad course is about to be served, so my grandfather and I consult the seating arrangement and see that we've been seated at a table with Josie, Colt's second cousin, Darrell, and Melly, who's got the hots for Leonard. Perfect.

I'm not sure why Bianca felt so strongly about having me here but has stuck me at her reject table instead of upfront with the best man. Then again, I'm glad we don't have to sit near Colt and Bianca and field questions about Leonard.

Of course, as soon as we get seated, Melly immediately asks where Leonard is.

She probably isn't in the know about the doctor fakeout, so I say, "He couldn't come. He had a pressing medical situation to deal with."

"Oh," she breathes out. "What happened?"

"Sorry, I can't say. HIPAA."

And suddenly my chest hurts. I can barely breathe as I try to eat the stupid dry salad while Top 40 hits are blasted at us.

"Is it supposed to taste like this?" my grandfather asks me in an undertone that's probably heard by the three tables around us in addition to everyone at ours. Turning to Josie, he asks, "Can you see what they're serving us for dinner? Is it going to be good or should I plan on bringing my granddaughter to Texas Roadhouse?"

"Honestly, Grandpa," I say, rubbing my head against an oncoming headache that's part hangover, part this wedding, and part Leonard.

"It doesn't work that way," Josie hedges as she plays with the lettuce with her fork. Glancing across the table at Melly, she asks, "Were *you* allowed to bring a date?"

"You're pissed because Bianca didn't give you a plus one?" I ask in disbelief. "She must have just invited you last week."

"I wasn't," Melly says. "Did she say anything to you about your dress? She told me I couldn't wear light yellow. I'd already bought the dress too."

"No, but she asked me not to talk to her or look at her unless I have a premonition I need to bring to her attention."

Ah, there's the Bianca I've gotten to know over the last several months.

The salads are taken away and we're brought dinner—a rubbery chicken course that has Grandpa promising me a ribeye after we leave.

Josie pushes her plate away. "Maybe they should have kept the steak."

"But you said it would give half the people here food poisoning," I say in disbelief.

"We might have been in the safe half."

"Can I come to Texas Roadhouse?" Darrell puts in hopefully.

"I don't know who you are, son," Grandpa Frank replies. "And I don't want to trouble myself to find out."

Then the DJ announces it's time for speeches. Fantastic.

Grayson, the best man, goes first, delivering a long speech about Colt and "his girl" helping him after he accidentally ordered a hundred pizzas to be delivered to his house.

Except I'm the one he's talking about, not Bianca. We brought the pizzas to a local homeless shelter and had ourselves a party.

It's an unintentional mistake, I'm sure, but there are a few embarrassed coughs that suggest Bianca's not the only one who's picked up on it.

He settles back into his seat after confused applause, and Bianca takes the mike from the DJ.

"Thanks for that interesting story, Grayson. So glad you're here."

Colter has an *oh shit* face, and I catch him typing something onto his phone. Grayson picks up his phone and then goes pale. Maybe Colt warned him to take off, because he whispers something to his date, Melly's friend. Before Bianca says another word, they're booking it.

The bride clears her throat. "Now, I'd like to invite my maid of honor, Shauna, up to talk to y'all. As you know, Shauna's the one who introduced Colt and me."

"That's one way of putting it," Grandpa Frank says without lowering his voice.

"Good luck," Josie tells me in an undertone as I get up. "This isn't going to go well."

Fantastic. Exactly what anyone would like to hear from a psychic.

I flash her a thumbs up as I head over to the DJ stand and claim the mike from Bianca, whose smile looks like it has turned to stone. For a second, I have a flash of sympathy for her. She didn't want to be like her mother—the kind of person who holds everyone to unachievable ideals of perfection—but she's become that way. It's incredible, the hold people who are no longer in our lives can have on us. It's been like that for Leonard too.

As Bianca returns to her seat, I look into the crowd and catch sight of Josie, peering at me through that necklace.

Then I clear my throat and start to talk.

"I think we can all tell Bianca and Colter are perfect for each other," I say, waving a hand in the direction of the happy couple. She's whispering something to him. He has a dejected expression, but as soon as everyone glances their way, their faces crease into smiles. "I'll be honest," I add, "I wasn't thrilled when I found out they were getting married, and I only accepted her invitation to be maid of honor because she posed it like a dare. Any of y'all who know me know I'm not the kind of person who can pass up dares."

Someone gasps, but I continue. I'm not going to be a dick, but I decided to scrap my sawdust speech and be as honest as possible. Maybe Bianca figures it's best to sweep the past under the rug, but people remember—Grayson's speech is proof enough of that—and she's the one who wanted me to be here. Maybe this is what she needs to move forward. Maybe she needs me to forgive her in front of everyone.

I meant what I said—I won't forget, but I *can* forgive.

"I was hurt by the way they began their relationship, but I'm not upset anymore, because I've realized love does crazy things to us. They saw something in each other they couldn't pass up.

"I know what that feels like. Many of you have met Doc, who came to the...very memorable sleepover camp in the woods with some of us."

Someone laughs, and another person gives a hoot that isn't picked up by anyone else. I pause, swallowing. "The two of us hadn't known each other long, but when he found out my grandmother had made up a little white lie about me having this hotshot surgeon boyfriend, he insisted on following through and coming to the wedding events with me. I'm glad he insisted, because if he hadn't, then I wouldn't have fallen in love with him. So, what I'm saying is that I may be the one who introduced Bianca and Colter, however unintentionally, but they returned the favor."

I glance at them. There's an inscrutable look on Bianca's face, and I can't tell whether she wants to kill me or is accepting my forgiveness. "So I'm thankful to them, and I know they're going to do great things together. I mean...look at those pompoms." I gesture to a decorative arrangement hanging from the middle of the veranda roof, obviously a Queen Bee original. "Those are some big balls, Bianca, am I right?"

She actually laughs, and Colter hugs an arm around her. It's a nice moment, until someone shouts out, "Does this mean Doc's not a doctor? Because he gave me medical advice about a sensitive matter."

"Next time try not to ask for medical advice at a social event," I say, although I'm dying to know what he told the guy. Judging from the looks he's getting, we all are.

"So—"

Melly raises her hand from my table in the back. She has a pinched look on her face. Maybe Grandpa Frank just cut the cheese. He's been known to do that at inappropriate moments, and he usually blames someone else for it.

"Um, yes?" I say, because I was all about handing my microphone back to the DJ and taking Grandpa Frank up on his Texas Roadhouse suggestion.

"How come you got to bring two dates, when I didn't even get a plus one?"

"I didn't—"

Then my heart leaps, because I notice that she's looking behind me.

I whirl around and see Leonard, dressed in a suit without the jacket, the white sleeves rolled up to show some of his tattoos. His eyes have circles under them, like he hasn't been sleeping, and he looks so good I could positively consume him. He came. *He came.*

I wordlessly hand the microphone back to the DJ and take a step toward him. I hear people murmuring, but their voices are a shapeless buzz in my ears as Leonard and I make our way to each other, our eyes locked.

I take another step, and then I'm running, and so is he.

"You came," I say as I charge into his arms, tears pricking at my eyes as he wraps me up in an embrace.

"Of course I did. I couldn't not be with you on your birthday," he says, running his hand up my back and through my hair. Then he pulls me back slightly so he can look at me. "I'm not going to jail, Tiger. I just found out, and I couldn't wait to tell you. I meant what I said in my message last night. I'm trying. I'm still a mess. Maybe I'll always be, but I love you, Shauna. I love you so fucking much. I thought I was doing the right thing by walking away, but Burke told me once that you're the one who should have the choice. He was right about that."

His words pound into me. He loves me. He texted me last night. He wants to be with me. I'm full of relief and love and elation. I run my hand down his cheek, then grip the back of his hair. "I love you too. Don't you dare leave me for my own good again."

I kiss him, and he kisses me back hard, his lips branding me, and in that moment I'm so wrapped up in him—and he in me—that it doesn't matter that we're here, at the edge of someone else's wedding reception. We could be anywhere.

Then something cold is splashed onto our faces, and we break apart, gasping.

When I turn to look at who doused us, I'm expecting Bianca. But it's Colter. He's looking at Leonard, his eyes blazing. There's an empty champagne glass in his hand.

"What the hell, man?" he asks in a furious undertone. "I told you not to come because Bianca's worried about the cake. I thought we were bros."

The voices of the crowd have cut back in, and everyone's talking at once.

"I'm here because it's Shauna's birthday," Leonard says, nudging me behind him. "You're the one who figured it was a banner day to get married. Besides, you fucked around on my girl..." I step out to the side because I have the training to take someone down quickly if it comes to that. "We're not bros. Not sure how you missed the message." He taps his eye.

Colter growls something, and then he's charging at Leonard. Leonard could have sidestepped him, but his first act is to push me out of the line of fire, so Colter slams into him.

Leonard falls backward—right into the cake table.

A shriek fills the air.

"I'll bet the mourning dove shows up," Josie mutters as all of us rejects head toward the parking lot together. It's a small group of Josie, Grandpa Frank, Leonard, and me. Shelly's the one who asked us to leave, although she did it nicely—her lips puckered with disapproval for her son, who "hasn't been acting with half the sense God gave him."

I disagree—I think he was acting with *all* the sense God gave him—but I understand why Shelly would prefer to think otherwise.

"I was right about the cake," Josie continues. "Maybe that bird will make a mess all over her head, and next time she'll show more respect."

"The cake was Colter's fault," I put in. "If he hadn't shoved Leonard, it wouldn't have happened."

"The frosting tastes like shit," Leonard says, squeezing my hand. "He did everyone a favor." I wiped some of it off with a napkin before we got the boot, but it's still encrusted all over the back of his head and the top of his arm. If it didn't taste bad, I'd be tempted to lick it off.

"I don't claim to see every detail," she says, her voice sulky, "but I was mostly right."

I sigh, glancing over my shoulder. We're already too far to hear or see anything wedding related. "I really didn't want to mess up the wedding."

"I didn't care," Leonard says with a shrug. "But I didn't come here to mess it up. I was going to wait until the dancing started to talk to you, but I had to step out when I heard your speech."

"So this is the criminal," Grandpa Frank said in an amused tone. "I hear Constance has given you her approval."

"I'm lucky enough to have it, sir." Leonard gives him a sidelong glance as we hustle down the sidewalk. "I take it you're the cheating Grandpa Fruckface?"

I give Leonard a nudge with my side. "You trying to get yourself another shove?"

But my grandfather laughs. "He says it like it is. I value that in a person."

He means it. It's one of the things *I* value about him—and my grandmother. Part of me wishes they'd been able to work things out, but Nana deserves better than someone who'd step out on her, and I'm in a generous enough mood to think she'll find it. Maybe one of her five thousand activities will lead her to the senior citizen hotshot of the year.

"Where are we going?" Josie asks.

Laughter bubbles out of me as Leonard swings our connected hands. "You're coming with us?"

She shrugs. "I like Texas Roadhouse."

"You know, none of this would have happened if you hadn't told them I was going to fuck up the cake," Leonard points out.

"I know, ironic, isn't it?"

Well, she has a better understanding of irony than Alanis Morisette, I'll give her that.

As we approach the parking lot, I notice Leonard's friend Danny standing by a map of the grounds. He looks uncomfortable.

"Shit, who did that to you?" he asks, taking in Leonard's cake hair. We probably smell like stale champagne too.

"Fate," Josie says with no mark of humor in her voice.

"Can we ditch the psychic?" Grandpa Frank asks.

"She's killing the vibe," Leonard agrees.

She ignores them both, her gaze narrowing in on Danny. She lifts her ridiculous crystal ball necklace and studies him through it for a second before whistling.

Danny gives her a frown that reminds me of my eleventh-grade math teacher. No one says anything, Josie included.

"Okay," I say, curiosity prompting me to break the stand-off. "You clearly want someone to ask you what you've seen. What'd you see?"

"You're gonna be the fourth one to fall," she tells Danny after a second, watching him with a knowing look. "You've already met your soulmate."

"What?" Danny asks. It's not exactly eloquent, but he looks like he's a stuffed animal that just got all his fluff yanked out.

"You heard me." She nods at Leonard, then says, "I see five of you. Three of you have already found your soulmates, and you're the fourth. Except you made a bad impression on her. You've got to turn it around."

"Who *is* this woman?" he asks, lifting his gaze to Leonard.

"I'm Josie." She holds out her hand for a shake that he doesn't give. "I'm a psychic, and I have a feeling I'll be hearing from you." Then she looks at Grandpa Frank. "So Texas Roadhouse is a no?"

He's nonplused by her supposed vision. "A no for you."

"And for you," I tell him. "Unless you want to go with Danny. I'm bringing Leonard home." Just saying it makes me feel warm inside. Like I wasn't doused with champagne and asked to leave a wedding.

Danny shrugs at Grandpa Frank. "I'll bring you."

"So, we *are* going?" Josie asks. "I really like their hot wings."

"Not you," Danny says pointedly.

She lets out a huff of air and then shrugs and starts walking toward the cars, murmuring about ungrateful men.

Leonard shakes his head. "That woman gives me the heebie-jeebies."

"You're not alone in that," Danny says, watching her as she retreats. There's a thoughtful look on his face, though, like what she said didn't go in one ear and out the other.

I don't believe people can see the future—or at least I don't think I do—but it *is* a little eerie, the way Josie knows certain things. She's either a hell of busybody spy, or she has...some sort of insight.

You're gonna be the fourth one to fall.

Only there's just four of them, so she got that part wrong.

Except...

Drew. Drew moved to Puerto Rico with the love of his life. It's why Leonard's been staying in that little purple house.

A tingle travels along my spine because it is uncanny. *She's uncanny.*

I give Grandpa Frank a hug goodbye. Leonard reaches out to shake his hand, but Grandpa Frank pulls him in for a hug too. By the time he's done with us, he has frosting and probably sticky champagne on his shirt, but let's be honest, Texas Roadhouse isn't the kind of joint where they're going to care about that.

My throat feels tight with emotion, but I don't try to push it away.

Danny nods to us both—either he's not a hugger or he doesn't want a sticky shirt—and off they go, leaving us alone together.

Leonard regards me with warm eyes. "Looks like it's just the two of us, Tiger."

"Looks like."

He pulls a gorgeous little wrapped package out of his pocket and whistles. "It survived the cake."

"You got me something?"

"Of course I did. It's your birthday. I...I got it a couple of days ago."

"Did Becca from The Paper Place wrap this?"

He gives me one of his shit-eating grins. "I might have asked her to do me a solid."

Of course he charmed her. As far as I know, he's only interacted with her the once, but that's all it would take.

I unwrap it, and he takes the paper from me, stuffing it in his pocket. It's a little cardboard box, and I open it to find a pendant inside—the stone is tawny and beautiful, with a darker area at the center.

"Tiger's eye," he says when I look up at him.

I kiss his jaw. "I love it. I'm putting it on now."

He takes the clasp and helps me get it on, pressing a soft kiss to the back of my neck. When he's done, I turn to face him.

"I'm sorry I fucked up the wedding," he says.

I grin at him. "No, you're not."

He runs a finger along my jaw, ending at my chin. "No, I'm not. I told you I'd be there with you, and I'm going to keep my promises to you. It's part of being a better man."

I lean in closer, getting up on my toes. Only a few inches separate us, and we're sharing air, space. "What if I like you the way you are?"

One side of his mouth hitches up. "No one said you need to have good taste."

I lift up and kiss him, and he makes me shriek into his mouth when he picks me up off the ground and swings me, our mouths still pressed together.

When he sets me down, I frown at my sticky, frosting-covered hand.

"Let's get you home and into the shower."

He's studying me again. "That's the second time you've said that today."

"What?"

"You called your house *home*. Like it was home for both of us."

"Well it is, isn't it?" I ask, lifting my eyebrows. "We've all missed you. Even Bertie's not himself."

He grins. "So he's not a growling menace?"

"Exactly."

He swallows, his eyes glassy. Every emotion I'm capable of fills me up like helium in a balloon, making me lighter even though I used to think they could only make me heavier. "I've never had a home before now."

"Well, you'd better get used to it. According to Josie, you're my soulmate. That means you won't be able to shake me."

He cleans my frosting hand off on his shirt.

"Is that your suit?" I ask.

He gives a shaky laugh. "Fuck, no. But Burke has so many of them he could open up a boutique. He won't mind." Looking back into my eyes, he says, "You know, I think maybe Josie really can read the future. Because I want you to be my soulmate. I want to belong to you...and for you to belong to me. I can't think of anything I've wanted more than that in my whole life."

My heart feels too big for one person. Like it's going to consume my whole body and keep on growing. "I love you."

He kisses me softly. "I love you too, Tiger. Let's go home."

And so we do.

epilogue

LEONARD

THE NEXT MONTH rolls by without anything bad happening.

Seriously, the worst thing that happens is that Bertie takes a shit on the carpet at night, and I step on it with a bare foot. Not a great moment, but as the worst moment of the month, I'll take it.

I'm...happy. I'm over the fucking moon. I'm working with my best friend, and I have a family I love. A woman I worship who's five thousand times better than me—even though she scowls at me whenever I say so. A cat who seems to like only me and Reese, and a dog who's slowly becoming resigned to me. I've been working with my therapist, and a psychiatrist at her office prescribed me some pills that help me sleep through the night. For the first time in years, I can go to sleep without seeing my old man. That's a gift I'm not giving back.

Better yet, Burke's private dick dug up some old dirt on Joel. He found a few of Joel's foster kids who'd aged out. He'd beaten them too, and they're teaming up with Reese to press charges. Maybe nothing will come of it. Maybe that asshole will keep pushing people around because it makes him feel like King Dick, but Shane is helping them out pro bono, and he's the kind of shark you want on your side. Either way, it's given Reese confidence. So has working at The Waiting Place. He and Rafe finished a mural on the side of the building that got some buzz from local papers and blogs, and they're going to sell some of his art in The Waiting Place. I'm also helping him study for the GED, and I don't doubt he'll pass on his first go-round.

But you don't get everything you want. They never found the guy who was robbing houses in Mrs. Ruiz's neighborhood, although the robberies stopped just after the cops found the truck. We all still think Burke's parents were behind it, but they're good at keeping their noses clean. Maybe I'm the one who taught them to cover their tracks after I caught them all those years ago.

I'm not proud of that, but I've got a lot of other shit to be proud of, and I'm trying to focus on that. On the life I'm building on top of the ashes of all the other ones I've left behind.

Today is my girl's big day—Friday, October 30, the Halloween party she masterminded at The Waiting Place. The whole damn place smells like pumpkin spice, which must be a wet dream for Danny, since he famously bought himself a pumpkin spice candle because he liked the way it smelled. Given Danny's not the kind of guy to buy himself anything impractical, this purchase is discussed a lot—even though it happened over eight years ago.

That's what it's like when you've got friends like mine. I'm never going to live down that red suit either, even though I burned it in the firepit in Constance's back yard and almost caused a fire doing it.

There are food vendors selling caramel corn, spiced cider, and all kinds of delicious crap that'll knock your teeth out. Each of the art stations is leading visitors through a different craft, and they also have spooky shit for sale.

Shauna's beasts have sold out, not that I'm surprised. My tiger is talented.

She went through with her plan to give Champ and Bianca

statues for their wedding gift, and they sent us a handwritten thank you note that's the most beautifully passive aggressive shit I've ever seen. I framed it for her and hung it up in The Clay Place.

If we ever see them again, it'll be too soon, although I still got people coming up to me in the street and calling me Doc.

Shauna's finishing up her lesson—teaching people to make snake bowls so they can scare the kids who stop by their houses for candy—so I've been shooting the shit with Burke and Shane in the hallway outside The Clay Place. Constance, Delia, and Mira are all taking the clay class, so they're locked up too.

Burke's got on his Prince Eric costume. I'd poke fun at him for being a chump, but Tiger only agreed to dress as a hot tiger if I'd come as her prey, so I got makeup on that's been frightening kids all night. Which means I have no room to talk.

"Where's Danny?" Burke asks. "He wandered off about an hour ago, and I haven't seen him since."

"Hiding," Shane says with a grin. "This isn't his scene."

Shane is dressed up like...a lawyer is my best guess, because he's wearing one of his damn suits.

Burke laughs, his gaze shooting toward The Clay Place. "He probably figures he should get peace and quiet while he can."

Mira's moving in with him this weekend, on account of Burke and Delia having finally moved into their house. Danny has said he's fine with the arrangement so many times it's obvious he's not looking forward to it.

Burke rocks on his feet. "Maybe this was a mistake."

"I think it'll be good for him," Shane suggests. "Keep him on his feet."

"If it doesn't work out, I can find her another place."

She wouldn't let him do that. I happen to know that both she and Danny have insisted on paying rent to Burke now that he isn't living in the apartment anymore. Burke isn't happy about it, but he won't tell them no. He knows when someone's dignity is on the line.

"I'll go find him," I offer, patting my buddy on the back.

It takes me a minute, because I stop to peep into the window of The Paint Place to check on Reese. He's helping Rafe lead a class painting a black cat slinking along a wall—a Reese original of Bean, I'm proud to say. I make a big show of waving at him, and he looks like every embarrassed kid who's called out by a family member. It makes my chest feel warm and toasty inside.

Finally, I get a bead on Danny. He's found what has to be the only quiet corner in this joint and parked a chair there. He's sitting with a hot cider that smells like whiskey, so I'm guessing he's got a flask on him.

"My girl's a genius," I tell Danny. "Isn't she a genius?"

He smirks at me. "She makes a mean clay dick, I'll give her that."

I gave it to him for his birthday a couple of weeks back, and he looked at it for a solid ten seconds before he burst out laughing.

"We made it together," I tell him now.

"Just tell me you didn't have sex over it."

"No promises. Don't be stingy, brother," I tell him, pointing to the drink.

He smirks at me. "You're good at smelling out whiskey." Then he hands the flask to me under the table.

I take a swig before handing it back. "You hiding from the fun?"

"I've got something on my mind."

"Is it Mira moving in? Because I have a feeling she's gonna knock you on your ass. We all have money running on which of you is gonna try to kick the other out."

"Good to know," he says with a laugh. "But no." He plays with the top of his cider cup. "I just found out that Daphne works for the company that wants to buy the game. She's the one Drew and I'd be dealing with."

It takes me a moment to place the name. Daphne. The one who got away.

I whistle. "You're thinking about what Josie said."

"I am," he admits with a slight nod. Then he takes another swig from the drink. "I need to change her mind about me. This is my chance to show her I'm a different man."

"But you're not," I point out.

He shakes his head, almost smiling but not quite. "No. I guess I'd better start changing."

I'd tell him he shouldn't have to change for the right woman— that there's nothing on this green earth wrong with liking simple pleasures and small crowds. But I know a man's got to learn some lessons by himself. So, I nod to the party raging around us. "Ain't no better time. The Danny I know wouldn't, for the life of him, join in the fun."

"You may have a point."

"Of course I do."

"Do I have to actually have fun?"

"No, brother, but it might sneak up on you." I pat him on the back, and just like magic, I've got him up and heading toward the other guys.

He tells them about Daphne, and Burke and I exchange a *he's next* look.

Shane frowns at Danny. "Why would you give her the time of day? She called you basic."

"I *am* basic," he responds. "But that doesn't mean I can't change. People change all the time. Leonard used to be a criminal."

"Alleged criminal," Shane says.

"Nah, he's got a point," I say, giving Danny a nod. There's an uptick in the volume around us that suggests the class has finally let out. Good. I've been hoping I can convince Shauna to sneak into the bathroom with me. She's looking mighty fine in her tiger outfit.

I rub my jaw, trying to focus. *Danny. Basic. Daphne.* "But being a criminal is frowned upon, I'm told. There's nothing wrong with being basic."

"Are you guys talking about the cider?" someone asks from behind me. I turn and see Mira, dressed up like a pirate. Delia's behind her, and Shauna's behind Delia, too far away for my taste. "I tried to convince them to let me take care of it, but Shauna insisted people like basic shit. She's wrong, obviously. It tastes like one of those shitty pumpkin spice candles. I'll bet no one's drinking it."

Then she notices Danny standing across from her, holding his cup of cider.

"Hey-oh," she says. "Sorry about that, future roomie. I'll bet it's awesome."

"The whiskey helps."

She reaches her hand out for a high five, and he nearly fumbles it, because he's got his cider in the wrong hand.

Fuck, I think he really does need help.

I reach out and touch his arm. "If you want to convince this Daphne chick to give you another shot, we've got your back."

Mira beams at him. "You want a makeover? I was hoping he wanted a makeover, right guys?" she asks, turning to Shauna and Delia.

"I'm not comfortable with this conversation," Danny informs us.

"You'll get used to me," she insists with a bright smile.

Shauna's looking at me, so I gave Danny's arm a final pat and squeeze by Delia to get to her.

"How'd it go, Tiger?" I ask, putting an arm around her, settling it just above the tail sewed to her orange Lycra shorts.

"Half of the guys made their snakes into phalluses, so you're not the only one who has a preoccupation with your dick."

"I hope *you* have a preoccupation with my dick."

Constance snorts as she pushes her way past us. She's another one who didn't dress up. Said it was beneath her. I would have accused her of being lazy, but anyone who's known her more than five minutes knows that'd be a damn lie.

"Nana's one of the only women who also made a dick bowl," Shauna says wryly.

"It was a message for your grandfather, dear. I cut the head in half."

I don't see him now, but Grandpa Frank came to the class too. Maybe the scissored dick was enough to drive him off. A man's only got one dick, after all.

"We'll be back, Constance," I tell her. "I need to talk to Shauna about something."

"I know what you want to talk to her about, dear. I've had plenty of turns around the sun." But she leans in and kisses me on the cheek. "You make a handsome zombie."

"And you make one fine-looking old broad."

She swats me, and Shauna sighs. "Stop manhandling my boyfriend, Nana."

"She can manhandle me all she wants," I tell her with a wink. Then I lead Shauna away to an open pocket at the side of the hallway.

"We need to get your grandmother online dating," I say in an undertone as I push her up against the wall. "Wouldn't that be fun for us?"

She laughs, her nose wrinkling. "She'd never let us."

"Who says we have to ask for permission? We can tell her after we've made her dates with a few silver foxes." I lift up my hands. "Her words."

"Maybe." She glances at her grandmother through the crowd. "I'm not convinced she needs anyone, though. She's happy for the first time in who-knows-how-long. And she has us."

"Nothing wrong with having a little fun," I say, letting my hand drop to her hip.

"That's how this started." She grins at me, her eyes bright. "And now I'm stuck with you."

"Come on, honey." I rub her hip. "You don't mind it none."

She leans in and kisses me, too damn quickly, probably because there are at least a hundred people around us. "I don't mind it at all. So, Danny's trying to get someone to give him another shot?"

I explain the Daphne situation quickly, and her eyes light up. "So, Josie was right?"

"Or it may be another cake situation," I point out. "As in, nothing would ever have happened if she hadn't stuck her nose in other people's business in the first place."

"I don't know anymore," she says softly, glancing back at our friends. "She was right about a whole lot. She was right about us."

"Sure, but any idiot could see I was a goner for you."

She grins at me. "We're going to help him, though, right?"

I go in for another feel of her hip, her butt. "We'll help him the way he needs to be helped, sure. But I'm not convinced Daphne is the right woman for him. Let's table that for another day, though. I was hoping I could convince you to have sex in the bathroom. I've been staring at your ass in those shorts all night."

She laughs and takes me by the collar. "How did I know you like to have sex in bathrooms?"

"I want you anywhere and any way I can get you."

"Same," she says, pulling me down for a kiss. I give it to her good and judging by the way her tiger makeup's smeared when I pull away, it's probably all over my face. I hope so, because I'm a lucky man, and I'd like everyone to know it. She takes my hand and leads me toward the staff bathroom—the only one that has a lock.

Maybe Josie's psychic. Maybe not. But Shauna has a point...she was right about me...and not just about the jail thing. I guess she could be right about Danny too. Except my gut is telling me he has the wrong girl in mind.

I think he needs more of a tiger.

Then again, I can't understand why a man would want anything less.

"When was the last time I told you I'm madly in love with you?" I ask as Shauna pulls me into the bathroom and shuts the door.

"An hour ago." She slides a hand under my shirt.

"Well, damn, I've been slacking."

Her hand dips down to my belt, her lips lifting into a smirk. "Yes, you'd better do something about that."

"Oh, I plan to."

What's up next?

Danny and Mira in the grumpy sunshine, forced proximity, roommates romcom *You're so Basic*. It releases in Read on for the first chapter.

about the author

ANGELA CASELLA is a romcom fanatic. Writing them, reading them, watching them—she's greedy, and she does it all. In addition to her solo releases, she's lucky enough to collaborate with Denise Grover Swank. They have three complete series and more co-written projects to come.

She lives in Asheville, NC. Her hobbies include herding her daughter toward less dangerous activities, the aforementioned romcom addiction, and dreaming of having someone else clean her house.

Visit her website at www.angelacasella.com or Angela and Denise's shared website at www.arcdgs.com.

Made in United States
Troutdale, OR
01/21/2024

17051354R00235